infernal

infernal

MARK DE JAGER

DEL REY

1 3 5 7 9 10 8 6 4 2

Del Rey, an imprint of Ebury Publishing
20 Vauxhall Bridge Road,
London SW1V 2SA

Penguin
Random House
UK

Del Rey is part of the Penguin Random House group of companies whose addresses can be
found at global.penguinrandomhouse.com

First published in the UK in 2016 by Del Rey

www.eburypublishing.co.uk

A CIP catalogue record for this book is available from the British Library

ISBN 9781785033346

Typeset in India by Thomson Digital Pvt Ltd, Noida, Delhi

Printed and bound in Great Britain by Clays Ltd, St Ives PLC

Penguin Random House is committed to a sustainable future for our business, our readers
and our planet. This book is made from Forest Stewardship Council® certified paper.

MIX
Paper from
responsible sources
FSC
www.fsc.org   FSC® C018179

The common man struggles to understand men like us, we who have dedicated our lives to the mastery of magic. They rail against the powers that we command and cry to their priests for succour. And yet it is us, not the priests, who are closer to the gods, for in calling forth the language of magic we speak that of creation itself. Not one among them would deny that the gods threw down the Dreamsinger at the beginning of time, nor that they bound its bones to become the earth, its blood to fill the seas, its fire the sun and its wings the canopy of the heavens. From its living flesh they created man and all the beasts, both great and small, and set these upon the earth so that the progeny of their great enemy would love and worship them for all time.

But it is only us, the chosen few, who understand that the Dreamsinger was vanquished, not slain, and that its song reverberates through all things born of it. To hear the song of magic is to hear the name of the Dreamsinger, from whom all our names are born, and to know its name is to know the power of the gods.

An Introduction to the Path of Power
by Tiberius Talgoth, Archmage

Chapter 1

I woke to the sight of vultures circling, three blemishes against the cobalt sky gliding lower with each pass, almost lazily, as if taking the time to savour their next meal.

I sat up to rub my face, to clear some of the fog that hung thick in my mind, but instead I found myself staring at an unfamiliar hand. My hand, apparently, since it was attached to my arm, but I recognised neither. The vultures rasped their displeasure and returned to their overwatch as I steadied myself against a sudden lurching of the world, as if I had just fallen. I shook my head again, willing the numbing fog from it, but the more I struggled for clarity, the more it drew in around me, smothering the knowledge of where I was, or why I was there. A memory stirred within the depths of my mind, an indistinct shape of something that offered little more than a brief affirmation that this was exactly what I had been hoping for before it slipped away.

I flexed the hand attached to my new arm, and watched the five short fingers curl and extend. The skin creasing and folding around the joints was darker than I remembered mine being, but just as hairless. It felt entirely normal, but there was something about the movement that sent a shiver through me. As I struggled back into a sitting position, I felt a flare of heat at the back of my head, as if someone had touched me with a flaming brand.

It was the only warning I had that something was very wrong.

One moment there was simply the sweet scent of crushed grass, the rasping call of the vultures and the sparrows singing, and the next my senses were lost to a maelstrom of pain. Unsurpassed agony swept over and through me, unstoppable and unrelenting. I spent what felt like an eternity screaming and wishing that it would overwhelm me and send me back to sleep, or simply kill me, but no such relief came. I was awake yet could do nothing; my brain felt like it was tearing itself apart from within, and all reason was swept away beneath a torrent of sensation.

When I eventually came to my senses, I was once again staring at the clouds, but now my body felt as distant and unresponsive as a rock. The fog still cloaked my memories, but it was clear enough to understand that something had gone terribly awry. I felt the tug of distant memories, but again they fled from my mind before I could glean anything apart from a vague sense of frustrated urgency from them. I tried everything I could think of as I lay there, the sun bathing me in a heat I couldn't feel. I couldn't even grunt with the effort that I put into trying to move my arm. I tried a hand instead, and then a mere finger, but my efforts all ended in disappointment. Apart from touch, my other senses were still keen, but that was as comforting as it was useless.

The horror of my predicament was starting to give way to a sort of boredom when the first vulture reappeared in my field of vision. I willed it to keep flying, but wasn't really surprised when it ignored my silent entreaty and returned with its friend in tow. I tried to still the panic rising within me, but the return of the third bird put paid to that. They were descending in tightening spirals, emboldened once more by my distinct and terrifyingly persistent lack of movement. Lower and lower they drifted, until they disappeared from my line of sight. I heard the soft thumps of their landing moments later, followed by raucous cawing and clicking as they competed among themselves to decide which of them would be first in line at the feast of Stratus.

Stratus.

My name was Stratus. If I could have spoken I might have said it aloud a few times, but for now I had to content myself with thinking about it. Stratus.

I wanted to sob, to scream, to do anything but lie there waiting to be torn apart by their dirty beaks. But it seemed that my path was about to come to a messy end, and the only consolation that Fate could offer me was that I would at least be spared from the pain of my slow death. The first of the vultures loomed into view, clicking its beak as it waddled towards me. I tried everything I could to do something, anything, but nothing happened. I was a living corpse. I saw it dip its head and moments later my body rocked as it tried to dig into my flesh. When it sat back after the third such attempt, its fierce beak was daubed with a shining, wet smear of my blood. It bent forward again, then abruptly shot out of view, leaving only a single feather swirling where it had been a moment before.

Something that sounded like a particularly large and angry wasp buzzed loudly near me, and I heard a strangled squawk from near my feet, followed shortly after by the sound of beating wings. A few moments of silence followed before I heard soft footsteps coming towards me. Two pairs of them; I doubt I would have heard them if I hadn't been lying there unable to do anything but stare at the sky and listen.

A voice spoke somewhere off to my right-hand side. The language was unintelligible at first, but as I listened to it, something changed. Warmth flared somewhere inside my brain, but it was a far gentler sensation than the sharp burn that had preceded my convulsions. It passed as quickly as it had come, but in its wake the words being spoken arranged themselves into something I could understand.

'. . . be a mercy.'

'Perhaps, but it should be the Deacon's decision, not ours.'

A man crouched next to me, handing a curved bow to an as yet unseen comrade. He seemed unnaturally large as I looked up at him, a perspective and sensation that I found deeply unsettling. He smelled of sweat, leather and mud, and stared at me intently with eyes that were bright against his browned skin.

'Fair enough,' he said. 'You go fetch him. Perhaps he can help our naked friend here to tell us what happened to him.'

The other man didn't respond, but I heard him walk away, his strides long but quiet. My watcher began moving around the clearing while I tried to order my thoughts. The panic was still there, circling me like a wolf around a wounded stag, but I wasn't going to let this unexpected respite go to waste. And if this 'Deacon' could help me, I wasn't about to squander the opportunity. Not that I had a choice.

The Deacon didn't take too long to arrive, and soon after I found myself surrounded by a gaggle of men draped in long robes, their combined scent almost overwhelming. Orders were shouted and a canopy was soon erected over us. A man in a darker robe with a white sash kneeled next to me, examining my body while the others fell silent and stepped away. He lifted my left arm with a grunt of effort, and I found it strangely comforting that mine was far larger than his. He rubbed and scratched at my dark nails before lowering it down next to my body again.

'And you just found him here, lying on the ground like this?' My examiner's voice was quiet, his pronunciation far less guttural than that of my bow-carrying saviour.

'Yes, Father. We thought he was dead. There were vultures around him and he wasn't reacting, even when one took a lump out of him.'

'You did well to bring him to my attention. You may go.' He didn't bother looking up as they padded away. 'Jules, come over here, and bring my bag.'

'Right away, Father.' This voice was high and clear, a cub of some sort. No, the word found me: a boy.

The Deacon leaned forward until his lined face filled my vision and his softly spiced scent clouded my nostrils. His hair was white, marking him as old for a human, although not so old that his scent carried the touch of corruption that tainted the infirm.

'What a fine puzzle you are,' he said quietly.

'Here you are, Father.'

He sat back, out of my sight, and I heard the clink of glass and a rummaging sound. I concentrated on my hearing and tried to build a sense of what was happening around me. I could hear at least three different voices speaking, and the smell of horse and metal was heavy in the air. Without being able to turn my head it was hard to tell where they all were, but I guessed that the men had moved a dozen or more yards to my right, no doubt watching.

'Who is he, Father? I don't like him.'

The old man grunted. 'That is what I hope to discover. But tell me now, why did you say that? He is injured and needs our help.' He paused. 'You have not seen a man with such skin before, have you?'

'No, Father. Why is it black? Is he a demon, like in the stories?' The sour tang of fear drifted from his direction, but the old man only made a chugging sound which I took to be laughter.

'And what do you suppose a demon would be doing out here, lying in the sun and being chewed on by vultures?'

I might have laughed too if I could. Or at least until some traitorous part of my mind asked me why I thought that so unlikely, given that I barely knew anything but my own name. And my skin and nails were far darker than theirs. Why was that? Perhaps it would clear up once whatever was wrong inside my head was mended.

'No Jules,' the old man continued, 'the men of the southern islands off the coast of Illutia are known to have skin like his, sometimes even darker if you go further south. And yet, I must say that his frame is far heavier than any of theirs that I have ever seen, even among their warrior caste.'

'I don't think he's a warrior.'

'What makes you say that?'

'He has no scars. Even the Duke's champion has scars.'

'Well done, boy,' the Deacon replied. 'That is an astute observation.'

'So what's wrong with him?'

'I don't know, not yet. I do know that he's simply too big to have been a cripple all his life, so I'm expecting to find an injury of some kind.' He loomed over me and pulled my eyelids up, then sat back down and looked at me. 'Well, friend, I'm going to have a look inside to try to find the problem. We can take it from there.'

'What shall I do, Father?'

'Make sure that no one disturbs me until the ritual is complete. No one at all, do you understand? The magic is delicate.'

'Yes, Father.'

Magic. I knew about magic. I felt the idea of it resonate strongly with the memories locked within my mind, and for one all-too-brief moment I felt the answer to all my questions taking shape before the fog rose up and swallowed it again. It was enough for me to know that sorcery had brought me to this, and that it alone could help me now. Yet whatever capacity or talent I had once had for it now felt as distant and unresponsive as the rest of me.

The Deacon moved to sit down behind me. A moment later I heard a loud grunt and my world tilted crazily. I had a moment of complete confusion where I thought he'd cut my head off, but then I realised he'd simply lifted it. I could see far more now, and I was pleased to see that my guess as to where the rest of the men were waiting was a good one. Half a dozen males stood some twenty yards to my right, talking quietly among themselves while they soothed their steeds. They were clad in hides and vests of metal rings, although two of them wore a different sort with more flat, decorated surfaces that were polished to a bright finish. These two stood to one side with their hands upon their swords as they watched the Deacon. I didn't like the look of them at all.

'You have a heavy head, my dark friend,' said the Deacon behind me, drawing my attention back to him. 'Now normally I'd tell you to keep very still for this part but I think we both know that's not going to be a problem.'

With that, he brought his hands back to rest on my face and began chanting softly. I listened carefully, straining towards the sound with everything I had, suddenly as desperate for a crumb of magic as a starving man is for a morsel of bread. I understood magic, and even though I couldn't yet say how or why I did, I knew that it was the key to whatever I had done to myself.

He was reciting a prayer of some sort, a short one that he kept repeating, a phrase that meant little on its own but one that built up a magical cadence through repetition. My flesh couldn't feel the touch of magic, but my mind could. I felt the moment where his mumbling transcended a simple mantra and became a conduit between him and the Songlines, those pulsing currents that span the world. I didn't resist its touch, not that I could, and his magic slowly entered me. I saw it as a brightly glowing network of fine white roots that bloomed somewhere behind my eyes and began to gently unfurl. It reflected his intent to heal, an inflection that helped to still my mind's natural instinct to push back at the intrusion.

He was looking for damage, trying to feel out where my body was broken, and as I surrendered to his magic, I started to get a real sense of it. It was purely aimed at my physical body and as he wasn't spending any energy on shielding either it or him, I let myself be drawn into it, basking in its radiance until I was saturated enough to blend in with it. Now that I could understand the nature of the spell he was using, I sensed his painstakingly careful and methodical approach. He clearly had a grasp of human biology that I could never hope to equal no matter how many of them I ate.

Ate?

The thought set a string of questions firing through my mind, weakening my connection to his magic. I hastily suppressed these before it broke completely. There would be time to wonder about that later when I wasn't entirely helpless.

As I watched him work I began to get a sense of his steadily growing confusion as his magic drifted through my body and found no injuries. I felt his confusion grow and colour with something else, something that shifted his intention and sent his magic probing towards my mind rather than my body. I wasn't sure how I felt about this. If I was a demon of some sort, I suspected that he'd waste no time in having those two in the shiny armour carve me into pieces. I was still debating how to push him away when the tendrils of his magic flowed into my mind, but then I felt them recoil as something *within me* reacted to their burrowing.

Something that wasn't me.

There was a glimpse of something dark and bestial, a twisted, writhing mass of magic, flesh and sharp edges that radiated the promise of undiluted rage and bloodshed. It was terrifying, and I recoiled as much as the Deacon had. I felt him hastily pull his magic back, and I knew that he was withdrawing from my mind. It wasn't hard to guess since I was recoiling as much as he was, my thoughts resounding with a single word. *Demon.*

However, I also knew that if he did withdraw, he would take away what might be the only chance I would have of breaking free of whatever it was that had broken my body. I tightened my grip on his magic, clutching to it desperately. He felt this, and pushed back, the soft glow of his power darkening as something like fear bled into it. He chose to break off the spell, abandoning the trace of his power that I had grabbed rather than trying to wrestle it away.

For a moment, that morsel of power was mine alone, and the beastly thing within my mind pulled it into itself. I felt something at the base of my skull shift, sending a fierce heat racing through my body like a bolt of lightning. It brought my muscles to life in a series of violent contractions that left me spent and vomiting a clear, viscous gel while the Deacon's men surrounded me, their weapons drawn and gleaming.

Chapter 2

Someone was shouting at me, but I was still too busy spitting slime from my mouth and clearing my throat to pay them much attention. Once I could breathe again I slowly sat up and looked around, trying to ignore the multitude of clicks and crunches that my every movement seemed to elicit. I felt my innards shift as if arranging themselves into a more comfortable position, but there was no blood or pain, which was already a significant improvement as far as I was concerned. The Deacon was standing well out of my reach by this time, flanked by the two warriors in their shiny armour, and I wondered how he had interpreted his encounter with whatever demon lurked inside my mind.

'Who are you?' he asked eventually, and I felt some of the tension leave my shoulders.

I doubted that he knew how apt a question it was, or how hard I had to think before answering.

'I am Stratus,' I said. I liked the sound of my name.

'And just who are you, Meneer Stratus?' asked the Deacon, staring at me.

I was too stiff, hungry and confused to think up anything clever. 'I don't know,' I said, shrugging. More crunching from my shoulders.

'He speaks the truth,' said the Deacon, and a moment later I felt something drift across my skin. The sly old man had used his magic on me.

'Where am I?' I asked, not giving any indication that I was aware of its presence. I didn't like the look of the weapons ranged against me and thought it best to look as helpless as possible.

'Twelve miles west of Thasper's Crossing in North Aldo.'

That meant absolutely nothing to me and it must have shown in my expression, for the Deacon gestured and the men lifted their weapons away from me. My relief was short-lived though, for his next command was for them to bind me. Two men rushed forward and grabbed me by my arms and tried to haul me to my feet, but my legs weren't quite ready to support me yet and it felt like my knees were bending the wrong way, making the men stagger about as they tried to lift me.

'He's a bloody ox!' one of them muttered as my legs finally stopped wobbling so much. My balance was completely off-kilter and another of the men had to help steady me as they bound my wrists with a woven rope. I was taller and larger than any of them, and their scent told me that they were afraid of me, even though I was naked and unarmed, while they had swords and axes and coats of woven metal rings.

The Deacon came forward once my wrists were secure. I let him turn my head as he stared at me, his eyebrows bunching together. 'Fascinating,' he said. 'You are not what you seem, yet I now sense no malice within you, even though I know it is there.'

'Why do you bind me?' I asked.

He smiled and patted me on my cheek. 'Just a precaution, you understand. Tonight I will have you brought to me so that I can unravel your mysteries. Once I understand what I have seen, then we can consider your freedom.' He turned to one of the men. 'Feed him, and for heaven's sake get him some clothes. Then put him with the others. We've wasted enough daylight.'

'Where are you going?' I asked as he turned away.

He peered at me for a moment. '*We* are travelling to Thasper's Crossing.'

'Why?'

He sighed. 'Because that is where my master bids us go. Now go with these men. If you are innocent, you have nothing to fear.' With that he strode off, followed by the two shiny warriors while others moved forward to fold the canopy away.

I didn't resist as the men led me off towards a trio of wagons that were parked some distance away. There were more men here, all of them armed and reeking of iron and sweat. Several stared at me and a few laughed as I was led to the rearmost wagon where several other men were sat in the shadow cast by its linen canopy. Their wrists were bound as mine were, and a chain ran from their binding to a closed hoop at the rear of the wagon. They smelled riper than the warriors around them but seemed to be in a reasonably good state of health. The warriors had to loosen my ropes so that I could get dressed, but it was only when they handed me the clothes that I realised I wasn't sure how to get inside them and my first attempts were clumsy enough to make them laugh.

'Best keep him out of the sun,' suggested one of the bound men, prompting a wider round of laughter.

I took a calming breath and managed to complete the task without any further drama. The man who bound and chained me to the wagon also gave me a small, round loaf of bread and a cup full of something that smelled like old leaves. I took a cautious sip from the cup and managed to keep enough in my mouth to work out that it was some sort of ale. I wiped my chin and tried again, and with far more success. It tasted better than it smelled and soothed the ache in my throat. I gnawed at the bread and, after a few tentative bites, realised that I was ferociously hungry and ate the rest of it in three giant mouthfuls that almost choked me.

'So what did you do?' asked one of the chained men.

'I do not know,' I replied, which was the truth. The man simply snorted and shook his head.

'Well, I'm sure they'll think of something to charge you with by the time we get there. Hel, they may even tell you what it is before they decide on your punishment.'

'Punishment? Who would dare punish me?'

They all laughed at this. The man who'd spoken lifted his wrists and rattled the chain. 'They don't give you pretty bracelets like these if they want to be your friend.'

That made sense, now that I thought about it. I needed some time to reflect on everything that had happened, not least of all the possibility that I was a man-eating demon. Despite my ongoing hunger, I didn't feel any particular urge to take a bite out of the men around me, so perhaps I wasn't some ravening monster. I had been lying out in the sun for some time with vultures pecking at me, after all. I was still mulling this over when a series of loud shouts and whistles sounded along the wagons. The men around me stood up, and I copied them, keeping my curiosity about what was happening to myself.

After a bit more shouting the wagon we were chained to began to move, taking up the slack in the chains until we could walk behind it. It was hard going for me as I still felt woefully unsteady on my legs, and with my hands bound in front of me I found myself colliding with the men on either side as I staggered about, my weight sending them sprawling into the dust.

The chained men were still a bit surly towards me when the wagons drew to a halt shortly after sunset, and the two men I'd knocked to the ground seemed particularly put out. I had my own problems though, and so chose to ignore them, which, as it turned out, only served to inflame their wounded pride. Two of the guards came along to distribute more of the ale and bowls of some sort of warm but tasty-smelling mush. I was too hungry to care what was in it, and after paying careful attention as to how to use the tiny ladle provided, I began to eat. I had just taken my first mouthful when one of the two men shot his elbow back, knocking the bowl from my hand. It bounced and landed upside down, spilling my nice warm mush onto the ground.

'Oh dear, I'm so sorry,' he said, which was a blatant lie and not at all as funny as his compatriot made it out to be.

I stared at him as a surge of anger rose within me. I could have suppressed it, and I probably would have if he hadn't interpreted my moment of introspection as weakness and decided to spit on me.

I looked down at the sputum sliding down my leg and that anger within me flared into rage. I reached out and grabbed him by the throat, meaning to choke him into submission, but instead I felt a soft crumbly sensation under my hand. His eyes swelled from their sockets until I thought they would pop out, but not a sound came from him, only a rush of blood from his nose. I let him go and he sagged to the ground, the air wheezing from his lungs and bubbles rising in the blood that now covered half his face. The men around me scrabbled backwards, their food and drink forgotten as the stench of loosened bowels rose from the man's darkening trousers.

I stared at my hands, which I had thought somehow weak and ineffectual, while the others called for the guards. I was convinced that I had barely put any pressure on his throat at all, but he was most certainly dead. The guards arrived before I could give it any more thought, but seemed at a loss what to do as I wasn't doing anything except sitting there and looking at my fingers. One of them touched the dead man's throat and confirmed what everyone else knew already.

'What is this ruckus?' I recognised the Deacon's voice and scent before he pushed his way through the milling warriors. He glanced at the corpse, then looked across at me. 'What did you do?'

'Nothing,' I said with a shrug. 'He spat on me, so I squeezed him a bit.'

'You killed him!'

That much was obvious, so I didn't reply. The Deacon rubbed his face and gestured to two of the warriors.

'I should have known something like this would happen. Chain him up. Hands behind his back, and keep him like that until we get to the Crossing.'

Something stirred in my mind at the sound of his words, just enough for me to know that I didn't like the sound of chains at all. And, since I was thinking about it, I really didn't care for the ropes or being dragged behind a wagon either. It appeared that I had woken with a finite amount of patience.

'No chains,' I said. The warriors took a step back as I stood up. 'I am no beast to be bound at your bidding.'

As I spoke, one of the warriors in the shiny armour moved forward to take up a position in front of the Deacon. His head armour was open, revealing a florid but typically unremarkable human face.

13

'The Deacon has spoken. His word is that of the Sacred Church, and as such is the word of Drogah. You will obey it, or be branded a heretic.'

I peered at his armour, paying more attention to the ridiculously ornate carvings on the front bit. There were what looked like skulls in thorns around a symbol that looked like two crosses next to each other. However, the strangest part of it was that I knew I had seen it before. I didn't know from where or how, but whatever memory my unbroken mind associated with it wasn't a pleasant one.

'You're a pad . . . padaladin. A paladin,' I said, feeling pleased that a piece of my puzzle, albeit a small one, had fallen into place.

'I am indeed of the sacred brotherhood. We are the chosen of Drogah, his will made manifest upon this tainted earth.' His voice rose as he said it so that the last was a shout, as if I was deaf or had stopped paying attention.

'I hate paladins,' I said, more to myself than anything else. I didn't know why I was reacting to them so poorly, but I had a strong suspicion that I would never submit to being ordered around by one. Perhaps I was a demon after all.

'Then I have no recourse but to name you a heretic!' the paladin bellowed, drawing his sword and advancing on me, teeth bared and his eyes rolling like those of a maddened beast.

Without thinking, I lifted my hands, ready to defend myself against the sudden rage that gripped him, and the warriors fanning out behind him who weren't exactly radiating friendship either. Their cold swords would take a terrible toll on this body.

There was a momentary resistance as I raised my hands, followed by a ripping sound, and I joined the men around me in staring at the ropes that I had just snapped. I looked up first, and seeing them still distracted, I turned and ran towards the forest.

Or that's what I tried to do. My legs responded admirably for the first dozen strides or so, but by the time I saw the tree stump it was too late for my imperfect dexterity to avoid it. I careened off its gnarled surface and rolled a few times, giving my pursuers enough time to arrive and start beating me with wooden cudgels.

I tried to shield myself with my arms but they were too many and too quick. The first half-dozen blows left me gasping, but amid the pain I felt my anger growing. I reached for it, and perhaps because I was no longer focused on the blows, the pain lost some of its grip on my mind. I reached out and grabbed the closest of my attackers by his ankle and, as I had with the man who'd spilled my mush, I closed my grip and squeezed. There was a moment of resistance before I felt and heard his bones crack within my fist. He screamed and fell over, and I used the gap this created to scrabble back to my feet and make another dash for the forest, bowling another of them from their feet with my shoulder.

First among the things that I learned that night was to never run through a dark forest. I lost count of the bushes and roots that I tripped over and the number of times that I nearly lost an eye or worse from protruding branches. The only advantage to this was that my pursuers fared equally poorly, and my dark skin and lack of clinking armour made it easier for me to evade them. I hid behind a tree and listened to them until I was confident that they had lost my trail, then circled back towards the wagons.

There were a few men with torches clustered around where the other men were still chained up, but the light that was giving them comfort was also ruining what little vision they had. I passed them by and followed the scent of the cooking fire. A single man was sitting next to it, a large bowl resting on his legs as he spooned the tasty mush into his mouth in a steady rhythm. I moved up behind him as quietly as I could and grabbed him by the throat from behind. I ignored him as he desperately flailed at my hand, but as he hadn't done anything to me I didn't need to kill him and so took great care not to tighten my grip. I dropped him as soon as he stopped squirming and was pleased when he continued gasping at my feet.

I helped myself to a brimming bowl of the mush and ate greedily, enjoying the taste and warmth that the concoction imparted. Another two bowls saw the gnawing ache in my belly recede and left me feeling better than I had since I woke in that damned field. The voices from the forest were growing louder, a sign that the rest of the mob were returning. There was a large bag of some sort nearby, as well as a sword and a few other items. I stuffed as much as I could into the bag and ran for the forest with it under my arm. I was more than halfway there before the first arrow buzzed past me. With my stolen bag held tightly to me, I was already running as fast as I could without risking another tumble, and I had to trust to the darkness and increasing distance to keep me safe.

The second arrow hit me in the back half a dozen strides later.

Chapter 3

The impact was a sudden but strangely dull pain, like a particularly vicious strike from one of their cudgels. It threw my rhythm off and nearly sent me face first into a tree, but I somehow managed to recover enough to avoid it. With my legs still working, I told myself that I would keep moving until the injury forced me to stop, and yet as I bullied my way through the undergrowth I found myself growing impatient for it to happen. I could hear my pursuers behind me, but not knowing the extent of the wound was driving me to distraction.

When I could bear it no longer I stopped and reached behind me, but all that I found was a half-dried smear of blood. There was no arrow standing proud from my hide, nor any blood flowing across the back of my legs. I licked the blood from my fingers, hoisted my stolen bag and started moving again. Perhaps it had been a glancing shot, or weak from the distance. I couldn't be sure but did not care to wait for the scouts to find and enlighten me about it.

Unfortunately the scouts had other ideas, and they were far nimbler and accustomed to travelling in forests than I was. The first hint I had that they had found me was when an arrow embedded itself in a tree in front of me with a loud thunk.

'Hold and surrender!' called a voice from somewhere to my left. 'Or the next one is in your back.'

Given that they'd already shot me in the back, it seemed a bit strange to offer me the option now, but then men were strange. The forest had gone quiet, as if the small creatures within the canopy and undergrowth were holding their breath with me. I turned and squinted into the darkness at where the voice had come from. The harder I stared, the stranger my eyes began to feel, like they were swelling. It was a very queer sensation, although not painful as such, just unexpected and odd. I rubbed at them, but the sensation persisted. A fear that my vision was failing began to gnaw at my thoughts. I continued to stare towards where I thought the scout was, resisting the urge to blink for fear that my eyes would not open again, but instead the edges of my vision began to fade into a reddish hue, as if my eyes were filling with blood. This red glow washed across my vision before my fear could bloom into panic, and as it did the impenetrable shadows that had rendered the forest so strange and claustrophobic began to yield their secrets; it was as if the entire area was bathed in the light of a fierce, red moon. I saw the scout at last, crouched in a shallow dip, his entire body pulsing with a soft light in time to his heartbeat. I chuckled and only the bag in my left hand stopped me from clapping my hands together in glee as the odds at last shifted into my favour.

'I see you,' I called back, and I saw his head move. I followed the line of where he was looking and caught a glimpse of a similar reddish-yellow body on the opposite side to me.

'Throw out your weapons,' the first scout commanded.

I dropped my bag with some reluctance; I would need both hands for what I needed to do.

'No,' I replied, and leaped forward. I didn't hear where his arrow ended up, nor did I care. I cleared the clump of bushes easily enough and knew that I was out of their sight for a few moments at least; I used the time to move back at a sharp angle so as to slip back past them. I was expecting them to chase after me and they didn't disappoint. I was convinced that my hearts were beating loud enough to betray my position, but they passed where I was hiding among some roots without so much as a glance in my direction. They were wonderfully skilled in moving quietly, and avoided holes and grasping branches with an ease that belied the limitations of their stunted senses.

I waited for the closest of them to pass me by, then rose and charged him from behind. He turned as I leaped for his back, his eyes widening even as he loosed his arrow. It whipped past me harmlessly, and then I was on him. He collapsed to the ground without any real resistance, and stopped squirming altogether when I pounded a fist into his face, breaking bones and turning his scream into a garbled, wet noise.

'Allan!' shouted the second scout as he darted from tree to tree towards us. The unfortunate Allan wheezed in reply as I lifted my weight off his chest, but could do nothing except lie there and die as I moved to intercept his friend. My ambush was betrayed by an errant moonbeam though, and the scout had just enough time to raise his bow and loose his arrow before I could charge him down.

This one hit me just under my ribs and sent a sharp wave of nausea through me. I staggered as various muscles clenched, slowing me down long enough for him to reach for the tube of arrows at his hip again. I plucked the arrow from my gut, and was surprised when it popped out without any real effort. I flung it aside and leaped to the attack before he could finish readying his next arrow. I balled my fist and hit him square in the chest, and watched in wonder as he lifted off the ground and sailed into a tree trunk some ten paces behind where he'd stood. I was still staring when he dropped to the ground with the boneless grace that only the dead can manage.

I moved back into the moonlight, which looked far brighter than it had any right to be, and examined my wound. I could see where the impact had torn a small 'V' in my skin, but the wound wasn't very deep at all and had already begun clotting. I stretched and twisted carefully, testing whether there were any lingering pains, but there was only a dull and formless ache. It was another part of the puzzle that I needed to think about, but this too would have to wait.

After making sure no one else was skulking about, I bent over the second scout's body and stripped him of his weapons and coin purse. I tried to take his shirt too, but after several frustrating minutes of trying to shake him out of it, I abandoned the idea. I gathered my loot up into a bundle and headed into the deeper forest, marvelling at how much easier it was to travel through it now that I could see more, even if I was still a bit wobbly on my legs. Everything looked so much bigger now too. I kept walking until the deep dark of the night gave way to the promise of dawn, and with neither sight nor sound of my pursuers I felt comfortable enough to stop and take stock of what I'd taken from the dead men.

It took twice as long to work out how to belt on one of their swords than it had for me to squirm into my clothes, and even then it threatened to trip me on every other step. I practised drawing it from its leather sock and swinging it about a few times, and was pleased with the swishing noise it made. I chopped it into a tree as an experiment but managed to snap the blade, which was disappointing. I decided not to bother with the other sword and tossed the whole contraption aside and only kept their knives, which were far handier to use and carry.

With that settled, I spent some time just moving around and getting a feel for this body's range of movement and strength. The long walk had done much to settle my balance, which had accounted for most of the problems I'd had. Curious, I picked up the second sword and tried to bend it, but it folded in half almost as soon as I applied any pressure. Disgusted by the poor workmanship, I tossed it aside and tried the same with a nearby sapling. The green wood offered little resistance and snapped wetly within moments, which made me even more curious. I balled my hand into a fist once more, gritted my teeth, and struck a nearby pine tree. Bark flew, the tree shivered and needles rained down on me from above. I tried again, a little bit harder, and was rewarded by the sight of a wad of pulped wood flying off to the side and a pair of startled squirrels landing opposite me. Another two or three blows saw the tree sway before the damaged trunk gave way with a loud crack. My knuckles were scraped and a bit bloody, but the bones underneath still felt sound and strong. I winced as the tree crashed to the ground with a sound like thunder, dispelling any notion of continued stealth.

I flexed my arm and felt the muscles swell. I poked at them, and felt as much give in them as a stone. They were dense, heavy bulges, and I knew that my bones would be equally strong; the fallen tree proved that. As signs of dawn began to filter through the canopy, I turned to examine the wound in my gut where the scout had shot me, except that there was nothing to see, not even a scab. Satisfied that I had one less thing to worry about, I tried squinting my eyes again to see whether this . . . blood vision that had come to my rescue was permanent. I squinted, pressed my palms against my eyes and blinked hundreds of times as I tried to make it go away, so much so that a passing fox stopped to stare at me. However, watching the fox leave proved to be the key to returning my vision to normal; it had something to do with squinting while I changed the distance I was looking at. I wasn't entirely sure how it worked, but I tried it several times more until the transition was smooth and the sensation of my eyes swelling up felt less unnerving.

If I really had done this to myself, I had done it well. Apart from the missing memories and paralysis of course, but then no one was perfect. I was in good health, strong and free. And hungry enough that I found myself wondering whether I could tempt the fox to come back. Instead I emptied the bag that I'd snatched from the Deacon's camp, hoping that a nice ham had somehow escaped my notice, but most of it was herbs and dried flakes that tasted of nothing and dried my mouth out until my tongue stuck to my gums. With little enthusiasm I chewed some dried fruit that I found among the goods, then fastened the stolen purses to a rope around my middle and began walking. I didn't have a direction in mind other than making sure that I wasn't heading towards Thasper's Crossing like the Deacon was, which meant heading further west.

Between the time that it took for the sun to rise and the insects to rouse themselves into an annoying, biting cloud, it was actually quite pleasant walking through the forest, watching isolated beams of morning light spearing through the leaves and listening to the birds. However, the first mouthful of stinging flies put paid to any ideas I might have had about lingering there and taking more time to try to plumb the mystery of my origin. I concentrated on moving as quickly as possible, for to stop was to become a banquet for anything with wings and a stinger.

The sun was comfortably past its zenith by the time the trees had thinned out enough to no longer be considered a forest, a change that gradually replaced the flying pests with a pleasant breeze. I could now see how the forest was giving way to wide, rolling plains that stretched out as far as I could see. The uniformity of this sweeping vista was broken by narrow and crooked paths, clusters of monolithic grey rock and ragged hedges and fences that divided much of it into a yellow, green and brown patchwork. Wherever I was, it wasn't a wilderness.

I was still mulling over which way I would go when I caught the distinct scent of men on the breeze, their usual pungency underscored by the sharper tones of metal and oil. Armed men, then, and drawing closer to me. I suppressed a groan. I was no friend of the forest like their scouts had been but I had thought my progress had been rather good; however, I had entirely forgotten about man's annoying habit of riding horses. The slope offered little in the way of cover aside from a shattered tree wedged between two rocks by some violent storm. I scrambled over the fallen trunk and had barely hunkered down before two horsemen came into sight a hundred or so paces down from me. They slowed and separated, occasionally stopping to stand up for a better view. It was a strange thing, but despite the danger, the smell of the horses was making me salivate. The thought of all that good, dark flesh was quite intoxicating.

They were moving ever closer to me, so I wiped my mouth and forced the thought of food from my mind as I started weighing my options. Their scents were familiar, which quickly quelled any notion I might have had that they were simply passing by. I felt confident with my balance now, but I knew that there was no way that I could compete with a horse for speed. I needed a slightly more sophisticated plan than running straight at them, and one came to me as my foot slipped on a loose rock.

When I stepped out from behind the trunk shortly after, they quickly drew their swords and urged their steeds closer. I stumbled towards them, clutching at my gut as if I was in pain. They edged even closer, and I continued with my mummery until they were both within range.

Then I straightened up, cocked my arm back and threw the first of the rocks I'd picked up at the man to my right. I knew it was a good throw as soon as it left my hand and I didn't bother watching its flight; by the time it smashed into his chest I'd already turned and cocked my arm towards the second man. He seemed to be undecided, and I saved him the indignity of further indecision by denting his skull with another fine throw, even if I had been aiming for his chest.

To say that I was pleased with myself was an understatement, and I wasted little time in gathering the reins of both horses and tying them to the tree trunk. The man who I had hit in the chest was still alive, although the blood on his lips suggested that would change very shortly. I dropped him next to his dead comrade and left him to wheeze out some sort of prayer while I rummaged through their bags.

'What is this?' I asked, rubbing the dry flaky stuff through my fingers. 'You're all carrying it.'

He frowned at me, then spat out a glob of blood. 'Oats, you bloody fool.'

'Oats,' I repeated. 'It's terrible eating.' I emptied the rest of the bag and picked out some dried meat and fruit. I watched him watch me as I chewed a mouthful.

'What are you?' he wheezed.

I shrugged and took another bite of the tasteless and entirely anonymous meat. 'Why are you chasing me?'

'You . . . killed our men.'

'You chained me up and then attacked me.' I swallowed the mouthful while he drew a few rapid breaths. 'You're dying,' I offered, but his only response was a short fit of coughing that left his chin red.

23

It was clear that he wasn't about to offer any insights into my predicament, so I busied myself with relieving him and his dead companion of anything useful, notably their knives and purses. The dying man didn't waste any of his remaining breath with questions or protests, which was wise of him since I'd have ignored either.

I settled back and emptied their purses, as well as what I'd taken from the scouts, onto the dead man's cloak and examined the mismatched coins that lay before me. There was little uniformity to them in either size or appearance, so I divided them into piles according to the type of metal they were made from.

'What is this?' I asked the coughing man, holding up a hexagonal silver coin with the stylised image of a bird, and waited patiently as he stared at it and me in turn.

'A double.' His voice was barely audible over the wind.

'Is it more valuable than this?' I held up a round silver coin. For a moment I thought he'd died, but he coughed up some more blood and blinked at me like an owl.

'Is it?' I prompted him.

He stared at me long enough for me to wonder if I had spoken my question out loud or just thought about doing it.

'Yes,' he gasped eventually.

'Ah.' I wanted to ask him more questions, but in all honesty the blood leaking from his mouth was making him look quite grotesque. I left him to die at his own pace and turned my attention to the horses. Those big, succulent horses.

I led one to the side and killed it as painlessly as I could, then used my newly acquired knives to butcher it, an endeavour that had seemed so simple in my mind but turned out to be anything but. The man was still wheezing when I had finished, and watched me as I rinsed the worst of the blood off me using one of their water-skins. The other horse was showing the whites of its eyes at me, but it wasn't going anywhere and I left it alone.

'Do you know how to make a fire?' I asked.

He mouthed something, but no words came out. I moved closer and straddled his legs. I meant to ask him to say it again, but instead something far more curious and grander happened. His gaze met mine, and as he looked into my eyes I felt something inside my mind shift, a sudden release of pressure that I hadn't been aware of. The dark of his eyes seemed to yawn wider until they swallowed me up, and I stood there in the blackness as images flashed past me at a tremendous speed. I saw myself stumble out from behind the trees. I felt his pain and surprise as my rock smashed his ribs inwards. I saw glimpses of men laughing around a fire and tasted strong wine upon my lips. I saw cities and towns, women with long hair, a fierce battle with goblins and an even fiercer one with hundreds of men in lumbering, square formations stabbing and hacking at each other. I saw this and more before the images faded and the black released me to tumble from where I had been sat on him, my chest heaving for air.

I sat up and took several deep breaths to steady myself as the sensations faded and reality reasserted its presence. I looked to the man, whose name I now knew to be Matthias, but whatever had just happened had cost him the last embers of his life and his eyes now stared sightlessly up at the clouds. I rubbed at my face as I rose to my feet. His thoughts and memories were mine now, and while I was still reeling from this latest revelation of my demonic powers, I was also actually quite pleased. I now knew where I was, and that no more riders were looking for me as the Deacon was eager to meet with his master. And, more importantly, I now remembered how to start a fire. Thinking was always best done on a full stomach and I was soon roasting horseflesh over a fine blaze and feeling pleased with my morning's work.

While I waited for the meat to char to my liking, I sorted through the pile of goods that I had emptied out of the riders' various bags and pockets. There really wasn't much of anything that I found interesting, and a few of the items were entirely baffling. I ignored these, or threw them over my shoulder, and finally settled on a nice sharp pair of knives, a large hooded cloak, a gold ring that Matthias had been wearing and a full water-skin. The ring went into my steadily expanding purse and the rest into my bag. Satisfied that I was now suitably equipped, I set to my roast and ate until the skin on my gut was as taught as a drum. I wrapped the leftovers in the shirt that I had cut from Matthias's body, jammed this into my bag as well, and resumed my journey west in good spirits.

Chapter 4

Despite the initial discomfort of walking with such a full stomach, the forest and poor dead Matthias were a good many miles behind me by the time a cloudless night spread itself across the sky. I wasn't particularly tired or cold, but the idea of a fire woke something akin to a thirst inside me, and so it was that the darkest hours found me stretched out alongside a glowing bed of coals. The slow procession of the stars overhead provided a glittering backdrop as my mind replayed the day's events and took a tally of what I had learned.

I was still at a loss as to how I had come to be in that field, and even more so, why. I knew only that the body I wore was not truly my own, but also that it was strong and resilient. In a way, I owed the men who had chased me a debt of gratitude, for without their pursuit and the confrontations that had followed, it may have taken me far longer to discover so much about myself. And yet I still knew so little. Was I truly a demon? Was it that heritage that made the idea of fire so appealing? And if I was some Hel-born creature, why was I wearing a man's body?

I stared up at the stars as I tried to coax a memory from my mind. I had woken with a sense that I had succeeded in whatever I had wanted to do and a vague sense of urgency, which suggested I had done this to myself purposefully. I couldn't have been hunting something, not if I chose a human form. Or was it that I was being hunted? A shiver rippled down my back at the thought and I felt it ring true with something inside me. I *was* being hunted, but by what? If I didn't know my enemy, how could I protect myself from him? Or her. Or even *it*, if I was indeed a demon that had somehow escaped from some terrible Hel.

And if I had not been able to defend myself with a whole and sound mind, how could I hope to do so when I couldn't even remember the rest of my name? Whatever terror pursued me, I had clearly believed that my greatest defence was the anonymity a human form offered.

With such thoughts in my head, I tentatively reached out and held my hand over the nearest clump of embers. I could feel the heat, but it wasn't at all uncomfortable, and hardly seemed to increase as I slowly lowered my hand. Intrigued, I picked up a large ember and let it roll into the centre of my palm. Despite the golden red glow that suffused it, I could hardly feel any real heat radiating from it; if anything, it felt quite pleasant. I experimented more, gradually adding more coals until my hand was covered in a small mound of them; only then did it start becoming uncomfortable. Curious, I pulled myself up into a seated position, scooped up a few coals and stared at them, willing them to burst into flame. I remembered how right it had felt when the Deacon's magic had suffused my body and how it had seemed so natural, but whatever I had felt then steadfastly eluded me now, no matter how much of my infernal will I bent to the task.

I dusted the coals off and lay back down, but now an ache began to bloom within my head, throbbing in time with my heartbeat. Groaning, I sat up again, hoping that a bite of horse meat and a gulp of the warm, vaguely goat-flavoured water in the skin would settle it, but before I could fish either out of the bag, my nose began to bleed. It ran freely, and I had no idea how to stop it. I tried pinching my nose, but it felt like it was oozing back into my mouth, so instead I simply hunkered over the coals and let it sizzle away. It didn't last long, but the ache grew worse once it stopped. I rubbed the sides of my head, then squeezed at them, but nothing I did made any impression. Whatever this was, it was inside my head.

I settled into a comfortable position and tried to concentrate on the pain, which was harder than it sounds. I closed my eyes and stopped fighting it. Pain is normally centred on an injury, and is simply your body warning you that you've done something stupid. Your flesh and mind know this, and so both will try to shy away from whatever is hurting you; it is an instinctive reaction and one that takes discipline to overcome. I knew I hadn't hurt my head, not physically, which meant it had to have something to do with what I had attempted with the coals. I tried it again, and the pain swelled in response. Much of me cried out to stop what I was doing, but I forced myself to keep trying, to keep pushing at the thoughts that brought the most painful responses.

The thing about pain is that it you can become accustomed to it, like plunging into an icy lake where at first you can barely breathe. If you endure beyond the initial agony though, you discover that there are a thousand inflections of it, nuances in intonation that those with courage can read and use as a guide to understanding what lies beyond. This is what I did now, and I knew that I was bleeding once more, but it was a distant concern now, a single discordant note within a far greater whole.

I heard the ghostly echo of the Deacon's magic within my mind, and there, amid the roaring pain, I heard another note. It was weaker than the Deacon's and somehow incomplete, but I knew it as my own. I reached for it with my mind and felt it respond, and as I drew it towards me I felt a lessening in the insistent weight of the pain. It was a small fragment of power, but magic was the one constant to all that had happened to me and was perhaps the only part of who I had been that I had carried with me. It was the key, both to understanding who I was and what I was seeking, and to my continued freedom.

I felt the sorcery hidden within me wake and call to the Songlines. There was no pain, nor any strange heat racing through my body as the call was answered, only an improved awareness of some of what I had lost. All magic has harmony at its heart, just as every living thing has a true name, its own unique song that forms part of the greater whole. Unlike most, I had known my true name but my memory of it had somehow fragmented or been taken from me. What I had found was only a piece of it, a single note from a forgotten song, but it was a start. Aside from opening a crack in my mind's refusal to share memories, it gave me a point to start searching from, and by the time the more active part of my brain began to register that dawn was breaking, I had gathered three other such fragments. I slowly rose from my trance-like state, the half-dried and midge-infested blood from my prolonged nosebleed crackling as I lifted my head. While I had sat there, locked within my own mind, utterly vulnerable and uncaring, the sun had risen high into the sky, basking me in warmth that I hadn't felt.

In my mind, the gathered fragments of my true name spun and harmonised themselves into a firmer whole, and I shivered in ecstasy as a steady connection sparked into life between me and the Songlines. I had never felt anything like that before, but I imagined it was how a blind and deaf man would feel if he woke to find his senses fully restored. I opened my hand and watched in wonderment as the air over my palm began to shimmer with magic. It was slow to gather, a dribble as opposed to the torrent my ghostly memories teased me with, but it was *mine*. I maintained my focus and it slowly returned to me, filling some of the void within me with a pleasant throb.

Despite the fact that I was trapped in this human form, I felt surprisingly good. All my wounds were healed, I was strong, healthy and hopefully not far from recovering my full power. I made myself comfortable and began crafting a few simple sorcerous constructs, making each more complex than the one before until the transitions became smooth and fast. The moon had risen again by the time I had satisfied myself that I was in full control of my power. The struggle to reclaim it had exhausted me though, and after stoking the fire back to life, I ate what was left of the horse meat, closed my eyes and knew nothing more of the world until the following morning.

The campsite was half a day's walk behind me when I saw my next human, a hunched-over figure pulling a covered handcart. According to my recently acquired memories, I was on the road to a small town named Five Elms where the local wheat beer was quite good, but hopelessly overpriced. The man with the handcart passed me by without even looking up, which was a bit of a novelty but encouraging, as I'd donned Matthias's hooded cloak in the hope that it would make me less noticeable.

The town came into sight shortly after I passed the man and his cart. The road ran straight down towards a wide pair of gates set into the sagging wooden palisade that encircled it, beyond which I could see a good number of low buildings and dozens of townsfolk walking about doing whatever it is that humans did in a town that wasn't on fire. I pulled my hood up and squatted in the shadow of a large boulder as I weighed my options.

The gates were wide open and by all accounts unguarded, unless you considered the portly figure sleeping against the wall with a spear on his lap a viable defence. If these people were aware of the war that Matthias had known of, they gave little sign of it. Dozens of figures were milling around on the road that ran through the middle of it, along with a number of wagons of various sizes. They didn't actually look to be doing anything other than standing there and occasionally gesticulating at each other, and the more I thought about it the less I liked the idea of going down there and drawing attention to myself. I had some of their coins now, but would it be enough for a meal? Matthias's memories suggested they would be, but even so, it seemed an unnecessary risk given that the lands around me were home to myriad free, tasty animals. And I rather liked the feel of the coins bouncing against my waist. I rose and put Five Elms to my right and headed towards the citadel Matthias's memories had hinted at.

Chapter 5

I felt good about my decision to bypass Five Elms even if some part of me was curious to discover what wheat beer tasted like. My own thoughts and problems were quickly eroding the finer details of Matthias's memories, leaving me with only a vague recollection of there being a sizeable citadel some distance ahead. I had nothing to compare how his idea of 'some distance' related to mine, but the sun was shining and I was strong and free, so it didn't really bother me. I let my mind wander as I strode along, mostly in the hope that thinking of nothing in particular would help soothe the questions nagging at me.

The walking was easy, and my mind wandered, so much so that I barely noticed that the sun had set as I strode along, now and then humming tunes whose provenance I had no recollection of. It was only when I saw the warm yellow light shining from a distant homestead that I began to pay more attention to my surroundings again. I was hungry, not alarmingly so, but I suspected that would change by morning. I contemplated visiting the homestead, but instead opted to simply help myself to one of the many sheep in their fields. Unfortunately a treacherous gust of wind sent my scent among them, spooking the ram, and soon enough the whole herd was bleating and charging about in a panic. The farmstead's door opened and that same warm yellow light now silhouetted the figures of angry, shouting men and the blurred shapes of hounds charging out of the house.

I sighed and rested my head against a fence post. Was everything in these lands always this complicated? I only wanted one little sheep. Wolves and dogs, for all of their barking and drooling, were good companions and even better eating when circumstances demanded it, but this wasn't the time or place for that. I drew upon my sorcery and projected an idea into the lead dog's head that my scent was in fact heading off in the opposite direction, and watched with both amusement and relief as the pack hared off across the fields, followed soon after by the swinging lanterns of the farmer and his farmhands. I hopped into the paddock, grabbed a confused-looking lamb and made my escape long before the dog came to its senses.

By the time that the sun rose the next morning I had already risen from my ferny bed under the stars and was striding along the road. It wasn't that I was particularly eager to reach the citadel, but I had it in mind that something so grand as to be called that would surely have a sage or two, men whose brains I could plunder for clues about myself in one way or the other.

The landscape was changing as I travelled, the wild hedgerows and outcroppings of rocks and trees diminishing and steadily being replaced with level, fenced fields dotted with men and women wearing large hats. Most of these worked fields also sported bands of armed men with large hounds that started barking and whining as soon as they caught my scent. I ignored the men's stares, and for the most part they ignored me as well, although some walked parallel to me until I passed beyond their territory, their spears and swords close at hand. I left them to their posturing and kept walking, pausing only to drink from the occasional stream.

My sorcery was far more effective than a snare when it came to providing myself with food, and I became remarkably adept at winkling out hares and a fat but surprisingly quick ground-bird that I discovered to be extremely tasty. I couldn't win though, as using sorcery made me hungry, which in turn made me want to find food more often. It was an amusing distraction nonetheless, and the habit of watching out for small prey served to at least keep me more alert.

The next morning had seen me set my feet to the road while the dawn was still painting the sky and I was in the mood for a decent breakfast. I was tasting the air for any trace of a suitable volunteer when I caught the scent of men, which was at best disappointing. I slowed and took a deeper breath. The road here meandered through a series of rocky outcroppings, turning sharply upon itself several times as it wound through some low hills that offered little grazing for anything except the most determined goat. I wondered why I could smell at least a dozen men ahead of me and no trace of a fire or cooking. Men were, however, as unpredictable as they were savage, so while their presence was a bit unexpected I wasn't overly concerned. They would have their own incomprehensible reasons for their behaviour.

I'd heard and smelled them moving long before the first of them strode out onto the path in front of me. There were five of them, all clad in various layers of hide and each with a blue sash tied about their waist. Their hands rested upon small shields and the handles of the swords that hung from those complicated-looking belts.

'Halt!' shouted the one in the middle.

I looked around and wasn't at all surprised to see that another five were on the road behind me. That left two that I couldn't see yet.

'Good morning,' I offered.

'Not for you, laddie,' the speaker replied, which made the men alongside him bare their teeth in smiles that were bright against their dirty faces. 'You armed?'

'Obviously,' was my immediate reply as I raised my hands. It was only when I said it aloud that I realised he had meant my weapons, which made me laugh.

'Are you sassing me?' he said, the humour of it obviously wasted on him.

'I'm not used to carrying weapons,' I said.

'Well, you're carryin' them now, and that's against the law.' He smiled at this though, which I found baffling. 'That means you're going to have to come with us.'

'You have more weapons than me.'

'We are soldiers of the Crown,' he said, tugging at his sash. 'And you, *sir*, are carrying arms on Crown lands in a time of war.'

'It's not my war.'

'It is when you're going about armed.'

I waited for him to continue, but he stood there with his thumbs hooked under his belt. One of them coughed behind me, but for a few moments the only sounds were the soft jingling of their buckles as they fidgeted about.

'Well?' said the speaker. 'You going to surrender them?'

'I don't think I will.'

'And I don't think you have a choice. Come now, look around you. It'd be a shame to ruin a fine morning like this by dying.'

It was a fine morning, but I had no intention of dying. I was about to say something similar when a thought came to me. 'Why are you here?' I said. 'Who sent you?'

One or two of them laughed at that, but the question seemed to have confused them. 'Do you know who I am?' I ventured.

'I know what you are,' the man in the middle said, and the presence inside me stirred as my hearts surged with anticipation.

'Yes?'

'Out of luck and, in the name of the King, under arrest.' He glanced at the man next to him while disappointment made my shoulders sag. 'Take his weapons,' he said.

'Down! Down! On the ground!' this man shouted as he advanced on me, his hand finding his sword. I felt the coiled, hidden thing inside me shake itself awake as he drew closer. I didn't want this fight, not when twelve men were ranged against me, but the beast only gave a dry, ghostly chuckle at the thought. A shiver rippled across my hide as its alien mind rose to meet mine, a tide of anger rising with it and filling my senses with the need to fight. To kill.

I was moving before I realised that I had made the decision to do so. I watched with a strange, detached interest as I caught his sword arm and swung my fist up into the bottom of his jaw, shattering the bone and severing his tongue. An inarticulate cry rose up around me as his fellows belatedly leaped to his defence, the steel of their weapons flashing in the morning sun as he fell to the ground, clutching at his face.

I charged at them too, a growl bursting unbidden from me which made them falter, particularly the squat little man who was unfortunate to be the closest and thus first in my path. His thrust was weak and poorly timed, whereas the slash I aimed at his neck wasn't. I ripped my blade free as I stepped past him, and so didn't have a chance to see the blood jetting from his torn neck. I kept moving, stabbing and cutting with my stolen knives until a more skilled opponent among them smashed both from my hands, cutting one deeply. The pain was sharp and sudden, and the dull roar that had filled my head faltered. The foolish bravado that the beast had lent me fell away and I cradled the bloodied hand to my chest.

A spear flashed, and I felt it bite. I grabbed it, snapped the shaft and drove the splintered end into the wielder's back as he tried to get out of the way. But more blows were hitting home with every moment that passed, and already more than one sword glistened with my blood. A blow struck my brow, sending blood into my eyes. I waved my hands wildly, caught hold of something and squeezed. An unseen man screamed. Something hit the back of my head, and suddenly there was grass against my face and my body was shuddering with the impact of the remaining men taking their vengeance upon me. It was a strange thing, lying there in my own blood like that. It felt important, a reminder of something familiar and important that I had to remember, but I was too dazed to think clearly. Images and voices waxed and waned, and I didn't know if I was actually hearing and seeing them or only remembering them.

I slowly rose back to consciousness some time after the sun had set. The awareness of my body's weight and form came first, encasing my spirit, and the residual pain of my injuries and the burning ache in my shoulders did the rest. My left eye was swollen to a slit, and the right was gummed up with something that crackled when I eventually forced it open. It was night, and I was tied to the stump of a rough barked tree on the edge of the men's camp with a prickly but stout rope. The embers of a small, neglected fire glowed dully in the centre of six or seven shapeless and snoring lumps. One figure was sitting with his back against a rock, and after a few minutes of concentration that set yet another ache pounding in my head, I managed to discern that he too was asleep, his heartbeat slow and steady.

I woke my night vision with difficulty, sending more sharp pains stabbing through my head. I couldn't keep it focused, and barely had time to sweep the blood-red tint across their shabby campsite. There was no sense to it, and if some night-prowling predator were to spring upon them, at least half would be running into their comrades' way or tripping over the arms and armour each had laid next to him. To the side of the little dell I could see five darker mounds, one of which currently sported a pair of industriously digging jackals who'd scented the dead men beneath as easily as I had. They weren't buried very deep, which I took as further evidence of my captors' laziness.

Finally I looked to myself. Scabbed clods of blood mottled my skin, most of it my own, and a grubby-looking strip of cloth was bound around my left thigh. This was ripe with a mixture of human blood and my own, and I guessed it was a makeshift bandage cut from the clothing of the dead. More interesting than that was the small metallic token that had been tied into the knot. My vision wouldn't behave itself long enough for me to pick out the details, but it was a triangle with something on the inside, and glowed softly in a way that clearly had nothing to do with moonlight. It hurt too much to keep my night vision awake and I blinked it away, sighing as the pain in my head went from viciously stabbing to merely throbbing cruelly. The skin on my face felt tight and dry as I grimaced, and a cautious bit of probing confirmed that I had another no doubt equally dirty bandage wrapped around my head.

A gentle pressure against the tree told me that I had a swollen wound at the back of my head, and the sudden pain that followed such a tentative touch made my neck and shoulders clench sharply. Even seated, it made my vision blur and left me feeling unbalanced. There was no point in even attempting sorcery while I was in such bad shape. A twinge of pain like that at the wrong moment could be disastrous, no matter what I was attempting at the time. Sorcery was a boon, but like a storm that can drown a city or flatten a forest, it was a natural force that offered no loyalty and was ruthless to those who disrespected it. Losing control midway through a construct would be like lighting a fire while standing upon the kindling.

I took what comfort I could from the thought that they hadn't killed me while they had the chance, a mistake that I silently promised myself they would come to regret. My body would heal itself given time, so all I had to do was wait until the right moment came and try not to get killed in the meantime. I slowly bent my legs, clenching my teeth against the new aches and pains that announced themselves, and rested my arms upon my knees and my forehead upon my arms. Once the initial discomfort passed, it was tolerable enough a position that I managed to drift into a fitful sleep.

It didn't feel like I had done more than close my eyes before someone kicked me in the ribs. The jolt of snapping into wakefulness hurt more than the kick, and my groan of pain seemed to please my tormentor.

'He's still alive,' he said.

I felt utterly helpless as he stood there looking down at me, and I was. All I could do was bare my teeth at him, careless of the cuts that reopened.

'Unlike your friends,' I snapped back at him. 'Untie me and you can join them.' It was mere bravado, and the scant pleasure I took from saying it was not worth the beating that followed. He was sweating by the time he grew tired of kicking me, whereas I was bleeding again from where his attack had reopened a few of the previous day's wounds.

38

'Shut your bloody mouth,' he said, punctuating it with a gobbet of spit as he marched away favouring his left leg. I had at least managed to hurt him in some fashion but it wasn't a method I'd care to employ again.

I lay there and waited for them to do whatever it was they were making so much noise doing. I smelled them cooking something that smelled bland enough to remind me of the oats they all seemed to have, and soon after they gathered their belongings and pulled me to my feet with no little amount of cursing from both sides. It felt like the ground was swaying beneath me as I clung to the tree for support, the horizons bobbing up and down at the edges of my vision. It was all I could manage to keep upright and walk, so didn't pay much attention to my surroundings as they coaxed and prodded me along one path after another. I did manage to get a good look at the charm tied to my bandage along the way though. It was an eye within the triangle, the bronze stamped with typically angular rune marks, their meanings lost to me without my sorcery to probe them with. That said, it was a poorly made thing, and I doubted it could contain anything more than the most rudimentary pattern of magic. They weren't doing anything to me that I could feel, so perhaps they thought it would guard me from getting wound rot or something similar. It lost its novelty soon enough and my attention wandered as we made our way across hillsides that all looked much the same as any other.

They stopped some time after the sun reached its zenith, and I was given a cup of water that I gulped at greedily. There was little rest though, and the remainder of that day and the next followed in a similar stupor, with the rocks and hills softening into woods and finally level grassland once more. Here we met with more soldiers, who were herding several dozen men between them. The two groups of soldiers met in a tangle of backslapping and handshaking, and I supposed they must have known each other. Many turned to point at me, but I was too sore and tired to either pay attention or care what they were saying. It wouldn't change anything in any event. They kept me apart from the other prisoners as we resumed our march, and I didn't miss that these others seemed to be enjoying considerably more freedom and food than I was. But then most of these looked either too young or too old to stand a reasonable chance of killing their attackers.

It was past sunset on the day we had met them when I saw our destination. I smelled it first, a combination of woodsmoke, men and animals, but it was the scale of the encampment that surprised me. A wooden wall that must have cost the life of half a forest surrounded rows and rows of tents, the true extent of which would only be revealed by the morning's light.

'What is this place?' I asked one of my captors, but rather than answer me the lout simply shoved me again and told me to keep walking.

After a few rounds of men on the walls shouting at the men around me, a pair of gates opened and we entered the camp. It smelled as bad as I had expected, and I kept telling myself that it was just mud that I was walking through in the hope that I'd start believing it. The path through the camp turned at sharp angles every hundred paces, which gave me some time to look around. It looked chaotic at first, with men marching here and there on some unfathomable purpose and the air choked with the smell of cooking food, horses, men and everything that went with them. There were so many that I stopped trying to count them; there were at least four or five to a tent, and there were rows upon rows of these.

Somewhere near the middle of the camp we were ushered into a smaller block of tents surrounded by a flimsy palisade that I could only assume was meant as a boundary rather than any real defence. Our captors pushed men into tents at random until they came to me. After a bit more shouting, one of the less belligerent ones led me to a smaller tent and told me that I was to go inside and stay there until they called for me. I peered inside and was pleasantly surprised to see that not only was it nice and dry inside, there were also some blankets. I scraped the worst of the mud from my feet on the threshold and lowered myself onto the blankets. I'd barely folded my arms under my head before a deep and dreamless sleep took hold of me.

I woke to the blare of something that sounded like a distressed goose shortly before dawn. The sound was briefly repeated on every side of me before it faded; I sat up and waited, but nothing happened and I slowly relaxed again. I felt better than I had since the fight, and decided to carefully unwrap the bandage from around my head. I was pleased to feel that the swelling at the back was no longer the size of a small egg, and wasn't anywhere near as sensitive to touch as it had been. It was my first real chance to take stock of my injuries since they had happened without being kicked, or having my head feel like it was splitting open, and I didn't want to waste it.

I sat comfortably and closed my eyes as I turned my attention inwards, concentrating on my breathing until the sounds of the camp faded away. The more superficial wounds and bruising that I had received were mostly faded already, my body's robust healing process having dealt with them quite effectively. The few penetrating injuries that I had taken were well on their way to being healed too, with new tissues growing through the wound paths and pulling them closed. My head remained the only injury that truly troubled me. I tentatively reached for my sorcery and felt it answer, although it was weak and uncertain, no doubt the lingering effect of the blow I had taken to my head. The throb of discomfort that emanated from the injured area was, however, far less intense than it had been when I had tried it on the way here, and I didn't even have a nosebleed, which was a marked improvement on my last attempt. It was still frustrating that I could not speed my rate of healing, but I was pleased that it was on the mend and that I was able to start building my strength again. Provided matters didn't turn too violent here for the next few days, I could bide my time and, once healed, shore up both my strength and my sorcery before continuing my journey.

I let go of the thoughts and sat there, breathing. Slowly but surely I felt my muscles begin to relax, the unnatural stiffness that my body had taken on in response to the injuries loosening. The noise and smell beyond my little tent faded away until it was just me, my breath and the sound of my hearts beating, the double thump comforting and familiar. Outside the tent men ran to and fro, doing whatever it was that so many men together found to do. The sun sailed its familiar path across the sky, raising the temperature in the tent to a level few beside me would have found pleasant.

It was only when the sun dipped towards the horizon that I stirred myself, stretching out my senses to build up an image of the encampment around me. The smells were different here, carrying more scents of horses and animals than those near the entrance of the camp. I could smell fire and food, mostly bread, and the scent of the men around me carried enough to tell me that they were restful. The occasional whinny of a horse reached me, the sound rising above the noise of hammering and groups of men talking. The other prisoners around me were becoming louder and more animated, and as the pitch of their conversations rose I could also hear more shouting from the entrance to our little paddock. I shook off the last of the meditative state with some reluctance and rose to my feet a few moments before the front bit of the tent was pulled wide open. Three men stood there, two with brass lanterns and clad in similar-looking arms and wearing the blue sashes around their waists, unlike the man in the middle. He was older than them, bearded, and wore a fine coat of gleaming metal rings under a long red shirt.

'Is this him?' he asked the one on the left.

'That's him.'

'Well, you weren't exaggerating,' said the bearded man, folding his arms as he looked me up and down. 'And here I thought you'd cooked the whole thing up just to weasel your way back into the camp.'

'Never, Sergeant,' said the man on the left.

'As fascinating as his size is, I still don't understand why you didn't just kill him. We're an army, not a circus.'

'He's not . . . natural.'

'I assure you that there are plenty of black men in the world, although I would wager they're all smaller than this lump, of course.'

'No, it's not that. Didn't the page write it down proper, about him cutting Owen's head off?'

I didn't remember cutting someone's head off. I'm fairly certain that I would have, as while it was a suitably demonic thing to do, it would also be terribly messy. I stayed where I was, curious to see what else they would say.

'Yes, but that's hardly revolutionary.'

'With a knife.'

'Again, hardly shocking, Corporal. The Elfadi have been doing it for years to discourage trespassers into their so-called homeland.'

'In a single stroke?'

'What? That's impossible, unless your idea of a knife is more sword-like.'

'With this.' The corporal held up a knife, and I recognised it as the one I'd taken off the dead scouts. That seemed like a long time ago already.

'There's no way—'

'We all saw it.'

I remember slashing it at someone's throat, but I hadn't stopped to see what happened afterwards. I suppose it was possible that they weren't lying. The knife was sharp, and I was enormously powerful compared to them.

The bearded man thumbed the edge of the knife and stared at me, then it, for some time. The corporal was smiling.

'You see? Told you it was weird. He's big, but still. Unnatural.'

'Perhaps, perhaps.' He tapped the point of the knife against his gloves. 'You there,' the bearded man said, looking at me directly for the first time. 'Do you speak our language?'

'I do,' I said.

'Good. Do you know who I am?'

'I have absolutely no idea.' I didn't even know who I was. 'Maybe you could ask one of them.' I pointed to the men alongside him.

'I'll make a note that you think you're amusing,' he said before turning to the man on the left. 'I've seen enough. Organise a watch guard and bring him to the command tent. The seneschal likes curiosities.'

My stomach took that moment to remind me that I really hadn't had much to eat. 'I would like some food,' I said, though I suspect that the grumbling had told them as much already. 'Lamb, if you have it.'

The bearded man didn't reply, unless you counted the loud snort he gave before he turned and marched out of sight, leaving the other two staring at me. The one on the left bared a set of yellowed teeth at me and hooked his thumbs under his belt.

'Not so tough now, eh?'

'Tougher than you.'

'We'll see about that when the rope goes around your neck.'

'What rope?' I asked.

'What d'you think?' he said, ignoring my question. 'What colour do you think he'll turn?'

'I dunno, Lev,' said the other. 'Maybe he'll go white.'

'What rope?' I asked again.

The one called Lev showed his ugly teeth again. 'You killed my mates, you ungodly bastard. I'm going to enjoy watching you die.'

'Threats? Is it your intention to bore me to death?' The gurgling of my stomach was stilled by the far more sinister stirring of the beast. I hadn't felt its presence since the fight and had quietly been hoping that the lump on my head had somehow dislodged it.

'The Church don't threaten, you should know that. But they do like a good hanging, and I'm going to be right at the front to watch you kick about and piss yourself, you bastard.'

I was still trying to make sense of what he'd said when they stepped back and slapped the tent covering closed. I heard him instructing some unseen men to break my legs if I even so much as looked outside.

I could sense that the thing inside me was restless and agitated. I felt a similar way.

'What do you want from me?' I said, looking down at my empty hands. 'What are you?' I didn't expect an answer, so the images of blood and torn flesh that flashed across my mind were as shocking to me as a slap to the face. It wasn't simply the images that surprised me though, but the impression of an almost elemental fury rising just beyond the borders of my mind, a crimson and gold furnace that wanted to scorch the world. I felt it pressing against me, and the sensation was enough to fold my knees and send me to the floor. I could sense the beast watching me from within those red depths, its presence so alien and violent that no other name seemed apt. To all others I might have seemed alone in the tent, but I knew that, in truth, I was not. I could sense its scrutiny upon me like that of a caged predator, patient and coiled to attack at the first sign of weakness. Would the weakness that precedes death be enough to free it, and what would happen to me if it was? Could I hope that it would save me, or would I burn away in its unleashed rage?

Who would mourn me, if I did not even know who or what I was? The only ones who would care about my death were those inflicting it, and if that happened, then my wish would be that the beast would tear loose when the time came. As if sensing my thoughts I felt the pressure of its scrutiny lessen and the weight of it withdraw, leaving me to fall back onto my blankets, suddenly aware of how my breath was coming in short gasps.

'What are you?' I asked again. 'What are we?'

It gave no further answer, and I was still wrestling with my feelings when the guards arrived to take me to my doom.

Chapter 6

It is our duty to seek out new knowledge and embolden our minds. Remember always that of all things, only knowledge is sacred. Let it be your god, and your teachers its prophets.

An Introduction to the Path of Power
by Tiberius Talgoth, Archmage

The guards that waited outside were arrayed in armour from head to boot, and stood with their weapons held ready. Tokens similar to the eye and triangle that still hung from the tattered bandage on my leg also hung from each of their belts, while more adorned their weapons or wrists. I was impressed by the profusion of these charms, but also curious how they possessed so many. I doubted any of them were particularly powerful, but it was still no easy thing to imbue an inanimate thing with even the meanest of charges. And certainly not in such numbers.

The man called Lev was standing behind the guards, and waved at me as they told me to lift my hands so that they could clasp metal rings to my wrists. I think that Lev was smiling, but the sharp stirring of the beast drew my attention away from his grimy visage. It didn't like chains, and I found myself in agreement with it. The links that joined the manacles were flat, rectangular things of cold iron, and I comforted myself with the thought that if I applied myself and didn't mind a bit of chafing,

I would most likely be able to snap them. It was more than the manacles themselves though, it was the submission that they represented. Submission and the dominance of another, neither of which sat well with us.

Even as I thought it, I felt something pulse from the beast, a sliver of an emotion that might have been approval but was stained with so many other sensations. I stumbled to a halt trying to reach for it. This was the closest I had come to an actual glimpse that this *thing* was something more than blind anger; understanding it was the key to understanding what I had done to myself.

The butt end of a spear dug into my back as I slowed. I started walking again, the moment lost and the beast having sunk back into whatever dark crevasse of my mind it inhabited. I glared at the guards, but they studiously ignored the violent death that I was sure my gaze promised. They had formed a square around me as they escorted me to wherever it was that I was to be weighed and measured, their scent betraying the curiosity that they were trying so hard not to show as we walked along.

The same couldn't be said for the men watching from the tents nearest the path, who were openly staring and called out to their fellows to tell them what was happening. By the time we arrived at one of several larger, red-roofed tents, we had attracted a score or more of curious onlookers who gave a muted cheer as the guards led me into a clear square in front. It was perhaps twenty paces to a side and of firmer ground, unmarked save for a thick, square post aside a single block of wood with deep gouges upon the top. The guards stepped away until they stood on the edges of the square, keeping the curious back, and me trapped in the centre.

I brushed away a few of the more persistent flying insects that seemed to be everywhere and waited for something more exciting than a boy lighting the torches in the corners to happen. The novelty of the situation was wearing thin by the time the entrance to the nearest tent was flung open and a man in the same sort of armour, but with a green sash wrapped about his waist, stepped out.

'Come,' he said simply, crooking a finger at me and making me dislike
him immediately. I didn't move and a moment later he stepped back outside.

'You. Come here. Now.' Now he helpfully pointed to the ground in front
of him as if I was some dog to be called to his heel. I stayed where I was,
and even kept the smile from my face when he strode over to stand in
front of me in what I took to be an attempt to intimidate me. He was a
bit older than most of the men I had seen in the camp, and from his scent
he also enjoyed a richer diet. This reminded me how hungry I was.

'You will obey!'

'Why?' The question seemed to surprise him.

'I represent the seneschal of this army, prisoner, and if you know what's
good—'

'Is there a law against good manners?' It was a petty thing, but the
combination of hunger, chains and his rudeness irked me.

'I . . . You.' He stuttered into silence while one or two of the guards
coughed quietly around us. 'Come with me now. Please.'

Even I could tell it was entirely insincere, but it was a victory of sorts
and cheered me a bit. I nodded my assent and followed him across and
into the tent, which was far larger than the one that I had slept in,
although half of it was taken up by a horseshoe-shaped table with three
men sat around it, one of whom was the bearded man from earlier. The
other half of the tent also had tables, but those were more ramshackle-
looking contraptions and had younger men hunched over them, staring
at piles of papers by the light of shiny lanterns in between stealing glances
at me. I was pushed into the middle of the horseshoe and stood there
quietly while the three men took their time scrutinising me.

'I would like some food,' I said, spotting a tray of small breads and
fruits.

'Silence!' shouted the green-sashed man who'd beckoned me in. 'You
will speak when spoken to.'

I don't have a very high tolerance for being shouted at, and particularly
not when I'm hungry and someone is considering whether to kill me.

'You offend me. Shout at me again and it'll be the last thing you do.'

His mouth opened but no words came out. He looked to the men at the table and I realised that he was just a peon of theirs, a chained dog, much like the men in the camp outside.

'What is your name?' asked the man sitting in the centre, whose head was almost as bald as mine but as wrinkled as a vulture's throat.

'Stratus.'

'Just Stratus?'

'Yes.' I didn't think of it as a lie since I didn't actually know what the rest of it was. I decided to be polite as well as honest. 'What is yours?'

'Aron, Seneschal of the first army.'

'What do you want from me, Aron Seneschal?'

'What *we* want, Meneer Stratus, is to know who and what you are,' said the bearded man, his words muffled by the hand stroking his face. It looked quite lush, and to be fair, if I had a pelt like that I would have spent much time grooming myself too.

How could I answer that though?

'I am no one of import. Just a wanderer who was attacked and defended himself.'

'A wanderer who looks like he can wrestle a troll and killed . . .' He paused and looked at some of the paper on the table before him. 'Five of our men, and injured two others.'

I forced myself not to shrug at that. The deaths seemed to matter to them. 'As I said, they attacked me; twelve of them, if I remember correctly. Is a man not allowed to defend himself against such tyranny?'

'We are at war, if you had not noticed.' Another stroke of the beard. 'Killing the king's men in a time of war makes you the enemy.'

The war again.

I remembered that there had been something about a war in the thoughts I'd dredged from the scout's mind, but the details and implications had slipped from mine.

'More than that though, is the disturbing report that you decapitated a man with a single stroke of what is quite an unremarkable knife, a feat that not even the stoutest of knights could hope to replicate.'

'Perhaps he simply had a thin neck,' I offered reasonably, but he waved it away.

'Do you know what this is?' asked the third man, who hadn't said anything up to now. He was dressed in a long gown of sorts and was very thin, almost as thin as I currently felt, and clean-shaven apart from some hair on his chin that gave his face a goatish look. He tossed something metallic onto the table, and I saw it was the same eye-in-a-triangle that I had tied to my bandage.

'Yes,' I said, 'I have one tied to my leg.' I lifted my knee and showed them. 'Who are you?'

'My name is Alexander.' He gestured to the token on the table. 'Pick it up, please.'

I slid it to the edge of the table and lifted it up for a closer look. It was heavier and of far better craftsmanship than the rough-edged one that I had. The runes were sharper and deeper too, and though I didn't know much about rune-craft, I knew that neat, sharp lines were of utmost importance. They were the channels that magic and intent would follow, and having the wrong sequence touching it would be as dangerous as pouring energy into a badly made spell or sorcerous construct. My fingers tingled as I held it and I wondered what it was reacting to.

'Do you know what that is?'

He had to know what it was, so I guessed that he meant something other than a bronze eye. 'A ward, but I'm not sure against what.'

Goat-man smiled, revealing square teeth that only served to reinforce my initial impression of him. 'Yes. But it is interesting that you say that. Most men would answer that with "a ward against evil".'

'I am not most men, and evil is hard to define.'

'Is it?' he asked.

'Of course. Evil is a motivation. You cannot ward against motivations, only the acts they motivate.'

They took a moment to look at each other before the goat spoke again. 'Wisely spoken, Meneer Stratus.' He leaned back and twisted at one of the rings on his slender, almost fleshless fingers. I felt the ward in my hands begin to vibrate, buzzing like a trapped insect. He was a wizard! 'But, answer me this, Stratus, what are your motivations? Who are you?'

I felt his magic bloom from the ward, which was more than that; it was a conduit attuned to the pitch of his magic. It was an idea that was as cunning as it was simple. Taking an item like the ward and tuning it to your magic increased the power of your spell as far less of it would be lost in the sending of the power. Giving that ward to someone you planned to target was a step further, because the mere act of willingly accepting it would erode their ability to resist whatever it was you sent at them. In this case, it was a compulsion to speak honestly. I tried to push back at it, but between my injured head and gnawing hunger I had as much chance of fighting it as a sick child does a bear. I felt his magic boring into me.

'I am Stratus . . .' I tried to say the rest of it; I really wanted to, but I couldn't. His magic was sly and cunning, but it wasn't strong enough to reach a secret that was buried as deep within my mind as it was. 'I am going towards the city.'

'Which city, Stratus?'

'I . . . I don't know. The closest one.'

'Why, Stratus?'

'I seek the counsel of your wise men.' I had an inkling of what he would ask me next, and I really didn't want him to ask it but had no way of stopping him. Every word that the spell coaxed from me strengthened its intent and power, like a chain being forged link by link.

'What is the counsel that you seek, Stratus?'

'I . . .' The strain of my mental struggle against the compulsion was spilling into the physical word, the chain that linked my wrists rattling as my body tensed. 'I want to know . . . who . . . what I am.'

'Who do you think you are, Stratus?'

The magic curled its way through me, and before I knew it was happening, I heard my voice saying, 'I do not know who I am. I have no memory older than the week.'

The three men were leaning forward now, their full attention levied upon me. I ground my teeth and my muscles began to tremble at the strain of it.

'Why did you say you want to know *what* you are, Stratus?'

That was the question I did not want him to ask. If I answered truthfully, that I did not know but thought I was some sort of conjuring or freed demon, it was no great stretch of my imagination that they would do far worse things than chain me. I felt my tongue stirring as the magic pried the answer from my mind and tried to force it into my mouth. I focused on my jaw muscles, willing them to stay clenched. It must have worked to some degree, because the goatish wizard prompted me with another question.

'Are you an agent of Penullin in any form?'

It was a mistake on his part, of course, but a boon for me. His impatience had changed the focus of the spell, not by much, but enough to loosen its hold on me. An ongoing effect such as this compulsion required single-minded concentration and repetition. Now that he had allowed one question to go unanswered, and more importantly, hadn't said my name, he'd disrupted the pattern he had established and the precise targeting of the spell. Even a portion of someone's name could influence how magic affected them, and the combination of these errors meant that some of the power that had driven that question into my mind had now lost its purpose.

Like it had when the Deacon pulled himself from his mind, the beast reached out and drew that tiny mote of power into itself. My mouth and throat were telling the wizard that no, I was no agent of Penullin and that I had never even been there before, but in my mind I was seeing a glimmer of light play across something with sharp angles and molten eyes. Then the glimmer was absorbed, and the coiled and terrible menace disappeared back into the impenetrable darkness. But it had left me a gift, a token of partnership, in that it had somehow healed what remained of my head wound.

It had made two things possible, one physical and one not. The first was the bruising that had clouded my brain had subsided, and the second that I could once again feel my sorcery. The pressures had changed, both of which combined to further loosen his magic's hold on my will. I doubt he had noticed amid all my previous struggles against it, and that was the sweetest irony of it, for now a portion of the magic that he was chan-nelling into the spell was in fact feeding my strength. I could feel the amulet reacting to it, but my hand was large enough that I could curl my fingers around it, hiding any glow from their sight.

'What is your earliest memory, Stratus?'

'Waking in a field and seeing vultures circling over me.'

'Why were you in the field, Stratus?'

I still felt a need to answer, but now it was more a suggestion than a command. I almost had the note of his magic in my mind and wanted to prolong it a bit longer.

'If I died, I wanted to die in the sunshine.' For a moment my careful plans slipped. Where had that come from? His spell had clearly burrowed deeper than I had realised.

'Why did you want to die, Stratus?'

'I didn't **want** to die, but if I had no choice, I wanted to die in the light.'

'Is this going to take much longer?' asked the bearded man in a whisper, and I almost smiled because the interruption caused enough of a slip in the goat wizard's control for me to hear the note of his magic. Now I could mimic and subvert it, and I wasted no time in flexing my will and taking control of his spell. It was laughably easy, for whoever had taught him had not expected him to meet any real resistance.

'Alexander.' He looked up as I said his name, blending the sound of his magic into it. A wizard should know better than to give someone his name, even a part of it, even if only in conversation. It granted no power over him but it made it that little bit easier to focus my intent on him. I had made the same mistake but as long as I had my sorcery I had at least a defence against its misuse. Alexander the goat had made no such preparations, and it was amusing to watch his reaction as he suddenly realised that something had gone very wrong for him. He tried to dispel his magic, but I wouldn't allow him to. I neatly reversed the compulsion and pushed it back into his own mind. I felt his will squirming, but there was little he could do against his own magic.

I could see that the bearded man and the seneschal were staring at us, and I knew from the wizard's thoughts that they wouldn't wait very long before acting on their suspicions. I had one advantage right now, and I had to act on it without hesitation if I wanted to retain my freedom. The first and easiest part of my tenuous plan was to order the wizard to stay in his seat and be quiet. The second step was to free my hands from the manacles, something that was almost equally as easy to accomplish. I could have broken the chains, but instead I lifted them, called up some of the magic that I was siphoning from the wizard and sent it into the lock, where it expanded in all directions at once, pushing the mechanisms and making them spring open.

This was the part where it became impossible to hide what was happening, and my only advantage was the heartbeat and a half it took the men to comprehend what they were seeing and start reacting to it. I grabbed one of the falling iron rings and swung it in a tight arc, smashing the other end of it into the side of Aron the Seneschal's head. It struck with a loud metallic clatter that hid the sound of the bone breaking beneath it. The bearded one was scrambling to get out from behind the table, but his haste saw his legs, and the legs of the chair, tangle long enough for me to drop the chain and twist and punch him in the forehead, making him slump like a puppet with its strings cut. The wizard watched all of this with a calm demeanour, his will smothered and bound by his own magic.

'Guards!' screamed the man behind me, the really rude one with the green sash. I turned to him but he was already dashing towards the front of the tent, and as much as I wanted to catch and break him, I knew that I had to let him go. His flight was the spur for the other men in the tent to scramble after him, their papers and ink pots forgotten. Had any of them bothered to look over their shoulders, they may have seen me cutting a hole in the back of the tent and darting out with my pet wizard in tow, but none did.

'Take me to the nearest way out of the camp and make sure no one stops us, Alexander,' I instructed him, and he hastened to obey. I let him walk in front of me and forced myself to keep to a walking pace. Running through the camp would be tricky unless we stayed on the cleared road, and if we did that we might as well have hoisted a flag to show them where we were. Darkness and man's poor night vision were my greatest allies at the moment. Behind us the commotion grew, and I heard the goose-honk sound of war horns being blown. Around us men rose to their feet and stared back the way we had come, but few paid us any attention for now.

We were less than a hundred or so paces from the gates before they began to organise themselves, which was a pity. Alexander was useful, and I would have learned much from him. I gave him his final instructions and sent him on his way. Fate does have a strange and cruel sense of irony. Here I had finally found myself a wizard of my own who might be able to give me some answers, but I couldn't read his mind without releasing the compulsion. And I could not release the compulsion because I needed him to do something he wouldn't normally do. All so that I could escape to go and find another wizard.

I waited behind one of the larger tents as Alexander staggered away on his chore. I had to trust that he truly believed it was both his idea and the best one he'd ever had as he slipped out of my line of sight; I still had the token that linked us, so I would know if he managed to shake off the compulsion. Touching the token would give me enough of a warning to plan something equally reckless if this plan failed. I squatted down and tried to ignore my stomach's plaintive grumbling while I waited.

A column of flame as thick as an ancient oak and at least as high shot up from the centre of a cluster of tents not long after, and even from where I was hiding I heard the soft whump of the air igniting and felt a hot wind wash across me. Conjuring flame isn't difficult once you get the knack of it, but manipulating an existing fire is far more convenient. Alexander, who I imagined was currently crisping somewhere at the base of the fire, had thrown all of his magic into feeding one of the cooking fires, convinced that the column of light that would rise would help all his little friends find me in the dark. It wasn't the most nuanced of plans, but I hadn't had much time to work on it.

The effect was, however, as spectacular as I had hoped. The order that they had just managed to restore to seek me out fragmented as the men who had been unlucky enough to be close to Alexander's stunt became living torches, setting even more tents alight as they screamed and spun. In the chaos that followed I walked up to the gates, helping myself to a discarded backpack to replace the one I had lost on the way, and flattened the sole remaining guard as he turned away from the spectacle to confront me. I tossed the wizard's now useless charm into the mud and put the camp to my back as I marched off into the night.

Chapter 7

The first blush of dawn was on the horizon when I found a hollow where I could examine the backpack I had stolen. I had intended to keep walking at a good, punishing pace until full light, but I had found my mind wandering and my vision blurring as my hunger grew from a nagging annoyance to a constant ache. I had felt my strength was ebbing even as I forced myself to ignore it and stride on, but after I walked into a tree I realised that I had perhaps pushed myself too far. As strong as this body was, it needed fuel like any other. I tore the pack open and quickly discarded the clothes and other mundane accessories of human life while I set the foodstuffs aside. There wasn't much at all aside from a nice enough knife and a few shiny coins, although both were scant compensation for what had been taken from me.

I went through the pack twice more before sitting down and staring at the meagre offerings: a small flask of something that tasted of apples and warmed my throat; a single, slightly blackened loaf that was almost as hard as a rock; and a pouch of those interminable oats. I poured the apple drink onto the loaf until it had softened enough to break into smaller pieces, each of which was still an exercise in chewing. As hungry as I was, I left the oats for the crows. I simply couldn't stomach them.

As I stood and started walking again I tried to convince myself that I did feel marginally better, but it didn't ring true, and by the time the golden disk of the sun had lifted from the horizon it felt like my stomach was hugging my spine. All I could think about was food, and I watched the land in front of me for any opportunities for a quick feed. I was to be disappointed though, for the seneschal's camp and his outriders had stripped the countryside bare, killing anything that they hadn't scared away or stolen. I even tried to use my barely recovered sorcery to roust something from the undergrowth, but there was nothing there that anything save a sparrow would consider worth the title of 'meal'.

As always, the use of my sorcery only served to stoke my hunger, and soon enough my pace slackened and I began to stumble as the thought of food overwhelmed all others. Eventually I happened upon a stream and bent to drink from it, hoping that a bellyful of water would at least give me a chance to recover some of my wits. I had barely swallowed the first gritty mouthful when four men followed me down into the small dell.

My first reaction was to think *I'm more exhausted than I thought* rather than that I was in any kind of danger, which should have been apparent from their blue sashes and the weapons in their hands. I hadn't even smelled them in the state I was in. Two came from the front, and two from behind, three of them armed with stout clubs and the last with a blade that was somewhere between a knife and sword.

'You,' called the knifeman, gesturing at me with his weapon as I sat back on my heels. 'You're coming with us.'

Being tired and hungry, I was too slow to recognise the tightening of my gut and the pressure at the back of my head for what they were. By the time I felt the rage blooming within my breast, it was too late to resist the rise of my inner demon. The anger that spilled from it was as intoxicating as ever, promising a relief from the hunger and weakness, and even though some small part of me knew that it was pressing on my mind, not within it, the magnitude of it was enough to send my hearts pounding and my fingers curling into hammer-like fists. A fire does not need to touch you for you to feel its heat.

The knifeman was speaking again, but I couldn't hear his words. They were nothing to me, after all. Nor was he. Nor were any of them. Who were they, to challenge *me*? To threaten *me*? He had time to widen his eyes before I grabbed him by the throat and lifted him off the ground, making him squirm and kick like the vermin that he was. I closed my fist and as he kicked one final time, I felt a moment of serenity where the fog of the rage and confusion that had dogged me since I woke fell away. It was like the sun burning its way through a heavy cloud, but even as I tried to hold onto it the clouds swallowed the light once more, and I heard myself cry out in despair, the sound of my voice echoed by the silent, plaintive roar of the beast within me. I wanted that light, that perfect peace.

I searched for and willed it to me as I slew the next two soldiers, tearing them apart as if that peace was something hidden within them. The last man surprised me by attacking with vigour, his club cracking down across the back of my shoulder and then my arm as I flinched away from the blow. I knew from the beating I had taken from the Deacon's guards that a blow like that would hurt but was unlikely to do me a serious injury and so I carelessly lunged for him again. He skipped back and cracked me across the chin with the club, hard enough to make my teeth squeal against each other.

It was a jarring hit and as I staggered back I felt the beast's dismay as its hold on me loosened. He pressed the attack as I tried to regain my footing. Several more jarring blows hit me, and although I managed to protect my head, it was galling to be beaten in such a way by a man with what was essentially a big stick.

It was a combination of that feeling and the heaviness of my limbs that made me use my sorcery rather than the strength of my arms to defeat him. Fire was still on my mind following my escape from the camp, and so it was flame that I reached for as I fell back once more.

The construct was a familiar one and came readily, and before he could land another blow I threw a ball of condensed heat at him. Fire needs air like we do, and the more you squeeze it, the more desperate to breathe it becomes. The ball of fire that I launched had expanded to the size of a large apple by the time it struck and spread along his arm, hissing like a cat as it drew in the air it needed and began burning through his skin.

He screamed and dropped his club in favour of flailing at the flames. Somewhere inside me the beast was watching and laughing, but as amusing as his leaping about was, I didn't need the smoke and screaming to attract any other soldiers who might be looking for me. I picked up his club and hit him hard enough to snap both it and his neck, stilling his screams. I sat down on the muddy bank and concentrated on breathing. The sorcery had come as quickly as it should have, but it had been even more taxing than wrestling him to the ground would have been.

There was no sign that any of them had any food with them, which was sorely disappointing. I needed to replenish my strength and soon. With the connection to the Songlines so weak in this area, using my sorcery was not only using up what meagre reserves I had siphoned from the wizard, but also taking its toll on my body. I was eyeing a meagre frog in the stream when I caught the scent of charring meat, and I followed my nose to where the dead man's gently smoking arm was draped over his chest.

I barely noticed the drool escaping from the corner of my mouth as I hacked the roasted limb off with his companion's long knife. I weighed it in my hand for a moment, caught between the desperate, hollowing hunger within me and the knowledge that this idea was perhaps not entirely mine.

That debate barely lasted as long as the telling of it, and any residual hesitation I had vanished as soon as I took the first mouthful. It wasn't that much of a revelation that the taste of human flesh was familiar to me, but the additional row of teeth that had descended from my palate as I ate the arm certainly was. The sound and sensation of enamel grinding against bone is even more uncomfortable than it sounds, but these were a predator's teeth. A demon's teeth, made to tear flesh and crack bone, and that is what they did. They stripped the meat better than any knife could have and put paid to any lingering concerns that I might have had about simply being a human in the grip of some terrible delusion.

With darkness imminent and the stream in a natural dip, I decided to risk another fire, albeit one fuelled by kindling rather than myself this time. I built it up with their clubs and set the rest of my dinner to roasting. I finished my meal without further interruption and felt immeasurably better for it, even if I had to endure the grind of my secret teeth receding into my jaws again. As I had with my eyes that first night in the forest, I then forced myself to do it over and over again until I felt that I had some control over the mechanism. Unlike my eyes though, the sensation didn't grow any less unpleasant the more I did it. Eyes were, after all, malleable whereas there was only so much space in a human-sized skull where you could hide teeth like these.

The sudden glut of food had made me drowsy and, reasoning that my body needed time to absorb this bounty, I moved a small distance away and laid down in a shallow ditch. I had only intended to rest for a short while but sleep pulled me into its depths almost immediately.

I woke while the morning's mist still clung to the grasses and simply lay there listening to the soft sounds of the morning for a while before rising. I felt immeasurably better as I shook off the dew and lingering lethargy. There was still a stiffness in my jaw that may have come from practising with my demon's teeth or simply the cracking blow from the dead man's club. Perhaps it was a combination of both, but either way I felt better than I had for some time. I moved along with new-found swiftness but also more caution than I had exercised before, tasting the air constantly.

However, my luck seemed to be improving and aside from a single, distant glimpse of several riders, I avoided all human contact the entire day. Despite the hours I had walked, I didn't feel the need to sleep but I forced myself to rest until the moon rose anyway, sharing my grassy bed and some of the leftover meat I had been carrying with a little jackal, who could count himself lucky that I hadn't come across him the day before. I fell into a light sleep with the jackal stretched out against my side, and I woke when he rose to continue his own moonlit hunt. It was a beautiful, clear night, and I almost stumbled twice by spending more time tracing patterns in the stars than I did watching the ground in front of me.

The sun was still rising towards its zenith the next morning when I found myself following a path that was meandering towards a larger, raised roadway in the distance. I stopped for a drink of water and just watched the scene for a while, straining for any hint of hidden pursuers or an ambush. When I found neither, I turned towards the high road, which was far busier than any I had seen before, but at least I knew that I was heading in the right direction.

I made my way down the slope and through some densely planted fields, pausing only to wave in what I hoped was a friendly manner to the workers who lifted their heads to watch me pass. Only one returned the gesture but that was enough. They bent back down to continue whatever strange and meaningless task they were busy with while I followed the path up to a small ramp that brought me onto the high road, which was far wider and topped with smooth stone.

I greeted a few people as I came abreast of them, but of these hardly any bothered returning the greeting with anything that I would have considered genuine enthusiasm, even in my most charitable mood. Most shied away and slowed until I passed, and I suppose that if I had actually cared about their opinions I might have been offended. I spent a few miles trying to puzzle it out by assuming different approaches to the groups I was passing, but all that my extra effort attracted was a new level of aggression from some of the males. It was exhausting and confusing, and eventually I abandoned my attempts and simply pulled up my hood and concentrated on walking.

A brownish haze rose in the distance, and as the road continued to climb I realised that this murk was the by-product of the morning fires in the citadel, which cheered me as I had come further than I had thought. I paused when the enormity of the city came into view. I had never seen such a thing before, and although the beast seemed to think differently, it gave no clue as to the how or why of its scorn. Five Elms would have been lost in the shadow of the great stone walls and fortified towers that surrounded it. It was an undoubtedly impressive feat of human construction that spread across the horizon, the sheer number of buildings giving the impression that were the wall to crack, half the city would come spilling out in a flood. I tried to imagine how many men it took to fill a place like that, but that thought fell apart when I started thinking about the prospect of being trapped inside those walls with all those thousands around me, inevitably chasing me with sharp weapons.

I needed to get my thoughts in order before I walked into the city if I didn't want a repeat of the seneschal's camp. I sat on one of the carved stones by the roadside, which had an elaborate arrow carved into it, pointing towards the city, as if anyone could miss it squatting on the landscape. The passers-by were generally ignoring me, which was fine, but the reaction of the armed men escorting a coach gave me pause. I'd been watching the coach, a grand thing painted a bright red and decorated with glinting baubles, with some interest as I'd never seen the like of it before. Perhaps I had been paying too much attention to it for their liking, because two of them brought their horses to a stamping halt in front of me. They didn't say anything while carrying out their little territorial display, and I expect that the sound and size of the horses and the polished spears they carried would have put the terrors in me if I'd been a man. They had no way of knowing that my first thought on seeing them was to wonder which out of their horses or them would taste the better.

I sat and watched their display, but they were so close that I could hear, and almost feel, that taut booming of the mighty hearts in their steeds. Human flesh was nice enough, but if I had to choose between it and horse, the men would usually live to see another day. My mouth filled with saliva and I groaned with new-found hunger, or perhaps simple greed, but the sound of it was lost in the jangling of their armour. The coach had passed though, and with one final flourish they charged off after it, while I chose to sit there a while longer until the smell of the horseflesh lost its grip on my senses.

I was still sat there when an old man came ambling up to me, the oversized pack on his back hung with all manner of copper pots that rang like bells with every other step. He made a strange wheezing noise and bared most of his remaining teeth at me, an image that made me recoil until I realised that he was laughing.

'You sure got balls, sonny.' His voice was a cackle and he favoured me with another of his broken smiles, his bristly eyebrows rising and falling. I assumed that he wasn't asking a question and simply shrugged in return.

'You simple?' he offered next.

'I am not.'

He bobbed his head as if I'd just said something profound. 'Just wondering. Man's likely as not to get his eyes poked out if he goes staring at that lot.'

'Which lot?'

'You sure you aren't simple? The holier than thous in the coach.'

I shrugged. 'I simply found the red quite striking.' *And all that delicious horseflesh.* He fairly hooted with delight at that and leaned heavily on his stick as he caught his breath.

'Who are they, these holy people?' I asked.

'The Stahrulls.'

I stared at him. 'The Stahrulls?' I knew that name, and for once my brain served up a usable memory. 'From the line of the kings of Krandin?'

'No, the famous chimney sweeps. Of course the bloody royals.' He shook his head. 'And what'd you do to your eyebrows anyway?'

I touched my brows. Unlike the hairy bushels that looked to have exploded from his forehead, my brow was as smooth and hairless as the rest of me.

'I don't think I've ever had any,' I said, feeling unexpectedly defensive about the flaw. 'And I don't think I could have spun any without something to start from.'

'Eh?'

'Never mind that. What can you tell me about the Stahrulls?'

He sniffed loudly. 'Son, I'm a tinker. If there's gossip to be had then I've heard it. But you'll have to get off that black arse of yours and walk with me if you want to hear it.'

I stood and began to dust off some of the dirt kicked up by the horses, but then saw how filthy my makeshift tunic was and didn't bother with the rest. The various bloodstains had dried to a dark brown, and the material was covered in leaves and burrs from where I'd been sleeping in the undergrowth.

'Heh. You're a big bastard.' He thrust a bony hand at me. 'Name's Crow.'

I took his hand carefully, not wanting to crush it. 'Like the bird?'

'You don't miss a thing, eh?' He held my grip while his magnificent eyebrows crept a little higher. 'It's considered good manners to offer your name in return around these parts.'

I made a mental note of that. 'Stratus.'

'You foreigners sure have some funny names. Where're you from?'

'Lots of different places.'

'All right, all right. Foreigners.' He tutted, then shrugged his enormous pack a bit higher with a loud jingle and began walking. 'So why are you so interested in the royals anyway?'

'I have my reasons.' I didn't add that I just wasn't sure what they were.

He grunted and sucked at his teeth noisily, but didn't say anything for some time. I was enjoying the experience of a conversation that was more than a series of escalating threats and so was content to wait. He began speaking just short of a quarter mile further, haltingly at first, but soon enough the trickle of words turned into a flood. Part of me wanted to simply shake him until he told me what I wanted to know, but his rambling monologue was also giving me a perspective into aspects of human society I'd probably not been exposed to previously, even if it was almost painfully tedious at times.

The war between the kingdom of Krandin and the Penullin empire seemed to be the most pressing thing on everyone's mind, Crow's included. He didn't seem surprised that I knew so little about it, or perhaps he was just enjoying the sound of his voice, but over the next few miles I learned much about it. They had been waging their war for almost ten years with something almost approaching civility, the way Crow described it, but over the last year or two it had become altogether more vicious since the Penullin emperor discovered a new fondness for wizards. He spoke of battles that had seen tens of thousands of men killed and left to rot under the sun, of cities and towns burned to the ground, their inhabitants having simply vanished without trace. When I asked him who was winning, he spat the most enormous gobbet of phlegm into the bushes.

'Depends who you speak to, but as I hear it, those Penullins have taken most of the south. It's that damn army of wizards and the bastard that leads them.'

I felt the thing inside me stir uneasily as he said that. 'Are you sure they're wizards?'

He chuckled wetly. 'That's what I hear, and I've gone and heard it from too many people to keep believing that it's just gossip. The way I hear it is that they're right bastards, raining fire into towns and setting folk alight or worse, from what some have told me. They've taken to calling their leader the Worm Lord. I hear that he only comes out at night, and no one's seen his face.'

'Perhaps because it's too dark.'

He gave another of his gurgling laughs. 'Might be. Still, funny names aside, it's a bad, bad business. They're firing towns left, right and centre, even those that surrender, and killing everyone who don't submit to being taken.' He shook his head and slowed to retrieve a clay pipe of some sort and a pouch of dried leaves from one of his numerous pockets before continuing. 'It's bad news for folk like me who need to travel though, damned bad. Those that aren't off to war are dead, so the law's gone from the roads, and honour with it. There are folk out there who'd cut your throat for a chicken, or if they were just plain bored. I turned my back on all of that and started heading north as soon as I made my mind up that it wasn't just the war putting the frighteners up folk.'

I let this sink in. I really couldn't care what the humans were doing to each other, nor their reasons for doing it, but the chaos that surrounded it could make my travels that much harder. I looked over to Crow, who had stuffed bits of leaf into the bowl of the pipe and was now hunched over a small box.

'What are you doing with that?' I asked.

'Making a fecking pie,' he lied around the pipe clenched in his teeth.

I sighed and rubbed my forehead. As amusing as his rambling was, we were getting close to the citadel and I didn't have the time or inclination to keep waiting for him to get to the end of his tale, or even to a point.

'Crow,' I said, sharply enough to snap his attention back to me. He straightened and stared at me. I fed a pulse of power into my gaze as he met it and drew his thoughts into my mind. It left him slightly dazed, and while he recovered his composure I used the time to sort through the jumble of thoughts, images and sensations that I'd skimmed from him. Most were meaningless to me, memories of women who he thought he'd had a chance of copulating with and trades where he had gained the upper hand, but there was one nugget that I felt resonate strongly with the beast inside. I felt the weight of its alien and fearsome attention wake and turn on me, and even though it was a fleeting touch, the potential behind it was enough to rob me of my breath for a moment.

It was a name.

I might have been able to dig deeper into Crow's mind, but I wasn't back to my proper form and my control was crude at best. And while his death wouldn't pain me, he had been kind to me in his own way and it would have been churlish to kill him, even if the cause was just. And so I waited until he was able to start walking again before pressing him a bit more, like the polite demon that I was.

'Tell me about Navar Louw.'

Crow plucked the pipe from his mouth as if it had bit him and rounded on me with something akin to ferocity.

'Why? Where'd you hear that name?' He stabbed the end of the pipe towards me. 'You'd be best forgetting you ever heard it, and certainly not saying it out loud.' He peered about after he finished.

'That's not an answer. Who is he?'

He looked around again, then edged closer, and I smelled a trace of fear in his scent. He grabbed my elbow and tried to push me. Curious, I let him guide me and we walked to the edge of the roadway.

'What are you looking for?' I asked after he wasted more time looking around.

'Tell me where you heard that name,' he said, tightening his grip. If he was trying to intimidate me, it was a laughable attempt, but I suspected that he knew that already.

'I heard someone mention it. Something about him being part of the wizards.' I tried not to smile at my own guile.

'He's not just part of them. He's, you know . . . him.'

I didn't know. 'Who else would he be?'

'You sure you aren't simple?' he all but hissed at me. 'He's the chief wizard. The damned Worm Lord hisself.'

'Oh.' I thought about it. 'Well, calling yourself the Worm Lord certainly sounds a bit more intimidating than Meneer Louw.' I shrugged his grip off. 'And?'

'And what?'

'Why are you staring at everyone like that?'

'Because the man who told me didn't wake up the next morning.'

'So? Men die all the time.'

'Not by vomiting their own guts out and then exploding.'

He had a point there. I knew I'd seen a lot of dead men, even if I didn't know the how or why of it, but I'm fairly certain I'd have remembered something like that. I couldn't help but wonder how this Louw character had managed it, assuming he'd used magic to do it. It would take a bit of preparation, a steady focus and a lot more energy than a simple ball of fire, although it would certainly make more of an impression. This Louw had a cruel imagination and far too much time on his hands.

'I'm glad you're getting to understand what I mean,' Crow said, jolting me back from my thoughts. It still didn't explain what he was looking for, but I decided to ascribe it to his eccentricities and leave it at that.

'So what else do you know about him?'

'Weren't you listening?'

'Of course I was. It's hardly a big secret though, is it? It's not like he told you Louw's true name. Why would he kill in such a manner simply to hide a fact that most in his entourage would surely know already?' I was thinking out loud again but saw no harm in it. I was pleased to see that it had given Crow pause to think too, even if he did go back to fiddling about with his pipe.

'I don't know,' he said.

So why hide his name? Even thinking about it made the beast uneasy and the predator's teeth hidden within my jaws ache. It was without doubt that he was part of this, but how? Had he driven me to this body, or worse still, was I some conjuring of his? My frustration was growing, and with it my anger. I fought against it, pushing away the urge to seek relief in destruction, however intoxicating the idea was. Instead, I turned to Crow, who was still trying to do something with his little pipe.

'What are you doing?' I asked. 'And I know that it has nothing to do with pies.'

He snorted and chewed on the long bit of the pipe. 'Trying to light the weed.'

'Ah, it's an aromatic. Here.' I focused my sorcery on a point in front of my figure until a small flame manifested. He stared at it as if he'd never seen fire before, then leaned forward and sucked the flame into the bowl of the pipe a few times, almost setting fire to his eyebrows in the process. Scented smoke puffed out, the smell of it jogging a memory loose in my mind of a forest ablaze against a night sky, the air alive with the smell of the burning resin and the crack of exploding trees.

'Come on now, tell me. How'd you do that?'

I blinked the ghostly fires from my vision and refocused on Crow. His scent was still sour with fear, and his heart was beating faster. I guessed that he hadn't seen much sorcery up close, which I suppose wasn't surprising. Wizards are rare among men, and sorcerers were as rare among wizards. I could only imagine how intimidating the thought of an army of them was. I risked another look into Crow's eyes, just a fleeting contact, but given our recent connection it was enough to glean that he was now worried that I was an agent of the so-called Worm Lord.

I wasn't sure how I would go about convincing him otherwise so I opted for the subtle and efficient alternative of meeting his gaze once more, this time with my sorcery at hand.

'I am not one of his minions,' I said. 'I am like you, a refugee from the war. There is nothing to fear.' My sorcery passed between us, carrying my words past his mounting fear and planting them into his thoughts. It was effectively a reversal of the mind-reading that I could do, but far subtler than the compulsion that Alexander the dead wizard had used. I gently extracted myself from his mind before breaking the gaze.

He blinked a few times, then began a long and painful-sounding coughing fit. When it had passed, so had his concerns. I patted him on the shoulder, taking care not to use too much force. He waved the gesture away.

'Damned thing,' he rasped, emptying the bowl of the pipe onto the road. 'Always happens.'

I left him to mutter and cough as we began walking once more. I believe I'd learned all that I could from Crow, and the citadel now loomed large before us. Unlike Five Elms though, the entrance here was closely guarded by several men, all of them wearing the same blue sash as the soldiers at the camp. They were questioning people as they approached the gates, and as I watched they chased off two men who weren't nearly as bedraggled as I was, giving them a clout with a staff for good measure as they slunk away. There was a sizeable crowd of people waiting to enter and it was only getting bigger.

'What was that about?' I asked Crow, pointing to the two men as they limped off.

He gestured towards some scratches on a wooden board hung next to the gates. 'The Duke's imposed martial law, so they can pick and choose who gets in.' He looked at me. 'Vagrants don't stand a chance.'

'I am *not* a vagrant.'

'Well, pardon me for saying it, but you damned sure look like one.'

I didn't give voice to the retort that sprung to mind and instead made myself pay a bit more attention to the crowd around us and soon noticed my garb did seem meaner than most of theirs. Not a few of them were staring at me too, which I wasn't sure that I liked. Fear, impatience and a growing crowd were the perfect ingredients for a mob, and while a riot might be entertaining, being the focus of its attention was less appealing. I turned and made my way to the edge of the crowd, trying not to be too physical about it.

'Where are you going?'

I was surprised to see that Crow had followed me.

'I may not be a vagrant, but perhaps I do look like one,' I said, holding the tattered fabric of my tunic away from my body. 'I was going to look for another way into the city.'

'You can't do that,' he said, moving closer. 'And don't say it so damned loud. Look, if they catch you climbing the walls they'll put an arrow in you without hesitation.'

'I'll go in when it gets dark.' I rubbed my arms. 'No one will see me.'

'They've got lanterns, you know. And you're too big to go climbing a wall.'

'Are you always this negative?'

'There's an easier way.' He paused, then leaned in close. 'You could just buy some new clothes.'

For all of his age and feebleness, Crow had a valid point and I wasn't so boorish as to deny it.

'A fine idea, thank you.' He moved to stand in front of me as I turned.

'You don't have any money, do you?' It took me a moment to realise that it was a question, not a request.

'Not much,' I admitted, realising as I said it that I really didn't like not having money. All the different shapes and values were still a bit confusing to me, but I quite liked the idea of being rich. Perhaps I had been in my previous life, a thought that cheered and depressed me at the same time.

He clucked his tongue noisily and, with a grace that surprised me, swung that enormous pack from his back and set it down on the ground with a light touch. He looked far smaller and vulnerable without it, like a snail that had lost its shell, and it really wasn't a boast to say that I could have punched a hole right through him. I watched as he busied himself with one of the numerous wrapped bundles inside it and pulled out a ball of cloth. He flicked it with a flourish and it unrolled into an extremely long, light-brown tunic.

'Impressive,' I said.

'Go on, take it,' he said, holding it out to me.

'What is the price?'

He spat lightly to the side. 'You've already paid it. Take it. I wouldn't be able to sell it around here anyways. Not much market for robes these days.'

I took the robe, which still looked like nothing more than an overlong tunic to me. 'You are gifting this to me?' I asked.

'Yes, you simple bugger.'

I stared at the shrunken little man in front of me and struggled to understand what I was feeling. Even the beast pulsed with something like confusion.

'Thank you, Crow,' I said, finding my voice again. 'You are the first man to offer me such generosity.'

'It's nothing, really. It sounds like you need some luck, and I liked having someone to talk to.'

I held out my hand, like I had seen others do, and he took it in his own as best he could. I shook it gently.

'I will repay this debt, friend Crow.'

He patted my hand and turned to tie his bag closed again. After a few long moments he stood and cleared his throat.

'I suppose this is goodbye, then?' he said.

'So it seems.' I wasn't sure what else to say; he was staring at me as if he was expecting more but I had no idea what the convention for this sort of thing was. Saying thank you, or more correctly, saying thank you and meaning it, had already put me on uncertain ground.

'Well,' he said, rubbing at his chin, 'you're a strange one for sure, son. Good luck, and try not to get yourself killed.'

I leaped on this. 'And although you are old, I hope you do not die soon.'

His eyebrows dipped, which I recognised as a sign that he was thinking, and I began to suspect that perhaps I hadn't caught the spirit of his farewell after all. He croaked out something which might have been a laugh or just another bit of phlegm trying to escape his lungs and swung his pack up onto his back once more. With a final wave of his hand, Crow turned and ambled off, leaving me to throw off my dirty clothes and don the tunic-robe he had given me.

I felt quite positive as I struggled into the arm holes. That had been my first human interaction that had resulted in neither death, fire nor flight, and one that had left me with a freely given gift. I had lost sight of Crow, but I honestly hoped that I would have the chance to repay him before he died.

Newly dressed, I wandered along the periphery of the crowd to where some enterprising merchants had set out some benches and were selling refreshments. I didn't trust the benches to hold my weight, so I carefully paid for a cup of what they said was the finest wine in Krandin from my now meagre hoard of coins, and sat with my back against a wall. The wine wasn't nearly as nice as I had expected, but it was only really an excuse to linger and watch the ebb and flow of the herd outside the gates as it grew dark. The guards had shut the gates shortly before sunset to a chorus of disapproval from the crowd, but after it became apparent that they weren't going to reopen them, they began to disperse. Some sat where they had stood, while others drifted towards the refreshments as I had.

The smell of cooking began to rise shortly thereafter, and despite having been locked out like cattle outside a farmstead, there was an almost festive air to the impromptu camp. I finished the last, sour dregs of the wine and spent yet more of my precious coin on a small loaf of bread filled with some sort of sweet vegetable. It was adequate rather than satisfying, but there wasn't much meat to be had, at least not without risking my anonymity.

I looked for Crow, but the old man was nowhere to be seen, so instead I wandered over to where a minstrel was entertaining some of the travellers, alternating between juggling balls and singing what I assumed were folk songs. His voice wasn't particularly good by my standards, but it was a pleasant enough distraction to while away the hours until I felt ready to find a place to sleep.

Chapter 8

My new clothes fit me reasonably well; they were a bit snug around the shoulders but they were also far more comfortable than the rags I had been wearing. I still didn't have shoes, but the tunic-robe was long enough to cover my feet if I stood still. And so it was that I felt confident as I stood waiting in my new finery for the gates to open at sunrise. There was a fair amount of jostling as people surged forward, but comforted by my new clothes I didn't react badly at all, although I did chuckle when one pushy young man decided to elbow me out of the way quite viciously. I heard the bone crack over the noise of the crowd, and he vanished swiftly after that. Eventually my turn came and I was called forward by the two men who appeared to be in charge of the gate.

'Name?' asked the first, looking me up and down.

'I am Stratus.'

He offered a grunt in reply. 'What is the purpose of your visit?'

I decided to go for honesty of a sort. 'I wish to discuss a matter with your wise men.'

'Wise men?'

'Yes. Your Elders. Scholars, perhaps.'

'You a scholar?'

'Yes.'

'Have you got a sponsor, or family in the city?'

'No. Why?'

'The city is under martial law. We can't have any freebooters within the walls.'

I thought about the vagrants and what Crow had told me. 'I have no boots, but I do have money,' I lied.

'Let's see it then.'

I bit back the curse that tugged at my lips. 'Of course.'

His armour sported one of the protective tokens that had been so plentiful in the army camp, and I now regretted not taking the time to explore them and their purpose. I could have planted the idea in his mind that I had enough money, but if the charm was attuned to something like that it might warn him. And there were enough bows and swords about that I didn't want to find out how they would react. I made a show of fishing my purse from inside the robe to give myself some time to prepare.

I opened the purse, angling it carefully so that only the man I was speaking to could see inside it. 'Here,' I said, touching his elbow lightly as he leaned forward.

'Well now,' he said, nodding as he looked down into the near-empty purse. I forced myself to stay calm and to keep the image of close-packed gold coins firmly fixed in my mind, grateful that I had taken the time to study them. I was projecting the image into the purse, using the two coins left in it to anchor the illusion. Touching his elbow helped to stabilise it by narrowing the angle at which the coins could be seen, although it also meant that if he moved too much or someone else saw it, the image would become as hollow as it really was.

'All right,' said the guard, scratching in his book. 'I suggest that you make your way to the Fox and Hare while they still have space.' He and his companions smiled broadly at that. He waved at the men behind him and they stood aside. I wasn't sure I knew what going to a fox and hare meant, but I was happy to put that problem aside for later. I offered him and the men holding the gate open what I thought was a grateful smile and made my way into the city and the next stage of my quest. There was a wide, long passage behind the gates that had regularly spaced holes in the walls. I stopped and peered into one, and was surprised to find a man staring back at me.

'Piss off,' he snarled. He called me an idiot too, but I chose not to react. The glimpse that I'd had into the walls had revealed several armed men in there, suggesting that it was a defensive feature rather than a flaw. I passed through another set of gates and suddenly I was in the citadel. I walked out into a small, open square surrounded by tall buildings with narrow windows and teeming with humans of all shapes and sizes. Almost immediately at least half a dozen vendors approached me, each holding out various trinkets or vegetables and, in one case, a fish that had clearly been dead long before I had woken up in the meadow.

I ignored them all and pushed my way through the milling crowd until I emerged on the far side of the square feeling strangely hot and not a bit disoriented by the experience, my nose raw and stinging after the deluge of smells trapped within the crowd. Everywhere I turned men and women were shouting, arguing or laughing, the sound of it washing over me from every angle. I headed down the first road that I came to, but it was clogged with handcarts and small horse-drawn wagons whose drivers traded threats and insults as they scraped past one other in a space that was clearly far too narrow. The sounds echoed from the walls of the shops and houses that rose high above me on both sides, their bulging flanks dotted with open windows from which more faces stared and occasionally shouted some sort of encouragement to the mob below. I backed up, jostling the half-dozen or so men who were already forming another crowd behind me.

The starchy smell of humanity was everywhere, itself only one layer of the thick fug pressing in on my senses. Human waste, spoiled food, animal and vermin spoor, stagnant water and smoke were thickening the air, making it difficult for me to draw breath. There was no clean air to be had. I stumbled as I forced my way further down another road, human faces and voices all blurring into one as I shoved my way through them. I stumbled my way around a corner, and seeing no one around for the first time, I crouched down and hugged my knees in an attempt to force out the noise and smells that were smothering me. I wasn't sure how long I had been sitting there like that, but I was aware enough to feel the tap on my shoulder.

'Hey friend,' said a male voice, 'you all right there?'

I lifted my head slowly in case the smell and sound came crashing back. They seemed to have abated though, and I squinted up at the man who was standing next to me.

'Yes.'

'New to the city, eh?'

'Yes.'

'Chatty too, hey friend?' He squatted down next to me. 'Listen, I know what it's like. So why don't you let me help you? Tell me where you need to go and I'll help you find your way.'

I didn't want to risk tasting his scent, not now that I had just managed to find some sort of equilibrium in my senses. The offer sounded reasonable, and it wasn't as if I had an alternative plan. I nodded my agreement and slowly stood up, catching myself against the wall as an unexpected wave of dizziness washed over me.

'Easy there,' my new friend said, offering me a steadying hand. It was a nice gesture but I doubted whether he or the two men standing behind him would have been able to catch me if I had fallen. 'They grow them big where you come from, eh?'

'Yes. From the islands in the south.' I couldn't quite remember what the Deacon had said. It felt like a long time ago.

'Sure, sure.' He pointed further down the roadway I had been sitting on. 'Come on, let's go this way. It's quieter than those nasty, busy streets.'

It was quieter, but it still reeked of spoiled food and human scat, and my discomfort must have shown because my guide patted me on the shoulder and said, 'Don't worry, we're almost there.'

I turned to look at him, and even though I still felt a bit delicate I now paid more attention to what I saw. I would be the first to admit that my experience with men was at best limited, my broken memories notwithstanding. However, such experience as I had was mostly of the sort where harm or theft was intended, and with my brain now actually working a bit better it didn't take much to see that my ever-so-friendly guide and his friends would fit into either category.

'Ah,' he said, stepping in front of me. 'You begin to understand.'

I looked over my shoulder and was more disappointed than surprised to see that his friends now sported a club and a knife between them. The guide had produced a weapon too, a thin-bladed knife that I quite liked the look of.

'Hand over the purse, big man,' he said, holding the knife steady, ready to lunge at me.

I took a steadying breath as the beast swelled in response to the prospect of violence.

The guide tilted his blade and shook his head. 'It's not worth it, friend. No one's going to care about another foreigner, and even if they did, we'll be on a northbound coach by then. Hand it over.'

Given how little I actually had I did consider doing just that, but I couldn't bring myself to do it. It was the principle more than anything else.

'No,' I said.

'Have it your way,' said the guide, and gave the man standing behind me a helpful nod. I stepped backwards into the arc of the club, spoiling the blow and sending the attacker crashing to his back. His companion with the knife was slow to react and might as well have told me where and when he was going to try to stab me. I caught his forearm, bent it back on itself and pulled him forward so that his face met my rising knee as he fell. I heard and felt the snap of bone as the impact detached and drove his lower jaw into his neck.

The guide was staring at me through all of this, his sharp knife and cool arrogance apparently forgotten. He sprinted away when I took a step towards him, which was gratifying, but also frustrating. I had really liked his knife.

I snatched the club off the floor and backhanded it across the first man's head before he could run away as well, then helped myself to their purses.

They wouldn't be needing the coin, and I was still out of pocket after paying for the wine and bread outside the gates. Aside from the boon of my replenished hoard, the scuffle had also proved enough of a distraction that my head felt clearer than it had since I had passed through the gates. The stench was still there, but it no longer felt like I was drowning in it.

I left their bodies to the scavengers and made my way further down the narrow lane, which eventually emptied onto a wider road. It too was thronged with people trying to sell all manner of things, from shoes and hats to carved furniture. Despite their desperate pleas and the seemingly endless stream of people shuffling past, they didn't seem to be doing much trade. I joined the flow of people moving deeper into the city, stopping occasionally to peer at interesting stalls. I didn't buy anything, despite the vendors' best efforts, although a few cunningly crafted items of jewellery did tempt me. The road led to another square, and although this one was smaller than that by the city gates, it was the point where four roads met and was just as busy.

I kept to the edge of the crowd, but the sound of running water drew me towards a wondrous sight. In the centre of a round pool bordered by smooth stone rose a life-sized bronze sculpture of a knight upon a rearing horse. The workmanship on that alone was worth pausing for, never mind the water spraying from the fat children with trumpets carved into the base. These streams jetted out without pause, creating fine, glittering curtains of mist and rainbows that drifted across the water, yet the pond did not overflow. I walked around it a few times, admiring it from every angle. I had not seen anything like it, and it seemed bizarre that I seemed to be the only one even paying attention to it. But then creating something so majestic, then ignoring it entirely, struck some part of me as a tragically human thing to do.

There was an inscription at the rear of statue, but the scratchings were meaningless to me. I tried to ask a few passers-by, but they either ignored me entirely or flinched away. Eventually I snagged the sleeve of a plump, well-dressed man. He too stiffened but I let go as soon as he slowed.

'Apologies, friend,' I said, offering my best smile. 'But what does the inscription say?' I pointed to the horse's rear.

For a moment it seemed that he would simply bustle off, but he relented. 'I can't read it from here,' he said, brushing the sleeve I had grabbed. 'However, the statue is of Henkman the Vanquisher, the first paladin.'

At the mention of that name, the beast coiled inside me shifted with sudden interest. I felt the heat of its awareness press against the back of my eyes, making blooms of light dance across my vision. I must have appeared quite ill, for when my vision cleared, the plump but helpful man was hurrying across the square with some cloth pressed to his mouth, staring at me as he shuffled off with what speed he could muster. I walked to the front of the statue and stared into Henkman's face, frozen for ever in a silent shout no one would hear, seeking any trace of familiarity in the face or the lines of his body, but nothing had changed. I had another name now though, another piece of the puzzle. What did a self-styled dark wizard and a dead paladin have to do with me?

'Navar Louw. Henkman.' I repeated their names, trying different pronunciations and accents, but they were just words now.

Come on, tell me something useful, I silently entreated the thing inside me, which had lapsed back into its dormant state and remained stubbornly useless. If I, or it, couldn't provide any useful answers I would simply need to find someone who could, which meant that my original plan to find a sage remained brilliantly insightful. But first I needed food and somewhere to sleep. I sort of missed having Crow about; for all of his deficiencies, he had been a useful source of random knowledge and information. I approached one of the nearby vendors, who was busily packing away the last of the trinkets he'd been attempting to sell.

'Do you know of a fox and hare?' I asked. He didn't respond at first, other than to stare at me. 'I believe it is somewhere, rather than a thing,' I added helpfully, unveiling another of my friendly smiles, although it didn't seem to encourage him much. I closed my mouth and hastily tested my teeth with my tongue, but they were still the square human kind.

'Well, umm, what was it again?'

'A fox and hare.'

'Ah,' he said, still staring at me. 'Up that way. It's on a corner.' He gestured off past the fountain. 'I'd go elsewhere though.'

'Why? It was recommended.'

'Look, I'm just being friendly here, but the owner doesn't care much for foreigners. Whoever recommended it to you either doesn't know the place or doesn't like you much.'

'So there would be trouble if I went there?'

'Yes. You're better off heading upwards, closer to the palace. It'll cost more, mind, but you'll be glad of it.'

'Thank you,' I said, and left him to pack his wares as I wandered back to the fountain. I found the sound of the water quite soothing, and once the worst of the frustration had abated I made my way to the Fox and Hare, more out of curiosity than anything else. It was a large, gaudily painted building with a helpful but poorly rendered painting of a fox and a wretched-looking hare on a board next to the entrance.

I stepped inside and tried not to gag on the thick, stale fug that hung in the air in defiance of any breeze that managed to force its way through the narrow windows. That alone was enough to convince me that this was not somewhere I would choose to linger, even without considering the damp straw underfoot and the scores of men who sat with pipes far grander than Crow's in their wet mouths, sending clouds of smoke to cling to the stained rafters.

I turned my back to the inn and rejoined the press of people in the street outside. I would follow the vendor's advice and head towards the upper city.

Chapter 9

The road outside the inn was crowded with men and women carrying large bundles or pulling hand carts and I kept to the side as much as I could. The buildings here rose higher than others I had seen, with wooden constructions sprouting from the roofs of the stone levels below in a variety of fashions, perhaps in response to the narrowing roadway. I had lost count of the number of carts that had scraped my legs, and when an argument stalled the flow of humanity and began to form a tight mob around me, I knew I had to get away from them. Fortunately I was close enough to the edge that it took little effort to make my way down the nearest lane. It snaked around the back of several buildings and was narrow enough that I had to twist sideways now and then to avoid mounds of detritus that had been left in it. Overhead the buildings leaned together as if whispering to each other, either by poor workmanship or design, creating patches of shadow that were as deep as the night even though the sun still sailed through the sky. It felt oppressive; the air was thick enough that I felt close to suffocating and it stank like nothing natural that I had ever smelled before. No matter how many times it branched off into other even narrower paths and alleys, that smell remained. The foulest odours of the city seemed to have seeped into those narrow spaces, thickening among them until it became a single, choking miasma that would surely have made a fly vomit. And yet, more humans lived here among this stench, peering at me with eyes that were bright against their stained skin. Few of these wretches were dressed, and from the way their bones pressed at their skin I surmised that winter would take any who survived that long. They were agile though, squeezing themselves into crevices and clambering high up the sides of the buildings like spiders whenever I drew too close.

It was hard to tell how long I had meandered through those dank alleyways. The shadows were hard to distinguish from the general gloom and the sun was lost behind the creaking height of the buildings. It was only when I began recognising my own scent trail that I realised I was most likely lost, something that I suspect the bedraggled inhabitants of this pit had known for far longer than I had. They were watching me from the ends of exposed beams and various other perches, all but invisible in the murk. I stopped and stared up at a small group of them but, even with the advantage of my blood vision, it was hard to tell whether they were adults or children.

'Hello,' I ventured. They looked at each other and, having wordlessly come to a decision, one of the marginally taller ones descended, dropping down to the street with an enviable dexterity.

'Hello,' he replied in a quiet voice. 'You lost.'

It sounded like a statement rather than a question, and I simply nodded my agreement.

He smiled, and the breath that wafted between the remains of his teeth almost made me take a step back. 'Bad place.'

As he spoke, his fingers were curling around the handle of a small knife that hung from a thong around his neck. It seemed that they were human after all, but I would be carrying this stench with me for days already and the last thing I wanted was to have their blood all over me as well. I whispered to my sorcery, moulding it into a shape not far from that which I'd used to light Crow's pipe and a small ball of fire burst into being above my outstretched hand, its flame steady and unwavering. My control was improving, an achievement lost on the grubby creatures around me, who hissed and clutched at their eyes. Their speaker fared slightly worse than the others by virtue of being the closest and the one that the light was directed at. He staggered back, his knife forgotten, and I took the opportunity to draw one of my own and place the tip under his chin with just enough tension to make him rise to his toes.

'No hurt me, mister please!' he squawked. I dimmed the intensity of the compressed flame, but didn't move the knife.

'I don't want to hurt you,' I lied. 'I just want to find my way out of here and a good place to eat and to rest.'

'I show you, magic man. Easy quick.'

I doubted that this scabrous creature would pass up the opportunity to stab his own father if it meant some coin in his pocket, assuming that the rags he wore had pockets. I let him feel the sting of the point under his chin for a few heartbeats longer, then withdrew the knife.

'If you run, I will burn you,' I said, making the fireball bob up and down. The reassuring scent of his fear now mingled with the more mundane odours of his poor diet and extinct hygiene, and I knew that I had him. I rummaged in my purse and brought out a few of the coins I'd taken from the bodies of my most recent attackers. They were tarnished and quite ugly, but they made the man's eyes all but gleam with hunger.

'If you help me, you get these. Do we have an agreement?'

'Yes, deal.' Then he spat on his hand and thrust it at me. I stared at the wetness with a combination of horror and disgust, the fireball brightening in response and he swiftly lowered his hand.

'Deal deal. You follow me.'

I did just that. He picked his way through the now midnight-black alley with confidence, pulling aside cunningly laid timbers that had concealed other exits. He only looked at me once over his shoulder, and whatever he saw or heard made him bark out something that I didn't need to understand to know it was a curse of some sort. His pace picked up after that but, with his scent now known to me and my blood vision woken, I had no problem in keeping up with him. When we unexpectedly emerged onto a normal, wider street, the sudden rush of moving, untainted air was almost intoxicating after the foulness of the alleyways.

I had no idea where we were though, and said as much. My pet wretch grinned in the darkness and pointed along the road.

'You want rest, this is best place. Many inns and houses. Good food.'

'Where are the city gates from here?'

He pointed to the side and made a strange waggling motion with his hand. I copied the motion, which made him cluck his tongue loudly.

'Steps. You must go down to lower city.'

I was impressed by how far we had actually come. For all of the stench and discomfort, I was almost exactly where I wanted to be. I was pleased that I hadn't killed him.

'What is your name?'

'Jovar.'

I handed him the coins I had promised. 'Thank you, Jovar.'

The coins vanished faster than a viper's tongue. 'Good, magic man. We see you again.' He gave a short wave, then vanished back into the alleyway.

'I don't think so,' I said to the darkness, tempting Fate's sense of humour. I lingered where I was while my senses began recovering from the abuse I had just subjected them to. As I waited, a party of a dozen young males came walking along, laughing and shouting among each other, paying little or no attention to anything or anyone around them. I stepped out behind them as they passed, enjoying the waft of soft spices and oils that followed them. I was conscious of the various new stains that my diversion through the alleyways had cost me, and so was pleased that the group was loud enough to draw any attention away from me. When they bustled into one of the inns a bit further along, I decided to follow them in. Their arrival was met with a round of cheers, which was strange but suited my purposes well. The room within was crowded, and just as thick with smoke as the Fox and Hare had been, although it lacked the riper undertones of bodily waste and soured straw. Here and there ornate bronze lanterns were suspended from chains, the warm glow of their light and the dancing shadows they threw making the murals on the walls shift and glitter as if possessed of a life of their own. It was quite a captivating spectacle and kept my attention for too long, causing me to bump into someone. Since my usual luck was reasserting itself, he was large and surly.

'Who do you think you are?' he snapped at me and lifted my tunic thing in his pinched fingers. 'You stinking peasant. Are you black or simply filthy? Who let you in?'

His loud voice had drawn the attention of the young males I had followed in. They looked at each other, then burst out laughing.

'Good lord, Krykis, he's not with us. He's almost as much of a freak as you are.'

I expected this 'Krykis' to punch the man who'd spoken, but instead he just smiled.

'No one's as much of a freak as me, my lord.'

'You'd be surprised,' I offered conversationally.

The lord clapped his hands together and laughed a bit louder. 'Marvellous! How about that, Krykis, do you think he's freakier than you?'

'Maybe I should open him up and look inside.'

I couldn't help but sigh at that. *Three words*. I had spoken three words and already another human was getting ready to try to hurt me. The only part of it that surprised me was that I found myself feeling disappointed again, rather than angry. It was all so meaningless. Looking around me, I could see the output of so much talent in the fancy cups they were drinking from, the coloured window glass, the lanterns, and even the murals that decorated the walls. So much promise, and yet here I was confronted by this shallow-brained fool.

He stared at me, the challenge in his stance obvious enough that even a dog would understand it. I met his gaze and held it as I plundered his thoughts for any redeeming features. I saw a whirlwind of violence, of beatings given and received while crowds roared around him, and felt the glory of triumph and his sense of empowerment as he stood over his fallen opponents. I neither wanted nor needed this fight, but the hubris of his former victories and almost bestial need to show his superiority meant that he did. I fed a wisp of sorcery into my gaze and reached into his mind, letting him feel a measure of the rage that emanated from the demon like the heat from a furnace. I felt his arrogance wither as the coiled menace within me roused itself and extended its attention to him. It barely brushed the periphery of his mind, but it was enough. He blinked furiously and looked away.

'Be on your way,' he snarled at me, licking his dry lips. 'I'll not sully my fists with your blood.'

I stood where I was until he stepped out of my way, his gaze finding the floorboards. It was only when the hum of the conversations around us swelled again that I realised most people had been watching the confrontation, including the innkeeper. He set down the cloth he was carrying.

'That's all very grand, but we don't serve—'

'Don't say *my kind*.'

'Only if your kind are vagabonds.'

I showed him my purse and he seemed to relax. A moment later the man who Krykis had called lord came to stand next to me.

'A drink for the man who stared Krykis down, on my chit. What'll it be, friend?'

'A wheat beer. I hear they're good.'

'And you'd be right too,' the lord said with a smile. 'Two of those.'

'Your face is painted.' I hadn't meant to say it out loud, but there it was. To my surprise, his smile remained.

'Aside from occasionally being embarrassing, I am also nothing if not fashionable.'

'I do not understand fashion,' I replied.

'Clearly.' Our beers were set down in front of us, and he touched my arm. 'Come, sit with us.'

I shrugged my assent and followed him to one of the larger tables where I took care to ensure that the legs of the bench were right underneath me. The lord pointed to each of the men in turn and said their names aloud. I didn't care enough to pay any attention and sipped my beer instead. It was far nicer than the ale I'd tasted and I silently thanked the dead scout for the recommendation.

'So what's your name then?' the painted lord asked.

'Stratus.'

'Just Stratus?'

I opened my mouth to say 'of course', but I knew that it wasn't true. I had another name, but like my sorcery, it was broken and wrapped up with the thing inside me.

'Yes, just Stratus.' I remembered the protocol for this sort of encounter. 'And yours?'

'Lucien. Lucien Stahrull.'

I recognised that name, and he saw that I did. He tilted his cup in some sort of mock salute. None of the others reacted.

'Are you a soldier, Stratus?' asked one of the men next to me. 'You look big enough. What regiment are you with?'

'The blacks are with the auxiliaries. Has to be,' offered another.

'He's big enough to be a siege-breaker.'

'I'm not a soldier,' I said, setting my now empty tankard down. 'And I have never broken a siege.'

The same man who had asked me about being a soldier leaned forward and pointed to the lord. 'Would you like to be? His lordship can make it happen.'

Lucien spread his hands. 'It's true.'

'I'm not a soldier,' I said again. 'I have no interest in your petty war.'

Several of them thumped their tankards down noisily and began shouting at me. They were all still seated, and none had a weapon, so I ignored them. The lord, however, hadn't reacted and was staring at me over the metallic rim of his tankard. He slowly lowered it to the table, and the others fell quiet at the gesture.

'It isn't just our petty little war, Stratus,' he said in a measured tone. 'It's not about provinces or kingdoms any more. And while you may not wear the blue yet, you'll be a soldier before it's over.' He looked around the room. 'We all will be, because our enemy demands it.'

'That being the Worm Lord?' I ventured. No one else at the table was talking any more, and those that weren't staring at either him or me were peering into their drinks as if they'd lost something inside them. A woman sitting alone at a nearby table was watching us too, an untouched tankard of ale on the table in front of her and a sword resting against her leg.

'That's him,' Lucien said, dragging my attention back to him.

'He's just a man.'

'He's a *wizard*,' hissed the man next to me, who was starting to annoy me.

'Wizards bleed.'

'I like that!' said Lucien, a smile creasing his painted face once more. 'Wizards bleed. I'll drink to that.' He lifted his tankard and didn't lower it until it was empty. 'Olaf! Another round. We must drink to the bleeding of wizards.'

Fresh tankards were brought, each filled to the brim, and yet the innkeeper did not ask for payment. I drained mine in two great gulps, enjoying the way it soothed a thirst I hadn't been aware of. The others around the table begin calling out different ways to kill a wizard, and with each new suggestion they sipped their beers. After several more tankards, the suggestions were becoming incredibly lewd and intricate as they tried to think of new ways to kill a person, and their sips had become gulps that saw as much beer spilled down their tunics as their throats. I found that I enjoyed the seventh tankard as much as I had the first, and was waiting for Lucien to order another when he toppled off his chair.

I disentangled myself from the bench and went to check that he wasn't dead. He was laughing when I bent over him and offered to help him up.

'No! Not up! We must . . . find food. Something nice, with actual meat.' He pointed vaguely to the door, then rubbed his face, smearing the paint on it. 'I forget how strong he brews them.'

'Do we need to run?' I asked, glancing over to where Olaf was watching us.

Lucien frowned. 'Run?'

'We have not paid Olaf.'

Lucien roared with laughter and clung to my shoulder with one hand while pointing to the exit with the other. 'To the food! Olaf, farewell!'

I decided to play along and no one made an attempt to stop us, not even those men at the table who were still awake. It was full dark outside, but that didn't seem to bother him. 'That way!' he'd shout, and I would half carry him in that direction until he made me stop and go in another. I wasn't sure if he was lost, mad, or both. He made us stop at another venue, where he ordered us each a tankard of their 'finest ale' and made me pay for it after no one recognised him. I'd never interacted with a drunk human before and I found him quite amusing despite how much he clung to me, and so didn't really mind too much. 'Who are you, Stratus? Why're you so black? Gods, I can barely see you.'

He was leaning across a table made from an old barrel that was swaying almost as much as he was, squinting at me as if I were a great distance away. Perhaps it was something in the beer, or because I had never shared a drink with a prince of men before that I could remember, but I decided to tell him the truth. I took a steadying breath, pleased to see that he was waiting for my response.

'I don't know.'

Once I said it out loud it didn't really feel like that much of a dramatic revelation, but it did make Lucien laugh hard enough that he vomited across the table and fell from his chair again.

'He's had enough for tonight,' said a voice behind me. It wasn't one that I recognised, and like all sorcerers, I had a good ear for voices. I turned as I stood, and found myself looking down at a female of about the same height and build as Lucien, and it took a moment for me to recognise her as the sword-carrying woman who had been at the inn.

'Why are you following us?' I asked, more as an excuse to draw in a good noseful of her scent than any real desire to know. Smell is a more powerful sense than any other, but one largely lost on humans. I drew in her scent, which was strong given how close she was in this confined space. It told me that she was young, well fed and was recovering from an injury, but there was a strange tang woven into her scent that was familiar. She smelled of Lucien, but something else as well.

'. . . of your concern. You just need to step away and let me take him from here,' she said.

'I like him,' I said, stepping back.

'Everyone likes a prince,' she said, kneeling next to him. She turned his face and wiped it with a small cloth that she tucked back into a pocket. She watched him for a few moments, then sighed and wrapped his arm over her shoulder and, with a grunt of effort, lifted him to his feet. I thought this an impressive feat, given that he was at least as heavy as she was and most likely more.

'Where are you taking him?'

'Home. So you can back off now. You've had your measure of free drinks.'

I followed them outside and took a deep breath to clear the smell of the tavern from my head. The female was talking again, but I held up a hand to silence her. I took another long draw of the night air, trying to find the scent trail that I had just caught a snatch of. A scent trail that was subtle, but somehow fouler than anything I had smelled that day, even more so than the alleyways, but aside from that accomplishment there was something in it that set the beast to growling. I lifted my head and turned around in a circle, seeking it. I wanted to find it, to follow it to its source and make it tell me about myself. I took a few steps, testing the air as I went until I was confident that I had it. I turned to tell the female and Lucien, but they were already gone, their scent trail leading them and me right towards whatever was exuding the unnatural stench.

Chapter 10

The streets were quieter now, the darkness having driven even the most stubborn of men to their homes. The female had managed to get Lucien walking again, but it wasn't much better than a stagger and I caught them up easily enough. Another man had joined them, and by the light of the lantern he carried I could see that he was one of the sash-wearing soldiers. He lifted the lantern and his sword when he heard my approach. The female turned as well, and I saw that she had drawn her sword now, albeit a smaller one than the soldier's. Only Lucien smiled as I stepped into the light.

'Stratus!' he called out. 'You should really carry a lamp or something. I can only see your teeth. I thought we'd lost you.'

'Yes,' said the female through clenched teeth, moving to stand between me and him. 'We did. What do you want?'

'Oh, be careful. She's fierce,' said Lucien, all but shouting the last word before breaking into laughter.

'What do you want?' she said, ignoring the prince. Her sword hand was steady, and despite its small size the blade she held looked like something I wanted to keep some distance away from me.

I wasn't exactly sure how I could explain the significance of the scent I was following to creatures who could barely smell a roasting ox from ten paces.

'Something foul is in the air,' I said.

'That's what pomade is for,' said Lucien. 'We should get a pie. Where's that place that you like so much, Tatta?'

'Don't call me that.'

'Don't be so sensitive.' She stiffened as he draped his arm over her shoulders.

She shoved him away with a sharp movement. 'Please stay behind me.'

'I thought you loved me,' he said, rubbing his chest.

'You're drunk.'

The noxious scent was thickening with every moment we stood there, but even I wasn't expecting it to start affecting the light. Just when I felt like gagging at the reek of it, the light of the lantern began to dim, as if the soldier was slowly putting it inside a barrel.

'What in the Hel is this?' he asked, shaking the lantern.

'Magic,' hissed the female, stepping closer to Lucien and filling her other hand with a curved dagger from a holder at her back.

'No, not magic,' I said, 'this is something different.'

Magic didn't feel so tainted, like it was leaving a grimy residue on everything around it. Magic was part of the same energy that gave life to all living things, as necessary to life and the natural order as the rising of the sun. It could be dangerous, but like the thunderbolt that kills a cow or the water that drowns a careless child, it wasn't evil or malicious in itself. This taint suggested otherwise.

I woke my blood vision in the moment before the light failed, and the now familiar red tint washed across my vision. I saw the five loping shapes that the unnatural darkness had sought to hide. They looked like men but between their ragged clothing and the stench they brought with them I couldn't tell for sure. The long knives that they carried made their intentions sufficiently clear. The three humans were staring wildly, their eyes wide in a desperate but vain attempt to see anything. I called to my sorcery and sent a fireball into the air above us, to hover rather than explode, shedding a light no greater than a hunter's moon but enough to foil the surprise attack.

Unlike the soldier, the swordswoman did not stop to look at the light or wonder where it had sprung from. She leaped forward, forestalling the attack of the closest assassin, swatting his knife away with her sword and plunging her dagger into his neck and ripping it open. Two lunged for Lucien, and I knew that I couldn't reach him in time. My sorcery wasn't strong enough to manifest two fireballs. But it was enough to speed the knife that I threw to its target, nudging its path so that it flew true and speeding its flight so that it sank in with enough force to spin the attacker off his feet. The other dark shape slashed for Lucien, and I expect he was as surprised as I was when the prince swayed out of the way, grabbed the knifeman's arm and threw him onto the ground with unexpected vigour.

The two remaining attackers fell upon the soldier, who had realised his error in staring at my light far too late. The long blades of their knives found his neck and groin, and he fell to the ground with his life's blood flooding from wounds that would see him dead in a few heartbeats. These two angled towards me, but I was ready for them. I leaped towards the first of them and swept his blade aside with my arm like the woman had. I had no blade to hand, so settled for thumping a fist into his ear as the deflection turned him, sending him to the ground. The second man's knife was already stabbing towards me, and I knew that he was too close for me to do anything about it.

I felt the sting of it jabbing me under the ribs, then the long ripping scrape of it tearing my skin as it failed to penetrate and glanced away along a rib. I wasn't about to give him a chance to recover from his mistake. I grabbed his arm, pulled it as hard as I could with one hand and felt it snap out of his shoulder. Before he could release the scream his open mouth promised, I chopped the edge of my hand into the side of his neck, snapping at least one of the bones within. I left him to flop lifeless on the ground and turned to see the woman hacking at the neck of the man that Lucien had thrown to the ground.

'We need to take their heads,' she shouted. Lucien was leaning against a nearby wall, retching noisily.

'Why? Are they valuable?'

'Don't be smart,' she said as she sawed through some stubborn muscle. 'They're agents of the Worm Lord. If we don't take their heads they may rise.'

I snorted in disbelief. 'The only thing they're going to be doing is feeding crows.'

I left her to the hacking and dabbed tentatively at the wound on my chest. It was long but fairly shallow, and had already stopped bleeding. It still stung though. I dropped my tunic and went over to the one that I'd punched in the ear. I had tried not to hit him hard enough to kill him, and it looked like I'd succeeded. I ripped the clothing from him, revealing a fairly typical human male, albeit one with a number of drawings on his body and face. The spiral patterns were strangely familiar, but whatever memories they belonged to were buried too deep to glean anything useful from. He wasn't carrying anything aside from his knife, not even a few coins. I nudged him a few times, but he remained steadfastly unconscious, a state which changed when I gave his genitals a hearty squeeze.

He flailed wildly as he gasped his way back to wakefulness, then froze as he saw me.

'The beast!' He cried before I grabbed him by the jaw and held his head immobile.

'Tell me everything,' I said as I bent forward and locked my gaze to his. The presence within me stirred hungrily as I eagerly reached into his mind. Here was one who knew me at last. He struggled, both against my grip and mentally, but his strength in either attempt was found wanting. The lantern's light was returning, so I didn't hesitate in drawing the fireball's energy back into myself and using it to fuel my plunge into his mind.

I bullied my way through his most recent memories, past the ambush that they had set and the shock of their failure. I wanted to know why, and who they were. I felt him desperately trying to shore up his mental defences, and while it might have stopped an inquisitive cub, they were no match for my skill. I undermined them with ease, then pulled them away. I felt his suddenly exposed mind recoil with an almost tangible sense of mounting dread, but forged ahead regardless.

A dark room, the air thick with sacred incense. There are six of us, and while we do not speak, there are no secrets among us. We are the same, sworn to the Master and chosen for this task by him in person. We have waited a long time, each of us having come to the city by his own route over the preceding weeks. We have waited so long for our command, each day without the Master's blessing akin to a week without food or water for lesser men. Each of us felt the pressing of the Sending, and it was with eagerness that we prepared the vessel that Rorik had brought to the temple. She screamed like the sheep that she was when he raised the knife over her, ignorant to the last of the great honour being bestowed upon her. He carved the sacred words into her living flesh, then spoke them out loud. The runes unfolded like red petals, freeing the blood trapped in her tainted flesh to rise into the air, where it drew together to form the Master's face.

'I seek one that might come to the city, and you shall find him for me if he does. His skin is black and hairless, and he stands a hand taller than me. Send for me if you find him, and waylay him if you can. Be wary though, for his strength is great. Draw upon my power if you must.'

'Yes, Master,' we said as one, each bursting with pride at the honour being bestowed upon us.

'Watch the harlot that guards the prince, for this beast may seek her. Capture her if you can.'

'Yes, Master.'

The Sending ended, and we relished the heat of the now released blood, drawing in its latent power. We would eat well this night, then begin our vigil.

I pushed harder, seeking more of this master, but I felt something buried deep within the man's mind stir. At first I thought he had rallied his strength to resist me, but then I felt a single, sharp pulse of magic that illuminated the enchantment's structure for the briefest moment. It wasn't a particularly powerful or sophisticated trap, merely a clever one. The enchantment released a pulse that swept through his brain like a wave, one that rebounded from the bone around it, each ripple more violent than the last as they clashed against each other. His brain was liquefied by the silent attack within a few heartbeats, so that by the time I released his head it had already begun to leak from his nose in a thick soup.

I stepped back from his body, simultaneously disappointed that I hadn't been able to dig deeper but also pleased that I had managed to acquire another small piece of my puzzle.

'What the Hel is that?' asked the woman, whose clothing was saturated with the blood of the dead men. As the lanterns brightened once more I could see numerous scraps of gristle and skin along the length of her bloodied sword.

'You reek of their blood,' I said.

'Yeah, well, I don't have much choice in the matter, do I?' She kicked the dead man at my feet, prompting a bit more of the greyish ooze to spill out. 'What did you do to him?'

'That's what's left of his brain,' I said, and couldn't help but notice how her grip on the sword changed. 'It wasn't me.'

'Just like it wasn't you that made that witch light appear.'

'No, that was me.'

'Who are you?' she asked, her sword rising as she put some space between us. '*What* are you?'

'I'm an islander, from the coast of Illutia. I . . .'

'Cut the shit,' she said, slowly circling me. 'The truth, or the guard will find seven bodies, not six.'

'Six.' I remembered now. 'There are . . . were, six of them. I saw it in his mind. Six. Which means the last of them is still about. And they were looking for y—'

'I didn't fall off a turnip cart yesterday. The truth, and none of that weird shit.' She waved the tip of the sword at me.

I stared at her in confusion.

'Leave him be,' said Lucien, who had picked up the dead soldier's lantern. 'If it wasn't for his witch light we'd both be dead.'

'Yes, but—'

'No buts, Tatyana. This is neither the time nor place.'

She lowered her sword. 'Are you hurt?'

'No,' he said. 'I will hurt tomorrow, but I'm not injured, thanks to him.' He looked down at the dead soldier, who was only marginally paler than him. 'Stratus, can you carry him? I don't want his body left here with this filth.'

I nodded and lifted the soldier onto my shoulder, grimacing as I felt his already cooling blood seeping into my new clothes. The woman, Tatyana, was still watching me as she wiped the worst of the mess from her hands and sword on the dead men's clothes. Apparently satisfied, she moved to walk ahead of Lucien and we made our way through the deserted city streets towards the palace that sat at the heart of it.

Who was she, that the dead men's master thought I would seek her out? I watched her as we walked. She didn't seem at all alarmed at the violence that had just transpired, her heartbeat thumping along in a strong and regular rhythm. There was something in her scent that was familiar, yet I didn't recognise her at all, but I suppose that was to be expected. Accompanying them to the palace would give me the opportunity to stay close to her and investigate. I would need to be careful though. If she was cursed with the same enchantment as the man I had probed, there was the chance that too direct a question would also see her brain melted. I would need to be patient.

In the meantime, however, I would have a chance to see a palace. I didn't think I had ever been inside a palace before. I was intrigued by the prospect, but the beast inside me rippled with mocking laughter.

Chapter 11

The palace was a disappointment. It seemed to me to be little more than a nice but overgrown inn with armed guards, none of whom seemed pleased to see any of us, not even Lucien. At least there wasn't anyone trying to kill us, although there was a definite sense of threat when I dropped the dead man at the guards' feet, despite it being at Lucien's request. I'd almost forgotten that I was carrying him.

'What happens next?' I asked Lucien as I watched three of the guards lift the body onto a blanket with poles down the side.

'Nothing for now. In the morning I will go speak to my brother Jean, although he'll already know everything by then.'

'No, I meant with him.' I nudged the dead man's foot with my own, prompting another round of cursing and empty threats from the other guards. 'I've not seen funerary rights from this perspective.' I had a distinct memory of someone important being boiled and his bones carved and inlaid with precious gems afterwards, but I had no context for it at all. 'Do you boil him right away? What do you do with the meat afterwards?'

Lucien was apparently no wiser than me about their death rituals because he said nothing for some time and simply stared at either the floor or me. 'We'll talk about this in the morning,' he said. By this time the guards had lifted the body and were already carrying it away on the pole-blanket. 'Tatyana, can you find him a room, please?'

She had slipped away soon after we arrived, and had taken the opportunity to rinse much of the blood from herself. 'Of course. I won't be long.' She made her fingers click loudly and gestured to me. 'This way.'

I followed her down another unremarkable corridor until she stopped at a door some way along it. 'Here.'

I peered into the dark room beyond. It was a simple rectangle with a bed and a tall box with a basin of water upon it. The floor was covered in a woven mat which I thought was very nice.

'It's very nice,' I said, stepping inside.

'Don't break anything, and don't leave it. You understand?'

'Of course I understand. But why can't I leave?'

She pinched her nose. 'Because any of those guards will be looking for an excuse to teach you some respect. Just stay inside until we fetch you.' With that she slammed the door shut and walked away muttering.

I opted not to waste time trying to make sense of it and to rather make the most of what appeared to be a clean and quiet place to rest. I pulled my clothing off and used some of the water to scrub the worst of the blood that remained from me before it could attract vermin. Then I carefully lay down on the bed, which wasn't as soft as some of the ferns I'd slept on but had fewer crawling things in it. It only took a few deep breaths before sleep took me. It felt like I'd barely closed my eyes before Tatyana was there again, kicking me awake.

I swam back to consciousness as she switched from cursing me to rubbing her foot.

'Did you sleep in your armour or something?'

'I don't wear armour,' I said, rising.

'Oh for gods' sakes,' she said, 'put some damned clothes on already.'

'My clothes stink of blood. I will need to get some more.'

'Just wait here. I'll go see if there's anything in your size in the stores.' She stared at me a moment longer before leaving, no doubt appraising what would fit me. I used the time before she returned to practise a few different constructs with my sorcery. It was good to practise, and it helped put the remnants of the half-formed dreams that had plagued my sleep to rest. The Songlines resonated quite strongly here and the rest I'd had, however short, had seen them replenish what power I had used the night before. Even the wound the robed cannibal had given me was gone without trace, and I found myself to be in a very good mood. Good enough that I wasn't irritated by Tatyana's laughter as I struggled my way into the clothes she had brought me.

'Now we can breakfast,' she said, finally satisfied that my shirt was facing the right way. It was tighter than the other clothes, but not so much that it hindered my movements. It was soft too, and smelled vaguely of crushed pine needles.

'Oh yes. I am very hungry,' I said, suddenly aware of how hollow I felt. 'I could eat a horse.'

'Me too.'

'Liar.'

I followed her to a large room with a tall ceiling where at least a dozen men were eating. I copied what she did, not wanting to draw more attention than I already was, and soon enough I was sat at a table eating chicken eggs that someone had thought to cook, along with red fruit and bread. She only spoke again after she had finished her second serving and I was on my fourth.

'So what's your story?' she said. 'You appear out of nowhere, and shortly after we're attacked by a troop of assassins. You're no islander either; I've served with some of them and aside from that hide, you look nothing like them. They're lean, like the great cats, and you're a bloody cave bear by comparison.' She picked at a tooth. 'You don't sound anything like them either. So start talking.'

I set down the loaf I'd been chewing on. I had been expecting something like this since Lucien had raised it the night before, reasoning that if he could sense something was amiss in the state he was in, it wasn't a far stretch of the imagination that the matter would come up again. I'd decided to try the truth then, and I would do so again now.

'Would you still want to know if the answers aren't what you want to hear?' I looked over to the other table, where the men were conversing in low tones. 'Is that why they're still here? To beat me if you don't like what you hear?'

She snorted. 'Firstly, I wouldn't ask a question if I didn't want an answer to it. And second, I'm no soldier, not any more. That lot over there don't give a shit about me, aside from bitching that I earn more than them.' She rudely tore a chunk off the end of my loaf. 'Talk.'

Neither her scent or heartbeat changed as she spoke, so it seemed that she was telling the truth.

'I don't know who I am,' I said, watching her closely. 'I woke up in a meadow several days past, with no memory of how I came to be there. I was paralysed at first, but a Deacon helped me regain the use of this body.'

'You just woke up in a meadow?' She snorted. 'Come on, you must remember something. And there just happened to be a Deacon there?'

I told her about the vultures and my rescue, but she kept shaking her head, so I stopped. 'Why do you keep doing that?'

'Because you're full of shit. Deacons don't go wandering about the countryside with armed escorts and prisoners, and least of all with paladins. What really happened?'

'It is the truth.'

'Fine. So, after this wandering Deacon heals him, how does a once-paralysed black wizard end up in Falkenburg drinking beer with a prince of Krandin?'

I told her what had happened since I escaped from the Deacon's men, although I may have glossed over elements of my capture by the seneschal's men. She didn't interrupt me, but just sat there, gnawing on the same soggy piece of bread. She lowered the bread when I told her about the infernal presence in my mind and the barely contained rage that surrounded it, and dropped it entirely when I told her about eating the soldier's arm. Even though I occasionally struggled to find the right words, it felt strangely normal talking to her about it, and I felt a sense of relief at being able to give voice to the thoughts I had wrestled with for so long. I finished with the events of the previous night and sat back, curious to see her reaction.

'Well, this is awkward.' She said, dusting the crumbs from her hands. 'It's not that I don't, um, appreciate the honesty, but it's a lot to swallow. However, if it's any help, I don't think you're a demon. A cannibal perhaps, but not a demon.'

'How can you be so sure?'

'I'm no priest, but I've read scripture and while the idea of you eating someone is the most fucked-up thing I've heard in a long time, it pales in comparison to actual accounts of demonic attacks. The idea of a demon complaining that his clothes are a bit smelly and then having eggs for breakfast is frankly ridiculous.'

'That's very kind of you to say.'

'So, in short, your story still stinks. I'll admit that you have a few impressive tricks up your sleeve, but again, it's hardly much proof of anything. I've seen hermits pull rabbits out of their arse for a few pennies.'

'Really?'

She waved the question away. 'I've also seen what war can do to some people, not to mention a good hit to the head, and what you're describing could all just be in your mind, and to be honest, it quite likely is.'

'Even the sorcery?'

'Even wizards can lose their minds.'

Wizards were a separate breed to sorcerers, but I didn't bother correcting her. I had been expecting outrage or fear rather than such complete dismissal of the whole matter. I toyed with the idea of forcing the row of fanged teeth to descend, to show her that it was more than a daydream, but it wasn't a nice sensation and if she chose not to believe me, so be it.

'Look,' she continued, 'all I am concerned about is Lucien. What is he to you? What do you want from him?'

'Do you love him?'

'What?' She froze in place as she said it, her eyes wide as her brows crashed into each other. 'No. What, why would you say that?'

'Lucien said it last night.'

'Lucien was drunk.' She folded her arms across her chest. 'He's my charge. I'm his personal guard, that's all. Our positions were agreed a long time ago. And don't change the subject.'

'I wasn't trying to. I think Lucien is linked to whatever I am somehow. The thing inside me, the beast, reacted to the name Stahrull.'

'The beast, eh?'

'It's what I've taken to calling it.'

'The delusion might be better.'

'Call it what you will, but it is part of the puzzle. It has only reacted to three names. Stahrull, Henkman, and—'

'Henkman?' she said.

'Yes, he was the first paladin. I saw a very striking statue of him yesterday.'

'I know who he was.' She leaned closer. 'But why did you – it – react to the name?' She stared at my chest as if expecting something to burst out.

'That's what I am trying to discern.' Her heartbeat had increased when she asked the question, which intrigued me. 'I know little or nothing about him, and am at a loss as to why either you or I should care about a dead paladin.'

'He's been dead a long time. About seven hundred years, so maybe you just like bad sculpture.'

'I thought it was quite striking, actually.'

'It's rubbish. The armour is all wrong for that period. Back then they mostly just wore chainmail. And his helmet would have been a pot, not visored. And those antlers on it? Ridiculous.'

'So you have seen it then.'

She picked up a knife and stabbed at some of the leftover fruit. 'My grandfather unveiled the damned thing. He hated it and didn't stop carping on about it until the day he died.'

105

'Your grandfather?'

'Aye. It was a big occasion back then, the seven hundredth anniversary of his *"triumphant and glorious death"*. There was bunting hanging from the buildings, troupes of minstrels and not a few of the nobles in attendance. I was only a child, but it was a big thing for the family, and I remember feeling like a princess that day.'

'You are not a princess though.'

'You noticed that, eh?'

'What was so special about his death?'

'He killed the last dragon. Right about the same time that it bit him in half.'

I must have heard this story before as I felt the echo of it inside my mind, but the why and how of it remained infuriatingly out of reach.

'Personally, I would have celebrated his life and his victories. You know, the minor stuff like single-handedly defeating the Demon King, but I suppose everyone enjoys a good death.'

'Unless you are the one dying, I would imagine.' She gave a grunt of laughter at that. 'So, if you were not a princess, it stands that your grandfather was not a prince. So why did he receive this honour?'

She didn't reply immediately and sat there, turning the small knife over and over in her fingers.

'My name, my family name, is Henkman. He was kin to me.' She looked up as the beast shook itself awake within me. Whatever else she said was lost to a deep, broken-sounding growl that I could feel in my chest but only I could hear.

Chapter 12

I doubled over as the corded muscles across my gut clenched with a sudden viciousness that almost had me smash my face into the table. I clutched my middle and felt them writhing under my skin, as if something sinuous was trying to find its way out through them. I groaned at the thought and fought against the clawing pain, pushing back at it, but whether real or imagined, it felt like the beast would surely tear me apart.

Flashes of red and black filled my vision, swamping the image of Tatyana rising from her chair. I didn't feel myself falling from mine, nor hear the shouting that ensued, but I had fallen. The beast within was trying to shake itself free and it didn't care about the blood that it would cost. It *wanted* Tatyana, to burn and tear at her. The patches of red and black spun across my vision, fracturing again and again into smaller fragments until they filled my mind like a stormy sea, glittering with a thousand different shades of blood. I felt myself sinking into that sea, its blood filling my mouth and silencing the roar on my lips. There was no taste and no sound after I slipped beneath the surface, just a perfect silence and the swirling shadows that briefly coalesced into images before melting away.

A mountain spewing fire. Paladins with swords that shone with white heat charging towards me. A burning city surrounded by a field of blackened and broken bones, thousands upon thousands of them. A long-clawed hand gripping my own, gone before I could see it.

And in the dark an impossibly large shape moved and began to rise, flickers of red playing across it like dying embers fanned by a sulphurous wind. I felt a sense of a deep and bitter rage rising with it, stretching towards me. Beckoning to me. Calling to me. *Stratus. Stratus.*

'Stratus, goddamn it!'

The voice was suddenly in my ears, not my mind. I felt the weight of my body return, and with it the sensation of a cold floor beneath me and air, not blood, in my mouth. I gasped and opened my eyes to see Tatyana straddling my chest, her arm raised over her shoulder, a flaccid glove held ready to deliver another stinging blow to my cheek.

'Please, stop.'

She hit me again, then stood up. I sat up, carefully testing my gut for any trace of the clawing pain, but there was nothing. The splintered remnants of the chair were scattered about me.

'You want to tell me what just happened?' she asked, propping her hip against the table. 'We were talking and you went about as white as I've ever seen you and fell over. For a moment I thought someone had stabbed you.'

'I . . . don't know.' But I did. *It* had wanted *her*. I could still feel it inside me, subdued for now but still awake, its presence a dull pressure behind my eyes. The dead assassins' master had been correct in believing that she and I were somehow linked, but how did he know and not either of us? The *beast* certainly knew, but it wasn't one to share its secrets. I hadn't felt its presence so clearly before, and as I stood I wasn't looking at the hall or Tatyana, but the images that had come to me through the blood and darkness that had filled my mind.

As before, I had no context for what I had seen, and could only guess that they were memories. I had no idea whether they were mine or the beast's. The memory of the charging paladins suggested a reason why I'd reacted so strongly to those that had travelled with the Deacon, but it also implied that the memory was a shared one, or at worst, my own. Why would a score or more paladins charge at me if I wasn't some demonic abomination? I didn't particularly feel like one, but the feral rage I had felt emanating from the beast suggested that perhaps that element of me was not buried as deep as I had thought. If it kept growing stronger, would I still be able to force it down? What would happen if I couldn't?

The images of the dead men and the burning city weren't helpful; from what Crow and Tatyana had told me, scenes like that were being played out across their kingdom as we sat there. But the mountain was something specific; its profile had been clear against the red of the fire that had engulfed it. The burning mountain. If I could find that, I would at least have a place to start. I was snapped from my thoughts by the slap of Tatyana's glove against my cheek.

'There you are. You had that look again. Did you hit your head?' she asked as I blinked the memories away and looked at her.

'No.'

'So what happened? Or is falling off chairs just a thing that your people do?'

I chose to ignore that. 'Your name. The beast reacted to it. Very strongly.'

She huffed out a sharp breath. 'You said that already.'

'Yes, but that was about a statue. You . . . are a *living* Henkman.' I resisted the impulse to touch her. 'It is quite a different thing entirely.'

'Aye, well, don't get your hopes up too high. I didn't like them when they were alive, and not much has changed since.'

'Who?'

'My family.'

'They're dead?

'Aye. I'm the last of the line. Poetic, really. Seven hundred years of heroic tradition and the only one to survive is the disappointment.'

Somewhere deep inside me, the beast gave a slow laugh that was far more chilling than its usual growl. It was pleased with what it heard, and as the laugh faded I felt it sink back into the depths, as if sated. It made me want to know why, and as Tatyana was still muttering about it, I forced myself to pay closer attention.

'Why were you a disappointment?'

'Paying attention really isn't one of your strongest attributes, is it?' She turned away, but then exhaled loudly and dropped back onto her chair. 'In case you haven't noticed, I was cursed with the burden of being a woman. It makes being a respected member of the Church a bit of an impossibility.'

'I noticed. Your moon is coming on and the scent is quite distinctive.'

'Sadly for my family— Wait, what?'

'I am paying attention.' I smiled to show that I was enjoying her telling, but it took some time before she continued.

'Anyway. The problem for my dear, departed father was that I wasn't a man, and to boot I was a difficult birth and ruined my mother. He resented me from the start, and my mother for not dying and giving him a chance to marry again. The Henkmans had a proud tradition of dying in battle, and that required lots of sons.' She bared her teeth as she spoke, and I felt her heart thud with new effort as she did so. I wasn't one for human emotions, but I was familiar enough with anger to know it when I felt it.

'That seems unfair.'

'It got worse after my only brother was killed. Suddenly there was no male heir to carry on the family name and traditions. This was, of course, somehow my fault too. I walked out of the house when my father tried to marry me off like some brood mare and I never went back.' She stared at me and shook her head. 'I can't believe I'm sitting here telling you this.'

'And then they died?' I prompted her.

She tapped the small knife against the table for a while before replying. 'Yes. My mother stabbed him in the neck while he slept, then opened her own veins. As you can imagine, that didn't do much for the family fortune.'

'Was that a tradition too?'

'Are you trying to be funny? Because you're really not.'

'Not at all.'

She stared at me for a few moments, then just shook her head again. 'I don't know what happened.' She tossed the knife aside and stared at the juice it had left on her fingers. Before she could say anything else though, the doors at the end of the room opened and a man with shiny clothes came striding towards us.

'Prince Lucien requests your company in the east wing reception.' His voice was high and clear, but his scent was definitely that of a male. He spun about and strode off as soon as he'd finished speaking, leaving behind a fading scent of some sort of sweet flower.

'Who was that?'

'Just a page. They're everywhere, and they're all like that. Come on,' Tatyana said, rising from her chair. 'You may even have the privilege of meeting Jean, Crown Prince of Krandin.'

It looked like she was expecting a reaction. 'How exciting.'

'I think that you and I have very different ideas about what exciting means.'

Lucien looked and smelled far better than he had the night before, so much so that had I not expected to find him there I might not have recognised him. With so little to differentiate them I found it hard to separate human faces from each other at the best of times, so I had made a conscious attempt to remember Lucien once I knew who he was. However, even with the attention I had paid, the combination of more colourful clothing, colour in his cheeks and a better posture made a visible difference.

There were several other people in the room, most of them clustered around him. Their conversation paused as we entered the room, which looked barely furnished. Tatyana made a show of deference to him, bending over almost far enough to expose the back of her neck, albeit briefly. She looked to me afterwards, which I thought a bit strange, but I offered her an encouraging smile while I helped myself to an apple from a bowl on the small table marooned in the centre of the room. The others in the room were watching me as if they'd never seen someone eat before, and I found their scrutiny a bit unnerving. I took a sniff of the apple, but it smelled perfectly normal and just on the right side of ripe.

'Stratus is a visitor to our lands,' Lucien said, coming over and clapping me on the shoulder. I took a bite of the apple, pleased that at least someone had believed my story.

He leaned in towards me while I chewed and whispered, 'You should bow when you enter my presence.'

'Why?'

'In here, I am a prince of Krandin.'

'I am not from Krandin.'

'It's protocol. It doesn't really mean anything.'

'Then it doesn't really matter,' I replied around a final mouthful of sweet apple.

He grabbed my arm, and I got the sense that he was trying to squeeze it. 'Listen to me. I don't care, but Jean does. Bow to him or it could go badly for you.'

'I won't bare my neck to any man.'

'He's not any man. He is—'

Before he could finish, the other door opened and another brightly clad man stepped inside. 'Prince Jean invites you to join his war council.'

'War council?' muttered Lucien, straightening his tunic.

'I thought we were seeing him alone,' said Tatyana.

'Something must have happened,' replied Lucien.

'Stay at the back with me,' she said, touching my wrist.

I nodded my agreement as I had seen them do before, and they seemed satisfied. Once he and everyone else had gone through the door, I picked up another apple and followed them into a wide hallway, offering the page at the doors my friendliest smile. The passage on the other side was more of what I had expected from something called a palace. There were large windows filled with glass of fantastic clarity and a multitude of colours, and a number of statues of men and animals, both large and small. Some were rendered with such skill that I was half tempted to test them for traces of magic. Boldly coloured tapestries and pictures hung from the walls, each an expression of the better facets of humanity. I found it very soothing and would happily have spent the day admiring these but Tatyana returned and bade me hurry up, which I reluctantly did.

The chamber where Prince Jean waited made up for it though. It was a circular construction, and the top of the dome was again inset with great panels of that glass that bathed the room below in a rainbow of light. The centre of the room was dominated by a large circular table, which was currently surrounded by a score or more males of various ages. Beyond them was another, larger set of doors, and next to these stood four paladins. The beast saw them too, and I felt it stir within me, but lazily, as if it sensed that I now shared its view on them and no longer felt as threatened.

No one paid any attention when we entered, so I took the opportunity to admire a small statue of a rearing stallion before making my way over to see what they were all talking over. It took me some time to understand what I was seeing, but I eventually recognised it as a map. I didn't say anything and listened closely, and was eventually rewarded by someone pointing out the symbol that represented Falkenburg. Once I knew where we were and where north was, it became far easier to follow what it represented. There were even little blue figures of men and horses, which apparently stood for Jean's forces, and red ones for the Penullin armies, and even to me it was obvious that there was a rather alarming imbalance in favour of the reds across the map.

'If the reds are the Penullin armies, what are the black ones?' I whispered to Tatyana.

'Those mark the locations where the Worm Lord's wizards have been seen.'

Admittedly it was only a human war, but I liked the idea of the map and the cleverness of the tokens. It was, I thought, a bit like a game I had once played. I didn't remember much about it other than that you had to go around your opponent's tokens in a certain way to capture them. Quietly pleased that I'd teased a memory from my miserly mind, I nibbled my apple and tried to make sense of what was being said.

'Your Highness, we cannot simply abandon them.' The speaker was just about average in every manner, aside from the bright red that was blooming across his cheeks. He jabbed a white stick at a small clump of blue 'soldiers' on the table. 'We can ill afford to lose that much equipment, let alone weather the impact on morale.'

A rush of voices rose as he finished speaking, some of them in support while others used the moment to point their own sticks at various other tokens. Amid this hubbub a single man stood absolutely still, drawing my attention. He was short, and while his clothes looked finer than any others, there was no hiding how fat he was. He stood with his arms folded across his rounded belly, staring at the table for a while, then raised a hand, at which the room fell silent. I guessed that this was the highness the man had been addressing. Prince Jean, no doubt.

'Do you think I don't know that?'

His voice was surprisingly bold and strong, and certainly made up for what he lacked in stature. He moved closer to the small cluster of blue and the half-circle of black and red that surrounded it. 'We cannot use the southern pass, so how do you propose we break the encirclement? Bellamy's army is in pieces and is barely holding Aswald, and the Red Guard is fighting on two fronts.'

The original speaker tapped at a block of blue somewhere between the two blue icons that the man I assumed to be Prince Jean had indicated.

'Baron Guderian's heavy horse can break them. All they need is an opportunity. I know Fischer, Your Highness. He'll get his men out if he has half a chance.'

A man on the far edge of the table gave a loud snort. 'In case you've forgotten, Guderian's a Neustrian, through and through. Fischer's mother was an Alamannian. You'd have better luck convincing a fish to fly than for those two to rescue each other.'

'Perhaps if this was just another border skirmish, but there's more at stake here than a few sheep and some peasant women.'

'You don't spend a lot of time with Neustrians, do you, Sardis?'

Before the first man could reply, Prince Jean's stick slapped the map, the sudden crack of it making several men jump.

'Do you even know how to read a map?' he asked, pointing the stick at the man called Sardis, then at a series of squiggles. 'What are those? Answer me, damn you.'

'Low hills, Your Highness.' *Tap*. 'High hills, Your Highness.' *Tap*. 'Grasslands, Your Highness.'

'So far so good. Now what are these?' He pointed at little arrow-shaped marks around the blue icon in question.

'Trees, Your Highness.'

'Trees indeed. And what does so many little trees together suggest?' The man who had spoken had grown ever more flushed as Prince Jean spoke, and the men around him had slowly edged away. He mumbled something in reply.

'Louder, my Lord.'

'A forest, Your Highness.'

'A forest. Well done. And do you want to venture a guess as to why I chose not to send my heavy horse into the bloody Gudsberg forest?'

'No, I mean, yes, I understand, Your Highness. My apologies.'

Jean tapped his stick against the icon a few times before replying. 'Do not misunderstand me, gentlemen. If we had the men available, I would have tried it.'

'Has there been any word on their situation?' asked a man with a profusion of hair on his upper lip.

Jean did not reply but gestured to a grey-bearded figure in a blue robe, who cleared his throat noisily.

'We scryed Lord Fischer's camp shortly before dawn. His forces appeared to be at a third of their original strength, and of that, perhaps half were wounded.'

A wizard. A surge of excitement fizzed through me. He was exactly what I had hoped to find; if anyone could tell me about myself, it would be him. His voice was resonant and commanding, as the voice of a wizard who had spent long years practising his art should be.

'Is Fischer alive?' asked another man.

'We don't know. The enemy countered our scrying before we could find or contact him. We did, however, manage to see several companies of the enemy preparing for battle, and in my opinion if Fischer was alive then, he most likely isn't any more.'

'Assuming that your so-called scrying was accurate, Fronsac.' This from a man standing somewhere on the other side of the pillar I was leaning against. His voice sounded pinched and nasal in the wake of the wizard's commanding tone. 'Forgive me for repeating myself, Highness, but your faith should be placed in the Church, not an order whose members flocked to our enemy's banner like whores to a merchant's bed.'

'Four of my apprentices have already given their lives in service to the Crown, Cardinal.' He spat the last word out as only a wizard could. 'Including my own son.'

'All that proves is that your order is as incompetent as it is prone to betrayal.'

'Enough!' Prince Jean's command snapped out crisply, silencing both the Cardinal and the wizard along with everyone else in the room. I had felt the wizard's connection to the Songlines swelling as his anger called his power to him, but he bit down on whatever it was that he was about to say or do and the surge drained away. He didn't take his eyes off the Cardinal though.

Prince Jean spoke first. 'Cardinal, you are out of order and I will not tolerate any more of this bickering.'

'As you command, Your Highness,' the Cardinal said with a small bow.

The wizard spun on his heel and marched out of the room, and I was torn between following him and a curiosity about what would happen next. Had the wizard not been so angry I might have gone after him instead, but I chose to stay. The prince gestured to a younger man, who handed him a cup of something. While he drank, another began moving some of the pieces on the table. The gathering watched in silence until he reached out and, with a look to Jean, removed a blue square and replaced it with a red one. This drew a round of loud gasps from the room, as well as a chorus of groans.

'Your Highness, it cannot be true!'

'Surely there is some mistake!'

The city we were in was marked by a similar blue square, so it stood to reason that it meant that a town or city had fallen to the reds. It was now the tip of a narrow wedge of red that split the remaining blues in two.

'There is no mistake. He would have told you himself,' said Prince Jean, 'but the magus Fronsac and his coven saw Garreton fall yesterday.'

'Do we know who took it?' The speaker wasn't dressed in finery like the others, and the width of his arms and neck marked him as a warrior.

'What does that matter?' asked the man next to him.

'Garreton has walls as high as Falkenburg and a larger garrison, yet it fell within a week. Don't you think it is worth knowing who managed that, and how?'

'Baron Karsten is correct once more,' said Prince Jean before the other man could voice a reply. 'The city fell to Lord Novstan's fourth army.'

'The same as who sacked Aknak,' said Baron Karsten. 'Do the wizards still ride with them?'

'They do.'

I felt Tatyana stiffen as he said it, and a soft undercurrent of fear tinged her scent a moment later. I wanted to ask her about it, but Prince Jean was speaking again.

'. . . I have called this council.' He finished his drink and handed the cup away. 'Novstan's fourth has been in the forefront of the push into our . . .' He stopped talking, and it was only when Tatyana tugged on my sleeve that I looked up to see him and everyone in the room looking at me.

'And who are you?' Prince Jean asked.

I remembered Lucien's insistence that I show some sort of deference to him, but I found it difficult to do. There was nothing about him that immediately commanded respect, at least not to me. All I could bring myself to do was stop leaning against the pillar and stand up straight before I answered.

'I am Stratus.' I heard a hiss of indrawn breath from Tatyana, so added a 'Your Highness'.

Another man, dressed in red and black robes and as tall as the prince but older and thinner, stepped around the pillar. He stopped in his tracks as he saw me, his mouth opening but no words coming from it.

'Stratus is here at my invitation, Jean,' said Lucien, brushing past a few of the onlookers. 'I apologise for not introducing him earlier but I hadn't expected a full council.'

'And for not asking my permission to drag a complete stranger into a private council too, surely?'

Lucien inclined his head towards Jean. 'Yes, that too. Of course.'

The old man in red and black was still staring at me, and when I lifted my gaze to meet his, he flinched away. Intrigued, I sniffed the air and found his scent. It was everything I expected from an older male, but it was also redolent with fear and something even more sour, but the air was too crowded to follow it.

'Cardinal?' said Prince Jean. 'Do you know this man?'

'No,' the Cardinal said, his voice low, as if he were struggling for breath. 'Forgive me, Highness, I had not realised the hour. I am due to deliver a benediction to the new arrivals.' He abruptly turned and hurried from the room as soon as Jean nodded, casting one last look at me over his shoulder.

The Cardinal. I didn't know much about men and their gods, but I recognised the title. He was a senior priest, and precisely the sort of man who I would expect to recognise a demon when he saw one.

Chapter 13

I don't remember much of what was said after the Cardinal's departure, but Prince Jean did not seem pleased with how things were going. I was still eyeing the map table when Tatyana grabbed me and told me to leave. I resisted at first, but she was persistent and I eventually let her lead me from the room. She marched us out, back along the passage with the nice art, and I took a moment to pull myself from her grip.

'What are you doing?'

'I want to look at the sculptures.' I pointed to a naked female clinging to the back of a running wolf that had been done in a red stone. 'Especially that one.'

She glanced at the display, then shrugged her shoulders. 'What for?'

'Because it's exquisite,' I replied. And it was true. Every line of it was in perfect proportion, even the undulations in the wolf's fur. 'Is it not?'

'Statues aren't my thing,' she said, dropping gracelessly onto a small bench nearby.

'Then you're poorer for it.' I didn't hear what she said next, and kneeled down to study it until I had it committed to memory. 'Where are we rushing to?' I asked when I stood up again.

'We're meeting Lucien in his chambers. He wants us to get our story straight before Jean gets there.'

'What story?'

'God's teeth, Stratus, are you being purposefully thick?'

'No?'

She stared at me, then just shook her head and walked away. 'Come on,' she said.

I followed, and as I walked along my thoughts turned to the Cardinal and how he'd reacted to me. No one else I had met in this body had responded like that. If he had recognised me as a demon or some other strange conjuring, what would he do? Would he not have called upon the paladins there to attack me?

'What do you know about that Cardinal?' I asked.

'Polsson?' Another shrug. 'Not much, aside from him being as narrow-minded and joyless as most senior Churchmen. He's quite a firebrand, which might be why the Orders like him so much. Why do you ask?'

'He seemed to recognise me.'

'Hmm. You're right, he looked like he'd seen a ghost.'

'Or maybe he can see what I really am.'

'You're not back on that demon nonsense, are you? Maybe he just doesn't like wizards or black men.'

'That makes no sense. Firstly, I'm not a wizard and secondly, if he doesn't recognise me, why wouldn't he like me?'

'Forget it. Go ask him if you really want to know.'

'I think that I will.'

'No! Don't be a fool,' she snapped, rounding on me.

I stared at her in confusion. 'But you just said that I should.'

'I know that, but I wasn't expecting you to agree. Gods.' She stepped into a doorway and beckoned me closer. 'Look,' she said quietly, 'I don't know much about Polsson himself, but I know his type. I spent most of my childhood listening to my father rant about them. If you get in his way, he'll come for you. You don't want to get dragged into any sort of fight with the Church, trust me on this. The best you can hope for is that he forgets about you.'

'He didn't look particularly dangerous.'

'Not by himself, no. But he has the loyalty of the Orders and the Church's money behind him, and that makes him someone you don't want to tangle with.' She looked around, then started walking again.

'What are the Orders?'

'The paladins. There are three kinds, but they're all the same kind of fanatic when you strip away the ceremony and armour.'

'I don't like them.'

'Only people who don't know them like them.'

I still didn't understand why I couldn't ask the Cardinal about myself. But there was fear in her scent when she spoke of him, and if one as capable with a knife and who was friend to a prince was afraid, then it would be foolish for me to ignore her advice. I would need to formulate a plan to speak with the Cardinal, to somehow convince him that I was no threat that had to be put to the sword.

'What about the wizard?' I asked just as she knocked on a door. 'Could I speak to him?'

She opened the door and stepped inside instead of answering me. I followed her and found myself in a rectangular room with several tables laden with possibly more trinkets, books and clothes than I had seen in the marketplace.

'What is this place?' I asked, fighting an immediate temptation to start rummaging through them.

'This is one of my private rooms,' said Lucien from across the room as he struggled to open a glass bottle. 'I collect things.' The bottle opened with a pop and he set to filling some cups with a strongly scented wine.

'Posh junk,' muttered Tatyana, but Lucien didn't seem to hear her.

'Me too. Or, at least I used to,' I said, frowning as a ghostly memory teased the fringes of my mind.

'What sort of things?' asked Lucien, offering me a cup, which I took. It was wine, but it smelled quite spicy. I inhaled the aroma and closed my eyes as my superior sense of smell explored it. I recognised some of the components, and with the smell filling my senses I could almost remember where I had last tasted them. Somewhere hot and arid, with a sun that had baked me with a wonderful heat.

'Statues,' said Tatyana, as if from a distance. 'That's why we took so long. He stopped to stare at some of them in the east gallery.'

'Not just statues. Sculpture. And unusual rocks,' I said, my eyes still closed. She gave a short laugh, but I chose to ignore her. The wine had yielded the last of its secrets and I took a tentative sip. It was nicer than I had expected, so I finished it.

'Take it easy with that,' said Lucien. 'We need to be ready for Jean.'

'We should get our story straight,' I offered.

'Yes, exactly,' said Lucien. He seemed pleased at my insight. 'Look, Stratus, I'm going to be honest. Last night was very stressful, and the ale didn't make it any easier. The fact is that I,' he paused and nodded towards Tatyana, 'that is, we, don't know anything about you.'

'I have told Tatyana much about me this morning,' I said.

'Oh?'

'He did, and we need to talk about it,' said Tatyana.

'It was very helpful. I learned some things too,' I said. 'Did you know that she is a Henkman?'

'Yes, I knew that. It's one of the reasons that I accepted her service. But this isn't about her, it's about me being realistic. You saved our lives and I fear that it's a debt that may not prove so easy to repay in the current circumstances.'

'Lucien, we need to talk,' said Tatyana. 'Before you say anything else.'

I understood what she intended. 'Should I tell him?' I offered.

'No, I think it best if I do,' she said. 'Can you wait outside?'

'Why?'

'Just do it!' Her tone made Lucien pause, his cup halfway to his lips.

'I'll wait outside, then,' I said, moving to stand outside the door, which one of them promptly locked. Tatyana, from the sound of the footfalls. I let out a slow breath and teased a wisp of my sorcery out and into the door. It wasn't warded, so the sorcery passed through it as easily as if it wasn't there. In my mind I saw it spread, growing outwards like a spider's web, every noise in the room making the strands of it vibrate, carrying them directly into my waiting head.

'He's mad, Lucien. I don't know how or why, but he's definitely unhinged. He thinks he's a demon for gods' sakes. I barely stopped him from going off to confess all of it to Polsson.'

Lucien laughed. 'A demon?'

'Yes, a bloody demon.'

'As in the armies of Hel kind? Why would he even think that?'

'Well, let's see. He can do magic, his nails and skin are as black as charcoal and—'

'You said he looked like those Southerners you served with.'

'At a glance maybe, but he's nothing like them. They're brown, a deep brown, but he's more grey. Or blue, at night. And who has black nails? Oh, and you'll love this. Apparently he got into a fight with some soldiers on his way to the city and accidentally ate one of them.'

'What? Are you serious? God, you ate. But that's insane. How in god's name do you accidentally eat someone?'

'Well, from what I could gather it's not the first time either. Look, I think he might have gotten hit on the head or something. You know what happened at Aknak, so maybe he came across something similar and it fuddled his brain; I know it made more than a few of my men get the jitters and they were hard, you know? But even so, I don't think you can let him speak to Polsson. Or Jean.'

'God's teeth, no. If so much as a rumour of that got out the last three months would have been for nothing. What do I do? Jean's probably on his way here already.'

Out in the passage, I grimaced. She'd clearly not been paying attention to what I'd told her, but even so, hearing it summarised like that did make it sound quite unflattering. On one hand, did what they thought of me really matter? I had been honest with them, so my conscience was clear on that. There was of course the matter of them somehow being part of whatever had happened to me, but then what did I have to support that, besides the dumb reactions of the presence that haunted my mind? They didn't know me at all, and their memories were intact, so where did that leave me? Short of pinning them down and progressively stripping their memories out of their mind, I had my doubts that anything useful would materialise from being in their company.

Perhaps it was time for me to look elsewhere. There was still the sixth assassin to find, as well as that wizard who I could approach. I drew my sorcery back, reshaped it and sent it into the lock. By the time I had closed the door behind me again I had reabsorbed the power. They watched me in silence as I walked in, and if they were impressed by my skill they gave no sign of it. I didn't miss how Tatyana's hand strayed towards her sword though, which I found hurtful.

'Stratus, please, we're not finished. Could—' Tatyana said, but I ignored her.

'I heard what you were saying. You still think that I am mad. And perhaps I am, but it is not a madness that you would know.' Lucien made to rise but I held up my hand and he stopped. 'You wanted to know me, and I have told you what little I know. I am seeking neither charity nor sympathy, only answers.'

'We don't think you're mad, just maybe confused,' said Lucien. 'I have read many things, including histories that some would consider forbidden, and I can tell you that I have yet to read of a demon who would save someone's life or who likes eggs for breakfast and fine sculpture.'

'The sculptures weren't for me, they . . .' The words spilled from my lips, seemingly without telling my brain. I had stopped them before the final three could come out, but I said these now, in a quieter voice. 'They were for her.'

The beast within reacted strangely to that, shying away as if stung rather than meeting it with its usual growl or sneering laugh.

Her.

My thoughts were crashing together, and whatever insightful reply I had intended for Lucien's insipid remark was lost in the turmoil. This was important; *she* was important. *Talk to me, tell me something,* I silently implored the beast, but it remained silent. It didn't feel so menacing now, knowing that there was a she to it. To him.

'Do demons mate?' I asked, interrupting whatever it was that Lucien had been saying. I hadn't seen him stand up.

'Not now, Stratus. Please. We can talk about it over wine afterwards.'

I felt strangely remote as I watched him open the door and invite his fat brother and two other men inside. I helped myself to another brimming cupful of that spiced wine as the men began talking at each other, wondering if I had been alone to that hot, arid place where I had smelled the spice. Did I have a mate, a wife, and where was she now? It seemed that for every clue I uncovered I also found a dozen new questions.

I felt a hand on my arm and turned. Tatyana was there, gesturing towards the men. I was tempted to walk out of there right then, to leave all of this pretence behind and find my own path, but for all of their faults they had been kind to me and there was still the chance that they could help answer some of my questions.

'My brother tells me that you saved his life,' Jean said. 'From his telling you're quite the hero.' He looked me up and down, and if he felt inferior he didn't let it show.

I inclined my head, both as a way of placating Lucien's concerns about showing respect and also to give me a chance to take a good noseful of his scent. I didn't have much chance to sift through it, but there was enough to reinforce my initial opinion of him. He had a rich diet, though one with far less wine and beer than Lucien's, but there was something lacking in it. There was a weakness in him, but it would take more than a casual sniff to know it.

'I am no such thing,' I said.

'Tell me what happened then, in your own words.' His tone was quiet, but there was something in it, some echo of the command for silence he had given in the war council. It was intriguing.

125

'I had a suspicion that something was afoot, but the tainted men struck before I could think any more on it. We killed them.'

'Well, you're certainly less poetic than Lucien.' He sipped from the cup of wine that Lucien passed to him, smacking his lips noisily. 'Very nice, brother,' he said. His gaze drifted back to me. 'My brother collects wine, along with everything else.' He took another small sip but didn't look away. 'Why do you call them tainted men?'

'Their scent. It carries a stench that is like no other, one that hangs on the air like an oiled mist.' I struggled for the words to describe it. 'You need only scent the smallest trace to know that whatever created it is nothing wholesome.'

Jean gave a brief smile. 'It seems strange to condemn men to death for their odour. By that token we'd have no one left in the fields.'

The others laughed at this, and it sat badly with me that they dismissed my words so easily. 'Perhaps I do not have the words for it,' I admitted, 'but I know that it is the truth of it. It is not something that a natural life could produce.'

'And you know this because of your wizardry?' asked Jean.

'It's sorcery, not wizardry, but yes.'

'Pretend that none of us here know the difference. It shouldn't be difficult.'

I sipped at my own cup of wine as I considered how to explain it in such a way that they could understand it this time, and it was a discarded harp lying among Lucien's treasures that provided the answer. I pointed to it.

'If magic was a harp, a wizard would learn to play it from a teacher. He would learn a few songs. A sorcerer, by contrast, could just pick it up and compose his own song.' I was quite pleased with that.

'So you're better than a wizard.'

'Undoubtedly.'

Jean gave a laugh at that and turned to one of the men who had entered the room with him. 'And what do you say, young Damiano?'

'I'd say he's read too many stories,' Damiano replied.

I coaxed some of my power to wakefulness and looked more closely at him. The bracelets on his wrists were glowing softly, and I could see faint lines running across what skin of his I could see. A wizard, then, and not a particularly strong one from the look of it either. Wizards channel their power through their bodies, and the repeated drawing of their powers creates a sort of scar in their body's pathways over time. His scars were faint, and mostly confined to his arms, which to me suggested that he drew most of his power from the enchanted bracelets that he wore. That smacked of laziness.

'I do not read,' I said. 'But nor do I lie.'

I was still watching him, but even without my sorcery aiding my sight it would have been obvious that he was reaching for the power in his bracelets. With him helpfully staring into my eyes in what I expect he thought was a challenging manner, I used the opportunity to prepare and implant a simple suggestion into his mind that the bracelet had exploded and severed his wrist. It was hard work to enchant an item, and I couldn't imagine that a skilled craftsman would have bothered with that sort of cheap trinket. Judging by the way that his mind accepted my suggestion he already harboured his own doubts about it. I severed the connection and even had enough time to glance across at Jean before the young wizard let out a screech and fell to the ground, clutching one perfectly healthy hand with the other.

Jean's gaze now met mine as the man whipped about, and I wasn't about to pass up the opportunity that this presented. I slid into his mind, but had barely scratched the surface of his thoughts before I sensed a powerful ward flaring into life to shut me out. I quickly retreated, taking little from him except a sense of fatigue and general resentment. I blinked the attempted intrusion away, but Jean gave no sign that he had even noticed.

'What is this? What have you done to him?' he said, also blinking as he turned to watch Damiano, who was staring at his hand in confusion as the suggestion melted away. They were all staring at me now, and it would be a lie if I said that the tinge of fear in the air wasn't pleasing to me.

'Enough to prove my words,' I said, hoping they wouldn't attempt a further test. The third man helped the wizard into a chair as Jean sipped his wine and continued to watch me.

'Intriguing,' he said, setting the cup down. 'I had it in mind to have you thrown into a cell for a few days to see what you're made of, but it seems that my brother's judgement may actually be improving.'

'Well, it's funny you should say that, because we were—'

'Let me finish, Lucien.' He turned to me. 'You have seen what we face, Meneer Stratus. I never thought the time would come when my brother would be made a war leader, and you must understand that I say that with love. He was made for summer and ballrooms, not the battlefield. But the times are what they are, and this war is like no other that I have studied.' He gestured to where Damiano sat staring at his hand. 'Because of them. Wizards. Half the army hates them, and the rest don't trust them, but they all clamour for more. And now my brother rides to lead men to war and I have few to spare even him.'

He paused to sip his wine once more, and I actually found myself straining to hear what he said next. He wasn't much of anything, but with a voice like his he might have done well if he'd had the inclination to be a wizard.

'I want you to take the vow and ride with him.'

'Your Highness!' Damiano rose from the chair, favouring his one arm. 'My master—'

'Your master will still need to approve this, yes, I understand that. But my waters tell me this is the right decision. What say you, Meneer Stratus?'

I looked to Lucien and Tatyana, and even to me it was apparent that Jean's decision was a surprise to them. It seemed that Fate was determined that our paths intertwined.

'I'm no wizard, but I say yes.'

Chapter 14

Prince Jean and his pet wizards had bustled off not long after Damiano agreed to arrange a meeting between myself and Magus Fronsac, who was apparently still too angry with the Cardinal to be approached directly.

'Did you do that?' asked Lucien soon after they had left.

'Do what?'

'Make him invite you along as my . . . our personal wizard.'

'I'm not a wizard. And no, I did not. In truth, I doubt I could have even if I had wanted to with all the wards placed on him.'

'So you tried?' Lucien said, his voice rising.

'Not really. I was simply curious.'

'What does "not really" mean?'

So many questions. 'It means that I did try to look into his mind, but only out of curiosity, not out of some secret purpose. I will say that I am pleased with his decision though.'

'Why?' asked Tatyana.

'Because I am tired of having more questions than answers, and I believe that I am more likely to find them inside these city walls. I will speak to this Fronsac tonight, and then we shall see.' And in the morning I would begin scouring the streets for the sixth assassin, but I didn't tell them this. I was growing tired of their endless questions and talking.

'Stratus, about the wizard. You cannot tell him that you think you're a demon. It would be suicide.'

'If he has any great talent I won't need to.'

'What will you do then?' asked Lucien, setting his cup down.

I sighed. 'That depends on what he does. If he attacks me, I will defend myself.'

'You can't,' said Lucien. 'We need him. It's hard to explain, but you simply must trust me on this.'

'No.'

'No?'

'No. I will not sit by and be attacked simply because you said so.' A hazy memory flickered across my mind's eye of a sandy arena, heavy with the smell of blood and magic. *My blood, but not my magic.* It drifted apart before I could grasp at it, but it was enough to set the beast to growling.

'Stratus, as a prince and a friend, I ask you to trust me. Submit to Fronsac and do not harm him.'

'I care nothing for your titles, nor for a friendship that would bid me walk to my doom like a sheep.' The rousing of the beast had shortened my temper as always, and perhaps I said it in a sharper tone than I would have for Lucien rose in a rush.

'You would do well to obey me.'

'Spare me your threats, little prince.'

For a moment I thought he would strike me, but instead he pressed his lips into a thin line before walking from the room with no little speed and slamming the door heavily behind him.

'That was poorly said.' Tatyana was staring at me, her arms folded across her chest and her heart thudding loudly. 'You should show him some respect.'

'You agree with him? That I should show this wizard my belly and let him do what he wills?'

'It's more complicated than that.'

'No, it isn't. You warn me that honesty would be suicide, then tell me to let him kill me? It is foolish.'

'Not that kind of suicide, you stupid oaf.' She ran her hands through her hair, and I could not help but wonder what that felt like. 'It's this place,' she said after a few moments, gesturing at the walls. 'You spend enough time here and you forget that not everyone thinks in the same way.'

'I do not understand.'

'Of course you don't. Fronsàc must not think that we, that is Lucien, knowingly let someone, particularly a wizard who may be a demon, into Jean's presence. Even if it wasn't true, if word of that got out it would weaken his reputation and, with it, the alliances that have been built around the royal family's personal involvement. I know it's complicated, but you have to trust me here.'

I knew little about the intricacies of human politics and quite honestly, I had no desire to improve my knowledge. However, the wizard and princes were clearly immersed in it, and if I was to get the answers I needed from Fronsac, I would need to take some care. I tried to mask my reluctance as I asked her to explain it again. After three or four more rounds of explanation I had a workable grasp on some of the treaties and promises that kept the city and soldiers supplied and the wizards supporting the war, a fair accomplishment given Tatyana's remarkable lack of patience.

Soon after, one of the servants brought a message for Tatyana, which made her curse and hurry from the room without a farewell of any sort. From the way that some of the tension left my shoulders once I was alone, I think I have always enjoyed the quiet. My mood improved even more after I drained the remnants of the spiced wine and eased myself into Lucien's enormous chair. It felt like the softest mound of grass, even if it didn't smell as nice.

For a while I didn't think about anything at all, and at some point I drifted into a light sleep. I was woken by another servant who was carrying the cups and now empty bottle from the room. I struggled from the depths of the chair as they apologised and left the room, but in truth my mind was still too fuzzy to notice, with the remnants of the images and half-formed dreams that it had conjured while I rested. Of these, the only ones that I remembered were a long convoy of wagons on a dusty road, and a stone pillar with spirals carved upon it, neither of which seemed remotely familiar to my waking mind.

However, the sleep did one thing for me, and that was to jar the memory of the darkened room that I had glimpsed in the assassin's memories just before his brain melted. Aside from Lucien and Tatyana, the assassins were the only other piece of the puzzle that I had, and as I had no idea when Lucien would be leaving, and me with him, I could see little point in wasting more time.

I pulled myself out of the seductive comfort of the chair and strode out of the door, ignoring the stares of the guards and servants. I had a purpose now and I would not be turned from it. It was a conviction that soothed me as much as it set a fire within my breast, but after a dozen hallways that were mirror images of each other and several flights of stairs, my strides had shrunk to the pace of a man. I had passed perhaps a hundred doors, but all of these led to more rooms and passageways, and the sense of purpose that had gripped me was being overtaken by the idea of smashing through the wall and making my way over the roof. I had resolved to do just that when a young man stepped out of a door ahead of me carrying a bundle of swords.

'Is everything all right, sir?' he asked.

'Where is the closest way out?'

'Through the exercise yards by the barracks, if you don't mind coming out on Coffin Lane.'

'I don't care.'

'Follow me.'

I did just that, and after a few more doors I finally stepped out into the sunlight. I felt my backbone straighten now that I had no roof above me and I took a few deep breaths. The air was rich with the scent of men, iron and mud, but it was still more welcome than the stagnant air within the palace. I took another breath and tasted a familiar scent on it; Tatyana was nearby. My young guide was saying something and pointing to a door in a high wall, so I guessed that was the way out. I simply nodded at him and followed Tatyana's scent to another, smaller yard. There were at least two-score men here, most of them young, all standing in a rough square around Tatyana as she and a younger, burlier man circled each other, their swords bared. A few of the bystanders were cheering, and I was on the verge of sending a ball of fire flying at her opponent when an older male began walking around the edge of the square. The cheers died as he began speaking so I stayed my hand and listened.

'Now, that sort of battle makes men react like animals. They look for weaknesses, like the lion seeks the old or the injured. You'll do it too. When it happens, it feels natural and right. But like the strength that comes from anger, it's a lie. You cannot trust your eyes. Who would you fight? Me, or her?' He pointed at Tatyana, and a murmur rippled through the young men.

'Her, but only if we was wrestling!' called a voice, prompting a brief round of laughter. In the square, the man stepped forward and whipped his sword back and forth, making it whistle in a manner I thought quite impressive.

Tatyana changed the grip on her sword so that the blade now pointed straight up. The man noticed too, and his sword suddenly shot forward again, almost too fast for me to track. There was a crash of metal on metal, and suddenly Tatyana was on his opposite side, out of reach, while her blade now rested on his shoulder. It would have been a killing blow. The man swung again, grunting with the effort, but it met nothing but air while her sword now fell onto his opposite shoulder. He launched a series of attacks then, each more vicious than those before, but on his third step forward she kicked his leg so that he spun away and smacked the flat of her sword against the side of his head, felling him. The men, who had cheered the man's every attack, fell silent as Tatyana returned her sword to her shoulder.

'Rash decisions will get you killed as quickly as overconfidence,' the older man said, stepping forward once more. 'Do not judge your opponent by what they seem to be. Expect everyone you face to be better than you. Faster. Every fight should be fought as if it were your last. Now, who's next? Carter, how about you?'

I made my way back to the gate. I had wondered why a prince merited only a single guard, but I understood it a bit better now. I made a mental note to kill her from a distance or while she slept, if matters ever came to that.

The sun already hung high in the sky when I eventually put the palace grounds behind me, its muted light turning the clouds above into silver. I made my way along the overcrowded lane beyond, following the boundary wall of the palace until I found the entrance we had originally used. From there I could begin to retrace the path we'd taken, although this proved harder than I thought.

Streets that had been empty were now clogged with crowds of noisy humans kicking up clouds of dust, and the shapes of buildings that I had glimpsed in the night were now distorted by the sunlight, however soft it was. Perhaps it was because I was feeling annoyed, but the men on the streets seemed louder, and more agitated than I remembered. It was only after an encounter with a particularly loud vendor that almost ended in violence that I became aware of the flat, sour tinge of fear that mingled with the omnipresent odour of their spoor. Once I noticed though, I could not clear it from my nose, not until I found the scene of the ambush. The stench of our attackers still lingered where their blood had stained the cobbles, potent enough for me to pick it out despite the plethora of smells competing with it.

I squatted down where the man's brain had leaked out. It wasn't hard to find as despite how thronged the streets were, most passers-by swerved around the spot. I doubted they were even aware that they were doing it. If I'd had the power to spare, I would have been interested to watch them through my sorcery, to see if I could find the moment when whatever tiny speck of the Songlines that lived within them flared in warning, steering them past a threat that only it could sense. I almost pitied whoever had been tasked with moving their bodies. The additional benefit of this behaviour was that no one wanted to linger near me or ask me what I was doing, which suited me just fine.

I used a twig to brush the dust from between the stones until I found some of the still moist remains of his brain matter. Not even the flies were interested in it. I dipped the end of the twig into some of it and lifted it, curious to see if it reacted to sunlight like the flesh of the blood-drinkers of old, but it just hung there, swaying like a pendulum while an idea formed in my mind. The time and heat that had passed since it was spilled hadn't done it any favours, and even though I knew it wouldn't do me any permanent harm, the thought of what I was about to do made my stomach lurch and clench as if it were pleading for mercy.

I dipped my finger into the goo, and then lifted it into my mouth. I would rather eat the southern ends of a thousand northbound vultures before I ever subject myself to anything remotely as unpleasant as that again. If the smell had been terrible, the taste of it multiplied that unpleasantness tenfold. It didn't so much fill my senses as erupt through them, scouring all else away. I could no longer recall the smell of grass, nor even the taste of the wine I'd enjoyed, only the reek of corruption and the spoiling dead boiled down to its purest essence. I gagged, and staggered about like a moon-touched madman as it burned through me, but eventually it passed, leaving me sagged against the bulwark of a nearby wall. The taste and smell of it was imprinted on me now, and it would be a very long time before it faded. It was, however, a price I was willing to pay if it brought an end to the questions rattling around in my mind.

There was one other facet of it that I had not expected, which was that in eating the foul soup it had somehow given up a ghost of a memory that it had once carried. It wasn't much, a shadow of a perching gargoyle glimpsed between one blink of an eye to the next, but it was enough to give me a direction, and that alone was almost worth the price. I circled out from where the man had died until I found the place where he must have stood to have seen the little gargoyle to remember it at the right angle.

It was right next to a rough-finished wall, and as I pressed my face against it, my newly attuned senses found the faint trace of their scent. They had all stood here, one behind the other, all pressed up against the wall.

I moved along the wall until the scent trace faded, then slowly moved further down the road. They had moved in the darkness, but whatever gifts their strange magics had granted them, the ability to see at night wasn't among them. Here they had felt their way past fixed tables, there the post of a shelter over a shop entrance. Small, easily forgotten traces. When the trail threatened to die away completely, I teased out a wisp of my sorcery and bound it to my sense of smell, amplifying it. It left me with watering eyes and the taste of blood in my mouth, but also a new trace to follow.

Night had won dominion over the sky by the time I found their lair. It was near the edge of the upper city where the houses were still crammed together, but only a few had shopfronts on the street level. Some even had small, neat gardens, but not the house that their trail led me to. It was a dark shape in a row of brighter homes, a missing tooth in a healthy jaw. There were boards across the windows and the main door, and whatever had once grown in the garden out front had long since withered and blown away, leaving stone trenches that looked like emptied graves.

The shadows hid me as I pressed my hand to the door and carefully probed it for wards, but there were none that I could sense. I braced my legs and hammered my fist into the wood, and after three blows the length that held the hinges splintered. It creaked and squealed as I forced it open, but the darkness beyond seemed to soak the sound in. I readied one of my knives and stepped inside, listening for anything more than the rats in the walls. My senses of smell and taste were in tatters from the foulness of the brain and would be of little use for some time, so I had to rely on sight and hearing.

I took a moment to wake my night vision, and soon enough the red tint bled into my sight, giving depth and shape to the darkness before me. The ground level was a large, single room with a few broken chairs, an overturned table and a pair of doors on either side of the steep stair-case that rose to the upper levels. I didn't like the idea of anything creeping up behind me, so I made my way through each of the doors near the bottom of the staircase, my knife ready. The first room was empty save for piles of discarded clothing, much of which was dotted with mould. Something moved in one of the larger piles and I stepped and kicked it apart, sending a dazed and disgruntled rat scurrying for one of the holes in the wall.

The second door opened to reveal a room that had been stripped of everything save a low table upon which lay the body of a woman. Or most of it anyway. Between her killers and the rats there wasn't enough left for anyone to say who she once was, and I found myself staring at the corpse for longer than I had intended. She was just another dead human, but there was something about the way she had died here, alone and terrified, that made me pause. Yet there was nothing anyone could do for her now, so I left her to the dark and turned back towards the stairs, shaking my shoulders vigorously to try to dispel the strange melan-choly that had gripped me. Fortunately the beast was waiting at the edge of my mind, ready as ever to transmute any emotion into anger, and for once I welcomed its efforts.

The wood groaned and clicked loudly as the stairs took my weight, but they held. Ahead of me was a small hallway with four doors and another, smaller set of stairs that looked to have been made by a blind man and would clearly never be able to hold me. I moved to the first door and paused next to it. My sense of smell was still little short of useless, so my sorcery would serve me instead. I closed my eyes and concentrated on my hearing as I spun out the same sort of web I had used to listen to Tatyana and Lucien.

I let it drift through the rooms, but all I could hear were the normal sounds of vermin and dripping water. I was on the verge of collapsing it when it caught the soft scrape of what could only be human feet from above me. I focused, and as the footsteps stopped I could hear a heart beating even faster than I would expect from one being hunted by me. I knew where he was now, and quickly drew the sorcerous construct back to me, greedily reabsorbing the unused energy. There was no way that I could climb the stairs, so I would need to draw him to me somehow.

However, before I could do anything more than think about it, I heard the familiar creak of the stairs behind me. Either I had missed someone, or the assassin had sent for help. If they thought that two of them would scare me, they were about to get a sharp lesson in disappointment.

I moved to the opposite wall and readied one of my knives as well as my sorcery. I wanted answers before I killed them, and with the house this dark a good flash of light could be quite catastrophic for human eyes. The tip of their sword came around the corner first and I felt the light construct buzzing within me as if eager to be released.

Two things happened as they stepped around the corner. The first was that I saw it was Tatyana, and the second was that an invisible hammer smashed me into the wall.

Wood and dust exploded around me, and it was only a particularly thick vertical beam that kept me from flying through the wall and out into the street. I rebounded from the beam and fell back against the splintered floorboards, my vision and hearing distorted as if I were under water. I tried to stand, but another hammer blow lifted me into the roof, the impact cracking the timbers and tearing at my flesh. I managed to roll onto my back as I crashed to the floor again, and so glimpsed my attacker landing, catlike, a few yards away.

'Pathetic,' he said, slapping his hands together. A moment later another blow smashed into me, driving me through the floor entirely so that I ended up in the entrance hall, impaled on a dozen or more splintered floorboards and unable to even shield myself as most of the house cascaded down on me.

Chapter 15

The fires raged around me, devouring the city and those too slow to escape its advance. I could hear their screams amid the roaring of the inferno and smell them roasting on the winds that buffeted me. Those that had survived my initial attack hid themselves from me, cowering like the vermin they were amid stones already hot enough to sear any skin that touched them. I left them to their fate and watched as another building collapsed into embers and sparks, and as the smoke cleared it revealed my goal beyond. It angered me that the cathedral's spire still stood, but I knew that I would change that soon enough.

I could still smell the smoke and charred flesh as I jerked myself back to wakefulness, spooking the rat that had just decided my face would make a good meal. It and its less adventurous fellows leaped away as I gulped for air. What I drew into my mouth was laden with something far less pleasing than smoke or rat though, and if the stench wasn't enough to wake me, then the pain and memories that came with it certainly did. I was lying upon a bed of splintered wood and nails, not a few of which were embedded in my flesh. The combination of dry wood and jagged ends meant they were stuck fast.

I looked around as best as I could. I could smell but not see Tatyana. I could smell her blood, and I twisted as far as the wood that I was impaled on allowed me to, seeking any sign of her. I must have turned as I fell, for my left side was largely free of injury, unlike the right.

Not only were both my arm and leg pierced in several places, but there was at least one sizeable splinter in my side. I wasn't coughing blood, so my ribs had at least kept it from my lungs. I was being optimistic, given that I still had a ragged chunk of wood half the length of my arm wedged deep in my flesh.

'At least you're still alive,' said a voice somewhere behind me. It startled me, and I felt a painful tearing as I twitched in surprise. 'If you were not promised to my master I would take those beautiful gleaming eyes of yours right now and watch you bleed to death.' Cloth rustled, and I caught a sickly waft of sweet spices as my tormentor moved to crouch just out of sight behind me.

Gritting my teeth against the pain, I swung my left arm back and up, fingers wide in an attempt to grab any part of him. I felt something draw a hot line across my palm, and a moment later the smell of my own blood reached me.

'She's probably dead already, your little harlot.' I caught a glimpse of the long dagger he'd cut me with, the steel softly lit with runes. 'Shall I bring you her head?'

'I'd prefer yours.'

'Your voice is not what I expected. I wonder if you still sound the same when you scream?' Another shuffle. 'Let's find out.' He lashed out with an unseen foot, catching the end of the long splinter wedged against my ribs and driving it a bit further into its tunnel of flesh. The pain was shocking; it felt like he'd thrust a lit torch inside me. He did it twice more, and by the third kick I couldn't hold the scream behind my teeth any longer.

'Yes!' my attacker cried, dragging the word out into a hiss. 'Again!' I gave voice to the pain once more as bright flashes burst across my vision. When they cleared, I could see him squatting to my right, a darker shape only visible against the moonlight that filtered from a broken shutter.

'Your blood is exquisite,' he said, his voice a whisper. 'I can taste its potency. I begin to understand why my master seeks you with such vigour.'

I spat a gobbet of the same blood from my mouth; it tasted like nothing more than defeat. The stake in my back had missed my lungs, but it was exerting a constant pressure on my ribs, making it hard for them to expand. I could hear my blood dripping from the wounds between my gasps for breath.

'It is time to go to sleep, monster,' he said. The knife was joined by something altogether more terrifying. It was a coppery cylinder with a long, tapering point from which dripped a fluid that shone with an enchanted glimmer. 'The Master—'

'Can go fuck himself,' said a voice behind him.

The assassin leaped up, turning as he did, the copper device swinging in an arc. I glimpsed Tatyana slipping under it and into the rising path of the dagger in his other hand.

I saw it sink into her, the shock of the blow straightening her, and as she arched away from him two things happened: his hand released the dagger he'd just buried up to the handle in her left side, and she drove her own dagger into the side of his neck. Unlike him though, she did not let go of it as she fell backwards and her falling weight ripped his throat open, spraying us with his reeking blood.

'Tatyana!' I shouted, although I did not have the wind to make it any louder than my normal voice. She gave no answer beyond a rasp of air as she collapsed to the ground. The wood tore at me as I tried to push myself up, setting a storm of lights dancing across my vision once more. I felt my injuries tearing as the jagged wood sawed into me, bleeding me of strength as well as blood. I fell back with a cry that was equal parts pain and frustration.

In my mind, it was answered. I could feel the beast, the demon, rising. I felt its scorn and contempt wash over me, but there was another note underlying all of it. *Fear.* It was a fleeting impression soon lost beneath a rising tide of anger. Like a flame to kindling, it lit my own anger as well. I held onto that anger and fed all of the frustration I felt into it and the cry of pain on my lips became a snarl, and by the time I pulled myself clear of the wreckage, bleeding from dozens of embedded splinters, the snarl was a roar that echoed what I heard in my mind. I reached behind me and curled my hand around the bottom of the splinter he had kicked so deep into me. I twisted it until the blood flowed more freely, making the channel it had torn slick once more, then ripped it out with a roar that sent the remnants of the shutters tumbling from the window.

I staggered to Tatyana and fell to my knees next to her, the cushion of my rage already weakening as my blood spilled from me in a dozen places. Her hands were wrapped around the dagger's handle, but she did not have the strength to pull it all the way out. She was drenched in blood, and I could hear a tremble in her heartbeat, an imperfection that would grow fiercer as her blood continued to pump out of her.

'I'm dying,' she said through clenched and bloody teeth.

'You are,' I said, tugging her hands away from the wound.

She no longer had the strength to keep pressure on it, much less resist me. I didn't need the Deacon's skill to know that her wound was fatal, the blade having cut into the muscle of her heart. She was fading away before my eyes, and with her went whatever secrets that were hidden in her head.

I looked at the dagger, now wet with her blood instead of mine, and I leaped onto the idea that bloomed in my mind. I bit into my finger, my sharp demon teeth puncturing the tough skin so that I tasted my own blood. I let it flow unchecked as I reached into my dwindling reserve of sorcery and formed it into a healing construct. I had become rather adept at them, and something robust enough to work on my bulk would certainly be able to act on her slim frame quickly enough to make a difference. I felt the shape complete, then pulled the dagger free and plunged my finger into the wound in her chest. I hadn't had enough time to customise the healing for a wholly human body, so my blood would serve as a binding agent; the healing would start where the concentration of my blood was the greatest, something that the blood on the blade had already facilitated.

She tried to scream, but she didn't have the strength to raise anything beyond a long hiss. I could feel the damaged wall of her heart against my finger, the weak beat of it as irregular as the fluttering of a moth's wings. I felt it lurch as my blood and sorcery spread across it, penetrating the damaged tissue. Binding it, repairing it, and becoming part of it. I felt it happening, and I saw the gossamer lines of force connecting us. To stop it now was to kill her, so I let both blood and sorcery flow as it needed to until her heart began to pulse with a new strength and vigour, drawing my blood into it and sending it through every part of her body. I felt her muscles knitting around my finger, becoming a gentle and insistent pressure that inexorably forced my finger from her flesh.

The numbing effect of my anger was all but spent, and it took everything I had left to stay awake as her body reacted to the new energies coursing through it. I held her head steady when the convulsions threatened to crack it against the floor. These passed swiftly though, and her breathing deepened into something more wholesome. I had enough time to congratulate myself before the spots of light in my vision won their battle against my will and swelled into a sun before abruptly going black.

The smell of food woke me, the growl of my empty stomach heralding my rise back into consciousness. I opened my eyes to see Tatyana sitting across from me, a gravy-laden hunk of bread paused midway between the bowl on her legs and her open mouth.

'Smells good,' I said, hesitant to move in case the absence of pain was an illusion.

'Welcome back.'

'What are you doing here?'

'Saving your sorry black hide, apparently.'

'I did not need saving.'

'So impaling yourself and bleeding to death was part of a larger strategy? You are truly most cunning.'

I chose not to reply and instead shifted to a more comfortable position. 'Why did you follow me?'

'Why do you think?'

I tried not to growl at her tone. How was I to know what any of them were thinking?

'It is of no import now. How long was I asleep?'

She smiled as she stuffed the bread in her mouth and spoke around it. 'All of the night and most of the next day.'

I lifted my right arm. It was bound with cloth stained with my blood; my leg was similarly wrapped.

'It's your back that I'm worried about,' she said. 'I picked out as much as I could and washed the wound with wine and honey, but I can't stop the bleeding.'

'Thank you,' I said, my gratitude genuine. Crow's gift aside, it was the nicest thing that I could remember a human doing for me. 'I will take care of the rest of it.'

I closed my eyes and turned my attention inward. Fortunately I didn't need to be able to see the wound to work on it. The healing construct came to my mind readily, and I sunk my consciousness into the wound with its energy. There were still a number of fragments lodged in flesh that had swollen around them; given time the pus and fluids would have pushed them out, but it would have been as uncomfortable as it was unpleasant and could have triggered problems of its own. I wrapped gentle fingers of sorcerous energy around each of them, solidifying the fluids to create smooth edges, then set my flesh to expelling them. It was pleasantly pain-less but it did coax the hunger I already felt into something truly monstrous.

I opened my eyes and slowly sat up while tiny lumps of wood and blood slid from the ragged and wet scar on my back. Tatyana was watching me closely and set her now empty bowl aside as I slowly pulled myself to my feet.

'Your back . . .'

'It will stop bleeding as soon as the last of the splinters work their way out. You did very well.' I looked around at the wreckage of the stairs. Looking at the mass of dry, sharp debris now, it seemed that we were both lucky to get away with as little harm as we had, especially her.

I stepped over to the dead man and flipped him onto his back with my foot. Thanks to the gaping wound in his neck his head hardly moved.

'Do you know him?'

'No.' She drummed her fingers against the bowl. 'What happened, Stratus? What did you do to me?'

I had been too preoccupied to think about how she would react, although I suppose I had expected an outpouring of gratitude more than anything else. 'I healed your wound,' I said, keeping it simple.

She shook her head. 'How? I've seen enough bladework to know I should be dead. But I'm not.' She tossed something at me and I caught it without thinking. An arrowhead. 'That fell out of my shoulder this morning. I've been carrying it in the bone since Aknak fell.'

'Bronze?' I turned the tapered head over in my fingers. 'How quaint.'

'The mountain tribes still use it but don't change the subject. What did you do to me?'

I took a moment to think about it. I had targeted the healing at her heart, not anywhere else. I rubbed at the surface of the arrowhead, the rough whorls on my skin scrubbing off the last traces of her blood. That was it – her blood, and more importantly, my blood, now mixed with hers. Rather than simply providing a temporary conduit for the healing, somewhere in the process of transferring the energy and the actual rebuilding of her heart, my blood had somehow permanently fused with hers. And if it had continued the healing process after I had apparently severed the connection, it was still somehow linked to me.

'What's the matter? Why are you looking at me like that?'

I kneeled in front of her. 'Do you trust me?'

'No, why?'

'I need to test something before I answer you.'

She rubbed at the bloodied shirt she wore, then nodded her agreement. It took me longer than I liked to wake my sorcery, but once I had it arranged, I gave her what I hoped was a reassuring smile and stabbed her in the arm.

She sprung back with a yelp, clutching her arm and shouting. I ignored what she was saying and kept watching through the veil of my sorcery. I saw the light of the healing construct wake within her, the glow of it overlaying her bones, then flow to the wound on her arm. If I hadn't been watching through my sorcery I would have missed the thin filament of light, no thicker than one of her hairs, that flickered to life between us, drawing a tiny measure of energy from me. I dispelled the veil and stood.

'Move your hand,' I said.

'Fuck you, you bloody maniac.'

'Tatyana. Move your hand.'

She muttered something vile but slowly lifted her hand and stared at her unblemished arm. 'What the Hel? How . . .'

'Sorcery,' I said. 'When I healed your wound, I . . . left a bit of myself inside you.'

She rubbed at her arm. 'I'm not entirely sure how I feel about that.'

I shrugged the comment away. 'Not liking it won't change it.'

'Will that always happen?'

'I suppose it will, until I die. Be warned though, healing like that comes at a price. The construct will heal wounds and sickness, but if you're not eating well, the amount of energy it costs your body will hollow you out.'

'Well, that sounds terrific. Thank you so very much.'

'You're welcome.' I looked down at the dead man. 'And now I need to do something you probably won't like very much. I know I won't.'

'You're not stabbing me again.'

'No,' I said, pointing to the body. 'I just need to eat his brain.'

Chapter 16

Tatyana stared at me without saying anything for long enough that I began to wonder whether I had said it aloud, or simply thought it. As I was about to repeat myself, she turned her gaze to the dead man, then back to me.

'You're going to eat him,' she said. She made it sound like a statement.

'Just his brain,' I corrected her.

'His brain.'

'Are you repeating everything for a reason?'

'Yes, if I have to! You can't do that, Stratus.'

'Of course I can. I have to, since you killed him.'

'It's sick, and just plain wrong in so many ways. And if you hadn't been flat on your back and bleeding like a stuck pig, I wouldn't have had to kill him.'

I chose to ignore the last. 'Well, it is not something I particularly want to do. I wanted to find him to get answers out of him, but I can't any more.' I was thinking back to the vague image that the bitter-tasting brain matter in the street had yielded, and how much more potent a result might be had if the brain were fresher and not a melted mush. 'But it's the only way I can hear a dead man speak.'

'You can't,' she said, still shaking her head. 'That's *necromancy*.' She whispered the word.

'Necromancy?' It wasn't a word that I had heard before. I knew enough of the language to understand that *necros* was an older word for the world of the dead, but I'd not heard it applied in a specific context. 'You do know that necromancy implies the use of magic that affects the dead?'

'That's what I said. Like the Worm's lot are doing.'

She gave no indication that she was making this up simply to dissuade me from eating the brain, and that worried me.

'Are you saying that the Worm Lord's magic affects the dead?'

'Am I stuttering? They started pulling the dead out of their damned graves, if that's what you mean by affecting them.'

'That's impossible.'

'I faced the dead at Aknak, so don't you dare bloody stand there and tell me it's impossible or that I'm a damned liar.'

'I have heard this Aknak mentioned several times. What happened there? I know it is a town that fell but little else.'

She sat and stared at her hands for some time before starting to speak. As she explained it, she and her now dead comrades had been in the employ of one of the mercenary companies paid to hold a city named Aknak. They had been doing a good job of it, having held up the Penullin advance for several weeks. Then the attacks began, not from the soldiers without the city walls, but from those who had fallen within them. I asked her to repeat the story as it was too incredulous to believe.

'The dead rose and attacked you?' I asked for the third time. 'You're sure?'

'It's the truth. I saw them myself, and I fought them with these hands. I don't care how sick or mad someone is, you stab them in the heart or cut their throat and they bleed. They die. I'm telling you, the dead walked. They were unstoppable unless you smashed their head in or lopped them off.' She spat on the dead man at my feet. 'Of course, we only found that out after they'd overrun the walls, and by then it was too late to save him.'

'Save who?'

She waved the question away. 'It doesn't matter.'

I had to agree with that, and stood up and began to pace, something that had always helped me think. I couldn't even begin to contemplate why, let alone how, they would do such a thing. All magic came from the Songlines, and they in turn were part of the life force that animated every living thing. It was the very antithesis of the cold, negative energy that separated this life from the world of the dead, and the idea of someone twisting and corrupting that power so as to reach through the veil and pull the dead back into this world was one I found almost impossible to comprehend. Negative power wasn't a form of energy that any living creature could wield; it and the Songlines were opposites, like fire and water.

'And you believe this was the work of the Worm Lord's wizards? His *necromancers*?' I asked.

'We captured one of them. The captain put the question to him and I tell you what, no matter how fanatical someone is, a bit of fire soon resets their priorities.'

'I would imagine so.' I didn't mention that a good fire would probably improve my mood.

'By the time he got talking he was pretty badly burned up, so it all came out in bits and pieces. He kept saying that his shadow brothers would come for him, and that the goddess of death they served would never let him die.'

'Did she?'

'What?'

'Let him die.'

'Oh yes. He scared the boys, see, and they didn't react well to that.'

An idea began to form in my mind. 'I would like to speak to one of these necromancers while they are still alive too.' I squatted down next to the body. 'But for now, I will start with what I have available.'

'You're still going to do it?'

'Yes. His brain isn't getting any fresher.'

'I can't watch. I can't even think about it.'

'Then wait outside. When I am done I will need food, real food.'

'You'll eat? After doing that?'

'I will be hungry, so yes.'

'Fine.'

With that she clambered up the side of the hole and vanished into the gloom of the ground floor. With nothing left to delay me, I drew one of my knives and set to opening his skull.

'Let's see what you know about necromancers,' I said, cutting myself a generous slice of his brain and eating it before I let my doubts affect my decision.

At first I thought that perhaps I should take a slice from a different part, or that perhaps the image I had drawn from the other's man brain had been an anomaly. I held the cold brain in my mouth, its texture almost as disturbing as the thought that it didn't actually taste anywhere as bad as I expected. But then the accumulated residue of the corrupt magic that had flowed through his body overwhelmed me, and any thoughts vanished as I concentrated on fighting the urge to vomit. My stubbornness was rewarded as the first images began to form in my mind; they were faint to start with, almost ethereal, but the longer I kept my lips together the clearer they became, until I was no longer seeing it as a stranger, but as the man himself.

A great hall with thousands of scrolls and books, the dark overwhelming the few lanterns. Dozens of robed men kneel before him, and his eyes are lit with the moon's cold light. The Master's hand is on my head, the power within him such that his touch is cold enough that it feels scalding.

The images bloomed in my mind, then faded into a mist. Encouraged by the success, I dug deeper into his brain and squeezed another lump into my mouth. I couldn't taste it any more.

The grey-haired general prostrates himself before me. I command this army for my master now, not him. His honour and pride are no more; he knows only fear. A thousand new corpses lie in their neat rows around me, and my throat aches from the task of seeding so many with the Bloodseed. Soon they will grow, and the goddess will command them to rise and I will glory in the touch of her cold majesty.

What I had seen so far had been interesting, but hardly revelatory and I silently cursed Tatyana's efficiency with her dagger. This would have been far easier and less unpleasant if he'd been alive, or even still dying. I carved out another piece of brain, this time from the other side of his head.

The city streets are crowded with hawkers and shoppers. This will be the next city to fall and I laugh at all their petty fears and desires, these fools who do not know they are already dead. The crypt is guarded by the sacred marks of the Master, but the stone opens for me and I begin upon the long stairs that will take me to our great temple. I am shamed that I fled when the beast slew my brothers, and that I must now seek the help of the Crafter, that fool barely weaned from the Master's power. He shall have the glory of its capture now.

I tried to focus on the already fading image of the figure of this gate-keeper that the dead necromancer had pictured, but as the others before it had, it broke up into mist, and with it went the final dregs of my resolve. My stomach emptied itself with rare violence, and as the contractions stilled, I knew that my willpower would not be enough to make another attempt. Without another look at the man's corpse I made my way to the edge of the hole and pulled myself up, groaning as the effort it took to lift my bulk up tore open the newly grown scar tissue across my back. I managed to staunch the bleeding with the very dregs of my sorcery, and limped out to where Tatyana waited.

'Is it done?' she asked. I answered with a nod and she turned and began walking away. 'I know a place that's good when you're properly hungry. The cook is as fat as a barrel, always a good sign.'

I didn't have the strength or clarity of mind to offer anything in return and simply focused on walking and trying not to bleed to death on the way. It's strange how you neither notice nor appreciate how many stairs or hills there are in a place until you're tired or injured, and I had just about convinced myself that she was taking me on the cruellest route out of spite when she abruptly stopped behind some men standing on the side of the road.

'Are you going to stay here? I need to get back and speak to Lucien.'

'Where's here?'

'The eatery. You said you were hungry.'

I peered at the men behind her. 'Why are we standing in the road?'

'It's a queue. It's nearly dinner time and it's a popular place.'

'I will be here for as long as they can keep feeding me.' Assuming that I didn't succumb to the exhaustion that wanted me to lie down in the nearest doorway and sleep until my enemies died of old age.

'Save me a pie. I'll be back.' With that, she patted my shoulder and headed off with an enviable vitality.

The air was ripe with all the usual odours that I associated with the city, a smothering fug that the wind only occasionally stirred, giving the more interesting smells a chance to surface. Interesting smells like those wafting from the eatery's kitchens, which were rich with spices and flavours I had never experienced before. My stomach growled, loud enough that I wondered if I'd swallowed some creature without noticing. The two men in front of me turned at the sound, but neither seemed alarmed.

'His pies have that effect,' the taller of the two said. His companion simply maintained his grin, as if proud of his little yellow teeth.

'Fat men make the tastiest pies,' I offered, and was surprised when they agreed with me.

'Can't trust a thin man in the kitchen, as my dad always said.' The taller one looked up at me. 'So where are you from?'

'Five Elms?' I ventured.

He shook his had at that. 'Five Elms is a shithole, but it's a small shithole and no one's ever mentioned a clan of giant black men living down there before.'

I thought about what Crow had told me about the war and the towns that had been sacked, wracking my memory until one of their names swam into focus.

'It was Dawlish before that,' I said, hoping that the pause made it sound more dramatic.

My interrogator pursed his lips. 'A bad business that. I'm sorry.'

Fortunately that successfully curbed their interest in me, and the rest of the wait passed without incident while I listened to them quietly argue about who was responsible for the apparently infamous story of the burning of Dawlish cathedral and the congregation within.

I entered what was jauntily named 'The Pie Hole' and was quickly shown to a seat on one of the shared benches by a spindly boy in an apron. I was too busy tasting the air to pay much attention to where I was sitting until the bench collapsed under my weight without so much as a warning, spilling at least a dozen men and me to the ground, along with a fair number of cups and half-eaten pies. The fall jarred my injuries and I hauled myself back to my feet with a growl that was half pain and half anger. It did nothing to dissuade one of the men from shouting at me, and I was on the verge of doing something spectacularly violent to him when a man who truly was as round as a barrel came barging out from a side door, bellowing for calm in a voice that would make a wizard proud. His sudden appearance and manner was enough to divert my anger, and I lowered my hands as he came over and surveyed the splintered end of the bench.

'Looks like someone's had a few too many of my little beauties, eh?' he said to no one in particular, earning a round of laughter. 'All right, all right. We'll get you gentlemen some fresh pies, but you'll have to wait for seats.' He came over to me. 'And you, my very large friend, you shall sit over there where the benches are made of brick and stone!' More laughter followed as he grabbed my wrist and led me over to the far side of the room before winking at me and trundling away back to the kitchen.

One of the boys came over to my table and planted a pie the size of a man's head on the table before me. He loitered until I drew one of my little knives to cut into it, releasing a savoury cloud of steam that made me groan with delight. I inhaled as much of it as I could before slowly breathing out. Thick gravy was pooling on the plate while I steeled myself to begin eating, the hesitation born of a fear that the taste wouldn't hold up to the promise of the aroma. But I wasn't disappointed. I all but licked the plate clean, at which point the little man returned and started loitering at my table again.

'The plate please sir,' he said eventually.

I passed it over. 'Bring me another. And do you have any wheat beer?'

'Um, yes sir.'

I ate two more pies and emptied three tankards before the hunger subsided, then ordered another of each and simply sat and watched the room while I waited for Tatyana's return. No one bothered me, although plenty stared, hastily averting their gaze when I looked back. My body was attacking the food with great enthusiasm, and I could feel the strength returning to me as I sat there, and with it came a lessening of the residual pain in my wounds. Without the distraction of injuries and the need to put as much food as I could down my neck, I began to pay more attention to the conversations around me, particularly when Lucien's name was mentioned.

'My cousin, you know the one I mean, he works down there. He heard it too. Nothing but farmers and boys.'

'But Prince Lucien's got the knights.'

'The way I hear it, the only sword he's swung has balls at the bottom.' A round of laughter greeted this.

'The knights—'

'Bah. The Hel with knights! They'll not get their hands dirty saving the poor bastards in the middle.' The speaker was an old man with hair that seemed to be sprouting everywhere but on top of his head. 'They'll ride in when its nearly over and come out just as shiny on the way out, just you wait.'

'What about them wizards?'

'Wizards!' Laughter croaked from the old man's lips. 'Worse than women on a battlefield. Besides, it's hard to be a wizard with a sword in your head.'

'You see they're clearing out the lower markets? My cousin says they've flattened the lot of them to make space for the knights.'

'Your cousin's a worse gossip than my Ginny.' The old man picked at the crust of his pie. 'It's a bad sign that. The war's getting too close.'

'You going to leave?'

'I'd rather be robbed in my own home than out on the road. At least I can get a night's sleep in my own bed.'

I looked up as I caught Tatyana's scent. The men at the table fell silent as she passed them, their heads turning as one, and I heard the old man whisper, 'That's her, the one I told you about.' She was oblivious to this and their stares as she dropped into the seat opposite me and neatly whisked my pie and ale in front of her.

'So hungry,' was all that I could make out as she fell upon it. I waved to the little pie-carrier, who had become very attentive after I'd ordered my second pie. I asked for another two pies and ales and simply watched Tatyana eat. She hadn't had much fat on her to begin with, and the severity of her injuries would have seen the healing burn up what reserves she had. I'd always liked eating, but the hunger that sorcery gave you was hard to explain to someone who hasn't felt it. She could have been eating those horrible oats and would still think it the best meal she's ever eaten.

Our new pies and beers arrived just as she emptied my tankard, and for a moment I thought she was going to embrace me. Instead, she began an amusing battle between succumbing to the driving need to eat and cooling the pie enough that she could eat it without taking the skin off her tongue. The heat of the food didn't bother me, and I actually found it to be something of a balm to my tortured sense of taste. We ate in silence for some time while the men at the table debated whether she was attractive or cursed, something that I would need to ask her about at some point. Eventually she sat back with a groan, her plate gleaming.

'God, I needed that,' she said. 'But now we need to go back to the palace.'

'I wanted to discuss what I had seen in his br—'

'Don't say it, not right now, all right?' She drained her tankard. 'Come on. Fronsac has asked to see you.'

'The wizard?'

'The very same.'

Chapter 17

It didn't take me long to start feeling uncomfortable as I waited for my audience with the wizard. A surly guard had shown me the way to Fronsac's rooms, which to me didn't sound very wizard-like, but I did as I had been bid, making my way there in good time and with every intention of keeping my ideas on human flesh to myself. The rooms were just that, with not a tower in sight. They were far narrower than Lucien's was, but seemed even smaller given the number of books, scrolls and the five apprentices crammed into them. It was these apprentices who were starting to annoy me, three of them in particular who clearly had a far higher opinion of their magical abilities than they should have.

They cast their first spell almost before I had announced myself to the oldest-looking of the three. The casting was a tremulous thing of such poor construction that it would have struggled to manifest even if I hadn't brushed it away as effortlessly as a cobweb. Their second attempt was a far better effort, but slow enough to manifest that I had time enough to interpret its intent and decide what to do about it. I wanted to conserve my sorcery in the event that I needed it during my meeting with the wizard, and as the spell construct was a simple probe designed to identify hostile magic and hidden weapons, I left it alone. Unfortunately, they clearly interpreted this as a victory, or at least an affirmation of their supposed talents, and the rest of my wait was spent having to deal with a series of similarly ridiculous things. I had just stood up to confront them when the door swung open and the wizard, Fronsac, walked in.

From the latent energy that I could sense radiating from him, it was clear that whatever he had been doing before had been far more potent than anything his lackeys were throwing around. He looked me up and down and headed to a closed door on the far side of the room.

'Come along,' he said over his shoulder. 'I don't have all night.'

The room he led me into was far less cluttered than the one where I had been waiting, or perhaps the clutter was simply better organised. Here again books covered every flat surface, and the walls were hung with ornate and complicated-looking diagrams. I recognised a few astrological symbols amid these, but little besides. In all, I suppose it looked very wizard-like, and had I not been able to sense how little magical residue permeated the room I might even have been impressed.

The wizard lowered himself into a padded chair and offered me a similar one in front of his busy-looking desk before lighting a candle between us. I considered the likely strength of the wood and lowered myself into it with the care of someone trying to bathe in lava. It held, but not without protest.

'So, you're a wizard.'

'No,' I said, biting back on my immediate irritation. 'I understand the principles, but I'm not a wizard.'

He scratched at the beard that covered most of his face and fished some folded paper out of his pocket. A small light manifested above his shoulder, and I silently congratulated him on his control. I had neither felt nor heard him call it up. It was a minor conjuration, but after the poor displays I had seen from his underlings it was reassuring to see something akin to actual talent. After a moment, he tossed the paper aside and the light faded.

'I know what you are,' he said, sitting back and crossing his arms. I felt my heartbeat surge and only a warning creak from the chair kept me from leaning forward.

'Tell me then,' I said, my voice rasping from an unexpectedly dry mouth and throat.

'You're a sorcerer, and only the second I've ever seen in over forty years.'

'Oh.' I sagged back. 'Who was the first?'

'A charcoal burner's son, of all things.' He raked his fingers through his beard again, and I found myself wondering what it felt like. 'He was a nice boy.'

'What happened to him?'

'He lost control of his gift and exploded. He also destroyed an ancient cathedral, half the town, and everything we knew about sorcerers with it.'

I rubbed my own chin as an idea crawled into my head. 'How ancient a cathedral?'

'About five hundred years, give or take a few decades. Why do you ask?'

'Your cathedrals and other holy places are normally built on the paths of the Songlines, and sometimes a confluence of them. I expect the proximity of so much power overwhelmed your charcoal burner.'

His beard twitched and it took me a moment to see that he was smiling.

'But you already knew that,' I said.

'I was watching you in there.' He gestured to the room we'd entered through. 'It was quite extraordinary to see how quickly you could react. My apprentices will be having nosebleeds for the rest of the evening from the pace you forced on them.'

'That was a trial?'

He nodded. 'Indeed. If there is one thing I do not have, Meneer Stratus, it is time. Time to train my own apprentices as I should. Time to rally those that still call me master to answer the Kingdom's call. Time to mourn my sons. And, now, time to worry about the stranger who has somehow convinced the man I serve that I should allow him, a stranger with an undoubtedly dangerous gift and unknown motivations, to walk among us.'

'If I meant either of them harm, I would have acted by now.'

'I know, which is why I'm curious and you're not currently anchored to the bottom of the river.' I said nothing as he poured us each a cupful of wine. 'Where did you go yesterday?'

I sipped at the wine as I considered my reply. 'I tracked the last of the assassins who attacked Lucien.'

'And did you find him?'

'Yes.'

'And you killed him?' He toyed with one of the rune-inscribed rings on his hand as he spoke, and I could sense a subtle but deep stirring of power around me. I reached out with a wisp of my own power and quickly sensed the strength of the wards that he had just woken. They were carved into the walls and the floor, cunningly hidden from sight beneath the floorboards and behind the diagrams and tapestries. I could feel the potency of the power stored within them, the runes sharp and deep and buoyed by regular reinforcement. Given time I might have unpicked them one at a time, but they were clearly linked and quite deadly.

'No.' I took another sip of the wine and hid a smile as he frowned at me. It seemed he didn't know as much as he wanted me to think that he did. 'That privilege went to Tatyana Henkman.'

'She is quite formidable. Still, it is a disappointment that you could not take him alive.'

'I owe her my life.' *A debt repaid.*

'Then you do at least have something in common with Prince Lucien.'

I felt his magic flexing around me as he toyed with his rings, and a ripple of energy washed over me as he woke another ward. I drew in the stray energy greedily.

'What did you attempt with Prince Jean?'

I thought back to the wards I had felt shut me out of Prince Jean's mind, and this wizard crept up a little higher in my estimation. 'I'm impressed that you felt that. I barely looked at him.'

'Protecting the royal family is my priority,' he replied, and this time I felt him flex the power that the rings had woken. 'And it is a responsibility that I take very seriously.'

'As you should,' I said, making the effort to smile as I woke my sorcery and sent it into the defensive construct I had prepared earlier. Even with my sorcery having largely recovered, sitting here amid his carefully prepared defences I suspected whatever I could offer would be as useful as paper armour. But I didn't need to defeat his magic; I only needed to win enough time to cross the desk and break his jaw. An unconscious wizard is, after all, little more than a man sleeping in nice robes. I felt his magic flow across the skin of my own simple wards, the touch light, leaving me unsure how to react. The beast was paying attention too, but I sensed that it was simply watching for now.

Fronsac's scent was equally confusing, muddled as it was by the ingrained tang of herbs and magical residue from his preparations. Was this another test of his? If circumstances were different, I would have been over the desk already, forestalling any attempt at attacking me. He didn't reply but simply sat there watching me, so I did the same. He must have known the strength that he could bring to bear on me, but he was restraining it and seemed too relaxed to be on the offensive, so I resolved that he was now testing me himself.

I pushed the thought of the wards burning around me from my mind and began to concentrate on the feel of the magic that he was consciously directing at me, attuning myself to the tone of it until it rang clear to me, a higher note than my own. It was like pushing against someone's hand; you could learn a lot about their strength and how they used it, but because they were pushing back, if they were wise they could learn the same about you. He was meticulous, and not just because of the nature of spellcasting, pushing and probing one way and the next, over and over until he had explored every inch of my wards.

But his consistent, dependable approach was also his weakness. Wizards' spells are not flexible, and while there was no real way to tell what a well-trained wizard was about to cast, once the spell was released its purpose could be quickly divined and its outcome predicted. Unlike sorcerers, wizards couldn't adapt their spells as they needed to; they had to stop and recast them with whatever new inflection or purpose they needed, and that made them predictable. He slipped through my wards eventually, but the smile that flared on his face did not linger for long. His eyebrows rose as quickly as his mouth fell when he felt the tendril of my sorcery that had wormed its way through *his* guard, having burrowed through the minute spaces that he left free every time he changed his focus. With each contact, I had felt a touch of his intent, each of these brushes against his will building on one another until I had a sense of what lay behind it. There was no malice, only a deep sense of duty. There had not been enough time to wonder what he drew from me, or indeed if he had the skill to do both, and I had to hope that he had not sensed anything of the beast inside me.

I didn't know how long we had sat like that, but when we both leaned back the candle he had lit was a misshapen, sputtering blob on the desk. My head was throbbing painfully with every beat of my hearts, the prolonged mental wrestling having utterly drained my reservoir of sorcery. Had I not eaten such a hearty meal before making my way here I would have fared much worse, but even so, it had been gruelling and I would need some time to recover. I was as vulnerable to magic as any normal man now, and it was not a sensation that I enjoyed.

As painful and hollow as my head felt, I held myself ready to spring at Fronsac if he gave any sign of pressing a new magical attack on me. However, he made no move and only sat where he was with his eyes lidded as if he was about to fall asleep, but my vision was good enough that I could see he was watching me.

'You play an interesting game, Meneer Stratus. Few have resisted me so adroitly, and none have breached my defence as you did.'

'Just Stratus,' I said, ignoring the voice in my head reminding me that it was really only part of my name. I found my wine and drained the cup in a swallow, uncaring of the drops that stained my new shirt.

'I have the sense that you are a man with many secrets.' He refilled both our cups as he spoke and I accepted the drink with gratitude. My body needed energy and it didn't care where it came from, and if I had been left alone I might well have begun chewing on his desk.

'Everyone has secrets, Meneer Fronsac.'

'Just Fronsac will do for me too.' He sipped his wine. 'You are a dangerous man, Stratus. The kind that I would either see dead or sworn to the same cause as myself.'

I felt the wards buzzing against my skin and forced my muscles to relax. 'I would prefer the second option myself.'

'I find that I am pleased to hear that, Stratus. If you are dangerous to one who is prepared for you, I expect our enemies will find you a calamity.' He leaned forward, and I felt the weight of his power press against me.

'Stratus, will you give me your word to stand with Prince Jean and to oppose the Worm Lord in all endeavours?'

It was a solemn question, solemnly asked, and only a fool would rush to answer it. The giving of one's word is a potent thing, especially when given to a cunning wizard or sorcerer. It is more than a simple promise, or even an oath. To break from what you swore to was to gift your true name to the person you broke faith with, giving them a power over you, the like of which not even the gods knew. To give my word to Fronsac was to commit myself to Krandin and pit myself against this Navar Louw, who styled himself the Worm Lord. And yet, I had largely done so already, had I not? The snarl I sensed from the beast within me at the mere mention of Louw's name was an eloquent confirmation of its stance too, and enough to tell me that it would tear me apart from within if I did anything else but hunt him down.

'I pledge my word, Fronsac. I will stand by Prince Jean and oppose the Worm Lord in all his forms.'

Fronsac watched me in silence for a moment more before clenching his fist and whispering a command. I felt the wards subside, the release of the pressure enough to make me gasp in relief.

'I simply call him the Worm. He's lord of nothing but woe.' The wizard rose and stretched out his hand, and I admit that for a moment I panicked it was another test before recognising the gesture. I took his hand in mine and was careful not to crush it as we shook.

'I am pleased to hear you say that. I will convey the news to Prince Jean, and look forward to exploring your magic, Stratus. Preferably in a more comfortable chair and with a brandy.'

I was still unsure how I felt about trusting him with the secret truth of my origin, but as I left I consoled myself with the thought that mutual respect was a good foundation to approach him on.

'Likewise, Fronsac. There are matters I need to discuss with you before we leave the citadel.'

'I shall do what I can. Speak to my apprentices and they will arrange a time.'

He opened the door for me and I stepped through into the empty room beyond. His apprentices were absent and the room was dark, but the pale moonlight that filtered through the windows was enough for me to bypass the piles of clutter.

'Karl?' called the magus behind me.

Curious, I looked over my shoulder and saw that the magus had stopped in the doorway. 'Who is Karl?' I asked.

'My first apprentice. He was supposed to be monitoring the Watch Stones while I spoke with you.'

'Watch Stones?'

'They help us control the wards,' he said, waving his hand. 'He should be here.'

I sniffed the air, drawing in a noseful of the scents that hung about us. My senses were still attuned to, or possibly traumatised by, the stench of the necromancy and, despite the competing aromas, the foul tang of it was the first that struck me.

'Necromancer,' I said. To his credit, the magus didn't question me. I felt the pull of him readying his spellcraft, although with no sorcery left in my reserve I had no idea what he was preparing.

'I must get to Jean,' he said, and in a flutter of robes he leaped over a half-open chest and raced from the room, leaving a faint trace of leaked magic in the air that I absorbed. I made to follow him, but paused when the stink of the dark magic bit into my nose again. An empty bottle rattled across the floor at the end of the room, and I turned around as one of his apprentices rose to their feet from behind a desk, swaying like a drunk.

'Karl?' I ventured, but he made no reply except to lift his head and stare at me with blank, dead eyes that shone with a cold light.

It seemed that the shadow of the necromancers had reached Falkenburg.

Chapter 18

The creature that had been Karl began walking towards me while I stared at it, caught somewhere between fascination and revulsion. Was he truly dead, or was this some sort of macabre puppetry? I knew that I had the potential to modify my power of suggestion into a form of domination in the right circumstances, so it was possible that Karl was simply under a similar sort of enchantment. However, it didn't explain his lack of a heartbeat and the stench that grew stronger with every shuffling step he took towards me. Unguarded minds were like fortresses with their gates unbarred, and I doubted that Magus Fronsac would have left his apprentices' minds without some sort of ward. This had been a targeted attack.

With no sorcery at my disposal, I had no chance of probing whatever was moving him towards me, which simplified my options. I didn't want to kill him, not before I'd had a chance to study him, and so I used the time that his clumsy approach gave me to look for something to tie him up with. He was nearly on me by the time I managed to find something suitable. I was just getting ready to drape the musty tapestry over him when he lunged forward with a speed and vigour that had been entirely absent from his slow walk across the room. His hand latched onto my left wrist with surprising strength, while the hooked fingers of his other narrowly missed my face. It was my fault really. I had been too distracted by the 'how' of his progress towards me to give any thought to the 'why'. I snapped a punch into his guts without thinking, but all it served to do was send an odorous whuff of air and some spittle from his mouth.

He wasn't breathing. And it certainly didn't look like he was troubled by the blow, which I was fairly certain would have incapacitated a normal man. He took another swipe at my face, but I caught his wrist and tightened my grip until his bones cracked. He still gave no indication that it bothered him at all, and I could feel the jagged ends grinding against each other as he tried to pull it free. Without warning he lunged towards me, his teeth snapping shut a hand's breadth from my arm. His little square teeth wouldn't do my hide much damage, but the thought of his wet mouth on my skin was too much.

He may have been possessed of a manic sort of strength, but there was only so much force his still-human muscles could exert, especially when some of the bones beneath were cracked. I broke both his arms and kicked his legs out from under him so that he fell helpless to the ground. I quickly wrapped him in the tapestry, as tightly as I could manage, and secured it with my belt. It didn't stop him from snapping his teeth together every time I moved, but the effect seemed almost comical now.

I left him to squirm in the dark and stepped out of the room. The hallway beyond was blessedly free of the stink, and I took a few moments to clear my senses before finding Fronsac's scent and starting to follow it. The mage's rooms were almost on the edge of the palace grounds and were linked to the main complex by a long and narrow passage of inferior stonework. I strode along the passage, following his scent and listening to the growing number of shouts and screams coming from the main building. The doors at the end were open, and there was no sign of the guards who had been there earlier, although the hallways beyond certainly had enough of them to compensate. They were all going in the same direction as me, which made things easier but diluted the scent trail, and I had to slip into a recessed niche before I could inch back along the wall until I caught it again. It led to a narrow and entirely unremarkable door tucked behind a half-dead tree in a pot. It wasn't locked, and the disused room beyond was almost as unremarkable as the door was.

His scent led straight across the room to a large painting that I actually recognised, despite it being so terribly rendered. It depicted a knight, his antlered helmet suggesting it was Henkman the paladin, jabbing a lance at what looked like nothing more than an enormous swamp lizard with bat-like wings. It was as hideous as it was ridiculous; wings like that would never have supported its weight, and if it could fly, why was it bothering to fight on land where the man had the advantage of his weapon's reach? It was as ugly as it was ridiculous, and in a moment of pure spite, I reached up and tore it down the middle. It was a moment of wanton destruction, and yet it brought a smile to my face and even made the beast inside me twitch in what I took to be mutual amusement.

Tearing it yielded more than a fleeting moment of satisfaction though. As the ripped painting fell apart, it revealed a door hidden behind it. There was no handle to grab, and pushing it was like pushing against the stone of the wall, and I began to worry that perhaps it was attuned to Fronsac's magic, in which case I had no chance of getting past it in my current state. Yet it felt too old to be something the magus had put together. I pressed my face to it at around the magus' height and licked the stone. At first I only tasted dust, but as I moved down I found a trace of his scent, no doubt where he had touched the stone. After some experimentation, I found the right angle to push the hidden lever.

The door slid to the side and I ducked into the narrow but surprisingly clean passage beyond. It bent as I followed it, and in some places became so narrow that even turning sideways saw me scraping both walls. I could hear voices as I moved along, louder in some places than others, no doubt influenced by how thick the stone was. I also saw more doors, but since Fronsac hadn't used them, I too ignored them for now. His scent eventually led to one of these exits, and I leaned my ear against the door to gauge what lay beyond.

I could hear several men and at least one woman talking at the same time, but it was impossible to make out what any one of them was saying, even with my superior hearing. They sounded agitated, so I decided to wait a little longer before doing anything. The last thing I wanted was an overeager guard or paladin putting a few inches of steel in me. Apparently I wasn't the only one who didn't like the noise, because a moment later absolute silence descended on the room, followed by a ripple of magic, the tone of it now familiar to me. Fronsac had silenced the room to help him identify any magical threat before it could fully manifest.

The door I was pressed up against abruptly slid away, leaving me to stumble into the room and the drawn swords that waited for me therein.

I caught my balance just in time to avoid the closest of the sword points. There were four guards, two of them paladins by their armour, and none of them looked remotely pleased to see me. I held my hands out to show that I wasn't armed, but braced myself to leap out of the way if they decided to attack. I could see a dozen or so people behind them but didn't want to take my eyes off their weapons. It was a good thing too, because when Fronsac dropped the magical silence he had imposed, the sudden snap of sound made one the guards leap forward. I pivoted out of the way with less than a hand's breadth to spare and managed to resist the temptation to pluck the sword from his grasp. The resumption of sound also saw everyone in the room start shouting again, including the guards and paladins, who were taking turns to tell me not to move, to raise my hands higher and to get on the ground.

'Silence!' Fronsac's voice boomed through the room, the irony of it lost on the men and women who reeled back from him. He strode forward and pushed between the guards. 'Stratus. What are you doing here?'

'I followed you,' I said. It was the truth, after all. 'I thought you might need help seeing as your apprentice has been incapacitated.'

'Karl?'

'Yes, he was behind the—'

'Your Highness, Prince Jean, this is no coincidence!' I recognised the voice that rose behind Fronsac, and true enough, there stood the Cardinal. He had one hand on Prince Jean's arm while the other was pointing at me. 'He is in league with the Worm Lord!'

This announcement created its own, short-lived bubble of silence that was quickly replaced with cries of outrage and alarm. Not a few of them drew back, clutching at charms and medallions. I looked to the Cardinal, then at Prince Jean, who was staring at me.

It was Fronsac who spoke first. 'That's nonsense, Your Highness. He was with me at the time of the attack, being tested.'

'Indeed, another coincidence no doubt.'

'What exactly is that supposed to mean, Polsson?' I could feel Fronsac's magic flickering just out of reach as his emotions weakened his control.

'Nothing, of course. It was just a coincidence that the prince was attacked at the same time as the leader of a questionable coven and this . . . dark stranger were out of sight.'

'Enough!' barked Prince Jean, that resonance in his voice silencing the room as effectively as Fronsac's spell. He pointed to the guards, then to me. 'Take him to a cell.'

The beast reacted to that before I could. It didn't like chains, and it liked cells even less, but the combination of these and paladins sent it swelling and uncoiling inside me. I staggered and leaned against the edge of the door as it pushed at the edges of my mind.

'No,' I said, my voice sounding half-strangled. I felt that terrible, pent-up rage pressing against my mind. I fought it, but I could feel it leaking into my own emotions, the unexpected exposure revealing a hitherto hidden undercurrent of panic buried within it. There was no time to think about it though, not if I wanted to stop it from making me do something entirely stupid. I was shoved and pulled along the corridors, numb to everything except the intoxicating anger rising from the beast, the promise of a rare gratification if I would only give in to the unrequited urge to punch the Cardinal's face into the back of his head and tear into the paladins to feed its almost primal need for revenge.

Chapter 19

Of all the voices that rail against the power bestowed upon us as the Chosen, none are louder or more dangerous than the ancient order of the Paladins. Their purpose ended when the last demon was vanquished, yet their order has prospered. Their crude, slavish dedication to the teachings of the Church and the enforced ignorance of their creed has made them a blunt but effective weapon when wielded by a cunning mind, and care must be exercised in all dealings with them.

An Introduction to the Path of Power
by Tiberius Talgoth, Archmage

It was some time after the door slammed shut behind me that the beast finally retreated and I regained control of myself. It hadn't gone willingly, but all I had to show for the struggle were aching knuckles where it had managed to make me lash out at the iron-bound door in blind anger.

The irony was that the room I was locked in was better appointed than the room I'd been given as a guest of the prince. Even the carpets were thicker. Yet I had no doubt about the nature of the room; the windows were too narrow for anything larger than a crow to navigate, and a blow like the one I had given the door would have made a hole in any of the others I had come across in the palace so far. I sat down by the table and dipped my knuckles into the basin of cool water that had been provided and watched the water take on a shade of pink.

The tussle with the beast had left my thoughts and feelings jumbled and discordant, so much so that I was unable to say with certainty which were mine alone. It was a strange thing, to have felt its panic amid all that anger, an unexpected vulnerability. It had always felt dangerous and strong, but had I been too quick in my judgement? What sort of creature was it to harbour such anger and violence, yet panic at the thought of a cell and a distant, half-formed memory of a mate? Or was that part of its design, to undermine my certainty and create a weakness it could exploit?

When they came to my cell some time later, their arrival caught me by surprise. The door crashed open and five of the paladins marched in, their boots and voices sounding far too loud after the quiet of my solitude. I rose as they lowered short, stabbing spears at me, each tipped with a long triangle of gleaming metal that looked wickedly sharp. Their scent washed over me, thick with aggression and anger, and it wasn't a combination that I could ignore, not if I wanted to keep their spears out of me. I backed away, lifting my hands in what I hoped was a calming gesture, but they kept advancing until my back was against the wall.

'He's secure,' one of the paladins shouted, loud despite the muffling effect of his helmet. A moment later the Cardinal stepped inside, trailed by two others in reddish robes, each toting a large book.

'So,' the Cardinal said, looking about the room. 'Your villainy is at an end, praise Drogah.' He gestured, and his followers laid the books down on the table. 'You might as well confess now and save us all a lot of unpleasantness.'

'You have the wrong man,' I said, mindful of the unwavering line of spearpoints levelled at my chest. 'I have nothing to confess.'

'Everyone has something to confess.' He moved to the books. 'You might have fooled that cantrip-peddling amateur, but you will not find such fertile ground for your lies and wickedness among the chosen of Drogah.'

Drogah was the name they'd given their god, but from the way the spearpoints drifted a little closer to me, I suspected that his words were more for the benefit of the spearmen. I decided not to say anything just yet and watched as he rapidly paged through the book, catching glimpses of coloured borders and charts that looked remarkably similar to those decorating the walls of Fronsac's study. Again, I opted not to say anything.

'Ah,' said the Cardinal, smoothing the pages of the book out. 'Now we can begin. I am going to ask you a question in a moment, and I want you to consider that I will know if you are lying to me. Believe me when I say that the consequences of a false answer will be decidedly unpleasant. Do you understand?'

'I understand,' I said, although I was more intrigued as to how he intended to divine the truth of my answers. I hadn't felt any attempt at compulsion, nor an activation of his magics. And they were magics, no matter how these so-called chosen of Drogah wanted to dress them up; there was no difference between Fronsac's magic and the Cardinal's, other than the way in which they created the bridge between their intent and the Songlines.

'Good, then we shall begin.'

I watched and listened closely as he called out a series of odd-sounding words and waved a glittering wand in a strange pattern; neither of them resembled any kind of magic that I could ever remember seeing, and I neither sensed nor felt any measure of magic touching me. It was mystifying, and also troubling. The one thing I had remembered, and had been confident about, was magic. Now it seemed that my knowledge and skills were somehow deficient.

'So now,' said the Cardinal, raising the wand once more. 'Is your name Stratus?'

'I said it was.'

I neither saw nor heard the command he gave the spearmen, but a moment later one of them drove the butt of their spear into my gut. The muscle there was dense enough that it was neither painful nor in any

173

way damaging, but the surprise made me grunt in way that seemed to satisfy them enough.

'That was not what I asked. Is your name Stratus?'

'Yes,' I said, straining for any trace of probing magic, but again finding none. Perhaps my sorcery was too weak at the moment to sense it.

'That's better. Are you an agent of the Worm Lord?'

'No,' I said. I was surprised that he'd gone straight to that, seeing as I had already openly denied it.

'Liar. Do you know what this is?' He held up some paper.

'No.'

'It is the account of an attack on one of our army staging areas. I won't bore you with all of the military jargon, but it describes in detail how a dark-skinned wizard, who named himself Stratus, killed Aron, the seneschal of the first army and more than two dozen other soldiers before vanishing into the night. A seneschal chosen by Prince Jean himself to lead the counter-attack that would have thwarted the enemy's advance on this city.'

I bit the inside of my lip as I considered this. I should have guessed that they would manage to take offence at the way I had left things at the camp.

'And now we find you, a dark-skinned wizard naming himself Stratus, in the same city, and necromancy afoot in the royal palace. So, I will ask you again. Are you an agent of the Worm Lord?'

'I am no agent of his. I understand that it may seem—'

'Brother Elq.'

I didn't have a chance to wonder what that meant as one of the paladins drove his spear into my shoulder with a quick thrust, the slim, tapering point biting deep. The pain followed a heartbeat behind the impact. I'd been beaten, shot with an arrow or two, and even impaled on a floorboard, but these were nothing like the hot, stabbing pain that radiated from the wound. I clutched at it with my other hand and felt the blood force its way between my fingers. I could do nothing else as

Brother Elq's spear came forward again, stopping a breath away from piercing my other shoulder. I could see my blood dripping from its well-honed point, providing a scarlet backdrop for the faint runes that now burned along the blade.

'Are you an agent of the Worm Lord?'

'No,' I said, and a moment later Elq's spear punched into my other shoulder, the metal rasping against the bone. I tried to pull away, but I was trapped against the wall. The other four spears remained levelled at me, and I felt a twinge of true fear curl through me as I forced my arm up to try to press the new wound closed. I felt the heat of my blood as it ran down the backs of my arms and rained down from my elbows.

'Are you an agent of the Worm Lord?'

As he spoke, the bloodied spear moved in again, the point lifting until it was aligned with my left eye, the tip blurring. I pressed myself against the wall as if I could somehow become part of it. I should not have been so passive, but it was too late. My arms were sorely weakened, my sorcery had not yet replenished itself and I had nowhere to go but into their barrier of spears. What option did I have?

'Yes,' I said.

I hated giving in like that, but if the choice was between losing some dignity or making it through the day with both eyes, I would always choose the latter.

'Well, well. It seems that I was right, after all. By the witnesses gathered here and the power invested in me by Drogah, I declare you a heretic and prisoner of the Church. Take him into custody.'

Chapter 20

They didn't offer any help with my wounds until we arrived at an uglier room with stone walls as thick as any castle I'd ever known. There wasn't even a blanket or a rug, just a bed of various grasses that had grown spongey in the damp air that wafted through a tiny slit of a window. A priest I did not recognise attended to me while the three paladins who accompanied him held their spears to my throat. I was annoyed when he cut my tunic away, but he gave no sign of noticing this as he daubed the wounds with a sweet-smelling unguent before he began to chant in a far more familiar way than the Cardinal, the repetition of the prayer creating the harmony required to let the Songlines provide the energy to fulfil his intention.

I felt his magic sink into the wounds and sighed with the immediate relief from the deep ache that had been growing steadily worse as the hours passed, and I decided to forgive him for ruining my tunic. I tensed and re-tensed my shoulders, forcing the damaged muscles to expand and contract, creating small tears in the newly formed tissue, forcing him to keep the connection alive for longer than he had intended to. The priest was reasonably adept, but I was counting on him not noticing the subtle manipulation, or believing it to be a natural shiver. My body's natural healing would account for these small tears easily enough, so I wasn't worried about them. What I wanted was him to feed me some more magic that I could use to boost the regeneration of my sorcery, and in that he did not disappoint. I dragged it out as long as I could, until I felt the intent behind the spell altering as he became curious, at which point I made a show of expressing my relief, and he soon ended the spell.

'Thank you,' I said, but he barely acknowledged this courtesy.

'Hands out,' said one of the paladins. I recognised his scent as the one called Elq, and I took a deep, slow breath, imprinting his scent on my memory.

I would find him.

Not today and probably not the day after, but I would find him and repay the injuries he had dealt me tenfold. For now though, I had to stay alive and healthy if that was ever going to happen. I held out my hands and let them fix the manacles on me once more; I was pleased to see that they sported the same flat, iron links as those they tried to use in the army camp.

Elq gave the chain a good shake and tried to push me against the wall, but I was tired of being pushed and stabbed. I resisted the shove, which was feeble by my standards, and was surprised when he met my gaze. Given how superstitious and charm-laden the paladins were, it surprised me that he would look into the eyes of a self-confessed sorcerer. Were their teachings so inadequate? It was too soon for me to act on it, but it was a valuable nugget of knowledge. He shoved again, and although it was barely harder than the first time, I obligingly shuffled backwards. I could almost taste the sense of triumph that he was exuding. I craned forward and took a deeper sniff of his scent. There was something about it, something out of balance, like the scent of carrion amid a flowerbed. I would need to plumb his thoughts or taste his brain to know for certain, but there was something strange about him. From his scent he was reacting to this utterly inconsequential act of dominance as if he had just copulated or won a great battle.

'What are you doing?' he snarled at me, giving me another shove. I was curious to see what happened, so again I resisted him. He punched me in the gut with a gauntleted fist but between my dense muscle and thick hide I hardly felt it. I let him think that it did, of course. I had enough knowledge of what men usually looked like when they were hit to indulge in some convincing mummery, and the three of them left shortly after.

I straightened up as the locks turned in the heavy door, and listened to them march away. I was still holding the noseful of his scent that I had gulped in as I'd bent forward, and I let it filter through into my nose as I leaned against the wall. It was enough to tell me that something in Brother Elq was entirely unstable. While such easy rage was no doubt a boon to a warrior, it didn't feel natural to me, even with my limited experience of being human. It was decidedly strange, but it may have been nothing more sinister than something in his diet, and without getting into his head in one form or the other, the best I could do was guess.

With my wounds tended to, my sorcery regenerating and the walls too thick to break, there was little I could do now but wait. Soothed by the release from the pain, I laid myself down to sleep, but on the stone rather than the spoiled grasses. It wasn't easy with the manacles, so I took the opportunity to snap the chain. I didn't have the leverage to remove the cuffs, but it was nonetheless an improvement. Despite the residual discomfort, when I woke the fall of shadows told me that a full day had passed, and I felt much better for the rest, if hungrier. The priest's healing worked on the same principles as what I did for myself and by extension, Tatyana, but his included an element of energy injection. But now the energy that the priest had shared had been used up, partly because my body needed more than what he could give and also because a good portion of it had been utilised to shore up my reservoir of sorcery.

When I sat down and tried to clear my thoughts, the thing inside me was restive and its sense of being trapped was starting to infect me too. I pondered sleeping some more but that gentle oblivion was denied to me as well, so I turned to pacing instead. It helped at first, but it also stirred up faint, disjointed memories of another place and time and a sense of growing anger that I could neither understand nor offer an outlet for. I wandered to the slit that served as a window, but rather than helping, the cool evening air brought me the sound of humans and animals calling out to each other as they went about their lives freely. Their every cry seemed to mock me as I stood there in my new prison, and all I wanted was to tear the stone apart and fall upon them, killing until they were all silenced.

Where brute force had failed it, the beast had now employed its cunning to creep up on me, whispering where it had shouted before. I felt its chest swell in triumph as I gave voice to the swell of anger in me and sent it rolling from the window in a wordless cry that was half scream and half growl. I had to, for otherwise it would surely have burst out of me.

'No,' I said, pushing away from the window, the awareness of how far into the beast's influence I had wandered sinking in as the echoes faded. More than anything, it was the sense of kinship that startled me. For a moment, the anger hadn't felt alien or oppressive, it had felt righteous. *Deserved.*

And as much as I didn't want to acknowledge it, it was an unavoidable reminder that whatever was inside me was, and had always been, part of me.

I was still trying to digest how that made me feel when I heard the sound of voices in the passage outside the door. Now wasn't a good time for a paladin to put his face in mine, although the beast had other ideas about that. I could feel its anger reaching out to me like a flame seeking kindling. The door swung open and a paladin stomped in, his arrogance manifesting in his posture and scent, every clink and thud of his armour fanning the flame within me.

I could not remember wanting to kill something more than I did him at that moment.

My hands had already balled themselves into fists when Tatyana stepped into the room behind him, the sudden wash of her scent clean and familiar. I felt my sorcery flicker in recognition of the mote of it that lived within her and pulse the stronger for it.

'Leave us,' she said to the paladin. He plonked the lantern down on the table and slammed the door shut behind him with no little vigour.

'Tatyana,' I said, clearing the thickness that the now fading anger had brought on from my throat. She ignored me and dropped to her hands and knees to peer at the bottom of the door. When she rose she held a finger to her lips, a gesture I recognised.

'I bring a message from Prince Lucien,' she said, tugging at her ear and pointing to the door. 'He expresses his great sadness at your confession to collusion with our great enemy and the betrayal of the friendship he has extended to you.'

As she spoke she walked up to me and leaned in close, pressing her lips to my ear.

'Is it true?' she whispered. 'About the seneschal's camp?'

I understood her gambit now; the paladin was listening. 'Tell the prince that I still hold his friendship in the highest regard,' I said in my normal tone, then leaned in as close to her as she had to me. 'Yes,' I said, pitching my voice low. 'But it was not what they say it is.'

'I will convey your words to Prince Lucien,' she said out loud, then moved close once more and grabbed my arm, her nails digging into my skin. 'What did you do to me?'

'You have my gratitude,' I said out loud. Then quieter, 'You know what I did. You were dying.'

'I know you healed me. But that isn't all of it, is it?' she hissed, shaking my arm. 'What did you do? What of you did you leave inside me?'

'What do you mean?' I asked, not bothering to whisper it.

'The dreams,' she said, glancing towards the door. 'We don't have much time left before they realise Lucien didn't send me. The dreams, Stratus. You have to stop them.'

'The dreams,' I echoed, confused.

'Yes, the bloody dreams!'

'What dreams?'

She stared at me for a few moments before releasing my arm and taking a step back. 'You don't know.'

'Tell me,' I said. Something like fear had drifted into her scent, and at first I thought she wasn't going to reply, but she folded her arms and looked back up at me.

'It's dark.' The pitch of her voice quavered. 'I'm trapped somewhere and I'm in a room. A prison. No, a cage. It keeps getting smaller and smaller until I can't breathe and the bars burn my skin. I'm trapped, and someone keeps calling my name, telling me I promised them something.' She paused and took a breath that rattled in her throat. 'But it's your name, not mine, that they're calling.' Another pause. 'The voice, Stratus,' she said, and now it was fear that I could scent. 'I can't hear that voice again.'

'Does it sound angry?' I asked, an idea beginning to worm its way into my mind.

'Angry?' she said. 'God's beard, no. It's the most awful, heart-rending thing I've ever heard in my life. I've . . . done things I'm not proud of, and I've been witness to worse, and those are memories I try not to revisit. But when I hear it, it all comes back and I can't stop it.'

She took a shuddering breath and smoothed her sleeves with unnecessary aggression while I stared at her, momentarily dumbfounded. As far as I knew, I had never heard of such a thing. My memories and understanding of my sorcery were the one element that I was confident about, but this found no home among them. Was it linked to my healing of her, or was it something sinister, a sending of the Worm Lord's, such as those that Fronsac guarded the princes against?

'I need to see them,' I said. She had given up all pretence of whispering, so I did the same.

'What?'

'The dreams. I need to see them.'

'I don't want to,' she said, taking a step back. 'Just take your magic out of me.'

'It doesn't work like that, Tatyana. The wounds are healed, but my blood is now part of yours. Even if I knew of a way to extract it, doing it would most likely poison what was left. It would kill you.'

She turned and walked to the little window, taking deep breaths of the fresher air.

'I told you the truth when I said that I do not know who or what I am. These dreams may be part of that.' I took care to keep my voice even. 'The more I learn, the better chance I have of controlling my own future.'

'What about mine?' If my hearing wasn't as good as it was, I might have missed that. I took a few steps closer, close enough to hear her again and to let me taste the uncertainty and prevailing fear in her scent.

'I believe our futures may be linked, to . . .' I meant to say 'to some extent', meaning that I would surely be able to help her once mine was clearer, but she cut me off with a sudden turn and a jabbing finger that she nearly thrust right into my mouth.

'I know that, you idiot!' The finger jabbed at me again and I was hard-pressed not to snap at it. 'What do you think that lot' – now it jabbed towards the door – 'will do if they knew about what you did in that house? I'm guessing you haven't told them yet, or they'd already have strung you up.'

'I've told them nothing.'

'So you say, but Polsson is strutting around the palace like he owns it.'

I shrugged the comment away. It wasn't Cardinal Polsson that I was interested in. 'The dreams, Tatyana. I need them.'

She spun away as if I had slapped her. Strode to the end of the room and then back again, her arms still folded across her chest. It was interesting how her scent shifted as she worked through whatever argument she was having with herself. I couldn't help but wonder if it was because she simply had a stronger scent than most or if there was something in the sorcerous link that we shared that made me more perceptive towards it.

'All right,' she said after her third circuit of the room. 'Two conditions though. First, you're not stabbing or eating any part of me. And second, you stop doing that.'

'Doing what?'

'Sniffing me. Do you have any idea how unnerving that is?'

'I hadn't realised that I was doing it.' Which was untrue, but I simply hadn't expected anyone to notice. The people in the city seemed to have no hesitation in sneezing, sniffing and coughing all over each other continuously so I fully expected a sniff here and there would hardly be worth mentioning.

'Well, you are, and I don't like it.'

'You have an interesting scent.'

'Gods, Stratus. That doesn't make it better.'

I heard the dim echo of voices from the passageway outside. 'They're coming back,' I said.

'How do we do this? I'm not sure I'll be able to get back in here.'

'Where am I anyway?'

'Saint Tomas Sepulchre, near the lower east wall. The paladins have taken it and several other churches over as barracks.'

'What's a sepulchre?' My tongue stumbled over the unfamiliar word.

'Huh? It's a church for the mortuary priests. They hold services for the dead.'

Something stirred in my mind as she said it, but now wasn't the time to dwell.

'I need to get out of here.' The voices in the passageway were louder now and I could hear the familiar rattle of armour and keys.

'That's impossible. You'd need more than a catapult to break these old walls and there are paladins everywhere.'

I patted the ancient stones. 'Leave that to me. I will wait for you at their lair.'

She only had time to nod her agreement before the door swung open and several paladins raced in, their sharp, aggression-tinged scents quickly overwhelming hers as they fanned out, their wicked lances raised and ready.

'You. Harlot. You have no right to be here,' bawled one who I took to be in command by the white in his beard.

I saw Tatyana stiffen as he addressed her, but I touched her arm to distract her. It was going to be hard enough for me to break out of here, and I didn't need the added complication of having to free or avenge her at the same time. She shook off my touch and stalked away between the paladins, giving the greybeard a hearty shove that made him stagger when he refused to move out of her way. She stormed off before he could recover, leaving them to make a hasty exit from the room to catch up with her. She was fierce. I liked it.

Chapter 21

Faith is a strange thing. I do not think that I have ever had any myself, at least not the sort that humans do with all their churches and temples and incomprehensible rules given to them by their gods. No, I had never had that sort of faith, although I had encountered it. But the heart of faith, the truth of it, was that no matter what guise it took, in the end it amounted to believing in something that you have no reason to believe is real. Which made it a bit like sorcery in many ways, and adds to the irony that while a natural-born human sorcerer is extremely rare, men were able to create their own sorcery in churches. Like St Tomas.

I had no idea who Saint Tomas was or what he was famous for other than being dead, or perhaps for having died in some spectacular way, but the countless thousands of men and women who had come to kneel in the church and pour their emotions and intent into the stones had a different view.

It was no mystery that the oldest and grandest of man's churches were built either upon or close to places in the natural world where the veil was thin enough that the Songlines were nearly audible. I could easily imagine some long-dead shaman discovering that if he did his little ritual in one particular place he had better results, and so passed that secret on to his successors. And so on and so on for all those centuries until they finally stacked stone upon stone and named the building, an empowering act in itself.

With the church lying so near to a Songline, the focused devotion from all those hundreds of years of emotional rituals, sermons and prayers would have combined with the inherent magical radiation to thoroughly saturate the stone. In effect, by praying to a god who most likely did not exist, the humans' prayers had gradually willed it into being; it was the ghostly residue of their forefathers' prayers that offered the worshippers comfort, as theirs would one day do for as yet unborn generations.

I was thinking this as I lay naked upon the stone floor of my room, my limbs stretched out so that as much of me as possible was in contact with them. It had been hard going to sense the spirit of this place at first as it had no specific signature, nothing that resembled a single name or nature like a man's magic would. It was the product of thousands of different wills and personas, a choir of broken notes that time had fused into a new whole. I didn't chase after it, nor did I call to it. I waited and listened, until all that I could hear was the song of St Tomas.

I knew that I could never hope to replicate it, not all of it. But like with any pack or swarm, there were some within it who stood out. These were the ghostly remnants of those who had given more to this place than any others, and like a hunter selecting the finest stag, I carefully picked these ghosts out from the rest and learned their song well enough to attach myself to them. I could bind no more than a handful of these to myself at one time, twisting the echoes of their names together into a whispering, rhythmic chant.

It was a dangerous gambit, all of this was. If someone heard and burst in, I may not have enough time to unbind the energy safely, which could very well force it to manifest inside me in an unpredictable but spectacularly fatal manner.

So it was a risk, a grave one, but if I was to control my own destiny I would need answers and power, neither of which were going to come to me if I sat here and did nothing. I was confident that I could break through the door given time, but where to then? I knew that I was physically superior to men, but there were many of them and only one of me, and their enchanted spears could bite deep. Perhaps Fronsac or

Jean would champion me, but that meant remaining here, caged, and waiting to be rescued like some forlorn thing from a bard's tale.

The beast didn't like the risk. I could feel it stirring inside me, clawing and snapping at the fringes of my mind like an old wolf, but as it liked the idea of waiting for men to decide our fate even less, my hope was that it would leave me to fight this on my terms, rather than driven by its mindless thrashing.

I let go of that thought and began to concentrate on my breathing, letting the sensation of the air moving into and through my body become everything to me. My body grew lighter and lighter until I felt the chains that bound my spirit to it loosen. I rose above my body and opened my eyes. Below me my body lay as if asleep, connected to me by what looked like nothing more than a snake spun from newly poured gold. I could see dark, smoky shapes shying away from the light it shed and knew them for the spirits of dead men that had been too weak to cross over to the world of the dead. The air was strangely thick with them, but then this was a cathedral to the dead and they were not what interested me.

I flexed my sorcery and sheathed my form in the same golden light as that which connected me to my body and the cloud of spirits drew back from me like smoke stirred by a fierce wind. The light was born of the Songlines, from the essence of life itself, and was as unbearable for a spirit as the cold of death was to the living. I rose through the silent spirits and the roof beyond, up towards the flow of energy that beckoned to me.

The Songlines were not static; they flowed like a river, and created channels in much the same way. If you cut a wizard open carefully enough, you would see the faint scars in his physical flesh, especially if he used stored energy, like most I had seen did. New energies entering somewhere where a particular flow of energy is old and strong, like it was here, create an imperfection in the flow, like stones thrown into a smooth river whose ripples you could follow back to their source.

I could see the path of the tributary of the Songlines that flowed through St Tomas now as a bank of thick cloud shot through with golden lightning. I could feel its power greeting me like a warm breeze, but to take comfort from that was dangerous. Once I passed into the cloud I would be wholly within a realm of elemental power where reality had no place and a stray thought could spell my doom.

I had no lungs in this form, so had to settle for thinking about taking a deep, calming breath as I crossed into the cloud. Delicate filaments of lightning flashed from its depths, holding to me and pulling me into its thundering depths.

I sunk into the power of the Songlines like the river it was, letting that perfect golden light close over me. Rather than fight it, I let my consciousness be carried away on the flow as I concentrated on seeking the songs of the ghosts I had identified as belonging to Saint Tomas. My attachment to them would serve as my anchor, keeping me within the pattern of energy that surrounded the sepulchre and preventing me from being drawn deeper into the full majesty of the Songlines and being lost for ever.

Chapter 22

The skill to walk your dreams is a difficult one to master without any natural talent, but is essential if you would seek to progress to the deeper mysteries of our art. The magical energies we are exposed to can bestow a potency on dreams, and with the correct training, the strongest of us may reach into the material world. Acolytes who display an aptitude for this gift are marked with the touch of the Dreamsinger and should be kept apart from others for their own safety.

An Introduction to the Path of Power
by Tiberius Talgoth, Archmage

The flow of energy here was slower than the elemental surge of the Songlines, but any prolonged, direct contact with it was just as dangerous. Errant thoughts could seduce you, trapping you in a cycle of relived memories, and with time as fluid as the power that flowed around you, even if you broke free of the cycle you could find that you have returned to a body that had starved to death or been slain. A bad or violent memory could cause you to relive that pain or injury, your body opening and bleeding wherever it lay awaiting the return of your spirit.

The echoes that even now guided me through St Tomas had suffered such fates and had chosen to remain here and live in those same memories that had doomed them for all time, rather than face the cold and uncertainty of what waited beyond death.

I was conscious of all this as I drifted along what I saw as a golden river, gently absorbing its power and stretching out my consciousness to gain an impression of St Tomas as it existed in the material world. It was akin to the scrying that Fronsac did, although he used tools to navigate his way rather than exposing his naked mind to the power, demonstrating his wisdom. I had passed through St Tomas perhaps a dozen times, extending the picture of it in my mind with every pass, and had begun the process of pulling back to my body when the attack came.

The first indication I had was a glimpse of a fin cutting through the 'water' towards me. I froze at the sight of it. This was no figment of my imagination, and I barely had time to realise this before it dived under the surface and wrapped itself around me, the touch of it cold enough to make my concentration slip as it pulled me under with it.

I didn't need to breathe given that this form had no lungs, but as with all magic, the symbolism was more important. I had a glimpse of a mass of translucent flesh and too many mouths as it squirmed and thrashed around me, but the advantage of surprise was fading. I was a sorcerer, born to the Songlines, not some mere meddling wizard. I flexed my will and my hands blazed with energy as I gripped it and tore it asunder, spilling what looked like grease and blood into the water. As it dissolved into a foul stew, I saw the dull and unpleasant cord that linked it to the material word and hastened to follow it before the Songlines washed it away. It was difficult to see at first, but the images slowly resolved themselves into a dark, low-ceilinged hall lined with stone boxes and watched over by a skeleton carved of stone, a shroud swept behind it like tattered wings.

I let myself rise to the surface as the images faded, feeling pleased with myself as I did so. My discipline had slipped, and even as I realised that I should not be thinking about how quiet the beast was, I felt it wake within me.

Almost immediately the waters around me began to thrash and churn, as if a storm was about to hit. I tried to subdue it, but it could sense the power, the potential around me, and wanted to reach out for it. I did not even want to consider what the consequence of that would be, but more pressing was the way the semblance of the Songline was changing, the structure my will had imposed on it crumbling and twisting.

The presence of the beast inside my mind was disrupting the harmony of my connection to both the ghosts of Saint Tomas that served as my anchor and the Songlines themselves. I could feel the changes around me and I desperately tried to push the beast away but the damage was done. I was losing my anchor and being pulled back into the Songlines themselves.

I felt myself sliding into the depths where the power was strongest. The energy burrowed into me like ice creeping into a rock, slipping in where it could and seeking to crack me open. I knew that if it succeeded, it would grind my sense of self into its purest essence, returning me to a note of pure energy and harmony. Even if I'd had time to consider that it was trying to kill me without any malice, it wouldn't have been of much comfort. I held onto the golden cord that would return me to my physical body and the safety of reality and sent my spirit racing along it, pursued by a surge of power from the Songlines.

It was a race, and one that my mind interpreted as me trying to hold a door closed against a flood, and because of where I was and what I was doing, that image became my reality. I could feel the water rushing over my feet, and the coarse, iron-bound wood against my skin as I threw myself against it, pushing back against the elemental power that wanted to force it open and rush in, drowning everything that threatened its great harmony.

I felt splinters gouge my skin and the soles of my feet tearing as I ground and dug them into the floor, seeking more purchase to prop me up. My tightly controlled thoughts were springing loose, and each that slipped out weakened me. If I had no idea who I was, or even what, how could I hold myself together? I felt the door that was my will bowing under the pressure, small jets of glowing water spraying from the edges as it slid open by a fraction, then another. I heard the wood cracking, the sound as sharp and loud as the whips that had once cracked outside my cage. I was losing the fight, and even thinking it accelerated the process. The wood was going to give way, and I would drown in that power. I would float in it and slowly dissolve until there was nothing left of me.

I felt the beast stir to life once more and I felt its molten gaze upon me, but I could spare no ounce of will to fight it. I could feel it taking shape behind me and I tried not to wonder what it looked like. If it attacked me now, I had no idea what would happen to me, or it. But I knew without doubt that if I surrendered to the flood, I would vanish for ever.

We both would.

I could feel its presence strengthening behind me, and I felt the moment when it took shape, the strange reality we were in bending as its form distended the space and filled it with a hot, dry heat. For a moment, I could sense its curiosity and wonder but these were cut off by a wall of rage and frustration that slammed down between us. There was nothing I could do about that though and could only brace myself for whatever would happen next.

No attack came though. Instead I felt it slam into the door behind me, putting its shoulder against it, close enough to me that I could feel its breath on the back of my neck, scalding and foul with the reek of charred meat and swamp gas. I heard its purring roar in my chest as it pushed with me, closing the door that threatened us both, and slowly the waters that had been flowing out turned to narrow sprays as we forced it to close. As soon as the door was shut I felt its claws upon my shoulder, pulling me towards it.

I woke on the floor of my prison cell, my legs kicking me backwards so that my back hit the wall hard enough to spill dust from the ancient mortar. I sat there, slumped against the wall and still enough that the mice re-emerged from their holes, as my mind reassembled itself after the shock of its ejection from the Song lines. The mist slowly cleared from my vision, and soon after the ringing echoes began to fade from my ears. I could still sense the energy around me, but that was as much a side effect of my foray into it as the fact that my reservoir of sorcery had been replenished in full.

I felt whole again, despite the chills that danced across my skin when I thought of that breath on the back of my neck and the hand upon my shoulder. A shoulder that now had five pale marks scored upon it, like the scars where some forgotten claw had bit deep. The implications of what had happened were too much for me to even think about at this point. I needed to escape first, and whatever game the beast was playing would have to wait.

I rose from the floor and pulled myself into my clothes again. They had replaced my ruined tunic with a shapeless thing that was neither white nor brown and looked disappointingly like what the paladins were wearing. I contemplated going without it, seeing how much easier it was for my dark hide to blend into the shadows, but I had learned that a casual glimpse of a naked man would surely cause more alarm than one dressed in a simple garment.

I moved to the door and lay my hand over the lock, calling upon my newly restored sorcery with an ease that was a world apart from what it had been the day before. I couldn't risk the locks or door being warded against magic, or me. It would be a cruel folly to have my plans stymied at the first obstacle, but there was no such ward in place, only a well-oiled mechanical thing that clicked and rolled as I gently pushed at it with sorcerous fingers. The bolt withdrew, and I pulled the door open and peered into the passage beyond. It was a steeply vaulted and narrow space as if built for tall, emaciated men, but poorly lit and heavily decorated with carved skulls, and the close atmosphere was made worse by the lingering reek of old incense. I kept low and tasted the air, sifting out the sweet spiciness of burned resin and the older traces of man-scent.

There had been a guard nearby very recently, and from the dispersal of his scent I guessed that he was a roving sentry rather than the static kind.

One guard. I actually felt mildly insulted, the beast even more so.

I closed the door behind me and followed the guard's scent, my bare feet soundless on the stone. The air became fresher as I moved along, the source of the breeze a narrower passage that split off from the hallway up ahead. I crept around the corner carefully. This narrower passage was actually a walkway around the edge of an empty space that dropped away to a cobbled yard some five or six body-lengths below, the stones gleaming under the light of the lantern carried by the guards crossing it. I crouched down once more and willed my blood vision to life. The guard I had been following was now clearly visible where he stood talking to another. It looked like they were eating something, which immediately prompted an accusatory grumble from my stomach.

Two guards. There were enough shadows between us to make me feel confident about getting close enough to strike with an element of surprise, but there were also enough shadows that I could slip away without them noticing. I tapped a fingernail against my teeth as I mulled it over. As much as I didn't like leaving armed men at my back, stealth had its merits too. With one last look at the wrapped bundle they were eating from, I turned back to the main passage and made my way towards the narrow, winding staircase it led to. It was an awkward and tight space, even without the profusion of skulls and winged babies that protruded from every other corner. I took a moment to silently curse the builders as I scraped my way down to ground level. Freedom was only a few doors away.

Chapter 23

The lower level of the church was saturated with the smell of men, a fug that no amount of incense and cheap lamp oil could dislodge. The stairs that I had used led into a small hall with two ways out. The first of these was across the courtyard I had seen from above, and the second through a set of large doors flanked by two deep recesses that were crammed with human skulls. These were not the stone-carved ones that watched from every corner, but actual skulls, the skin and hair long since given to dust and their teeth for evermore bared in welcoming grins. For the entrance to the main hall of the church it wasn't the most enticing of vistas, even for me, and had I not taken the time to explore the building via the Songlines, I might have chosen the courtyard. The latter was a tempting choice, but I knew that it passed by several sleeping chambers that were full of men.

I sent a pulse of sorcery to douse the torches that were flickering along the wall, then moved forward through the shadows. I was perhaps halfway across the hall when I felt something familiar tug at my mind. Familiar, but unwelcome. Whatever I had encountered in the Songline was close by, and most likely directly beneath me. I might have passed without noticing had I not woken my sorcery, but now that I knew it was there I could not ignore it. I squatted in the dark, torn between the twin need to escape and to find answers.

Every moment I lingered here risked the discovery of my escape, and with it a gruesome end, courtesy of the swarm of paladins currently infesting the cathedral. Even as I thought it, I saw two of them move into the courtyard, one of whom was carrying a brightly burning lantern. As strong and fast as I was, those short, stabbing spears of theirs had proved more than equal to the task of making holes in me. Given the warriors' unstable emotional states, I doubted that it would take much prompting for them to switch from capturing to slaughtering me, something that both the beast and I preferred to avoid. Whatever I was going to do though, I had to do it soon because the conversation that had delayed the guards had now ended, and they were walking straight towards me, the light from their lantern stripping away the shadows that concealed me with every step they took. *Their lantern.*

I smiled in the dark as I wove a new sorcerous construct, pleased that I had kept it ready. Once I was satisfied with the shape of it, I fed some more energy into it and released it. It was soundless and invisible to all but me as it sailed out and wrapped itself around the lantern, joining with the existing light and flame and magnifying both a hundred times over before the man carrying it could so much as blink.

The glass exploded with a sharp crack, spraying burning oil across both of them. They bellowed as the blazing oil took hold in their beards and clothing. I doubted it would kill them, but that wasn't my primary intention. While they screamed and others rushed to their aid, I dashed through the remaining shadows and slipped through the skull-draped doors.

As it turned out, it led into the main church part of St Tomas, either the chapel or cathedral; the different names that they gave the same sort of place made little sense to me. I stepped to the side as I closed the door behind me and looked around. Aside from being taller and larger, the chapel was also more interesting than the building I had just left, with more leering skeletons and winged knights adorning each of the twenty-one pillars as if they were spilling from the roof. If the hall beyond had been awash with skulls and motifs of human death, the cathedral was positively drowning in them. Each of the columns was softly lit by globes of magical light, the golden ambience leaving the roof draped with deep shadows and making it seem as if the hollow-eyed menagerie was descending upon whoever was sat below. The workmanship was astounding, but to me it seemed as if their purpose was to cow rather than comfort the mourners gathered below.

I dragged my gaze away from the skeletons and down to the score of figures kneeling in front of the altar. They seemed oblivious to my intrusion and continued chanting quietly, the sound carrying far in the cavernous space, their white robes and heavier build suggested that they were paladins. Unfortunately, there were also a few priests in the chapel, their dark robes in stark contrast to those of the paladins. One such priest was making his way towards me, his hands hidden in his sleeves but a smile on his face. It was too late to back away or hide, so I stayed where I was.

'Greetings, brother,' he said in a quiet voice, his hands sliding from his sleeves. Neither held a weapon, but I stayed alert. 'Are you here for the Cardinal's benediction?'

'No,' I said, forcing a smile. 'I had one already, thank you. I was just leaving.' I gestured to the door on the far side which, by my reckoning, should have led to the main exit.

'To the crypt?' His smile was gone, but he was still being quiet.

I bit back the curse that threatened to spill from my lips and kept my smile in place instead. 'Yes. Thank you. Brother.'

'Of course.'

He stepped out of the way. I had been worried that he would be a bit more suspicious, but his smile was back.

'Thank you,' I said again, and walked towards the door to the crypt. I didn't need to look over my shoulder to know that he was still watching me. I pushed the door open and stepped inside as if that was exactly where I had always intended to go. It was dark in there, which fortunately wasn't a hindrance, and soon enough the clear, unwavering light swelled from the sorcerous orb floating just above my left hand, revealing a bucket and some torches nearby. However, I had no desire to add breathing greasy smoke to the list of things that were going wrong.

As I reckoned it, I was there already so I might as well go and see what it was that was disturbing the natural energies of the church. I sent the orb of light out ahead of me as I descended the stairs that the passage led to, its constant, even light letting me find my way to the small chamber at the bottom. It was little more than a swelling rather than an actual room, and had several ornamental slabs on the wall, each of these heavily carved with the usual incomprehensible human writing. Three equally dark passages led from the chamber, and I closed my eyes and carefully extended my sorcery until I felt the unpleasant tug of the dark magic once more, not so much pulling me to the right as telling me to avoid it at all costs. Of course, I ignored that advice and chose that passage, and the light that I sent ahead of me showed me yet more stairs, although far steeper and more numerous.

I passed several other small landings, each of which bore more inscriptions carved into the walls and not a few with niches stuffed with skulls, some half-smothered in wax or adorned with ribbons and cheap medallions that the air had long since turned green and lumpy. I was beginning to regret my decision to press on with this course of action since I would have to climb my way back up, something that would be long and tiring even without the prospect that I may have to do so in a rush. I put those worries aside as the undisturbed air noticeably began to thicken with the reek of dark magic. Even though I knew that it wasn't a physical odour like scat, I still found myself breathing through my mouth. By the time I reached the chamber at the bottom there were three doors again, two of which were plain wood and the third bound with iron.

I could sense the dark magic somewhere behind the iron-bound door, the stench of it hanging in the air and making me breathe through a folded corner of my tunic in a vain attempt to stifle some of it. A wooden sign was nailed to the door, whatever advice or instruction that was painted on it remained lost on me, as was the blob of wax with a pattern in the corner. As I saw it, anything that only merited such poor workmanship wasn't worth taking seriously anyway, and with a derisive snort for their efforts I tried to open the door. It was of course locked, but what was surprising was the discovery that it was warded too.

I picked myself up off the floor and shook my head to clear the painful ringing from my ears. The ward had triggered a thunderclap of sorts, and if I had been a human thief kneeled in front of the lock, rather than a lazy sorcerer leaning against the door jamb using magic, the explosive change in pressure might have left me trying to pick my face up off the floor instead. It was a stupid thing to have done, and a painful reminder that complacency could, and most likely would, kill me. I was quite certain that I was deep enough that the sound would not reach beyond the lower half of the stairwell, although there was a chance that whoever had laid it on the door might have felt it activate.

There was little I could do about it though, and I took some consolation in that now that the ward had expended itself, opening the mechanical part of the lock was as easy as I'd thought it would be the first time. The door swung inward, but whatever sound it made was lost to the ongoing ringing in my ears, and I sent the orb in while I peered around the edge of the doorway, my lesson learned. A hall lay beyond, albeit one that was wider than it was high, the roof a low, curving structure that rose to barely an arm's length above my head in the centre and tapered to meet the walls at the height of my waist above regularly spaced squares of paler stone. Four thick pillars stood in the centre, one at each corner of the stone crypt that squatted between them, one of the sides broken open. And there, perched on the lid of the crypt like some monstrous crow, was a skeleton carved of stone, its shroud swept behind it like tattered wings. The strange enchantment that I had encountered in my vision was anchored somewhere nearby.

I approached the crypt slowly, my sorcery testing the stone, floor and roof for any trace of wards hidden among the glyphs carved into them. I could sense traces of enchantments, but nothing active, suggesting that whatever protections had been woven into the chamber had been triggered or had dissipated through age and neglect. I did, however, sense that while the source of the taint I felt was near, it wasn't focused on the crypt. Intrigued, I stopped and turned in a slow circle, silencing the voice in my head that was berating me for spending my sorcery so freely, and concentrating on the slippery, unpleasant sensation of the dark magic pushing back at mine. It seemed to be everywhere, pulling at me from each side as I turned, and I felt my confusion turning towards a sort of panic before I realised why. A few long strides brought me to the closest of the pale squares in the wall, although I had to duck and shuffle to reach it beneath the low roof. I moved to put my hand against the stone but a crackling arc of purple light kissed my palm. *Interesting.*

I broke off a chunk of the skeleton's stony cape and used it to smash a hole in the pale stone, letting the ward waste itself on the masonry in a flash of hot purple light. As I had suspected, it was a covering for a void, rather than part of the wall. The stench increased sharply for a moment, then dissipated enough that my eyes stopped watering. I bent lower and sent my light into the hole, stripping away the mystery of the darkness and revealing several human corpses laid on top of one another. It didn't take much to sense that these weren't just dead men; the cold touch of the negative, dead energy that saturated them wafted out of the hole like the northern wind. I cringed back from the unnatural feel of it, then made my way to the next pale slab, and the next after that.

There were nine in total, each with between four and six bodies in each, save for the very last one, which held a long box packed with glass bottles surrounded by straw. I peered into the hole once it was removed, but there was nothing else save for a long-dead rat, its rank fur rippling with the maggots at work beneath it. Curious, I lifted a bottle out, smashed the top off and carefully sniffed it. **Wine.** I could smell nothing else and was almost tempted to taste it.

I set the bottle down and peered into the hole again, the unforgiving white light of my orb showing me the rat that lay at the back. I was about to move away when its head lifted and turned towards me, and despite its eyes being little more than sunken hollows, I knew it was *looking* at me. I watched in morbid fascination as it righted itself, limbs shaking as if palsied, and began pulling itself towards me. It was quiet enough down here that I could hear the click and scrape of its little claws and the wet burbling of its distended gut as it dragged along the bottom of the hole.

'What are you?' I whispered, hunkering down outside the hole, unable to tear my eyes from the impossibility of what I was witnessing. It is one thing to know *of* something but quite another to be confronted by it. Which is why it was nearly upon me before I even began to consider the possibility that I might be in danger. The shivering that had made its sides twitch had grown more frantic, until its loosened fur undulated like a pennant in the wind. The great muscles in my legs had just begun to respond to my mind's entreaty to move me away from the wretched creature when its jaws yawned open and, in a series of contractions whose violence broke all of its bones, the rat vomited itself inside out.

Cold mucus and jellied blood burst from it as I half fell, half leaped backwards, but it was not that bloody corona that made me cry out in horror. That honour was reserved for the mass of pale, writhing worms that coiled and uncoiled amid the slime and blood, the pointed tips of their bodies waving in the air like the rat's whiskers once had.

I hesitated only slightly before my sorcery burned them and the remains of the rat into a blackened crust. I stayed well back as the smoke rose and vanished against the roof. A movement on the floor drew my eye and I saw that several of the worms had been spewed far enough out that they had escaped the fire, and were now pulling themselves towards me. Even as I readied my fire once more, their movement faltered and became erratic. I waited, and in the span of a few breaths they sagged and lay still. I held back a bit longer, but they remained limp. Whatever they were, they were not very robust, although that was scant comfort. There was something terrible in the way that they had moved and I burned them from existence just to be safe. I stared at the charred remains of the rat, replaying the horror of it in my mind, the mockery of life that it represented.

'He vomited his guts out, then exploded.' I spoke the words, but my ears heard them spoken in Crow's voice. Two such deaths could be no coincidence, not when the thread of necromancy linked them. I poured the contents of the broken bottle onto the floor, and while I could see no writhing shapes in the wine, I had no doubt that it was somehow cursed. This whole area was steeped in dark magic. To feel it here, so close to the Songlines, was as sickening as it was worrying. It was a pervasive force, and while not strong enough to resist the constant, cleansing action of the natural energies here, like a splinter in the flesh over time, its presence could sicken the area. Men wouldn't be able to sense it as I did, but they'd start to feel discomfort nearby nonetheless, and as the worship faltered so would the stream of energy, and perhaps eventually enough for its taint to become the new normal. I knew that I had little time before the paladins and their ilk came looking for me, if they weren't already, but I could not bring myself to leave while this place festered so.

I needed a fire, one as hot and bold as I could manage, and while my sorcery could certainly start one, I wasn't yet strong enough to do more than boil the wine away. I wanted to obliterate it, to leave nothing more than a sooty stain as I had with the rat. And so it was that I found myself carrying the empty crate up the staircase. It was as exhausting as I had thought it would be, even more so with the awkward crate. Luck was with me for a change though, for once I was back in the upper passages I quickly found what I was looking for – a storeroom laden with supplies. I packed what I needed into the crate and began the arduous journey back down the stairs, strengthening my legs and back with sorcerous energy so that I did not reach the bottom at a speed I would not appreciate.

Moving the bodies was far harder than carrying the laden crate had ever been. I didn't want to touch them, but their skin was slick with a bitter oil of some sort and I was forced to grip hard to move them. Even the beast was disquieted by the feel of them, but as usual it offered no new insights as to why, and I cursed it while I laboured alone.

Eventually it was done, and I hoped it would be enough. I lit the first of the kindling, and basked my hands in the flame to try to rid myself of the itching discomfort left by the touch of all that dead skin. Whether it helped or not only time would tell, but I at least felt better for it. With a groan that would be repeated several more times, I climbed the stairs once more, cradling the two bottles of wine I had kept to my chest. I stopped on the topmost landing and, setting the bottles aside, put my hands to the large barrel that I had left there, ready to push it off the edge.

'What are you doing?'

I stopped and turned, surprise slowing my thoughts. Two paladins stood at the corner of the passage, sputtering torches in one hand and swords in the other. I silently cursed the priest as they advanced on me.

'Step back,' said one, gesturing with his sword.

'Just a moment,' I said, offering them a fake smile before straightening my arms and legs and tipping the barrel over the edge.

They raced forward as it fell. The first one let his curiosity overcome him, and it was a simple matter to shove him over the edge when he stopped to see the barrel smash into the ground below. As he fell I heard the 'whump' of the lantern oil igniting as it met the fire I had kindled. He might have screamed but I was too busy avoiding his companion's sword to notice. He was quick, and he might have been able to hurt me, but he made the mistake of calling for help, which was enough of a distraction for me to grab his sword hand and spin him around. A foot to the back sent him falling into the chimney that the stairwell had become.

I snatched up the bottles and hurried along to the exit. It was tempting to watch the flame race up the stairwell, but the smoke was too thick and choking. I found myself looking at three priests as I stepped out and shut the door behind me.

'Is the benediction over?' I said in the calmest voice that I could muster. 'Where are brothers Sando and Frederick?'

'They are . . . checking the storeroom. Brother,' I said in the same even voice.

The oldest of the priests stepped forward. 'I will go see about this. You will remain here.' He pointed to one of the other priests. 'Go call the guard.'

'Perhaps you should not disturb them,' I said, darting a look past him. The chapel was all but deserted aside from these three priests and two others who were busy at the far altar but not paying us any attention.

'Get out of my way,' the priest said in what he no doubt thought was a stern voice.

'As you wish,' I said, stepping aside. He opened the door and staggered back as black smoke billowed out at him. It was short work to kick him into the passage beyond, the smoke parting as if to welcome him. By the time he met the floor the two other priests were almost halfway to the doors and the guards that lay beyond. I was tempted to throw a bottle at them, as I'm a dab hand at throwing things, but instead I opted to punch one of them in the ear with a fist of condensed air. It wasn't a hard blow, not with so little preparation, but a clap of air like that was enough to throw a human off his feet and to let them experience the same ringing as I had endured when the ward on the iron door had triggered. Fair is fair, after all.

It also had the unexpected benefit of sending him crashing into the other priest. The trinkets and amulets they carried clearly weren't up to the task of protecting them against such an overt attack, which was interesting. I darted over to them as they began untangling themselves and cracked their heads together before they could rise. I didn't think it killed either of them, but it was enough to ensure that they certainly weren't about to stand up, let alone run off. The priests at the altar had turned at the sound of them falling, and I held to the hope that the dramatic but ultimately poor lighting was enough to ruin their vision. I waved to them, and to my great relief one waved back.

I ran for the other door as soon as he turned back to the altar and padded along the blessedly empty hallways on the far side of the chapel, and eventually made my way out through a small side door. I slipped through the shadows that hung across the graveyard and was already over the far wall as the bells began to ring out behind me.

Chapter 24

'You set fire to the church.'

'Asking it again isn't going to change my answer,' I said around a mouthful of bread and meat. Tatyana's wounds were all but healed; however, the energy the healing construct had demanded had left its mark, and she had thoughtfully brought enough to feed us twice over. She had been waiting for me in the now deserted house that the necromancers had used, and had cleared out the room that had been full of old clothing, which is where we were now sat, eating and talking by the light of a single fat candle.

'It wasn't a question. I'm just talking out loud and trying to understand why the Hel you would do something like that.' She waved her eating knife at me. 'I know, I know, the cold bodies.'

'Not just cold. They were something different, and I am as sure now as I was then that leaving them there would have caused more problems.'

'More problems than burning paladins and priests to death in a church? In a city that's now under the control of the clergy?'

'That's a different sort of problem. But tell me, what has happened to Prince Jean? I thought none but a queen or king could command a prince.'

'Well, that sort of thing gets a bit complicated. I've been with Lucien for a few years now and I barely get by. There's much that happens behind closed doors, you know?'

'Not really.'

She tapped the knife against the table. 'No, of course you don't. Well, neither the Church nor the royals can command one another directly, so they negotiate most things. They're supposed to work together, to keep each other honest.'

'I can understand that. But how is it that the Church is now in charge?'

'It's a few different things. For one: they have more men under arms in the city; and two: people are scared. And when people are scared they run to church, and that gives the Church a lot of weight. If Jean goes against them, he goes against the people. It gives the Church quite an edge in their negotiations, as you can imagine. When the war is over, half this province will belong to them in return for their defence of the city.'

'Your enemies are marching on the city. Surely that is more important than who controls it *if* it survives?'

'Why do you think people are so scared? Word has spread that an army of wizards is heading this way and as many people as are trying to get in are trying to get out. It's a goddamned mess.'

'Is there?'

'Is there what?'

'An army of wizards heading this way? I remember that a city had fallen and someone called Novstan was expected to come this way.'

'So you do occasionally pay attention. Yes, Novstan's fourth army took Garreton.' She leaned forward. 'Word is that the coven who rides with his army has doubled in size; they're not actually an army of wizards, not compared to an actual army, but it's the most we've seen in one place. There's a rumour that the Worm Lord himself might be travelling with them, and if word of that gets out, they won't need to lay siege to the city. The people will have torn it apart themselves.'

'And Lucien is to lead your army against them?'

She huffed a breath. 'Yes. I think he's starting to believe all the flattery that Jean's sycophants are heaping on him.'

'I do not understand.'

'Lucien's not bad at a bit of wrestling and I've been helping him with the sword, but the way they're talking about him you'd think he was some ancient hero reborn to save the kingdom. I'm sure Jean started it, but that counts for nothing with Lucien. He loves his brother.' She ran a hand through her hair. 'It's all part of an idea to bolster Lucien's reputation, to give the militias a bit of backbone, but the ridiculous part is that I think he's starting to believe them.'

'Is that why you have left him?'

'I didn't leave him. I don't give my word easily, and I don't break it.' She toyed with her knife, pressing it into her hand until it was on the verge of drawing blood. 'I tried to talk some sense into him, but he was like a small child. He sent me away and told me he didn't need my protection any more now that he had actual paladins to protect him. He said that, to me.' She stared at the drop of blood snaking across her palm. 'Just like that, never mind that he's only breathing because of me.'

'And so you found your way to me?'

'You're the only wizard I know. You know, personally.'

'Sorcerer.'

'Yes, that. I figured I might as well try to sort out my own head before I went back and broke his. Or before the Worm Lord's army do it for me anyway.'

'It's an apt but strange and discomfiting name.'

'Fear is a weapon.' Now she tapped the knife against one of the wine bottles on the table. 'So how does magic wine fit into all of this?'

'I'm not sure yet. At first I had thought it must be poison of a sort, but after seeing the rat I knew it was no poison. Everything in that chamber was steeped in what you would call necromantic energy.' I gestured to the bottles. 'Including these. They are imbued with the same magic.'

'Fine, but why?'

'That is the question I cannot answer.' I chewed on a bun as I stared at the dark liquid within the glass. 'Magic is just energy that is shaped by intent, like a woodworker shapes a chair from a tree trunk. I cannot fathom the intent here.'

Tatyana snorted. 'I don't know about you, but when I have wine the intention is to drink it.'

I paused with the remnant of the bun halfway to my mouth as something connected in my mind. 'That's it,' I said, dropping the bread. 'You are very wise, Tatyana Henkman.'

'I am? I am.' She set her knife down. 'But just to be clear, how is it that I'm suddenly wise?'

'The intent. This' – I tapped the nearest bottle – 'isn't the enchantment. It's part of it, a component, like a bracelet that holds charged power. The drinker supplies the intent. It's crude, but also quite clever.'

She leaned sideways and peered out of the door. 'I think my wisdom just left. What are you talking about? And no more about the magic singing rainbows that join us all together.'

'I need to speak to Fronsac.'

'That's not going to happen. They're looking for you everywhere, Stratus. Do you hear those bells? Those aren't marking the next service, they're an alarm. Every guard and soldier out there is looking for a large black man, and I don't know if you've noticed but there are precious few of those in these parts.'

'That's ridiculous. It was only a storeroom, and that below ground. It would never have burned any further.'

She rubbed her face with both hands. 'You killed three priests and two paladins. Inside a church. While under arrest for being a necromancer and having confessed to the same.'

'It's not that simple. They attacked me! I am innocent.'

'Setting fires and killing people isn't the way to prove it.'

I bit down on the irritation fomenting inside me before it woke the beast, and took a deep breath. 'Yes, fine. But the fact is, there is a necromancer in the city, and I think he's doing something to the paladins. And if he is, then their defence is hardly something you should be counting on.'

'That's not possible. Paladins are blessed and protected from such things. They're more than just skilled fighters, they're Holy Warriors. Each of them is a priest in their own right. Everyone knows that.'

'I've not seen much evidence of those blessings and protections.' I tapped a nail against the wine bottle meaningfully. 'Unless they're somehow shrugging off that protection without knowing it.'

She frowned, and I stayed silent, willing her to see it for herself. 'So the wine weakens their blessings?'

'Possibly. If the wine was somehow created or imbued with the intention that whoever drinks it is more susceptible to dark magic, accepting it voluntarily will carry that intent to whoever is drinking it, especially if they're of a similar mind already.'

She was frowning now. 'So if that woodworker made his chair with the intention that whoever sits in it will fall asleep, if you sit in it you'll fall asleep?'

I smiled. 'Especially if you were already tired, and more so if he warned you that you'll fall asleep, but yes, something like that.'

'They can do that?'

'It's the symbolism that's important.' I toyed with my abandoned bun. 'When I ate the necromancer's brain, I saw something else. I thought I had figured it out when I went down into the crypt, but it wasn't that.'

'What are you talking about?'

'Do you trust me?'

'Not a chance. The last time you asked me that you stabbed me.'

I acceded the point with a gracious nod. 'I want to show you what I saw. It will be easier for you to know what I am looking for.'

'How?' she asked, her voice loaded with suspicion.

'I want to show it to you here,' I tapped the side of my head. 'The magic that links us should make it fairly easy.'

A whiff of fear wormed its way into her scent. 'Can't you just paint it on the wall or something?'

Paint it on the wall. An innocent enough phrase, but I felt it resonate with one of the memories that my mind guarded so jealously, and for a moment I remembered a cave, warm, dry and lit by a great blaze, and my hands covered in paint as I finished shaping the antlers of a great elk.

'Stratus? Are you doing magic?'

'What?' The images faded as I blinked. 'Magic? No, I was remembering something. From before.'

'Before?'

'Sometimes I see . . . I remember things from before I became what I am now.'

'Do you think they're like the dreams?' The scent of her fear was strengthening.

'You have had them again?'

She looked down at her hands. 'Yes,' she said quietly.

I was pleased with my insight but didn't show it. I wanted to see what she had seen too, and it would be easier if she wasn't going to resist the attempt.

'You can let me see them at the same time. Perhaps I can draw them from you. That might be why you have been seeing them.'

'Do you really think so?'

'It can only help.'

She took a deep breath and released it slowly. 'Fine. What do I do?'

'Just look into my eyes.'

'Can I blink?'

I smiled. 'Yes, that will not affect us.'

'All right then.' She cleared the leftover food away and rested her elbows on the table, her chin propped on her hands. I woke my sorcery as I copied her, and being so close I could feel the latent enchantment within her responding to me. I could sense it snaking up from her heart and to the back of her eyes, so that when our gazes met, the green of her eyes was already glowing faintly in my vision. I heard her gasp as the sorcery sparked to life between us.

I could feel her confusion and fright as my will flowed through the connection, distorting her perceptions and joining our vision. She did not like losing control and fought against it vainly, thrashing about like a trapped animal, but she was fighting by the rules of the physical world, and those did not hold sway here. I projected a sense of calm at her and let her see an image of me as she knew me, and the thrashing subsided.

What is this? What's happening? You didn't tell me about this. I'm afraid.

Her thoughts spilled from her and I gently increased the sense of calm until it was more of a command than a suggestion, and her resistance finally subsided. I began by showing her the necromancer's body, but spared her the gut-wrenching awfulness of the taste of his tainted flesh. I had no idea whether a mental projection could vomit but I preferred not to find out inside my own head. I let the image fade, and then showed her what I had seen.

The crypt stands open, the entrance guarded only by a stone reaper. Slick stairs beneath my feet, the long path to our temple. The beast has slain my brothers, and I fear my Master's anger.

She understood what I had done, and with her interest focused on a single image and sensation, the last of the suppressed sense of panic surrounding her subsided and was replaced with elation. She knew of the crypt, and though I am sure that she did not know how or even that she was doing it, she showed me a long, narrow strip of muddied ground in the shadow of the citadel's walls. And there, proud among them, stood the crypt. Her memory of it showed her walking behind Lucien, bored and hungry, while he sketched the reaper draped across the lintel with charcoal and parchment.

I released the memory and sent more calmness at her, because now it was her turn to show me what she had promised. The dream. Turning her focus inward was easier than I had anticipated, and I could not help but wonder whether this was because of our mixed blood or some latent ability. Either way, the suggestion that she needed to show me the dream met with no resistance, which certainly made things easier. Nonetheless, it took some time before I understood what I was seeing; memories of something seen or heard were easily read, but dreams were harder to grab hold of by their very nature, and before I found exactly what I sought I had to swim through a confusion of half-formed memories and fantasies that broke apart to form new and impossible structures if I tried too hard to see them.

When I found what I was looking for, it was something of a bastion amid the otherwise fluid memories in this part of her mind, as if the fear and emotions that it generated had given it an actual mass. I slipped through the skin of it and sunk into the dream, deep enough that I could see it as she had.

I paced along the length of the cage, my footfalls silent on the rancid reeds and grasses beneath my feet, the dimensions familiar enough to be part of my very being. I reached for the bars, but drew back as the angled runes hissed to life upon them, their heat threatening to scorch the skin from my hands. It was dark beyond the bars, a primordial blackness that had lost all memory of light. But I sensed that it wasn't empty, that something moved in the heart of it. I felt the air stir as it moved closer with the sound of iron drawn across bone, and I knew that whatever dread monster lurked in the dark, it was looking for me. I shrunk away from it, fearing that if I saw its eyes in the darkness, something terrible would happen. I felt the bars press against my skin and then the sharp agony as their blazing runes blistered my back, and I cried out in a voice that wasn't my own. The thing in the darkness heard my cry, and I knew, even though I could still see nothing but the fading runes, that it was turning towards me.

'Stratus.' The voice was small and weak, a final entreaty formed from a dying breath. 'Stratus.' As it spoke, the metal around me twisted and shrieked, and I felt the roof crumple inwards as if crushed in a giant's fist.

'Where are you?' the words sighed from the darkness, and I could feel a hunger in them, a plaintive desperation. Around me the metal sung its song of pain as it buckled further, the bars pressing inwards, the hiss of the runes burning through my skin louder than the wretched sobbing that echoed from the darkness.

'It's cold, Stratus.' I could smell my flesh cooking as the torn metal pushed deeper into me in a dozen places, my blood bubbling as it ran down the shattered bars. 'You promised . . . you promised.' I felt my eye burst as the final bar pierced me and burned into my brain.

'Stratus!' the voice had changed. I backed away from it, and rather than broken metal, I felt wood beneath me. I drew a breath and opened my eyes. Both eyes. Both whole.

I looked around and released the breath I had not known I was holding as reality reasserted itself once more. Tatyana was kneeling next to me, the sorcery within her glowing softly as it repaired whatever damage had caused her nosebleed.

'Oh,' was all I could manage as I slowly sat up.

'You saw it,' she said, and I could only nod. I felt exhausted, as if I'd not just eaten several loaves and a haunch of cold meat.

'You are stronger than even I gave you credit for, Tatyana Henkman.' I meant it too. To experience it once was harrowing enough, but to have had that waiting for whenever sleep claimed me would surely have driven me insane.

'Is it gone now?' she asked, grabbing my hand. The contact sparked an echo of the dream in my mind, and a shiver passed through me at the memory of that voice. I did not shiver alone either, for deep inside my mind the beast was awake, but silent, the heat of its anger and lust for violence reduced to embers. As if sensing my silent scrutiny, the anger flared to rage once more, cutting me off from it, but not so quick that I could fail to sense the grief and shock that had cooled its fires at hearing her voice.

'*Her* voice,' I said out loud.

'What?' Tatyana sat back, releasing my hand.

'Her voice. It knows whose voice that was.'

'It being your . . . demon?'

'Yes,' I reached out towards the beast but it was gone. 'But it won't tell me anything more.'

'I want it out of me,' she said, rubbing at her chest.

'What sort of thing is it that lives within me,' I said, more to myself than her, 'that has dreams like that? Who is she? What happened to them?' *Us*, my traitorous mind whispered.

'I'm serious. I don't want it or your messed-up demon dreams. Just take it back.'

'I believe it is gone from you now. The message has been delivered to me.'

'It had better be. I'll kill myself if I have to hear it again.'

Chapter 25

'This is a bad idea.'

I slowed as we approached a corner. 'You keep saying that, yet you have not suggested an alternative.'

'I haven't exactly had a chance, have I?' she said, her whispers becoming louder. 'We need to sit and think it through.'

'We had a place to think. You're the one who insisted we leave.'

'Well, perhaps I would have reacted better if you had warned me there was a goddamned sacrificial altar in the next room.'

I peered around the corner while she tried to rationalise her overreaction to the corpse she'd stumbled onto. She was probably right about it being a bad idea, but it was the only one I had at the moment. We had been making our way to the crypt through the pre-dawn streets with great care and had already seen several armed patrols. The Cardinal was not wasting any time in flexing his new political muscle, a phrase that Tatyana had offered and one that I rather liked. Aside from the increased patrols, he had also implemented several new laws to keep people behind closed doors at night, which in Tatyana's opinion gave him a licence to arrest homeless refugees and 'the sort of people who only come out at night', a predilection that the Church clearly did not view favourably.

I was about to move around the corner when I heard the sound of voices on the air. I edged back a bit further and whispered a warning to Tatyana. They seemed to take an age to finally appear, and by that time the combination of the noise and an advantageous wind had already told me that there were at least a dozen men, all armed and armoured and therefore most likely paladins. What I hadn't realised until they emerged from a nearby road was that Lucien was among them.

'Lucien is with them,' I whispered to Tatyana and felt her twitch, her heartbeat increasing noticeably.

'Where?' she asked. 'Is he all right?'

By the time that the patrol had come to a stop in the intersection of the three roads, the nearest paladin to us was no more than thirty paces away, but even with my excellent sight it was hard for me to pick Lucien out among them.

'Damn it, Stratus,' she hissed as she pushed past me to peer around the corner.

'They all look the same,' I said. Trying to remember individual faces was hard enough, but when they were all wearing the same clothes it made it even more challenging.

'Now isn't the time for that,' she said and pointed to an armour-clad figure to one side. 'There. He's cut his hair, but that's him. With the blue pauldron.'

'I do not know what that is.'

'The armour on his shoulder. See there?'

'Thank you. Yes. He looks taller.'

'It's hard to slouch in that armour.'

'Shall we speak to him?'

She frowned and simply watched them talking for a while before coming to a decision. 'Yes, but you stay here. Don't start anything, you'll only make it worse.'

I thought that was unfair given that the paladins were the aggressive ones, but chose not to respond.

I caught her arm. 'If something happens, close your eyes.'

'What?'

'Trust me.'

'It scares me when you say that.' She pulled her arm free but nodded before she walked out around the corner.

There was no harm in being prepared though, and while she walked out and hailed Lucien, I began weaving a defensive construct that would hopefully combat their superior numbers if something went awry.

When I risked peering around the corner again, I saw that two of the paladins had stopped Tatyana several paces away from Lucien. I turned my head so that I could hear them better.

'I would prefer to discuss it with you in private,' she was saying.

Lucien removed one of his metal gloves and ran his fingers across his now almost bald scalp. 'I . . . we should be back at the palace in an hour or two, perhaps . . .'

'Forgive me, Highness, but a secret enclave with this . . . woman would be unseemly. She is unclean. You must have her taken into custody so that—'

'I heard you the first time,' Lucien replied, waving a hand at the paladin.

'This woman?' Tatyana snapped. 'Unclean?'

She took a step forward and one of the paladins lunged for her, but before his hand touched her, she grabbed his arm and kicked his legs at the same time, sending him crashing into the cobbles. It was a clever move, and one that I wanted to remember.

His companion let out a shout and several others also turned on her, their weapons drawn. The paladin closest to me had also turned to see what was happening, saving me from the trouble of having to employ stealth. I grabbed him from behind, one hand on his neck and the other finding his thick belt, and threw him into the nearest wall with a twist of my hips. As I had expected, it made a fantastic noise, attracting the attention that I wanted.

'The demon!' shouted one of those who had rushed towards Tatyana, and a moment later he was at the forefront of a whole jumble of men charging towards me. It was perfect. I took a breath, steadied my concentration, and released the construct I had prepared, closing my eyes as I did. An arm's length above my head, a ball of light flashed into being, bright enough that I could almost see the men's outline through my eyelids. The hardest part about creating light, which is a simple derivation of fire, is controlling the amount of power you put into it. I had simply ignored my habit and fed it far more energy than it needed, giving the men charging towards me the opportunity to look into a small sun.

I opened my eyes as the flash faded and stepped back as the paladins staggered to a halt. Some had been protected by their visors, but none had escaped without some effect. I hit the most lucid-looking of them to the ground, leaving a fist-sized dent in each of their pretty chest pieces, and made my way towards where Tatyana was supporting a dazed Lucien.

'Will he be okay?' she asked.

I gestured at the moaning figures staggering about behind me. 'See? They're all alive.'

'Stratus! Will Lucien be—'

'Yes, yes, he will be fine. They'll all be fine.' The lie came out easier than I had expected.

'Good.' She helped the prince to perch on a nearby trough and began whispering to him urgently. All around us pale faces were emerging from carefully opened shutters and cries of 'Murder!' and 'Help!' were echoing down the streets.

'We should probably go,' I said, and after repeating it for the third time she finally released Lucien. Several of the paladins were already back on their feet, albeit unsteadily.

'Stratus,' he called as we turned to leave. Curious, I stepped over to where he sat.

'Lucien.'

'Look after her.' He rubbed at his red and watering eyes. 'She doesn't trust easily.'

'You would do well to remember that too,' I said, resisting the urge to find out what his shorn scalp felt like.

It looked like he wanted to say something, but he simply bowed his head and kept rubbing at his eyes.

I hurried after Tatyana, who led us through a bewildering array of small roads and alleyways until we could no longer hear the shouting or see any faces staring down at us. She didn't say anything, and I was content to follow in silence.

The crush of buildings eventually gave way and we wandered out onto a narrow strip of land near to the north-eastern wall. It had a forlorn feel to it, and was dotted with scores of stone blocks and slabs that Tatyana explained were memorials to the dead, which I found ironic given the poor condition of most of them. At least the crypt was easy to find.

Aside from the mossy but otherwise well-rendered skeleton draped across the entrance, I thought it was quite an unremarkable, weather-beaten stone box. That all changed when I extended my sorcery towards it and saw the violet light gathering around the necromantic wards hidden near the entrance, thick enough that the air around it looked bruised. They were difficult to focus on, almost as if they were under several inches of water, a clear indicator of their potency. Whoever had set them there was no mere dabbler and had invested a significant amount of time and energy into ensuring the entrance remained undisturbed.

I looked up as Tatyana started walking away. Curious and a bit suspicious, I grabbed her arm as she passed me.

'Where are you going?'

'I am going to the market.'

'The market? Now? I thought you said they had all been closed.'

'What? Oh. Yes.' She rubbed her head, and I felt the tug of my sorcery within her responding to something. Something nearby, and much like the wards on the crypt.

Still holding her arm, I sent a pulse of sorcery into her, infusing the spark of myself within her blood with new energy, enough to thwart the wards. She gasped and staggered, but I held her up.

'What was that?' She rubbed her arms.

'The crypt is warded. You must have crossed into their sphere.'

'Shit.' She stared at the crypt as if expecting it to somehow lash out at her.

'I think the outer wards are there to deflect people away. You should be fine now, at least for a while, but stay behind me.'

'Will it take long?'

'It might, but I won't know until I start.'

'I'm worried about Lucien.'

I sat down on a weathered memorial and looked up at her. 'He will be fine. The light had no heat in it.'

'Not that. I'm worried about the paladins. What they might say to him. About me.'

I wasn't sure what she wanted from me. What was I supposed to say? She had to know that I had no idea what the paladins would say or do, not without using my knife on them anyway.

'He told me to look after you,' I said. It seemed to be the right thing to say as a fleeting smile creased her face and she sat down next to me.

I turned back to the crypt and, slipping off the memorial, inched closer until I reached the point where I could see the wards starting to react, then squatted down and carefully extended my hand until I touched the stone. The wards to send me off to the market were rippling with a dark violet light, while others were only now stirring to life. I kept my hand on the edge of the crypt, well away from the door, and slowly began to tease out a few more tendrils of my sorcery. If I was going to defeat them, I first needed to know how many there were and what they did, and that meant testing each in turn.

I was vaguely aware of the day passing us by as I worked on them. I felt Tatyana's restlessness as her patience burned off like the morning's mist, a distant friction against my sorcery. I felt it when she left some time after the sun passed its zenith and returned with food, but I didn't turn from what I was doing. Joining with the energies of the church had been satisfying in the way that it had commanded my full attention, but it hadn't ever felt like anything besides a means to an end. The wards were different. I didn't exactly need to do this, but I wanted to. They were alien and yet familiar, and the painstaking nature of their challenge wasn't just engaging my mind, it was exhilarating. With each rune that I mapped and negated, I felt a sense of pride swell inside me. Whatever or whoever I was, this was something that I knew, and working in the presence of magic like this was like bathing in the sun.

The night was gathering its forces when the deep purple of the final rune flickered and dissipated. I sat back, my numb legs threatening to send me sprawling.

'Stratus? Are you all right?' asked Tatyana, her voice thick with the sleep she'd been drifting in and out of for most of the afternoon.

'Yes,' I croaked. 'Do you have any of that food left?'

She did, and I ate it all as she watched and interrogated me with a dozen questions, eleven of which I ignored.

'Yes, it's open.' I stood and stretched, feeling remarkably refreshed considering the stream of sorcery that I had been steadily expending throughout the afternoon. I looked around again, then laughed. We were in a graveyard, and had I known how to, I might have laid a wager that there had been a church here once. And where a church was, there was usually some form of energy. Much of what I had expended had been reabsorbed as I'd worked, an unexpected benefit of the slow and steady approach I had adopted.

'Are you ready?' I asked.

'What? You want to go in there now?'

'Why not? Time is pressing.'

'Time? You just spent the entire day staring at a damned crypt!'

'I had to remove the wards. If you prefer wearing your lungs and liver on the outside of your skin you should have said something.'

She folded her arms. 'It's getting dark.'

'It's always dark beneath the earth. The time of day makes no difference.'

'Isn't it safer to enter somewhere like this during the day?'

I glanced at the sky, but it was too early to see the moon. I couldn't feel its pull either so it was probably still early in its cycle. 'No,' I said, 'that makes no difference either. A full moon might have, but tonight is not an issue.'

'I didn't bring a lantern.'

'We don't need one.' I sent some flame skittering across my fingertips and smiled as she ran her fingers through her short, pale hair and drummed her heels on the stone. She looked up at the rapidly darkening sky and swore loudly before standing up.

'Fine. Let's just get it over with.'

'I'll go in first.' My muscles swelled as I pushed the heavy door open, the stone grinding noisily. The smell of wet earth puffed out to meet us, the air almost damp with the odour of necromancy and thick enough to make me stagger backwards and clout my head on the low lintel.

'What is it? Are you hurt?'

I was too busy fighting to keep the food I'd just eaten inside me to reply, and she pushed past me, a long-bladed knife in her hand. She looked back at me from the gloom.

'Empty. Smells a bit miff though.'

I gulped some of the marginally fresher air from the entrance. 'Miff?'

She waved the knife about. 'You know. Damp and dirty.'

'You can't smell it? The taint?'

'Does it smell like the underside of an old rock or a froggy pond?'

'No.'

'Then that's your answer.' She put the knife away. *Sheathed it*, an errant memory prompted me. 'Next time we go crawling about inside an old crypt, remind me to bring you one of Lucien's scented kerchiefs for your delicate nose.'

'I will.' I could have let her smell it, but there was no point in making us both vulnerable to whatever may wait below. I took a tentative sniff of the air now that the open door had vented the worst of it, and while there was a marked improvement, the lingering tang of the brains I had tasted made me suspect that it would be a very long time before I forgot either the taste or smell of it.

It was at least breathable now and I moved into the small crypt and pulled the door shut behind us, ignoring Tatyana's small cry of protest as the stone slammed shut with a solid finality. Her fear spiced the air, the familiar tang actually rather comforting to me. It lessened slightly as I kindled an orb of sorcerous light, revealing a dozen or so narrow, empty shelves around us.

'That's it?' she asked, looking about. 'An entire day wasted for a steaming pile of bugger all?'

I ignored her as I followed the stench to a cleverly disguised door in the floor, blowing the dirt from the edges to show her.

'Clever,' she said. 'You don't need another day to open that one, do you? Because I'll wait outside.'

'No, this one is not warded. I should be able to smash it open in far less time. Stand back.'

'You're such a man.'

'Thank you.'

'It wasn't a damned compliment, you oaf.'

I watched her with no little confusion as she circled the room once, occasionally rapping the handle of her dagger against the wall. She muttered something to herself as she reached into what looked like a crack above one of the empty shelves, then turned and smiled at me as the door swung open to reveal several stone steps leading into an inky blackness.

'Impressive,' I said, genuinely impressed. 'How did you know?'

'Even a lady needs her secrets,' she said, peering down at the stairs. 'Well? After you then.'

I sent the orb down a few steps ahead of me and called up just enough sorcery to give me a chance of seeing any wards that might have been set on the stairs. Then I squeezed myself through the entrance and began a long and exhausting descent that had my shoulders scraping both walls for most of it. Had I been given the gift of precognition I may have stopped there and equipped us better for what lay ahead, but instead I led the descent with a sense of hope and enthusiasm.

The stairs led down at angles, turning sharply on themselves every twenty-five steps, and aside from a fascinating profusion of spiders, there was little of note about them, and the only time I felt in danger was when Tatyana fell onto my back after walking into a particularly thick web. Some ten turns of the stairs later we came to a stout door, the wood banded with iron. I did not sense any wards upon it, but the lock was an extravagant contraption and took my sorcery nearly three heartbeats to prise open.

The door swung open on greased hinges, revealing the first of the horrors that the darkness beneath the city concealed.

Chapter 26

The room was square, some twenty paces along each wall, and had an open archway on the far side. Between where we stood and the archway opposite lay scores of slack human corpses, layered one upon the other in two great piles on each side of the room, leaving a narrow passageway lined with sightless eyes and limp hands. The air was thick with the sickly sweet odour of putrefied flesh, and I doubted that the origin of the dripping I could hear was anything as benign as groundwater.

Behind me, Tatyana folded herself almost in half as her mind and body struggled to comprehend what she was seeing and smelling; I stepped away and let her fight through it. It wasn't that I found the smell pleasant in any way, but the repeated exposure to the strange and pervasive stench that hung about necromancy had given me something of a sensory perspective on these things. Decay was a natural process, and while not a particularly pleasant one to wade through, it was nothing more than natural gas. Dead men didn't trouble me, and I had little doubt that I killed my fair share in the past.

The obvious question that remained was what they were doing here, but there was nothing I could see that offered an immediate answer. The bodies showed little sign of having been abused or gnawed on by anything larger than grave rats, so it was safe to assume that this wasn't some bizarre larder.

'We should move on, there's nothing of worth here,' I said, moving my light towards the dark of the archway.

'Can't breathe,' Tatyana gasped, her voice muffled from where she had it buried in the crook of her elbow.

'Nonsense. The air's a bit thick, but its entirely breathable.'

She made a retching noise and squatted down, pinching her nose. 'Can't.'

She flinched as I moved back and set my hand on her hair. 'Keep still,' I said, sending a curl of sorcery through my touch and, using the healing construct within her as an anchor, I opened a bridge between us. Or rather, from my mouth to hers.

'Lift your head,' I said, breaking the contact.

She did, and took a tentative sniff. Coughed. 'What did you do? The stink's gone, but the air still tastes . . . moist.'

'It's my breath.'

'Funny. Seriously, I mean, it's much better, but it's . . . wet and meaty.'

'As I said, it's my breath.'

'Yes, I heard, and I stand by my earlier decision that humour is one of the things you should avoid.'

'It's not important,' I said, offering her one of the shrugs she seemed so fond of. There were more pressing problems than her worrying about such trivialities.

The archway led to a short passage, not even ten paces long, which opened into another similar-sized room with a moss-speckled door on the far side. This room contained yet more bodies, but where the piles we had just passed were still wet with juices and rotting, these appeared older and drier, and were stacked more neatly, although that may simply have been because they didn't have fat leaking out to make them slide to and fro.

'What the Hel is this place?' muttered Tatyana behind me.

'I don't know.' I rubbed the skin of the nearest corpse. 'Someone has taken the effort of dividing them into distinct types, but for what reason?' I tasted my finger but found only what I'd expect.

'You're not doing that,' Tatyana said in a strangled voice.

'Doing what?'

She gestured to the body. 'Eating him.'

'For one, I don't eat carrion,' I said. 'And secondly, I'm not hungry.'

That seemed to satisfy her as she simply pulled her coat tighter around herself and stared at the floor. I in turn closed my eyes and fanned my sorcery out, letting it drift through the room, seeking anything that might provide an insight into what this was. No answers came to me, but I felt the unpleasant pull of necromantic energy at the fringes of my perception. I let the sensation guide me to a small table in the corner and a pile of rags heaped on it. I carefully lifted the rags, which now seemed to be a single sheet of cloth folded about the strange object that lay in the centre. It was a thick copper cylinder a bit longer than my fingers were, with a needle-like protrusion on one end and a T-shaped lever of some sort on the other. It was mottled with dark stains, most of which had dried to a flaky crust.

'Interesting,' I said. 'The assassin whose throat you cut in the house had something similar. Do you have any idea what it is before I touch it?'

'He did? I thought it was a knife.'

'He had both, but he stabbed you with the knife.'

'Thank you for the reminder.'

'It is nothing.'

She sighed and leaned closer. 'It looks like something I've seen priests using in the healing tents.'

'Yes?'

'I don't know what it's called, but I remember how they jabbed it in a lump on someone's head and used it to draw the blood and muck out of it.'

Now that I had a context for it, I could see how that would work and the debt I felt I owed her grew slightly. I lifted it off the table and gave it a careful sniff. I could smell old blood, alcohol and spoiled fats, but something else too, a taste somewhere between mulch and old fur that I didn't have a name for. It was, however, something that was undoubtedly linked to, and quite likely born of, necromancy.

I turned the cylinder over and traced the fine runes and sigils that had been scratched into the surface, but none of them meant anything to me. I pulled and pushed at the T lever, and felt something inside it moving. I pushed harder and watched as a greasy black liquid began to drip from the hollow tip. I pushed harder and the drop of black liquid suddenly began to writhe, twisting back on itself as it stretched out like a snake that had been stepped on. Tatyana cursed loudly, the word unknown to me but the tone unmistakeable.

It looked like a worm, a pale thing wrapped in the sort of slime that grew on stagnant pools, but black and grainy. I aimed it at the rags and squeezed the handle until the worm-thing fell from the needle with a soft plopping sound.

'What in Drogah's name is that?'

I didn't bother answering and watched as the worm sunk into its own slime and fell dormant, a state in which it became almost indistinguishable from the dull jelly that surrounded it.

'I don't know.' I brought my light orb closer and focused its brightness on the slime, making the worm within writhe about furiously. I fed some more energy into the orb, combining the construct for light with that of heat, and boiled it in its own filth. It was a crude experiment, but the stench that rose with the smoke confirmed my fear – it was without doubt a necromantic creature, saturated with dark energy. I cooled my light and moved to the nearest corpse, a terrible suspicion crawling around in my mind, but its flesh was too mottled and wrinkled to discern any of the punctures such a thing would have made.

Tatyana watched all of this, her fear under control but her anxiety obvious. 'What was that, Stratus?'

'I don't know. I've not seen the like of it before.'

'But you suspect something, don't you?'

I acknowledge her astuteness with a nod. 'That thing, that worm, was not a natural creature. It might have been once, but it wasn't any more.'

'You think it came from the bodies?'

I lifted the brass instrument. 'This can push, or it can pull. Until I know which one they need these bodies for, I dare not speculate.'

She looked at the brass contraption, then at the corpse, then back again, her grimace deepening. 'Drogah's teeth! Those sick bastards.'

She flinched away from the nearest column of corpses, which made her brush against those on the opposite side, and only the shortness of her hair saved her from becoming entangled in their fingers. While she cursed and swore I debated whether I should take the injector tube or not. On one hand, it would be interesting to study, but on the other I did not particularly relish the idea of walking about with a canister full of necromantic worms on my belt. In the end, I decided to leave it where it was. The secretive nature of these chambers meant that it was unlikely there would be another exit so I could collect it on the way out if I still wanted to.

The mossy door in the far wall was surprisingly easy to open, and revealed yet another set of stairs leading deeper into a darkness that seemed to leach the brightness from my orb. I shouldn't have been surprised by the stench that rose from below, but I couldn't help it. Remembering the stink of it was an entirely different thing to being exposed to it afresh, particularly in a place like this where it had been steeping undisturbed for some time. I leaned against the cold stone as I fought through my body's reaction and concentrated on not emptying my guts from either end.

'Magic?' asked Tatyana simply, and it was all I could do to nod. She waited, her frustration evident, until I could stand on my own strength again.

'Necromancy,' I said, feeding my light more energy until it shone as bright as it had before. I could feel the darkness pressing against it like a current flowing the opposite way as it reluctantly gave way and closed up as soon as we passed, but more worrying than that was the increasing potency of the stink that clogged the air. There was more than just latent necromancy left down here; someone, or something, lurked below.

'What is this place?' Tatyana said, and even though there was no noise beyond the soft slap of our feet and our breathing, her words were faint, their potency stolen away by the darkness around us.

'It's your city, not mine,' I replied, keeping my eyes on the slick stairs in front of me. I had no idea how far we were from the bottom, and the thought of breaking a few bones while the stars knew what pulled itself out of the dark wasn't one I wanted to explore.

'Not mine,' she said, 'I'm from the north. Have you been to Balfont?'

'I couldn't say.'

'It's famous because of a huge battle that was fought there centuries ago, but in truth there's not much to look at really. A fancy fountain, the best brewery in Krandin and a big church, because of the graveyard. But there's lots of statues which you would like.'

She liked them, not me.

'It sounds pleasant,' I said, hoping that the tone I used would end the conversation. Anything sounded nicer than the dank hole we were descending further into, but I really didn't need the distraction of buried memories showing themselves right then. It was bad enough that I could feel the beast stirring within me, the steady exposure to the necromancy waking it from where it had been laying dormant.

'It was nice. I used to accompany scholars and chroniclers when they went to study the battlefield, which was the perfect excuse to avoid having to sit through endless lessons. The battlefield is supposed to be haunted, you know. Every few years the ghosts of the dead soldiers rise and fight and relive their deaths. Some of the scholars used to carry so many charms and sacred bells it was almost comical, but I only ever felt sad there, never frightened.'

'Is there a point you're trying to make?'

'What? No. Well, just that I'm not from here. No need to be so tetchy.'

'I'm not tetchy.'

'You're worse than a bear with a hangover. And at least bears don't go around poking around in piles of rotting bodies looking so very pleased with themselves.'

I stopped, and she cursed again as she walked into my back. I turned to look at her, and because of the level of the stairs we were eye to eye for a change. 'I am trying to prepare for whatever is waiting at the bottom of these stairs. It is not a time for levity and tomfoolery.'

She lifted her chin and gestured to herself with a wave. 'Does it look like I'm juggling and dancing back here?'

'No, it doesn't. But you're talking about inconsequential matters. It's distracting.'

'So what? I'm talking. It's what normal people do when they're following a madman who thinks he might be a demon down a staircase under a goddamned graveyard.'

'I didn't realise that normal people followed madmen who might be demons into graveyards.'

She folded her arms. 'Well, perhaps.' Her smile faded as quickly as it showed as she looked past me and shuddered. 'Look, I'm really not comfortable down here. The air is unpleasant, everything is slimy and if I start thinking about all that dirt pressing down above us and the kind of monster that could be lurking down here, I think I'll lose my mind.'

'You're afraid.'

'Of course I'm bloody afraid!'

'So am I.' There was no shame in admitting it, as it was the truth. For all of my strength and not inconsiderable skill with sorcery, my reserves were limited and I still had more questions than answers in my head, least of all about how necromancy worked in practice. If I didn't know that, how could I protect myself against it? I'd be an idiot if I wasn't afraid.

'You are?'

'Of course. I am many things, but I am not a fool.'

'I'm not sure if that makes me feel any better.' She let out a long breath and rested a hand on the handle of her sword. 'Look, let's just get it over with. I'm sick of this place.'

'I agree,' I said, and we were soon making our way down the stairs once more, but my concentration had slipped and I found myself wanting her to say something again, which was a peculiar enough experience to distract me for a while. Yet the stairs showed no sign yet of reaching the bottom of whatever this was and, perhaps because she had put the idea in my mind, I started feeling more aware of how far from the sunlight we were and how cold it was becoming.

'What I said earlier about not eating carrion isn't entirely true,' I said, slowing marginally. 'If you consider it, everyone does. It's really only the freshness that differs.'

'Is there a point you're trying to make?' she replied.

I smiled as I recognised my own words. 'I am not tetchy.'

'I'll be the judge of that.'

We reached the bottom not long after that, the sudden transition to flat ground after so many steps taking us both by surprise and pitching us to the floor with nothing bearing a passing resemblance of grace.

I brightened the orb as we stood and eased the tremors from our tired muscles. The walls around us were no longer the rough, raw stone that had surrounded the stairs but grey slabs worked by mortal hands, the joints between them now home to myriad pale, skittering things where the ancient mortar had crumbled. Before us loomed something too grand to be a mere gate or archway. It was half as tall again as I was, and several times wider. It was lined with statues whose grandeur had long since been lost to the endless drip of moisture from above, leaving behind the merest suggestion of what they had been. The blind, faceless shapes that time had left them were both unsettling and somehow tragic, and as the light of the orb played across them they seemed to stir, but it was only the colonies of pale insects upon them fleeing the light.

I had expected a curse or query from Tatyana, but she was silent, her sword drawn and held close to her chest as she stared into the absolute blackness that waited beyond my light. Had my sense of smell not been blunted by the constant assault of necromancy, I had no doubt that the sharper tang of her fear would have cut across it.

'It's the undercity.'

'You knew of this place?'

'No. I mean yes, sort of. I've heard it mentioned before. There's been a city here for many hundreds of years, and it's been sacked a few times. I guess the survivors found it's easier to build up than dig down.'

'Interesting.' Contempt radiated from the beast, but it passed quickly.

I rolled my neck and shoulders and silently fed some energy into a set of protective wards that I hoped would give us a fighting chance if we were ambushed. I looked back at Tatyana, who gave a sharp nod, and with that we walked through the portal.

Chapter 27

We passed beyond the entrance and its blind sentinels, and moved along the wider passage beyond. Unlike most that I had seen, the roof was curved rather than vaulted, and marked with archways of paler stone every twenty paces. Despite the damp that was eating away at the stone like a canker and the roots that had pierced the roof, the passage was actually quite remarkable in its construction and must have been truly impressive once. We came to a junction where it divided into two marginally narrower but equally unwelcoming passages, and here for the first time I could sense a distinct pull on my sorcery. Whatever lay down the passage on the right was the source of the miasma of dark energy that saturated this level.

'Why right?' asked Tatyana as I sent the orb gliding into the passage.

'This is the direction where the necromancy is strongest.'

'And what about the left?'

'What about it?'

'We should check it. I don't want some sneaky bastard jumping me from behind.'

'We could split up.'

'If you think I'm going to go crawling around in here on my own, you're sorely mistaken.'

'I could give you your own light.'

'No. It's a stupid idea. And we're going to go left first.' With that, she slapped my leg with the side of her sword. 'Move it.'

I swallowed my irritation at her tone, which wasn't helped by her concern being a valid one, and swung the orb back and out along the left passage. The floor was strewn with rubble and mouldy bones but it at least remained level, which was the only positive thing I could say about it. Had my light not been as bright as it was, there was a moment where we might both have walked straight into a pit that had opened in the floor at some distant point. Gripped by a shared curiosity, we kneeled by the edge as I sent the orb down into it, revealing a narrow wound in the earth that opened into another chamber at least a hundred yards down, its floor littered with shattered stonework. We moved with renewed caution after that, freezing at any movement underfoot and ready to leap to whatever false safety another patch of the same floor might offer.

It was soon after we had negotiated a patch of floor that had sagged and creaked beneath my weight that I heard something beyond the noise we were making and the constant dripping of moisture.

I held up a hand that Tatyana walked into with a squawk. 'Do you hear that?'

'Ow. Hear what?' She tilted her head to the side, and after a moment she nodded. 'Sounds like someone crying.'

'It could be anything. Stay alert.'

'I'll try not to fall asleep back here then, shall I?'

'That is probably best.'

I moved forward again, dimming the light of the orb but also preparing a surge of power that I could feed into it with a thought. A sudden blast of light would play havoc with anything that had become accustomed to the dark, and would use less energy than fire. The sobbing grew louder as the passage curved away to the left, and then became a scream as we rounded it.

And not just one.

A chorus of screams began, the sound of them echoing along the passage. After the relative silence up to this point, the shrill sound of them was shocking.

The passage straightened before us, and I fed a bit more energy into the orb, revealing four doors set into the left wall. The screams were coming from behind these doors, each of which had a small window set into it with three vertical iron bars. Raising her sword to the height of her shoulder, Tatyana moved to the side of the first door, then spun to peer into the little window, her sword level and ready to skewer anything that tried to leap out at her. I sent the orb whizzing past her to illuminate whatever was inside, which caused a whole array of similar screams to rise, several of which sounded remarkably like 'my eyes, my eyes'.

Tatyana didn't say anything but beckoned me closer. I peered into the window as she stepped away, her sword lowered. It took me a moment to understand what I was seeing, but eventually the mass in the far corner resolved itself into several men and women, their shapes rendered formless by the filth and blankets that encrusted them. It didn't help that they all had their faces covered by their hands.

'It's the same in the other three,' Tatyana said. 'Move your light, damn you.'

I had just been about to move it closer to try to make out some more detail, so I dimmed it instead, which seemed to satisfy her as she didn't swear at me again.

'Can you please stop screaming?' I asked, but I might as well have been speaking to the bricks. 'Can you do something?' I asked Tatyana.

'Me?'

'You're one of them. Say something soothing.'

'Can you open the door?'

I put my hand on the door. There were no wards, just a mechanical lock. I didn't want to waste any sorcery on manipulating it, and given that the wood the lock was bolted to was barely an inch thick, I improvised and kicked the lock out.

'It's open,' I said.

Strangely enough, this act of violence actually quietened their screaming somewhat. Tatyana stepped in, her sword still in her hand but held down and low.

'Hello,' she said, kneeling down in front of the closest of the figures. It shied away, but then slowly a face emerged, pale against the stiff blankets.

'Hello,' it croaked back.

'Who are you?' Tatyana said. The screaming in the other rooms was at least abating now and being replaced with weeping, which was marginally easier to bear.

'You . . .You're not one of them?'

'One of who?'

'The w-wizards.' The face turned towards me and the voice became a moan. 'Who's he?'

'He's a friend, do not worry. Did the wizards bring you here?' A nod answered that.

Five more faces had now emerged from the huddled mass. 'My son,' said one of these. 'Have you seen my son? They took him.'

'No, I'm sorry. Look, we're going to help you, but you need to tell us what you—'

'He's a good boy. He has red hair, are you sure you haven't seen him? I have to find him.' The person was crawling towards Tatyana now, the movements made awkward by a wooden strip bound to one of their legs. The bone was clearly broken, and from the way the flesh was straining at the bindings, wound rot had most likely set in.

'Help us,' said another, staggering to its feet. 'We have to get out!'

One of the others scrambled up and ran for the door. 'No, wait!' Tatyana called, but the figure, clearly a man now that it had stood up, shoved her hand away and ran from the room, flinching away from me before speeding off down the passage. It was a stupid thing to do given the absolute darkness, and I left him to his fate. I certainly wasn't going to run after him.

Inside the room Tatyana was backing towards the door as the prisoners advanced, their demands becoming strident and not a little bit hysterical. The one with the broken leg surged forward and grabbed her ankle. I'm sure she didn't do it out of spite, but Tatyana's immediate reaction was to lash out with her other foot. It was a good hit, but the woman hung on, crying out 'my son, my son'. The other prisoners were crowding her now too.

'Some help here!' she shouted, which I took to be directed at me.

I stepped in and delivered a swift kick to the side of the woman with the broken leg, the impact breaking both her grip and not a few ribs. She slid across the floor and tripped another of the prisoners, leaving just the one flailing at Tatyana. Even as I turned to send a fist into his back, Tatyana snarled and hit him in his forehead with base of her sword handle. He dropped immediately and fell at her feet in a tangle of limbs, mewling like a lost lamb. The other two prisoners retreated as far as the room allowed them to, their eyes wide, and just in time to hear a scream from somewhere up the passage. It faded quickly, and I guessed that the man who had run away had found the same hole that we had.

'God's teeth. What are you people thinking? We're trying to help you!'

The two prisoners flinched at her words and sunk to the floor.

'Their minds are lost,' I said. 'Let's see what's in the other rooms.'

'And what? Just leave them?'

'Well, yes. We could just kill them. It would certainly be quieter and we wouldn't have to worry about them getting underfoot.'

'We can't do that,' she hissed at me. 'They're not the enemy and are clearly here against their will.'

'I have no doubt of that, but they're of no use to us.'

'That doesn't mean we can just kill them!' The prisoners moaned and flinched at this.

'Then we leave them. Unless you would prefer to lead them out.' I gestured to the yawning dark of the passage.

She sheathed her sword with unnecessary violence. 'Bastard.'

I ignored her and peered into the next room, keeping the orb dim. Unsurprisingly, it and the room next to it were much the same as the first. White eyes, dirty skins and screaming mouths. The fourth was slightly different though. In there, a single female stood with a youth behind her and stared at me defiantly when I sent the orb in. She flinched at the light, sudden tears cutting clean lines through the dirt on her face, but she stood her ground.

'She might be of use,' I said, stepping back and kicking the lock out, an act which was strangely satisfying.

'Let me go in first,' Tatyana offered, slowly pushing the remnants of the door open. She had taken two steps inside when a black shape fell upon her; whatever it was, it had clearly been waiting above the door.

Before I could step in to help her she gave a quick twist and suddenly the dark shape was under her, one of its arms neatly twisted, pinning it in place. It gave a loud squeal but kept absolutely still. The female and the youth looked like they were about to join in, so I sent the orb straight at them, which made them stumble and cover their eyes.

'Magic Man.' The voice that came from the figure Tatyana had immobilised was familiar. I squatted down next to them and peered at the narrow features that were currently mashed against the floor. In normal circumstances his scent would have helped me place him, but now I had to rely on sight, which for me was always difficult with humans.

'Magic Man,' he said again. 'Not hurt Jovar.'

'Jovar,' I said, the memory of the wretch falling into place. 'You said you would see me again and you were right. Clever. Let him go, Tatyana.'

'You know this man?'

'Yes. Jovar helped me when I first got to the city.' I didn't think it necessary to mention anything about his assistance coming at the threat of being immolated. She released his arm and disentangled herself. Jovar stood as well, rubbing the arm that she had almost broken. The female and youth moved to where he stood and took what shelter his slender frame offered. On the floor behind him was a shard of metal, its gleaming tip the only remotely clean thing within the prison cell.

'What happened, Jovar?' I asked.

'Men came and chased us out. Brought us here.'

'Which men?'

'Church men. Red on their chests,' he said, gesturing to his own, making enough of the shape of the cross of Drogah that his meaning was unmistakeable.

'Paladins?' Tatyana asked.

Jovar nodded and spat. 'They killed many, took the others.'

'They brought you here?'

'Yes. Very scared.'

'How many of you are down here?' I asked.

'Was many, but they gone now. Other men come, take them away. None come back.'

'Tell me about the other men. How many are there?'

'You got food?' he asked.

I nodded to Tatyana, who passed him one of the hard breads that she had squeezed into her small pack. Jovar tore it in half and passed one half to the female and the boy. He gnawed on an edge for a few moments, then nodded.

'Five, maybe six,' he said. 'Always in robes with hoods. Sometimes only two come, but I only see five or six most times. Very cruel.'

'Five or six. That's not too bad,' Tatyana said.

Jovar shook his head and lowered the crust he was chewing on. 'Five or six men, but many dead men also.'

'Dead men?' I said.

'Dead men,' he said, nodding again. 'Very, very bad. The robed men speak and the dead men listen. Even our own people. Fathers take their sons, but they not care. Cruel hands, and sometimes they bite and robed men laugh.'

'Necromancers,' Tatyana whispered. 'But that can't be. The paladins . . .'

'Paladins bad,' said Jovar. 'They bring us here.'

Tatyana staggered as if struck, and even in the silvery light of the orb I could see how pale her skin was. 'Tatyana?'

'God above, Stratus. Do you know what this means?'

241

'The paladins are in league with the Worm Lord?'

'It can't be right, it can't be. They're the *paladins*. Do you understand what that means? Yes, they're judgemental and generally as much fun to be around as a wasp's nest, but they're the *paladins*. They're not . . .' She squatted down and pressed her palms against her forehead. Jovar watched her as he continued to gnaw on the crust, occasionally shooting a look at me.

'It may only be a few of them,' I offered. 'We will find the answers.'

Tatyana grunted, and eventually stood up and wiped her face. 'You're right, you're right.'

'Jovar is coming too,' Jovar said around the bread.

'That's not a good idea,' Tatyana said.

'Jovar good with knife,' he said, then pointed to the passage outside. 'And too dark to see.'

'I don't mind,' I said. 'He's quiet enough.'

Tatyana jabbed a finger at him. 'Fine, but you stay behind me, understood?'

He nodded his agreement, and so it was that five of us headed back towards the junction. If Jovar knew any of the others in the cells, he gave no sign of it and neither of us pressed him on it.

Chapter 28

'Do you trust him?'

We were crouched a score or more paces ahead of Jovar and his companions while I reluctantly sent the orb ahead to probe the darkness. In the absence of its light, I could almost feel the darkness pressing against me, like dry skin that had yet to be shed. I couldn't suppress an annoyed sigh as Tatyana's whisper knifed into my concentration.

'Yes.'

We had found our way back to the junction easily enough, having paused just long enough to confirm my suspicion about the man who'd run away. The right-hand passage was in a marginally better condition than the left, and while I suspected that the men who had attacked Lucien had been the same six necromancers that Jovar had spoken of, I wasn't keen on taking unnecessary risks.

'I'm only asking because he seems to have taken it all very well, bearing in mind that the rest of them had gone a bit loony.'

I called the orb back and turned to the patch of darkness where her voice was coming from.

'I think it's more important that he tried to kill you while he thought you were one of them.'

'Maybe.'

The light washed over us again, and as it pushed the dark back I saw that Jovar was sitting on his heels not two paces behind Tatyana, the female and youth just behind him. They really were superbly quiet.

'You can trust Jovar,' he said, making Tatyana jolt forward. His teeth flashed, almost as bright against his skin as mine were. 'I steal many things but not children.'

'Sorry,' muttered Tatyana. 'I didn't mean anything by it.'

I let them talk as I extended my sorcery down the passage again. Given the recent bout of screaming from the prisoners and that the only source of light was hovering over my shoulder, keeping them quiet wasn't going to do much to mask our presence. There was something about the passage ahead that didn't feel right, but I couldn't tell what it was. There were no wards that I could sense, but somewhere inside me an unnamed instinct was trying to tell me something.

'What are we waiting for?' asked Tatyana.

'I have a strange feeling about the passage ahead.'

'Strange how?'

'That we're missing something.'

She squinted at the stretch I had indicated. 'Let's see. Blind spiders, slimy puddles and bricks that feel like soggy bread. Seems normal.'

'Those are not normal things.'

'Well, we can't sit here for ever. You could be wrong, after all.'

'I suppose that is possible.' I stood and dusted a few stray spiders from my sleeve. 'Stay a few paces behind me.'

Tatyana grunted her agreement and I started forward again, my arms slightly out from my body and my wards glittering faintly as I squeezed some more power into them. I tested each step, but passed across the section without incident. I paused at the corner and gestured the others forward. Tatyana was barely two steps away from me when I looked back and realised what it was that we had missed. The passage narrowed slightly going back the way we'd just come, and at just enough of an angle to hide four shallow alcoves, each of which sheltered a dead man.

As if waiting for me to think it, the dead men lifted their heads, their eyes glowing with a cold light. I called out a warning, and Tatyana spun to the side, her sword sliding from its sheath and finding her hand in a silvered blur. Behind her Jovar turned in time to see the dead step out of the alcoves, maces held in their hands.

I cursed as I fumbled drawing my knife. With my senses numbed by the constant aura of the necromancy, I had missed their presence entirely. Whatever animated them had to rely on something beyond control by another party or I would surely have felt the command being given.

Tatyana was first to reach them, sending a fast slash along the arm of the closest of the dead as she sidestepped his mace, opening a gash that exposed the pale bone within. He tried to follow her with the mace, but with his muscles cut the weapon tumbled from its hand as the weight moved.

I pushed Jovar back as two of the dead men walked towards me with no sign of haste, giving me enough time to brighten the light and finally get my knife into my hand. I stepped sideways so that only one could strike at me, which it quickly did. The speed of the blow was far more impressive than his walking pace suggested and I flinched backwards with barely a finger's breadth to spare. His chest was exposed as the mace passed and I took the opportunity to drive the knife through his breastbone, hard enough that my thumb pressed into his flesh. It was a satisfying strike and sent him falling to the ground, but it also tore the knife from my grasp. The other one's mace swung down before I could move again and glanced off my arm as I tried to dart back, the impact hard enough to numb my outer two fingers. I barged into him with my shoulder, the solid weight of my body sending him sprawling.

The man-thing with my knife in its chest was slowly pulling itself to its feet with clumsy movements. I stamped down on its back, my weight driving it into the floor with enough force that the point of my knife broke through its back. Another stamp broke its spine and as it spasmed, I wrenched its mace away and caved its head in with it. I didn't know how they made the dead walk again, but I thought it safe to assume that the head was important.

When I looked up, Jovar was busily stabbing the one I had barged into with his sharpened metal spike, driving it into the thing's chest time and again. It didn't seem to care and as I watched, it reached up and grabbed at his face, making him curse and splutter as its fingers found his mouth. I stepped over and cracked its head open with a sweeping blow from the mace, forcing me to spring back to avoid getting its brains all over myself.

Tatyana, however, was having no difficulty dealing with her two opponents. They were a mess of cut flesh and exposed bone, and one even had an arm off, but they were still on the attack. I watched, fascinated, as one stumbled, the tendons in its leg severed by another viper-quick cut from Tatyana's sword. Whatever drove them, they were still subject to the usual mechanics of a human body, circulation notwithstanding. The amount of damage she had inflicted to the corpses would have bled both men out twice over if I was any judge of wounds.

She glanced in our direction, then slipped beneath a clawed hand and thrust her blade through the first corpse's eye so that a good hand's-breadth of steel emerged from the back of its skull. She released the blade as it fell, and sidestepped the other, the stump of its severed arm waving in a vain attempt to grab her. She kicked its knee out so that it fell, then stepped behind it and snapped its neck in a single violent movement as if it were a chicken rather than a man.

'Now do you understand what I meant by what happened at Aknak?' she said between gulps of air. 'They don't stop unless you smash them in the head.'

'Ah. I thought that perhaps you had forgotten. It is quite fascinating.'

I kneeled by the one I felled and put my hand on its chest where its tattered clothes had parted. The body was as cold as I had expected but was unexpectedly slick, as if recently oiled. It didn't smell like any oil that I recognised though. I stood and walked over to where Tatyana was quietly retching next to one of the bodies.

'Do you recognise this smell?' I asked, lifting my fingers.

She managed a strained 'Piss off' before her stomach wrung itself out once more.

'What is the matter? Are you hurt?' She shook her head. 'Did you ingest any of their fluids?'

'No, damn it.' She took a sip from a small flask, spat, then took another, longer sip. 'The dead. Fuck. Expecting them and seeing them are two entirely different things.'

'I know.' I kneeled by the one she had stabbed in the face and poked at the deep gash she'd put in its leg. No worms spilled from the flesh, which was mottled and barely moist.

'There was no command,' I said, more to myself than her.

'What?'

'There was no command. They acted from their own will, of sorts.' I shook my head, partly in confusion and partly in denial of what it could mean. 'It should not be possible.'

Jovar was off to the side, talking quietly to the female and youth, both of whom he'd given maces to.

'So?'

'So? So that means I was wrong. I thought they were puppets controlled by the Worm Lord and his cabal. If they are independent creatures, it means that more than the principle of the magic animating them is corrupt.'

'That means nothing to me. And why do I need to smell your damned fingers anyway?'

'Oh. Well, they're slimy, but I can't place the smell. My senses are a bit out of sorts down here.'

She grabbed my fingers and, staring at me the whole time, brought them to her tiny nose and sniffed a few times, her brows almost meeting as she did.

'Smells like the frogspawn from the old millpond.'

'Frogspawn.' I thought back to the worm in the injector canister in the room above us, and more pointedly, the dark jelly that had surrounded it.

I thrust my knife into the great wound in the creature's face, and with a grunt and my other thumb, pried its skull open. The confirmation of my fear lay woven into the blotchy mass of its brain, and as the light touched it, the engorged worm wriggled back into the depths of the dead tissue like an eel.

'The worms are the key,' I said, but Tatyana had moved away and was pacing back and forth with her hands on her hips. 'Did you hear me?'

'Yes! God, I wish I hadn't.' She rubbed her hands against her tunic. 'Goddamned fucking worms in their goddamned heads.'

I wiped my knife on its clothes and stood. 'The worms are only part of it.'

'I don't care!' she shouted, the sound echoing down the passage. 'I'm supposed to be a bodyguard, not whatever this is.' She gestured at the bodies and me.

'Calm down.'

'Calm down? There are dead men. With worms in their heads.' She emphasised each word as if I hadn't just told her about it.

'It's not natural.'

'Really.'

'Of course not.' I took a breath and released it slowly, hoping that the bridge between us would help carry some of the calm it brought me, to her. 'I am not sure I have the words to explain to you the very great degree by which this goes against everything I understand about sorcery. About the world. But what I do know is that it must be stopped. And to stop it, I must understand it.' I looked at her, challenging her to meet my gaze. 'And for that, I will need your help.'

Tatyana didn't say anything at first, but simply stared at the bodies behind me and chewed on her lip. Finally she nodded.

'Fine. I will help you. But I swear, if you show the slightest inkling of bringing one of those things near me, or eating one of their goddamned brains, I will feed you a foot of dendral at a speed you will not appreciate.'

'Dendral?'

'The steel, for god's sake.'

'So why call it dendral?'

She looked to the roof, then back at me. 'It is a type of steel. The best kind, from the north.'

'I thought perhaps it was the name of the sword.'

She laughed. 'I've known two people who named their swords. Both were morons and both are dead.' She waved her hand. 'Look, forget about all that. Do you understand the terms? I'm quite serious about this.'

'You will help me, but also kill me if I eat a brain with worms. Yes, I understand.'

'And the same goes for you, Jovar.'

Jovar simply nodded. He seemed inordinately pleased with his newly acquired mace, which he was cleaning far more fastidiously than he ever had himself.

'Good. Now listen to me. I have fought the dead before, and while you are strong and Jovar is good and sneaky, that will mean nothing if they come at us in any greater numbers, especially in a tight space. If they do, you will support me, one on each side. You don't rush off. You keep my flanks safe and let me open a space.'

'I should be in the middle,' I said.

'No. You're strong but you're messy.' I was about to protest but she made a chopping gesture with her hand. 'No. I don't tell you about magic, you don't tell me about this.'

I relented with a shrug. There were far more pressing things to worry about than what sequence the dead were going to try to kill us in. I did, however, refuse to relent about taking the lead as we advanced down the passage. Tatyana might have been good with a sword but she really was useless when it came to magic. With that settled, I sent the orb out ahead of us again, the brightness intensifying as it navigated the corner in the hope that it would befuddle the senses of anything waiting for us.

The passage beyond the corner widened into a long, vaguely oval chamber with a domed roof that seemed to be held up solely by the profusion of roots that had pierced it. Whatever grand purpose this chamber once had was now forgotten, although here and there signs of its ancient grandeur glittered under the light of the orb, golden shapes lost beneath centuries of accumulated grime. It was not, however, abandoned.

Chapter 29

'What is this?' Tatyana asked in a hushed tone.

I had no answer to give as the light drove the darkness back, revealing the dead that were arrayed before us. They filled the cavern, leaving me re-evaluating my earlier thought that nothing this day had left to offer could have surprised me more than being attacked by living corpses.

On one side of the cavern they lay side by side in two neat rows, looking as dead men should. On the other side, at least a score were suspended over barrels in what looked like metal cages. And in the centre between these stood a solid mass of the wakened dead. I angled the light towards them and fed it a little more power, driving the shadows back a bit further. There were easily more than a hundred of them, but to my great relief they remained slouched and unmoving as the light washed over their gleaming bodies. There were at least twice that many lying in the rows on the left, and the mere idea of being so close to three hundred or more of these creatures sent an unpleasant shudder through my flanks.

'They aren't reacting,' I said as quietly as I could.

'Small mercies,' said Tatyana who was clutching her sword. 'What do you want to do?'

I pushed the light as far ahead as I could before the tide of the strange darkness dimmed it, revealing a set of doors on the far side. 'The same as I did when we entered the crypt. Find some answers.'

'This is a bad idea.'

'So you said, but we have come this far, so we may as well see it done.'

She grunted at that. 'All right. Shit. Keep your eyes on the standing ones. If they start moving, we run before they get going. If we're lucky only the ones on the outside will see us. You got that?'

'It makes sense.'

'Jovar?' she asked.

He only nodded and pulled his mate and child closer. With that settled we made our way forward, each as quiet as we could be, straining for any sign that the dead men had become aware of our presence. Aside from the burble of their gases and an occasional twitch that made us all stop in our tracks, they remained where they were, their eyes dim and their jaws slack.

I headed for the closest of the dead who were laid out on the ground and squatted down next to it. The first thing that struck me about these bodies is that they were not like the partially decomposed and deflated-looking ones that we had stumbled across on our descent; these were relatively fresh by comparison. I brought my light in close, playing it across the body, and while it was always pleasing to be right, on this occasion it wasn't quite as satisfying. The body was as slimy as they all had been down here, but there was an additional layer of it on the face. A careful dab of my finger came away coated in that same strangely coarse, brackish jelly.

'They've got worms in them,' I said to Tatyana, wiping my finger against the floor several times.

'What?'

I pointed to the jelly under the man's nose. 'It's the same thing the worm was covered with.'

'Are you sure?'

'Go ahead and smell it.'

'No, it's fine, I'll trust your judgement.'

'I'd like to open its head to be sure, but if it is a single worm it may take too long to find.'

I tapped my knife against its head as I looked at the rows of corpses. I felt certain that the wine and the worms were related, but I was missing something.

'Magic Man.'

I looked up and saw Jovar standing near one of the bodies suspended in the cages, his mace resting on his shoulder. I sheathed my knife and joined him, taking care not to get too close to any of the standing dead.

'Yes?'

He nodded towards the cage, which was a tall, roughly circular construction, much like those that some of the street vendors kept songbirds in, only larger and more crudely made. It was tall enough that the bodies inside were able to be hung upside down without their heads scraping the bottom, and I saw now that the body strapped into the cage in front of us had a copper and glass contraption wedged in its nose, much like an outlandish pipe that someone had mistakenly squeezed into his nose rather than his mouth. His head was braced firmly by several brass rods, which I surmised were there to prevent it from dislodging or damaging the fine glasswork. I had never seen the like of either before.

'Well, that's new,' I said, leaning in and bringing my orb of light closer.

Jovar wasn't the most talkative man I had ever met, but even so I would have expected him to have warned me that the man in the cage was alive. If nothing else, it would have saved me from the undignified squawk that burst from my lips when the captive's bloodied eyes suddenly opened and stared into mine.

'Alive,' Jovar said helpfully as Tatyana hurried over.

The man's mouth opened, but rather than saying anything, he coughed out a mouthful of something bloody that slid over his eyes before he drew another wet, labouring breath.

'What? Let's get him out of there,' Tatyana offered.

'Wait,' I said, holding out a hand.

'Why?'

'The cages have magical wards,' I lied. They might well have, but I had neither the time nor inclination to be dragged into another moral dilemma about rescuing these wretches. Whoever had strapped them into the cages and manufactured the glass contraptions had put significant effort into it, which meant they were important. Tatyana relented and folded her arms while I sent a gentle probe of sorcery into the cage. I struggled to interpret what it revealed though; the glass contraption gave off the strongest pulse of necromancy, which did not really surprise me. However, the man was rotten with negative energy too, enough of it that he should have been dead. And yet his heart was still beating and his lungs filling with breath.

'Can you speak?' I asked. There was no point in expending my power if he could tell me himself. He coughed and groaned, which made the already engorged blood vessels in his face swell even more. I stepped forward and took hold of the cage, bracing my legs as I sent a carefully controlled slip of power into the iron chain that it hung from. It snapped with a pinging sound and I lowered the cage gently to the floor while the rest of the chain unspooled and fell to the ground with a loud clatter that drowned the man's moans. He continued moaning as I rolled the cage until he was looking up at us, pausing only to spit out thickened gobbets of blood and slime.

'Can you speak?' I asked again, and this time he rasped out a faint 'yes' in reply. I gave him an encouraging smile. 'What did they do to you?'

'Hurts,' he gasped, quite unhelpfully. I continued to smile. 'My head.' With the tubes in his nose it was distorted and sounded more like 'med'.

'How long have you been hanging there?' asked Tatyana from over my shoulder. I saw his eyes lift and widen as he saw her.

'Don't know.' He gritted his teeth and I saw that blood was starting to snake out of his abused nose and the corners of his eyes. His hands opened and closed, grasping at nothing until Tatyana unexpectedly kneeled and grabbed one. His eyes opened again, and he blinked the blood from them as he stared up at her. 'They . . . they're inside me,' he said, the words running together and tapering into a long groan.

'What's inside you?' Tatyana asked. It was a good question, and he seemed to be responding well to her.

'Buh . . . Buh . . . Bloodseed.' He took a shuddering breath, and through the filter of my sorcery I could feel the weave of the necromancy surrounding him strengthening. 'Can feel it. Inside. Buh . . . Burrowing. Whispering.' He clenched his teeth and I heard one crack as he ground them together.

'Tatyana,' I whispered. 'Let go of him.' *Bloodseed*. I had heard that before.

'I can't.' She tugged at his fingers, but his knuckles were whitening as he clung to her.

'Kill me,' he groaned, as his eyes filled with blood and began leaking. I didn't know how to tell him that it probably wouldn't change anything if we did.

'Let go,' Tatyana said, but whatever was happening to him seemed to have taken over his mind.

I reached into the cage and broke his fingers, allowing Tatyana to pull her hand free a mere heartbeat before blood began to ooze from his skin as if he were sweating it out. I watched with both horror and fascination as a change came over him, the transition from life to death, and then something else entirely. I watched him die with my sorcery-enhanced senses, and saw the spark of life energy within him lose its brave fight against the trauma inflicted by the necromancer's corruption. It should have returned to the Great Song, but as I watched, the dulled flicker it had become was pulled into his brain, and for the briefest of moments, played across the squirming jumble of string-like worms within his skull before sinking into the mass and falling dark. As it vanished, the blood that had oozed from his skin flickered with an absolute blackness that radiated an icy chill colder than anything this world could offer. I had never felt or seen its like before, but from the way it tore at my sorcery I knew exactly what it was.

Death.

I hastily pushed myself backwards, far from any of its blood and stared at the corpse, unable to digest the horror of what I had just witnessed.

255

I might have sat there for some time, my mind all but stupefied by the impossibility of it, had Tatyana not slapped me across my face once more.

'Damn it, Stratus, they're stirring. Get up!'

I dragged my gaze from the caged body, and looked across to where the last score or so of the mob of the dead in the centre of the room were turning in our direction, the silver light in their eyes kindling into a new brightness. The light of my orb strengthened as my focus returned and I stood hurriedly. Even as I watched, they began walking towards us, their gait stiff and unsteady.

'What did you do?' I asked.

'What? We did nothing. What did *you* do?'

'Nothing.' There was little point trying to explain it to her, not when even I was struggling to comprehend it. 'They must have sensed his death.'

'What should we do?' she asked, her attention now focused on the dead.

'As you said.' I could feel their wrongness pulling at me, and while part of me longed to wade into them and send the mockery of life that animated them back to the cursed realm where it belonged, the rest of me felt violated simply by being in their presence. 'Make for the doors. Run.'

It was unfortunately easier said than done. The dead spread out in all directions like ants from a kicked nest, making it more difficult to keep as much distance between us and them. Then Jovar's female companion strayed too close to one of the cages and a pale hand snatched at her hair in what I would guess was desperation rather than malice, but the result was the same. She gave a sharp cry and fell backwards, cracking her head against the bottom of the cage. The figure in the cage blubbered as she struggled to free herself from its grasp. The boy was frantically pulling at her hand, but he was too weak to help.

Jovar shouted something, her name probably, but I couldn't make it out. He reached in and began prying the fingers from her hair as the dead closed in.

Chapter 30

I could only guess that having your hair pulled was somehow uncomfortable, which left me uncertain as to whether she was screaming out of pain or from fear. Screaming from pain I could understand; I had done it a few times myself. I didn't think I had ever been afraid enough that wasting breath screaming about it would have felt like an appropriate response. However, Jovar's nameless companion had no such compunction and was positively wailing as he clawed at the caged man's hand in an attempt to free her.

I was about to tell him to hurry up when Tatyana dashed past me to their side.

'Move!' she shouted, and a moment later her knife flashed as she cut the woman's hair in a few deft strokes. It was a commendable effort, but it still left them exposed to the dead, who now closed the remaining gap with unexpected speed.

There were several barrels nearby, empty save for rat droppings and colonies of the pale spiders that seemed to be everywhere down here. I grabbed the nearest of the barrels and, pivoting on one foot, threw it into the dead. I couldn't hit those in front without putting Tatyana at risk, so I aimed for the side of the group. It struck high and hard enough to knock several of them down and into the path of those behind them, breaking up their attack.

Even as my barrel hit, Tatyana threw herself backwards as the first of the dead, an older female with swaying teats, launched itself at her with clawed hands. Rather than drawing her sword, she ducked behind the cage and swung the bottom of it up and into the dead woman's face, knocking her off her feet. She had barely hit the ground when Tatyana's boot cracked into her chin, snapping her neck with an audible crunch. Jovar swung his mace into the next of them, staving its face in quite neatly.

It was a fine effort, but again his companions spoiled it. The boy had foolishy slowed to watch Jovar, and the female reached back to grab him, giving one of the dead the chance to snag her arm. To her credit, she swung a fist into its face, but it was never going to be hard enough to stop it. The corpse was unarmed, but it had teeth and the will to use them, and soon enough they were sunk into her arm and another scream burst from her lips.

'Yenni!' Jovar shouted, and smashed his mace into her attacker's ribs, which did nothing to stop it from shaking its head from side to side like a dog with a rat. She screamed as its filthy teeth tore her skin, her blood painting its face. Jovar leaped forward with a wordless cry and swung his mace like a madman. It was perhaps the fourth blow that smashed the jaw from the biter's skull and the fifth that sent it crashing to the floor.

'Take him!' Tatyana shouted, thrusting the youngling at me even as she stabbed her sword into a dead man's mouth, the steel shrieking against his teeth. There was no time to discuss it, so I tucked the child under my left arm and stepped forward to grab the dead man who was about to pounce on the still-flailing Jovar. I took it by the throat and crushed its neck, grimacing at the sensation of the foul, death-tainted blood that surged from its nose. I gave it a good shake and tossed it aside. Inside me the beast purred its approval as the violence roused it and stoked the embers of its rage.

I felt something warm against my side and spun around, incredulous that something had wounded me, but there was nothing there save for the urinating youngling with his wide eyes. I dropped him without thinking, but before I could do anything else another of the dead was there, its unnaturally cold hands clamped onto my wrist and its teeth snapping.

I felt my anger swell, and I didn't care how it made the border between my will and the beast's rage blur.

I could feel the heat of it pressing back against my mind, its touch promising a release from all the doubts and fears I harboured about my sorcery, myself, and this new necromancy. Compared to all of that, the anger was beguilingly simple. Honest. There were no pretentions about it, just the release of giving into something that I knew I wanted to do. These abominations had no place in the world of the living.

The cocoon of the anger felt familiar and comfortable, more than anything that I had felt since I had woken, and I surrendered to it, not caring how the thing inside me roared with jubilation. My world narrowed to one of fury, broken bones and torn flesh, and I exulted in it. I gave the dead the peace that had been denied them, and in doing so brought another type of peace to myself. Hot blood splashed me but I thought nothing of it. Then, amid the glory of that magnificent red carnage, I heard something call to me. The beast roared and fed me images of more death, of more vengeance to be had, but the voice would not be denied.

Stratus.

I felt myself responding to it even as the beast gnashed and bellowed its wordless denial.

Stratus.

The grip of the fury that had fuelled me loosened, and as the mist cleared from my vision, I saw that I stood amid a ring of broken human bodies, none of which were whole and very few that could have been reassembled by even the most ardent surgeon. Their blood was thick and cold on my arms and body, and worst of all, I could taste it in my mouth. My orb of light was no brighter than a candle and I quickly fed it some more power to push back at the darkness that was pressing in on me. I dropped the shattered bone I had been holding and looked around. I was still in the cavern, and more of the dead were closing in on me.

'Stratus?'

I turned to the voice and could just see Tatyana's head above the barrels she was hiding behind.

'Of course,' I answered, and she stood up, the youngling clinging to her side like an oversized spider.

'Are you . . . recovered?' she asked.

'Recovered?'

'You went a bit mad there.' I could hear her heart beating as she edged closer, racing as if she had just run towards me, and I did not miss that her sword was still in her hand.

I glanced down at the torn and broken remains around me. I could remember moments of the fight, such as it was, but nothing consecutive.

'I have little patience when it comes to being gnawed on.' I looked to the remnants of the dead closing in on us. They seemed slower, their movements as clumsy as those of a young child. 'We should go.'

She didn't answer, but followed me as I made my way through the circle of torn bodies, my feet slipping on spilled viscera.

'Stratus.' She stopped several paces away. The youngling mewled and hid its head behind her shoulder. She let out a long breath. 'I think you were right. About you being a demon.'

I grunted with amusement and felt drying gore crinkling on my face. 'I thought it was all a delusion.'

'Then it is one that we share. Because what I saw you do just now was not anything a man could do.'

She seemed quite serious about it, and while her heartbeat had slowed, it was still thumping away like a hare's.

'Why are you so afraid? I told you this at the beginning. What is it that I did that you now believe me?' I looked around. 'And where is Jovar?'

'You don't remember?'

'That's a question I invariably have to answer with a no.'

'You killed him.'

'I did?'

'Yes!'

'Oh.' I looked down at the bloody mess on the floor, but between the sharp shadows and spilled blood I could see nothing that I could definitely say was his. 'I didn't mean to. He was . . . helpful.'

'You didn't mean to.'

'Not at all. I was fond of him.' I hadn't really thought about it until I said it, but I really had been fond of him in my own way. He was as close to vermin as any man I'd seen, but he had been respectful and helpful.

'You called him vermin and pulled his head off.'

'I pulled his head off.' I had meant it as a question.

'Yes, damn you!' She slashed at the air with her sword. 'And the boy saw it.'

'And the female?' I feared I knew the answer to the question before I said it.

'Her name was Yenni. And yes, you killed her as well.'

'Oh.'

It was a wanting response, but I didn't know what else to say. Tatyana seemed strangely aggrieved, given that she had known both for less than half a day, but I suspected it was the principle, more than the act, that had riled her so.

'I did not mean to,' I said again, hoping that my tone reflected that it was the truth as I knew it. I lifted my hands and looked at the thick gore that coated them, trying to remember any of it or at least why I had killed him, but it was all a blur rendered in shades of red. 'I would say this though, I did not name this *thing,* this *presence,* inside me the beast for a flight of fancy, nor did I raise the question whether I was a demon because of some knock on my head. It is real and it is dangerous, but it is not what I am. Who I am. I fear it as much as you do.'

'Do you?'

'I just said that I did.' I tried to hide my growing impatience. The dead had slowed, but they were still following us.

'Tell me this, Stratus. How do I know that you will not do the same to me? That you'll succumb to your beast's whispers and kill me and leave me to rot down here in the dark.'

I stepped out of the pooled blood and nearly lost my balance as a layer of meat and gristle slid under my foot. 'I would never do that.'

'How can you know that though? You say that you didn't mean to kill Jovar, but there he lies. How can I know that your demon won't tell you to pull my damned head off the next time?'

'I know this because you and I are more than accidental companions, Tatyana Henkman.' I gave her the warmest smile I could muster. 'Fate brought us together, and my blood runs through your body. You are kin to me now.'

Bizarrely, this made her curse loudly and lash out at the closest thing to her, which happened to be one of quicker dead. The wild blow sent its head bouncing across the floor, and before it came to rest the boy sprung from her side and ran off, a strange ululating cry rising from him, the tone high and clear.

'Come back!' she shouted, and began to run after him. He at least had enough sense not to run straight at the dead and she managed to recapture him. The movement seemed to excite the dead, and several turned to follow them, some of their clumsiness vanishing. They were still no match for Tatyana, even when she dragged the wailing, squirming boy back to where I was using my sorcery to probe the room beyond the doors for any threats. Sensing none and not wanting to risk another encounter with the dead, I hurried them through and shut the door behind us.

Chapter 31

No new horror was revealed as the door creaked open, the swollen wood grinding against the bowed lintel. The room beyond was even smaller than I sensed, much of it having collapsed. A narrow gap had been cleared through the fallen rock and masonry and led to a short span of roughly worked stairs that ended at a smooth, blank stone slab.

'It is interesting that the bodies that lay upon the floor did not rise,' I said. 'I wonder why that is?'

'What does it matter?' she said, setting the boy down but holding onto his arm. His cries had subsided to a snivel, and rather than trying to flee from her, he now hid behind her legs as I dragged a slab of carved stone over and dropped it behind the doors as a rudimentary lock.

'Leave him be,' she said.

'I won't hurt him.'

'I've heard that before,' she said, and I didn't miss how she shifted the grip on her sword.

'We don't know what we will find next and I would rather not have either of us getting killed because he can't control himself.'

'He's just a boy.' The boy in question peered around the side of her legs as we were speaking. I caught his gaze and held it, trapping his attention. His was an easy mind to manipulate, and I quickly drained the fear and stupidity-inducing panic that was gripping it so tightly. I remembered what Tatyana had said about him witnessing what I had done, and it was little work to find and draw the memory from his turbulent but shallow thoughts.

I felt a moment of disorientation as I pushed into the memory, my perception falling to the boy's level.

The hall is dark, and the dead men make little sound as they attack, but the tall figure in the middle of them is anything but quiet. The black man roars like a lion, the sound of it louder than anything he's ever heard, and he sees how the man's eyes gleam red, brighter than the blood that explodes into the air as he – it – rips the very bones from a dead man's back. He feels sick. His father is there; he is shouting at the terrible red-eyed man. It turns to him and he sees that its teeth are like a lion's too. His father shouts again, and now the lion man roars again and grabs his father by the neck, bending his head right back. He is screaming as his mother races forward to beat at the lion man's chest, but it doesn't even notice her as it grabs his father's head, its fingers in his mouth, and pulls and pulls and then there is blood, more blood than there was in the whole world. He covers his eyes as his mother starts screaming.

I drew the memory together and plucked it from him like an unwanted fruit. If he survived whatever lay ahead, he'd remember the day with a sense of apprehension and confusion, but little else.

'. . . blame him for it.' Tatyana's voice sounded quite loud as I broke the connection between myself and the boy. 'Are you listening to me?'

'Yes,' I said. Anything else would have only prompted her to repeat it. 'We should go.'

'Not yet,' she said, turning to the boy. He was watching her quietly, his arms at his side.

'Hungry,' he said, and patted his stomach.

'See?' I said. 'He's perfectly healthy.'

She looked at the boy, then back at me. 'You did something.'

'I simply took his fear away.'

'What? How?'

I sighed; this was fast becoming tedious. 'How do you think?'

She had barely started her next objection when I turned and walked away. I had come here for answers, not a debate. Between what I had witnessed and the beast's strengthening influence, I had more than enough to keep my thoughts in turmoil for some time without having to waste energy on anything so ultimately pointless as human morals. I made my way to the wall that the rough path led to. It had to be something more, like the hidden doors that Fronsac had used. Why else would someone make a path to it?

Tatyana eventually came to stand next to me. 'It's a door,' she offered helpfully.

'Indeed.' I tilted the light and saw several horizontal lines on two corners. Spreading my hands, I set my weight against it and began pushing towards the scratched corners. It moved slightly, but whatever counter-weight ruled it also served to secure it in place. I explained it to Tatyana, and we began searching for any sign of the mechanism to open it, but with little success. It seemed that the door could only be opened from the other side.

'Can you break it?' she asked.

I considered that. It couldn't be too thick, or the counterweights would be unwieldy and difficult to conceal. My sorcery was at a low ebb already, and I was loathe to expend it on something as mundane as a door, but the thought of turning back to the long and slippery climb back up to the crypt with little to show for it was equally unappealing. I kneeled by the slab, spread my hands against it once more, and cleared my mind. It might have been inanimate, but stone that remained so deep in the earth also remained part of a larger whole that the Songlines had shaped. If I wasn't to waste most of my reserves trying to force my sorcery into it, I needed to at least sense the tone of the energy here. That way I could go with the flow, rather than inadvertently pushing against or cutting across it. To my surprise, I felt the stone echo to my first and most tentative call.

It was unexpectedly familiar, and it was not long before I recognised it as the song of St Tomas. My surprise almost saw me lose my connection to it, but I calmed myself and, buoyed by my familiarity with its course, it was no great undertaking to divert some of its power to both open the door and start replenishing the power I had expended.

'Impressive,' Tatyana said as the stone slid aside with little noise. 'If you decide not to be a demon any more you'll make a great burglar.'

'I will bear it in mind,' I said, although I had no such intention. 'Tread carefully now. I do not recognise the chamber and there may be guards down here.'

'Hold on. You know this place?'

'In a way. We are beneath St Tomas.'

'What? How can you be sure?'

'The magic singing rainbow told me.'

She snorted but flipped her knife over in her hand and gently pushed the boy back. He stared at her mutely but didn't move when she let go, which was something. I peered into the square room that lay beyond. The walls were some twenty paces long and the far side had a shallow alcove with a few steps leading up and out to another chamber. A long table stood to the side of this exit, much of its surface covered in bulbous glass bottles of various sizes and delicate-looking tubes. I released the door as we stepped inside and moved to the table while Tatyana crept up the stairs, her knife in hand as the stone rumbled shut behind us.

'Nothing,' she reported not long after. 'A burial chamber about this size. There's an old coffin against the wall but whoever is inside is still wrapped up tightly.'

'Look,' I said, lifting an empty wine bottle from a stack at the end of the table. 'It's the same sort of vessel. Whatever was done to the wine was done here.'

'I don't see any though. No full bottles, nor a barrel.'

'There were barrels near the cages.'

'Shit. Those were big barrels too.'

'How many bottles do you think they will have filled?'

She scratched at her head with the bottom of her dagger. 'More than a hundred, less than two.'

I thought back to the number of barrels we had seen. 'That is not good.'

'No, it's bloody well not good.' With no warning, she flung her dagger across the room to clatter against the wall with a flare of sparks, then screamed at it. I was terrible at reading human emotions, but I was no stranger to anger. I did not try to stop her as she grabbed the table and tipped it over, sending the glass instruments smashing to the stone, the sound of their destruction as sharp as the shards that danced around our feet. It was an impressive feat, for that table was a sturdy, rough-hewn thing. She stood over the wreckage, her chest heaving and her hands clenched into fists. The boy was staring at her, his eyes wide.

'You're angry,' I said, knowing it to be true. She turned towards me then, but her heartbeat was already slowing as the fury drained from her.

'I'm not angry,' she said. 'I don't have enough anger to do what I'm feeling any justice.'

She took the knife I passed back to her without looking and held it loosely at her side. 'We should go.'

'And where should we go?'

'Up. Up and up again until we find the one responsible for this taint.'

'What does it matter? We've lost.'

'Lost what?' I asked.

'Everything.' She waved the dagger at the broken glass as if it explained anything, but my patience was rewarded soon enough.

'The wine, Stratus!' she shouted. 'All of this. Why are we bothering, when all those hundreds of bottles are out there, turning the people we were hoping to save us into monsters? We've been on our back foot this whole bloody war, and now our own people are stabbing us in the back. What does it matter what we do here? Novstan's army is going to descend on the city any day now. Even if we find who this necromancer is, it's not going to change a single bloody thing.'

'Perhaps not, but I am fairly certain that a dead necromancer can do a lot less harm than a living one,' I said. 'Someone once told me that even the greatest of fires start with but a spark.'

'Who?' she said, her arms crossed.

I smiled without humour. 'That is exactly why I am here. I do not know. These men, these necromancers, lie at the heart of what I am now. They have taken everything from me. They know me, and they're hunting me because of it.' I clenched my fists until the knuckles cracked. 'I am going to take that knowledge from them, whatever it takes. I would rather die whole than live like this.' I tapped the side of my head for emphasis. 'And there is one more thing.'

'What?'

I flashed my teeth at her in triumph. 'I believe I know who the necromancer is.'

'What?'

'Who, actually. The Cardinal.'

'What?'

'You sound like an idiot when you say it like that.'

'Get knotted. What do you mean it's the Cardinal?'

'Who else could do all of this? Who else commands the paladins?'

'That's . . . that's madness. He's in church every day.'

'And just look what lies beneath his church. And what does his presence matter?'

'It's Holy Ground.'

I gave a short laugh at that, which was clearly the improper response because she swung towards me, her heartbeat surging and her face colouring.

'What?' she all but barked at me. 'What now?'

'There's no such thing. The energy that suffuses this patch of dirt is no holier than I am.'

She shoved at my chest with no little vigour, and it was unexpected enough that I had to step back. 'Don't do that,' she said, her voice hard.

'Don't do what?'

'Blaspheme.'

'Blasphemy? It is a statement of fact.' Her posture remained stiff and belligerent, like a dog that is unsure whether it wants to attack or flee. 'It sounds like you did not leave your family's legacy behind you after all.'

'This has nothing to do with my family.'

'And my statement had nothing to do with blasphemy. All that I meant was that the power in this place is not in itself sentient as we know it; it is the will of whoever can harness it that gives it purpose.'

This seemed to placate in so much that she stopped staring at me from under her brow and began to pace the length of the room instead, her face strangely contorted. When she spoke her voice was pitched higher than it had been. 'You have no proof that he even knows about this. Why would he do it?'

I assumed that she meant the Cardinal. 'Why would anyone traffic with the dead? Who knows what thoughts his rancid mind churns out.'

'That's not good enough. If that was all it took to prove someone's guilt, we'd have been neck deep in chaos years ago.'

I smiled, but this time without the humour behind it. 'I am neither a sheh-riff nor a man. Your laws are not mine.'

'Something which I am sure Jovar regrets.'

'What does he have to do with the Cardinal?'

'Nothing. I only meant . . .' she trailed off and turned away. 'Forget it. I will say that you are mad if you think you're going to get anywhere near him.'

'Why would I? He is quite dead.'

'He is?'

'You told me I pulled his head off, so I would assume so, yes.'

'Not him, you damned fool. The Cardinal.'

That made more sense. 'I will not let you or anyone else stop me. I will have the truth from him.'

She waved her hands about. 'I'm not talking about me! I'm talking about the twenty-one paladins that form his bodyguard and, just maybe, the two thousand other Holy Knights who are currently here under his banner.'

I rubbed at my chin as I considered this. 'Those are steep odds.'

'That's what I've been trying to tell you.'

'No, it's not.'

'Let me finish. This isn't some old fairy tale where you can kick the door down and chop the evil king's head off. If it is the Cardinal, the only way we're going to get to him is through the Orders, and for that we need their support. And solid evidence of his corruption.'

'You would place your trust in the judgement of men who have not seen the snake in their midst? Who are most likely tainted by his vile concoctions and in his thrall?'

'You said it yourself. I can't believe that all of them are tainted. I won't.'

'To risk everything on that belief seems a fool's hope to me.'

'Well, it's my bloody hope. Feel free to put your opinion anywhere you like.' With that, she turned and climbed through into the next chamber before I even had a chance to try to make sense of her words, so I didn't bother and simply followed after her instead.

The next chamber was as she had described, although I was quite intrigued by the sarcophagus within. It was a grand thing of dark wood, finely carved with the same intricate religious symbols that covered the walls, but inlaid with gold thinner than the finest vellum and tiny mosaics of ivory and gemstones. The maker had built a cunning lock into it, but this was splintered and broken now, something that Tatyana assured me was not her handiwork. While an insult to the craftsmanship, it made it easier to pry it open and check the body within. It was quite small, and wrapped in linens that were browned with age and still smelled faintly of the resins they had been painted with, but it showed no signs of molestation.

'What are these lumps?' I asked Tatyana, poking at the largest that rose upon the corpse's breastbone. She was staring at the shrivelled shape with wide eyes.

'Talismans, I believe,' she said, her voice barely above a whisper as she squinted at the symbols carved inside the lid. 'To ward off evil spirits and ease the passage of the soul. Do you know who or what this is?'

'No, and I don't really care, but I suspect you're going to tell me anyway.'

'I think this is Saint Tomas.'

I shrugged. 'That would make sense, given where we are.'

'This is Saint Tomas!' She gestured wildly at the shrivelled corpse.

'Saying it louder will not make me care.'

'I don't understand. He shouldn't just be lying here.'

'You know what I find most interesting?' I poked at the lump while an idea bloomed in my mind. 'I can smell the resin.'

'So?'

'So? So I haven't been able to smell anything since we descended into this pit, not even you.'

'Thanks.' She reached out a finger and ran it along the browned wrappings.

'So why can I smell both the resin and you now?'

'Because you're special?'

'No, it's more than that.' I stood and walked back into the previous room, and as I did I felt the thickness of the air close in on me again, the soured reek of whatever had been spilled when Tatyana had toppled the table vanishing under the pervading odour of the necromancy. I made my way back to the sarcophagus and kneeled beside it, filling my nose with the cleaner smells of ancient cedar and my friend. She gasped when I drew my knife, and again when I slid it into the wrappings of the body and began sawing through the toughened fibres.

'What the Hel are you doing?' She almost shrieked the words.

'I would have thought that was clearly evident.' The smell of the resin sharpened as I exposed hitherto trapped layers of it. And there, amid the dust and torn cloth I saw the glint of gold. A few more deft strokes gave me the space I needed to draw it out.

'First murder, then blasphemy, and now this?'

I ignored her protests as I cradled the medallion in my palm. It was a flat, seven-sided disc, the centre set with a murky blue stone that was held in place by a mesh of golden strands as fine as human hair. Both sides of the flat expanse of it were marked with three rows of neatly incised runes, and even without waking my sorcery I could feel the potential within it like a light buzz against my skin. This was no mere talisman, but a potent artefact crafted by a master. It seemed that Tomas had been quite popular when he was alive too.

'This is a wonder,' I said, passing it to Tatyana, who at first held it in her hands as if expecting it to bite her. After much hesitation she tilted it back and forth in the light.

'It's beautiful,' she said, passing it back to me. 'I like the stone. But Stratus, you must put it back.'

I closed my hand around it. 'Would you leave a treasure like this for your enemies to find?'

She began to say something, but I was distracted by the familiar stirring of the beast inside me, a slow and languorous awakening like a lion roused after a large kill. It had risen strongly when my anger called to it, but this felt different. I could feel its presence, but more than as just a firestorm of anger and bloodlust. I could sense the mind lurking within it, the sentience.

'Interesting.'

'What is?'

I ran my thumb across the runes. 'As soon as I touched it the beast within me woke.'

'Should I be worried?'

'I don't know yet. I don't sense any rage. That is, no more than I always associate with it.'

'How about the kind that Jovar would associate with it?' Her eyes shifted to the boy, who was busying himself with trying to pick some of the gold off the sarcophagus with his soft and entirely useless nails.

'I meant that the rage that surrounds it is a constant feeling, and not focused upon any one thing.'

'That gives me no comfort whatsoever, but let's pretend it did. What does its awakening mean?'

'I honestly do not know. It has only ever risen in response to something, and then in a sudden rush.' I reached into my mind and felt the pressure of its awareness push back at mine. 'This feels different. Less frantic.' *And more worrisome.*

'And again, what does that mean?'

'I will tell you once I know.'

'Wonderful. If you need me, I will be twenty paces behind you.'

I looked down at the medallion and although I could not see it, I knew the beast was smiling.

Chapter 32

We left the broken sarcophagus behind us and made our way along a passage that was narrow for me but spacious for Tatyana. It was a revelation to be able to smell my environment again, even if there was only Tatyana's scent and creeping damp to enjoy for now. We passed through a heavily warded doorway, but thankfully the wards were all focused on whoever was opening the door from the other side. After that we passed two larger rooms that housed scores of what Tatyana explained were funerary urns containing the ashes of dead men. These were stacked like merchants' wares amid scores of stone coffins and sarcophagi, and while she did explain the difference between these, I did not pay sufficient attention to remember it. None of these seemed to have been disturbed, an impression confirmed by a brief sorcerous probe. Apparently the Cardinal preferred to save the more odious side of his evil practices for the deeper dungeons.

'We're getting close now,' I said, taking another noseful of the air. I had scented the almost sweet residue of an oil fire as we had climbed yet another set of wide stairs, and once I opened the door at the end of them the smell strengthened considerably and brought with it the hint of charred meat. The sound of men's voices reached us as well, and the end of the passage was lit by the yellow light of lanterns. I reabsorbed my own light and we made our way towards the junction, moving quietly. I stopped halfway along when the sorcery I had sent ahead of us found a strong trace of necromancy around the threshold of the last door.

'What now?' whispered Tatyana.

After making sure the surface wasn't warded, I put my hand against the rough wood and let my sorcery flow through it. It was smaller than most of the chambers we had passed up to now, although its contents looked much the same at first glance: urns and coffins, but also rough sacks and more crates. The door was locked but was a simple thing and my sorcery proved as good a key as ever. I woke my light as I entered, and let my sorcery lead me to the crate that was the source of the taint.

'Is it more of the wine?' she asked, kneeling beside it.

'It feels like it.'

The box was nailed shut, so she held the top and rocked it so that we both heard the muffled clink of glass on glass from within.

'Shall I crack it open?' she asked.

'Yes. Every bottle destroyed is a victory, however small.'

She wasted no time in hammering her knife in under the lid and prying it open. Eight bottles lay within, and after a brief discussion about how best to destroy them without betraying our presence or risking a cut from the glass, we agreed sorcery was our best option. It wasn't difficult to crack the glass once I had the idea in mind, and before long the sour tang of burning wine filled the room.

'Look at this,' said Tatyana as I broke the last of the bottles. I left it to drain before burning it away and glanced at the small square of paper she was holding. 'It was in the crate.'

'Speak the words back to me.'

'You don't read?'

'I don't think I ever saw the need.' I gestured for her to proceed.

She studied the paper, her brows creasing. 'It is a letter to the Master of Students at the University of Wizardry, congratulating him on the graduation of his apprentices.' I waited as she continued staring at the paper. 'It's written really formally, but the wine is a gift, a bottle for each of the students. To thank them for pledging themselves to the defence of Falkenburg.' She lowered the paper. 'It has Cardinal Polsson's seal on it.'

I opened my mouth to ask her about the University of Wizardry, but the beast closed it for me. It knew of it, and from the painful twist in my gut, it was not at all a fond memory. If nothing else, it confirmed that I was right about the Cardinal.

'. . . trust wizards,' Tatyana said, waving the paper at me.

'My apologies, I was not listening. Was it important?'

She sighed loudly. 'I said, it makes no sense that Polsson was sending them gifts. He doesn't trust wizards.'

'I thought it was obvious. He was poisoning them with the wine.'

'Well, yes, I know that. But why would the university be speaking to Polsson in the first place? They've always been at each other's throats.'

'I've never heard of the University of Wizardry.' I flinched as the beast buffeted my guts.

'Were you living under a rock? Until the war got serious it was everyone's favourite source of gossip.'

'Maybe there are no gossips in Hel, or just not any under my rock.'

'It's a long story, but you must remember that even as recently as my great-grandfather's time, people could go about their whole life without ever seeing a wizard, and if they did, they'd probably stone them.' She carefully folded the letter away into a pocket as she spoke. 'The university opened a few years before I was born, but these days they hold fairs to find new students, and some lords have found that peasants who once tilled their fields are now commanding the very forces of nature.' She smiled and shook her head. 'I remember my father ranting about it at length. Most of my earliest memories are of hiding on the stairs and listening in while he and other sour-faced men in stiff coats shouted and wrote letters about it in the parlour.'

I rummaged through some of the baskets stacked on the shelves as I waited for her to say something useful and was rewarded with the discovery of a few wrinkly apples that I wasted no time in eating.

'To this day the Church organises regular protests, and a few people have been killed. Every time it happens it's all people can talk about.'

'Why?'

She shrugged. 'Everyone has an opinion about wizards.'

'What is yours?' I asked with genuine interest.

'They're useful. I've only known a couple besides Fronsac, but they were generally nice enough. A bit pale and dull, but no different to priests really.' She laughed quietly as she finished and my curiosity must have shown. 'Sorry. My father would have had a fit if he'd heard me say that.'

'So the university is important?' I prompted her.

'Yes, more so now than ever. It started off small, founded by the last wizards in the lands, and was secretive and mysterious. And then they sent word across the land that they were accepting apprentices. A handful in the first year turned into a score the next, then doubled with each year that passed. It's now a town all unto itself with baby wizards from every kingdom.'

'So that's where the army of wizards comes from.'

'More or less. Every kingdom sponsors their own wizards so that they don't get left behind, so many went home when the trouble started. Penullin is a big place, and they had a lot of wizards studying.'

'And Polsson?'

'Well, the Church was opposed to it from the start, and came close to having it closed down a couple of times. Half the town was torched about five years ago in a riot after Polsson did a speech there.'

'I think I understand why you find it strange that he is now writing letters to the master of students.'

'Especially ones addressed to the master by name. It makes it sound like this isn't the first time. So where do we go from here?'

'Up.'

'Up?'

'Yes. Up.'

'You do remember that we're standing underneath the stronghold of the men who're hunting you, yes?'

'Of course I do. I am not an idiot.'

'I'd like to hear your plan before I agree to that.'

I finished my last apple before I answered. 'As you say, they are hunting me. Which means that many of their warriors will be out on the streets, or on the walls preparing for the siege, rather than waiting for me to step out into their fancy chapel.'

'That makes a sort of sense.'

'Thank you. And if our luck is with us, we might be able to find the Cardinal and ask him a few direct questions about his career as a wine-maker.'

'And his new-found friendship with the esteemed Magister Navar Louw.'

Navar Louw. I had barely a heartbeat between me recognising the name and the beast lurching into life.

'Ack,' was all I managed to say before my muscles began to cramp and writhe beneath my skin. I had no control over them, and it felt as if a nest of snakes had erupted within me. I staggered across the room, jaw clenched and my teeth grinding together until they squeaked, and the muscles on my arms bulged until I thought they would split my skin. Tatyana was shouting, but my mind was filled with a storm of fractured memories of blood and sand, of magic burning into me, and through it all rose the growl of the beast, a deep and primal vibration that left me deaf to her words. I could feel its thirst for vengeance and its raw hate pressing against the part of my mind that was mine alone, seeking a weakness, like a fiery storm battering a lone tower. I could almost glimpse the shape of something huge and horned amid the flame and darkness, but to focus on that was to weaken myself, so I turned away. The roar reached a crescendo before it broke and splintered into a thousand echoes that faded with a hiss, like a wave retreating from a stony shore.

Released from its grip, my muscles relaxed as one, spilling me to the ground, albeit with much of my usual grace.

'What the Hel, Stratus!' Tatyana shouted at me, her sword half-drawn. I wasn't sure if she meant to defend me or cut me down.

I pulled myself to my feet and didn't try to stifle the groan it brought with it. It felt like I had just wrestled with a cave bear and wasn't sure which of us had won.

'That name,' I said, the words sounding slightly strangled. 'I know it.'

'Louw?' she asked, her sword slowly lowering. 'Navar Louw?'

I felt another spasm twist me as she said the name again. 'Yes,' I grunted. 'That's him.'

'How do you know him?'

I leaned against the wall and waited for the shiver to leave my legs. 'I heard it on the road. From a man who was terrified of the knowledge.'

'You're not making any sense. Are you well?'

'Well enough. The beast. It recognised the name too. It felt like it did when you told me yours back at the palace, only worse. Sharper.'

I rubbed at my head to try to dispel the lingering echoes of its voice. It had not reacted like that when Crow had told me his story, so why now? The answer, when it came, was by way of the boy. I'd all but forgotten about him, but I caught a flash of gold in my side vision and turned in time to see him stuffing my medallion under his tattered shirt. He squealed like a piglet when I grabbed him and took it back, but I let him go without harm. *The medallion.* The enchantments that were bound to it were still strong, possibly because they hadn't been tested for most of the time that it had been safely ensconced in the sarcophagus, but they were clearly as cunning as they were powerful.

'Stratus?'

'The medallion,' I said. 'I believe whatever is bound to it is also affecting the beast. Waking it.'

'Tell me about the name,' she said, and it did not escape my notice that she didn't say it out loud, which pleased me.

'He is the Worm Lord.'

'Nav . . . Him? The master of students?'

'Yes.' I could feel the heat of the beast's attention. 'It is him.'

'Oh shit,' she said, sheathing her sword again. 'Are you sure? If that's true, then how do we trust any of our own wizards?'

'We may have more pressing problems,' I said, inclining my head towards the door. With her dull senses she probably could not hear the men moving towards us yet, but they were clear enough to me. There were at least four distinct voices, and the scrape and clink of metal suggested they weren't simply down here to look for apples.

Chapter 33

'We can't kill them,' Tatyana hissed at me.

'Of course we can.'

'Damn it, Stratus, don't be clever. You know what I mean.'

'I really don't.'

Before she could offer another retort, the scrape and shuffle from the passage stopped and a male voice called out.

'You in there! Come out now and you will not be harmed!'

Tatyana grabbed my wrist. 'Just follow what I do.'

Before I could tell her that I had no such thing in mind, she stood and opened the door halfway, keeping her sword hidden.

'Hello,' she said, her voice lighter than it had been with me. 'Can I help you?'

'Eh?' said the unseen speaker. 'Who are you? What are you doing down here, and what was all that shouting?'

'Oh saints,' she said, 'this is so embarrassing. I was just getting some apples for . . . uh, the Deacon, when my betrothed surprised me. You know.' She gave a blatantly false laugh.

'Oh,' the speaker replied. 'Well. You shouldn't be doing that down here, and especially not in the goddamned stores. It's not right. You'll have to leave.'

'We'll be right out,' she said, closing the door.

'I am not your betrothed.'

'That was me trying to get us out of here without a damned bloodbath.'

'I see. Cunning.'

She turned to say something to the boy, so I opened the door and
stepped into the passage. The men were carrying a lantern, but I had
assumed the combination of its poor light, their equally poor vision and
Tatyana's mummery would give me the element of surprise, and I was
right again.

I smashed the first man's face into the wall and punched the second
in the breastbone, cracking it and several of his ribs before the two behind
them even realised they were in danger. The one with the lantern hesitated, while the last ran. In a moment of inspiration I wrenched the
lantern away from the hesitant one and threw it at the runner. It hit him
across the shoulders, making him stumble and then burst alight as the
splashing oil found the flame. A swift fist to the lantern man's neck sent
him to the floor before the flames brought on the first of the runner's
screams. All four of them were down, without a single weapon having
been drawn against me and I was rightly pleased with my work.

'Hel have mercy,' Tatyana said behind me.

'Thank y—' She dashed past me before I could finish thanking her
for the diversion, only to stand next to the burning man's writhing body,
staring at it with her mouth open, which struck me as needlessly cruel.
The fire had by now seared his throat, stilling his screams but I was never
one to inflict suffering for no reason, and a quick blow from one of his
dead friend's swords stilled him.

'What is wrong with you?' she asked.

'I'm fine. They didn't land a blow.'

'No. Not that! This. Him!' She gestured to the burned man.

I shrugged and dropped the sword. 'I have never found joy in the
needless suffering of others. We should move on.'

'There was no need to kill them!' she shouted. 'They would have let
us pass, they're just labourers for Drogah's sake.'

'I didn't kill all of them.' I almost added that they were just men, but
it struck me that she was unusually prickly in the wake of my accident
with Jovar. 'Can you rant while you walk?'

'You're mad, utterly mad, aren't you?'

'Why would you think that?'

She didn't answer, save for pressing her palms against the sides of her head, before marching off ahead of me. I sent a pulse of sorcery through the connection that we shared, hoping that it would let me make some sense of what she was so riled about, but all it told me was that she was angry and anxious about something, neither of which was a revelation.

As I had suspected, we soon came to the area where the men had been working. The passage we had come down had actually run parallel to the one where I had burned the tainted bodies and wine on my first visit, and the heat had cracked the stone of the wall that separated them. The original hole it left had been widened and there were neat stacks of yellow bricks nearby along with a plethora of hand tools. I was curious to see where this passage led, since I hadn't seen any connection on my first foray, but Tatyana was already climbing through the hole so I followed her through. The walls of the chamber beyond had been blackened by the fire, and the workers had set three lanterns here which seemed excessive at first, but then Tatyana shivered and looked about.

'I don't like it,' she said simply, her heartbeat increasing fractionally again.

I pushed some energy into my vision and stepped closer. I could almost see the exact moment when she came within the aura of the medallion. She sighed and shivered again. Curious, I stepped back and watched as the fine hairs on her arms puckered and rose again.

'What is going on?'

'This is where I burned the bodies,' I said, stepping in again. 'I cannot see any active trace of necromancy, but it is as if the enchantment persists in the crusted fat.' I nudged a lump of the same from between the floor stones with a toe.

'Are you saying that's undead fat?'

'In a way, yes.' I crouched down to sniff at the lump, the medallion in my hand.

'That's bloody disgusting.'

'No, it's bloody interesting. Any half-competent wizard or sorcerer can easily exert a crude control over fire, but it is almost as disruptive as water when it comes to interacting with enchantments.'

'So?'

'So the framework for whatever the necromancers did to the bodies has been all but eradicated, but there's still *something* here.'

'Is that bad?'

'Bad? No, not in itself. It is, however, strange,' I said.

'Are you going to tell me why, or do I have to guess?'

I gestured at the blackened ground. 'It should have dissipated entirely.'

'Well, pardon me for not being a wizard.'

I stood as I considered that. Familiarity had made it easy to forget that she was of the warrior caste and no scholar. 'Think of the chair we spoke about, the one that makes you sleep.' She nodded. 'Now imagine that chair fell into a fire and was burned to ash. You would expect the enchantment to vanish when the chair burned, but instead, touching the ash would still make you drowsy.'

'And that's strange because the enchantment was for a chair, not the ash?'

'Yes,' I said with a smile, pleased at how swiftly she had followed the example.

'So perhaps you shouldn't touch the ash.'

'A good point,' I said, scraping the half-charred grease from my foot. 'It is something to think on when we are somewhere safer.'

'Agreed.' She turned and began climbing the stairs, the boy as close as he could be without tripping her. 'So what do we do if the chapel is full?'

'That depends on who or what it is full of.'

'You do have a plan though, yes?'

I grunted non-committally and hoped it would suffice. For as much as I had intended her to be my guide, it appeared that she was now following me, a position that I wasn't sure I was entirely comfortable with. Or perhaps it was because she was making a habit of asking questions I wasn't yet ready to answer.

After a not inconsiderable amount of cursing from Tatyana and a growing ache in my legs, we reached the upper levels and took some time to catch our breaths. I took a moment to dispel the connection between my breath and hers, since I judged we were now safely past the likelihood of encountering another chamber full of the rotting dead. I felt a pang of guilt for not having warned her what I was doing when she spluttered into a painful fit of coughing and gasping.

Remembering my manners, I asked her if she was in good health, which she answered with a wave of her hand and a deep, rattling breath.

'It's like. The air. Was just punched out of me,' she wheezed.

'We must have passed a ward of some sort,' I lied. 'Can you breathe now?'

'Yes,' she said, slowly standing erect once more. She took several progressively deeper breaths. 'Gods, that's so much better. It doesn't taste like we're walking around in a dog's arse any more.'

The lie I had just told forced me to keep my teeth together and swallow a sharp response about her ingratitude.

'Indeed' is all I managed before leading us along to the doors that opened into the chapel. I set my hand against the smooth wood and pushed my sorcery through, using it as my eyes and ears. The residual energy that had soaked into the door and chapel over the years distorted and pulled at mine, so that I could see little more than shapes in a thick fog of sorts. It was, however, enough to know that my lack of an actual plan had just escalated from a hiccup to a problem.

'Well?' she asked.

'Not at all. There are at least a dozen or more people moving about.'

'Huh. Are they paladins?'

'I couldn't tell. There is a surplus energy in the air that suggests they have recently held a ritual of some sort. It makes it hard for me to see.'

She folded her arms and the boy copied her. 'Have you tried opening the door and looking out?'

I limited my derision to a snort before opening the door a sliver. The chapel was as dark and laden with skulls as it had been before, but at least half of the benches had been removed from the middle section and replaced with narrow beds. Tables had been laid out along the edges of this area, each piled with linens and bottles, although thankfully not of the wine-filled sort. I counted just over a dozen figures, although given the dark robes most wore and their bland, hairless heads, I might have counted some of them twice. I closed the door and told Tatyana what I had seen.

'It's a hospital,' she said in a confident voice. 'Novstan must be close.'

'I thought it was a temple of the dead.'

'I'm not saying it would be the cheeriest place to wake up in, but even mortuary priests know how to stitch and sew.'

'Interesting. Now, if I rush in, I should be able to kill or disable at least half the priests easily enough. If you can block the doors on the left, I can finish the others off, leaving us to make our way out without the alarm being raised.'

'No,' she said. 'That simply isn't an option, Stratus. Just give me a moment.' She pushed past me and opened the door slightly, pressing her face to the gap as I had done, but for far longer. Eventually she closed it and rubbed her hands, the boy copying her again in a manner that was fast becoming annoying.

'I could only see three men-at-arms, and they are down by the altar. If we move fast and quiet we should be able to slip out while they're distracted,' she said. 'And you should carry the boy.'

'Why? The last time I tried that he defecated on me.'

'Because they're not looking for a man and boy, just a man.'

It was a simple ruse but clever enough, although the boy wasn't convinced. He squirmed and tried to run, but changed his mind once he was out of the circle of my light. Apparently being carried by me was less intimidating than being alone in the absolute darkness that waited in the bowels of St Tomas.

And so I entered the chapel of St Tomas for the second time, with Tatyana following close behind. We moved as quietly as we could and tried to remain within the deeper shadows that pooled against the walls. It was only twenty paces to the doors, and then another hundred or so along a straight passage to the outside, and I was starting to feel the first stirrings of optimism when I felt a change come over the boy. Or, more accurately, I felt the trace of the magic I'd implanted in his mind dissipating.

I didn't have time to curse my own stupidity. For all my clever tampering with his memories, I had not considered what effect exposure to the ambient energies of the church itself might have, let alone the medallion's indiscriminate influence. They must have started working on him almost as soon as I had done what I had, slowly unravelling my work. Such a short exposure would not affect Tatyana or myself, but a weak and pliable mind like the boy's was another matter entirely.

The boy's original memories reasserted themselves, his fears rising to the surface once more, most of which were focused on the man who was currently carrying him. He screamed as if I had set him on fire and kicked himself away from me, the combination of the strength his fear lent him and my surprise letting him succeed in wriggling free of my arms. He hit the floor and was up and running, another scream wailing from his lips before I could give voice to the curse rising in me.

As one, everyone in the chapel turned to us as the boy found himself a priest and leaped into the man's arms.

'Run!' shouted Tatyana, who was already taking her own advice. The doors were not locked, but they were heavy, and we stumbled our way into the passage beyond, chased by the men-at-arms and their cries of alarm.

Chapter 34

'Stop them!'

'Seize them!'

My luck, as far as I could tell, had always been a changeable thing. And now, as we ran towards the outer doors of the church, it seemed to desert me once more. There were three men-at-arms at the doors who were already responding to the shouts rising behind us, but these I am sure we could have dealt with easily enough. Then the main doors opened, revealing an entire troop of paladins and filling me with dismay. It was scant consolation that they looked equally surprised to see us, but that did not last very long at all. They dropped the boxes and helmets they were carrying and broke into a run, bellowing war cries as they came.

Tatyana's response was short, crude and surprisingly eloquent in the circumstances. I grabbed her arm and pulled her down a side passage on the right. There were more rooms along it, and already several men had spilled from these. I set my shoulder and barged through them, leaving not a few on the ground who would be grateful that there was now a hospital so close by. We crashed through the door at the far end and I swung us left, fully expecting to see a window that we could crash through to make our escape, but I found myself stood before a wall of thick, pitted stone.

'No,' I said, hammering at it with my fist, but it was no illusion.

A man leaped at Tatyana, but she twisted and grabbed his arm like I had seen Lucien do the night he was attacked, and promptly threw him onto his back hard enough to snap at least a few rib bones off his spine.

I felt the beast rising, and I could not tell if it was me snarling or it. Behind us the paladins were leaping over the bodies of those I'd knocked down and filling the air with yet more threats.

'We have to get out of here!' cried Tatyana, as if that wasn't my plan already.

'Follow me,' I shouted, and ran towards the door at the opposite end of the passage. It was narrow and filthy, and as I had begun to fear, it led back to the main passage where a dozen or more paladins and men-at-arms were waiting for us. I could feel the rage of the beast pushing into my consciousness. I hadn't wanted this fight, not at first, but there was something about the sight of them that made me want to pull them apart.

To tear them down and make of them a red ruin.

I felt the painful pressure of my demonic teeth grinding past the human approximations that I normally showed the world as I stalked forward, all but drooling in anticipation of the killing to come.

I didn't see or hear the attack that felled me, but it had to have been a blow of some force. The last I remembered was tasting blood, after which everything went black and silent until I awoke to a whole new world of agony.

Waking to find yourself upside down is a monstrously disconcerting experience, even more so when you have been severely beaten and cut while you were asleep. It took me several attempts before I could open one of my eyes. The other hurt badly enough that I feared it had been cut from me; the flesh around it was too swollen for me to sense anything else but the pain centred on it. I didn't dare try to do anything else. My body was a distant thing, held immobile by unseen hooks and chains and separated from my mind by a mountain of pain.

With my vision as limited as it was, I turned to my other senses. My nose was a dull weight, and from the taste in my mouth I guessed that it was blocked with blood that had trickled down from my wounds and dried within it. That left my hearing, which at first seemed as much of a mess as the others. With little else to do though, I focused on it, slowly separating out the sound of my blood thundering through veins engorged by my suspension, then the constant dripping which may have been water or, more likely, my own blood. It was much like standing beside a waterfall and trying to listen to birdsong. At first, there is only the roar of the water, but once you have heard all it has to offer, you begin to hear other things until you know every sound around you.

So it was that I listened and slowly built an image of where I was by the sounds around me. I was indeed dripping blood, but far more slowly than the roof was leaking water. From the muted squeaking above me I surmised that I hung from iron chains fixed to something made of wood, and the chamber I was in was not very large, probably no more than fifteen paces to a side and nowhere near as high. I listened keenly for anything new and tried to ignore how the pain I felt was growing more intense, as if waking had given it permission to start crawling into my awareness. No one came to me, and the only relief I had from the tedium of waiting was watching a pack of the albino spiders stalk an equally pale lizard across the wall in front of me. I heard its soft, plaintive cry as it succumbed to the spiders' venom, and listened as it was dragged into a crevice and devoured. As portents went, it was not particularly heartening.

'Farewell, little lizard.' My voice was a whisper, but to my ears it sounded as if I had shouted it.

With a firmer grasp of my situation I turned my attention inward, seeking my sorcery and a connection to the Songlines. I had expected it to be painful, and in that I was sadly not disappointed. To move beyond the pain that filled me, I had to acknowledge and work my way through all of it, and that meant feeling it all. I began at my feet and worked my way towards my head, and discovered that my injuries were too numerous to tally. My legs were scraped raw in places, no doubt from being dragged across rough stone, and were bound to the frame that I hung from by what felt like wire. My gut and chest had taken the brunt of the beatings and finding a part of me that wasn't bruised or scraped proved the harder task. If I had not been black before, I most certainly would have been now.

The pain in my chest was too sharp and insistent to be mere bruising, and it seemed that the Church's men had finally succeeded in breaking one or more of my bones. My arms were in a similar state to my legs, and my head too. I hadn't lost my other eye as it turned out, but the combination of the bruising caused by repeated blows and me hanging like this had seen blood and fluid swell my face to grotesque proportions.

Worse was that after enduring all of the pain once more, my sorcery remained hidden from me. I strained for it, but my only reward was a faint glimpse of violet light, followed by a pain inside my head that matched that outside of it. My captors had set an enchantment on me, robbing me of my most versatile weapon and the implication of this was not lost on me. I roused myself back to a more normal awareness and spent some time forcing the pain from my mind again, squeezing it back into a formless presence that was marginally easier to ignore. I was in trouble, that much was certain, and with every moment I hung there, remaining calm enough to think was becoming more difficult.

After what felt like an age of forcing myself to listen to the arrhythmic tap of unseen spiders and rat claws, I finally heard something new: the steady impact of something far heavier and two-legged. It grew close, and soon enough a door opened somewhere behind me, flooding the room with yellow light that seemed as bright as the sun and the sound of a heart beating too fast.

'There you are.'

I recognised Cardinal Polsson's voice a moment before I heard the faint echoes of Tatyana's screams in the passage behind him.

'I'm going to kill you,' I croaked at him.

He gave a short laugh and thumped across the floor towards me, and a moment later the world lurched horribly as he spun me about to face him. He seemed impossibly tall as I squinted up at him against the light.

'You will have to forgive my lack of fear, creature.' He walked around me, and I felt like one of the birds that were strung up outside the butcher's stalls in the market. He kicked me in the face as he completed his inspection. The pain was sudden, enormous and entirely disproportionate to the damage his frail legs should have been able to mete out, but I kept my teeth together and denied him the pleasure of a scream.

'You're pathetic,' he said, and I could hear the sneer in his voice. Another kick hit home, but this one was aimed at my shoulder and set me swinging like a pendulum, the chains grinding and clanking as the world swung around me.

'Look at you. Stripped, beaten and entirely at my mercy. How the mighty have fallen.'

It was hard to focus on his words while the new pain unleashed upon my once noble face was still ravaging at my senses. I caught glimpses of barrels and boxes along the wall behind the door; yet another storeroom then.

Polsson arrested my swinging with another sandalled foot to my face. This time he managed to tear some skin and I saw my blood spurt free in a long stream, driven by the pressure within the stretched skin. It was almost a relief. I spat more from my mouth.

'I am still mighty,' I said, which made him hoot with laughter and kick me again. I suspected that his ageing joints prevented him from kicking at anything that wasn't as low to the ground as my face was, although it wasn't much of a consolation.

He squatted down in front of me. 'I have sent word of your capture to my master,' he said, and I flinched as he touched the skin of my chest with a hand as unnaturally cold as any of the corpses I had destroyed. If I had harboured any doubts as to his complicity, the nausea that squirmed through me as he stroked my chest would have put it to rest. I would have preferred a dozen kicks to the lingering sense of wrongness that trailed behind his fingers.

'He spoke to me directly.' A shiver passed through him as he spoke, and he paused to lick his thin lips. 'My reward for capturing you will be great. I suppose I should thank you, given how easy your blundering and pathetic attempts to disrupt our plans here made it for me.'

I tried to twist away from his hands, but I was too weak to do anything more than rattle my chain. He laughed again, sounding like nothing more than gas escaping a body, and I was glad that my nose was blocked.

'And just who do you think I am?' I asked. He didn't reply at first and simply sat there, watching me with an adder's unblinking stare.

'So it's true then,' he said. 'Your mind is lost. That's as much a pity as it is a boon, I suppose. I would have liked to have understood why my master sought you with such passion, but it has also made you easy to capture.' He scratched at his thin beard. 'Although I suspect that even as tainted as your blood is, the power it carries would be quite something.'

I didn't like the way he studied me as he said that, and I liked it even less when he said, 'Yes, he said alive, but no more than that,' and walked out. He left the door open, which was something at least. I had had a bellyful of being in the dark and the light was welcome. Another scream echoed down the passage, muffled by the stone and closed doors, but it was unmistakably Tatyana's.

With access to my sorcery blocked, I had no way to tell whether the sorcerous healing that I had imbued her with was still functional. It all depended on the structure of Polsson's enchantment, but I could not even study that. Where was my rage, my beast, now when its mindless fury might actually be of use?

'Where are you?' I said, shaking my head. 'I know you're in there. Help me. Help *us*.'

If it heard me, it gave no sign of it, and I was midway through repeating my entreaty when Polsson re-entered the room, followed by another man carrying a wooden box. I didn't recognise the new man, but from his pale and emaciated appearance I suspected that he had been spending far too much time in a dark and wet environment.

'A fine specimen indeed,' the pale man said, his rictus smile revealing teeth that hadn't been as white as his skin for a long time.

'Isn't he just?'

'How much do we take?'

'As much as we can. My master expects him alive, but nothing more.'

'Shall I begin?' asked the pale one, opening the box on a nearby barrel.

'Of course,' said Polsson before squatting down in front of me. 'You should be honoured. Skibor here is by the far the most talented of my students and quite gifted in the art of turning blood into power. I am going to leave you in his capable hands while I go pay your little whore a visit. What's left of her anyway. Skibor's skill is quite something, but so is his enthusiasm.'

He had to be talking about Tatyana, and I felt an unexpected pang of emotion as the import of what he was saying sank in.

'I know you can hear her from here. I am going to discover just how many times she can scream your name before she starts cursing it instead. She will tell me everything.'

He left without another word, leaving me alone with Skibor and the whisper of the blade that he was honing on a leather strap.

Chapter 35

'Fascinating.'

He said it quietly but his breath felt like a fiery wind against the exposed flesh of my arm. 'I could study your arm alone for months.'

I clenched my teeth as he spoke, fighting the nausea that followed the pain as well as the urge to watch what he was doing. I had no fear of blood, least of all my own, but that was different to seeing it draining into bottles or watching the way he had sliced and pinned my skin back, exposing the striated bulges of the muscles beneath.

I had yet to give him the satisfaction of crying out, although I was surprised that my teeth hadn't shattered from how tightly I had them clenched. He had at least adjusted the way that I was hanging in order to bring my shoulder level with the table he had set up. The relief had been immediate and acutely painful, but nothing compared to what I had endured as he prodded and cut his way deeper in to my arm, occasionally commenting on what he saw. His thin, pale lips were red now, but with my blood rather than a flush of his own. According to him, I had an exotic and thrilling taste that could only be complemented by a fine searing and the best wine. He'd laughed when I tried to take a bite out of him in turn and had simply tied my arm down and gone back to work on it, cutting his way up from the wrist to the elbow and inserting hollow glass rods, connecting them so that my blood flowed steadily through them and into his bottles. The rods I recognised from the contraptions we had seen wedged into the noses and mouths of those in the cages below, a realisation that made me strain all the harder against my restraints.

I turned away again as he slid a thin blade into the muscle and started opening it up, blowing the blood that welled up away with short, sharp breaths that felt like liquid fire against the newly opened flesh. I had not heard any screams from the passage since he started cutting, and rather than provide any comfort, the effect of the silence was entirely the opposite. Tatyana was only human, but she had a been a good companion, honest and bold.

I would avenge her when I broke free.

That was easily said but seemed as remote and unreachable a goal as the moon then. Skibor's blade was cutting deep now, and while I did not scream, it was too much to hold back a groan that was born of a combination of pain and despair.

'Did that hurt more than the others?' He pressed his blade in again and the pain hit me like a bolt of lightning. 'Fascinating. There is what appears to be a muscular tube lodged between the bones, but I cannot fathom its purpose.' He paused to lick some blood from his fingers. 'Let's see what is inside.'

The pain was terrible, a combination of fire, ice and lightning that consumed the whole of the left side of my body. It was all I could do to tell myself that I had survived worse, that this paled to the intensity of the agony that had followed my reawakening in that damned meadow. It was only pain, and I knew they were not going to kill me. Skibor was focused on digging out the sheath in my arm and I ground my teeth as I tried to push past the sensation. I felt something tear in my arm and saw that Skibor had pried the tube free, and it was strange enough that for a few moments I forgot that it was the internal workings of my own damned arm that he was squeezing and pulling at. The tube, as he had called it, was pale and rigid, and about the width of my finger at its widest part. It looked to be the full length of my forearm, and as he squeezed it I could see there was something dark within it.

Something dark.

The thought chimed with something in my mind, but I didn't have a chance to explore it any further. I am not sure which of us was more surprised by what happened next. He had bent forward, still examining the tube, and had moved to cut it free at the base when it flexed, much like a throat swallowing, but with far more force and vigour. As it did, what looked like a single, ebony claw shot from it and skewered him quite neatly through the neck.

He threw himself backwards, which was when we both discovered that the ebony talon was barbed. It was too late for him to stop though, and with my arm firmly anchored to the barrel when he fell back, it was his neck that lost the struggle. I glimpsed ribbons of meat and the ragged ends of his great arteries streaming from the wound as he toppled in a spray of blood. He made one desperate grab to steady himself and to try to stem the fountaining blood, but his strength had already fled and all he managed to do was grab the edge of the box he'd carried his tools in.

I laughed as I listened to his bowels emptying. Killing a necromancer had a delicious irony to it, and to do it in such an unexpected fashion was even funnier. It didn't alter my situation though, and as the humour in it dwindled I turned my attention back to the talon that had killed him. I had no idea how it had gotten there, but from the way it was bedded into my body I was sure that it had to have been something that had been part of me before my transmogrification to human form. As I watched, it began to withdraw, the muscular sheath slowly expanding to swallow it again, tight enough that Skibor's blood and flesh were rubbed clean from its length.

A movement from his hand caught my eye. He could not be alive. Or was he rising from death? I waited, and as it moved again, I breathed a sigh of relief. His fingers had spasmed as he died, and it was simply that the weight of his body was pulling at the box. It scraped forward a hair's breadth at a time, then suddenly slid forward and toppled from the edge of the barrel.

The noise had barely faded when I felt something twist *inside* my head. There was pain; but if anything, it was a good pain, like that when a festering splinter is finally pulled from your flesh. It faded as swiftly as it came, and as it left I felt a touch of something softer than any breeze. I reached for it – my sorcery – and I felt it thrum against my soul as if welcoming me back.

The enchantment binding me had been broken. I didn't question how or why but reached for the Songlines with all my will, plunging myself into its power. I drew deeply on it, almost foolishly so, and let the intoxicating thrill of it course through me, driving the pain from my body and igniting a wholesome, healing fire in my injuries. It was laughably easy to sever the wires that bound me so cruelly, although I did regret rushing to do that when I fell to the ground.

Even with the energy flowing into me like it was, it took an unusually long time and no little concentration to heal my injuries. The demands of the healing burned through the small reserve of fat left in my body before I could complete the process, but my arm was whole again, the strange black talon once more hidden. Even though I knew it was there I still had no sense of it, not even now, and I could not help but wonder what other secrets my body was hiding from me.

I could force the rest of the healing now, but without food or drink to fuel it, I would create something of a vacuum in my body and would need to draw on the Songlines constantly to prevent my body from consuming itself. I couldn't take that risk, nor would I, even in the best of circumstances. The injuries that remained were uncomfortable and ugly, but they would not be enough to stop me pulling the Cardinal apart like an insect. I threw the bottles of my blood against the wall. I didn't know what they wanted it for, but I would rather not find out.

With that done, I set about cutting Skibor's head off, both because I wanted to and as a precaution. Aside from the measure of satisfaction it brought me, moving the body also revealed the medallion that had spilled from the fallen box and broken the enchantment. I lifted it out and smiled as I ran my finger across the runes. I was becoming more fond of it every time I saw it, and I owed whoever had buried it with the long-dead Tomas a great debt.

I took a moment to clear the blood from my nose, then shook the feeling of compression from my back and neck, eliciting a startling variety of brittle noises. It was time to collect the blood debt the Cardinal owed me, something that was now true in every sense of the word, and I felt the beast's approval pulse from within.

I stepped out into the passage, seeking the old man's scent, but the two men-at-arms standing outside a door some sixty paces along made it unnecessary. They saw me almost immediately and began shouting even as they charged along the narrow passage. I was angry enough on my own, but within me the beast was rising too, and before I had even thought it, I was baring my demonic teeth at the guards and filling the passage with a roar that would make the great cats of the plains shrink away. I smashed into them as they faltered, the knotted mass of my knuckles making a mockery of their armour and bloody kindling of their bones.

Behind them the cardinal burst from the doorway. He began shouting too, but I was too busy disentangling myself from the spilled guts of the second guard to pay his words any attention until it was too late. It was a spell. I should have expected it, but despite having known that we were chasing someone of more than rudimentary skill, it still took me by almost complete surprise.

Blood-red forks of lightning flashed down the passage, splitting the air with a deafening crack and hitting me like the kick of a giant. They sent me tumbling and skidding back, my senses scrambled, the smell of burned flesh thick in my nostrils as I slid to a sudden halt against a wall. I tried to lift myself, but my limbs still twitched with the dregs of the bolt's energies and refused to obey me. I managed to lift my head in time to see him casting another spell, but could do nothing as a wall of flame rolled down the passage towards me with a booming roar.

Chapter 36

Fire.

The most beautiful of the elements, twisting and dancing as if celebrating its brief life and burning in a thousand shades of red, gold, white and orange. It rolled over me like a wave, burning the filth and blood from my skin and filling a void within me whose depth I only appreciated as the heat and flame filled it. I had felt something of this when I had lain on that hill and drew the heat of the campfire into my hands, but then I had taken it as a sign of my demonic heritage and shrunk from the implications.

This fire was not one I could turn from, and it wrapped me in an embrace I could not have escaped from even had I wanted to, silencing my doubts and leaving no part of me untouched. I drew it into me like the desert sands drink in an unexpected storm, but the flames were gone all too soon, and I almost cried out in frustration when I opened my eyes and found myself in the steaming passage once more. The edges of the stones around me were brushed with a fading orange, giving them a strange beauty, and as my hearing returned I could hear them clicking and cracking as damp air rushed in to replenish what the fire had breathed in.

The remnants of my clothes and the gore from the dead guards fell from me in a fine cloud of ash as I stood up. A steady rumbling filled the passage, and it took me several moments to realise that it emanated from me. Or rather, the beast inside me, and I could not tell for sure if I was hearing it with my mind or my ears. It clearly liked fire even

300

more than I did, which made sense if we had come from same burning pit of Hel.

The Cardinal was staring at me where he had stopped, mid-stride.

'We have matters to discuss, priest,' I said, my voice thick with the beast's growl.

He took a step back, then several more, each more rapid than the last until he was back at the doorway he had emerged from. I followed him, but at a slower pace, my feet crunching through the crisped remains of the guards. Polsson looked inside the room and flicked his hand. I felt his magic bloom, and a moment later the bright glow of a fire burst from the room accompanied by a high-pitched wailing.

Tatyana.

He turned and ran, and even though my muscles were bunched to spring after him, I hesitated as another scream tore along the passage. The Cardinal's head held the secrets I yearned for and he was so very close, but to stop him meant leaving Tatyana to burn to death. I let the Cardinal run and set my teeth, ready to repel any attempt by the beast to stop me from helping her, but none came.

Apart from being ablaze, the room she was held in seemed exactly the same as mine had been. She too hung from a cross-shaped wooden contraption, but not upside down as I had been. In the confined space Polsson's fire spell had filled the room entirely, setting anything remotely flammable afire, including Tatyana. She was thrashing against the frame she was bound to like a trapped animal, her skin already blackening in a dozen places and her hair ablaze like a torch. I channelled a strong pulse of sorcery to her, enough to smother her senses and render her unconscious before turning my attention to freeing her and snuffing the fire. Cradling her carefully in my arms, I made my way back to the room where I had hung and set her down.

I could feel her injuries drawing from my sorcery, but her body was healing from the inside out, choosing the most critical wounds first. Yet if I was going to carry her, the open wounds on her skin would be acutely distracting for both of us, particularly the deeper burns where the skin had crisped and the fats had begun to run. I drew my sorcery up and took some time to prepare the construct. Healing a cut was fairly easy: you simply squeezed the sides together and let the body's own fibres stitch together. Burns were, however, a far greater test of skill because of the way they affected the skin and flesh, transforming it from something that was part of a living body into something delicious.

My third attempt at creating the healing construct was successful, the first two having failed because of the same distractions that I was trying to prevent. The skein of energy settled across her body like a soft blanket as I released the sorcery, and while it looked quite beautiful in my mind, I knew that if she had been awake the pain it would have caused her would have been almost as bad as what the fire had inflicted. To heal a burn, you need to skim the burned area until healthy flesh is revealed, and only then can you begin restoring it. I knew this because I had been awake when my newly reformed body had relived the agony of its creation in exquisite detail. As painful as it had been, it had at least left me with a robust knowledge and experience of how to do what I needed to do. It was an expensive process in terms of how much power it took though, and if it had been anyone else but her I would have broken their necks and left them.

Once the sorcery finished its work and dispersed into a golden mist, I gathered her up once more and stepped out into the passage again, intending to make my way back towards the damp and crumbling dungeon that coiled beneath St Tomas and the long climb back to the abandoned crypt we had originally entered through. I could not, and would not, risk the chapel again. Not yet. There was no guarantee that Polsson's minions would not be waiting for us at the old graveyard as well, but I felt confident enough that if they were, they would not be in the numbers that the chapel could yield.

It was not long after I had stepped into the passage that I heard the first voices, and then the thud and clatter of men in boots and armour. It seemed that Polsson did not want to lose his prize so soon. I slung

Tatyana across my shoulder and hurried in the opposite direction, scanning the walls and floor for any sign I could recognise. It was perhaps fortunate that she had been bleeding when they brought us here as it was the faint trace of her blood that guided me back to the network of tunnels that was more familiar. I was halfway down the stairs that led down to the chambers where we had found the medallion, when the first of the Cardinal's men-at-arms saw me. His shouts echoed down the stairs but I didn't bother looking up, not then and not when the sound of hurried footsteps sounded behind me. It took a little coaxing in the circumstances, but I relieved the pressure in my bladder as I walked and, I will admit, took no little pleasure in doing so.

That stolen pleasure was multiplied tenfold when I heard the surprised squawk of their fastest man turn into a scream as he slipped on the doubly slick stairs and fell past me and broke upon the bedrock some thirty body-lengths below. The stairs were smooth and treacherous when dry, and as I had hoped, a good wetting had made them lethal. The beast was still awake within me and I felt a flush of pleasure from it and, just for a moment, the omnipresent aura of rage that surrounded it lifted. A flash of sparks and the whine of metal on stone broke the moment and made me recoil and nearly lose my own footing, which would have been a terrible but poetic irony.

I risked a glance behind me as the broken arrow fell away into the darkness. There were at least a dozen men behind me, of whom four were archers. I shrugged Tatyana off into my arms and cradled her to my chest, offering them my back as a target rather than her; I had been shot before and their little pricks held no fear for me. They loosed their shafts just as I cleared the last of the stairs and two hit my back, the impacts sudden and acutely uncomfortable, but I knew their sting would fade swiftly.

'*Kill them.*'

To say that those words took me by surprise was an understatement, and it was something of a miracle that I didn't fall over as I stumbled into the small antechamber at the foot of the stairs. The voice that spoke them was rich and deep, a voice that I would pay gold to listen to, such was the harmony within those simple words. But it wasn't the beauty of the voice that arrested me so, but that they spilled from Tatyana's lips.

'What?' was my eloquent response as I looked down at her. 'Tatyana?'

'You heard me.' Her lips and throat worked, but she didn't lift her head or open her eyes as she spoke.

'Tatyana?' I asked again.

'Don't be a fool.'

That voice. Tatyana. I staggered as I realised where I had heard it before. The dreams. The dreams of the lonely thing in the darkness and the voice that had cried out in the cage.

The beast.

'You speak.' I looked behind me as the paladins and their companions spilled out into the small antechamber, their voices shrill and insubstantial.

'Kill them or we die here.'

I warily laid Tatyana down and turned to face my pursuers. The paladins were, unsurprisingly, the loudest of them, and I could sense the coldness within them. The archers loosed another volley of shafts and I let them break against my hide. The fear that bled into their scent at the sight of their impotence was worth every mote of pain. The archers fell back behind the paladins, who closed their helmets and advanced upon me. They each carried one of the short stabbing spears that I knew could penetrate my hide, while the men-at-arms that walked between them simply carried swords.

'Some help would be nice,' I said, which made the men-at-arms glance at each other.

'No one is coming to help you,' said the centre paladin. 'Today you face your judgement.'

They advanced as one, and I felt my anger at the beast stirring. 'So is this your grand scheme? To see me ended like this?'

I edged away from where Tatyana lay and raised my arms. I would not die so easily.

It was a noble thought, but one whose impact was lost when the sudden ache in my forearms sharpened into something searing and made me gasp. I felt my wrist bones grind together and without me thinking it, my hands curled into fists, neither of which paid the slightest heed to me telling them to open. A single, curved ebony talon as long as my forearm slid from a bleeding tear between my middle knuckles on each hand.

I had a heartbeat, perhaps two, to gawk at them before the paladin to my right leaped to the attack. He charged forward and drove his spear at my chest in a single powerful motion that would have driven it clean through me. I flinched away and felt a solid contact as one of my new black talons clipped the shaft and knocked it away. My hands were still locked into fists, so I simply punched him with the other hand, driving the talon through the coat of rings he wore and piercing more than one important organ inside him.

'Demon!' screamed another of them as I kicked the dying one from the now slick length of the talon. A man-at-arms swung for my legs, but the extra reach I now had let me intercept his blade. I punched him too, with even more spectacular results given that he wore little more than stiff leather. The remaining two paladins closed in with a flurry of fast stabbing attacks, several of which cut into me despite my best efforts. I was bleeding like a cracked bucket by the time I felled the last of them by punching a talon through the eye slit of his helmet, and I couldn't even clutch at my wounds since my fists still refused to open.

I slid down against a wall and gulped in some air. 'Something a bit bigger would have been better,' I said. It seemed the beast was listening now, as no sooner had I spoken than I felt my bones twisting again and the talons slowly withdrew into my arms. I shook my hands as the hurt faded and then set to examining my newest collection of injuries. I coaxed the dregs of my sorcery into staunching the worst of them and sat quietly to let the dizziness fade. This could not be sustained.

I hauled myself to the nearest of the dead men and, with a grunt of effort, smashed his head open against the floor. By the dimmed light of my orb I scratched through the glutinous mass that leaked from it with the point of a fallen sword. Nothing squirmed or swam within the fluids, which was good enough for me, and I wasted no more time in butchering him. It was unfortunate that I didn't have enough power in reserve to start a constant fire, but he was still warm and soft and it proved easy enough to gulp the fresh meat down. I could feel my body attacking it even as I swallowed, and with each mouthful the dark rings around my vision receded and my thoughts fell back into a more useful order. I stood and marvelled at how easy that simple act now felt, and I had to forcibly remind myself that this new strength felt greater than it was simply because of how weak I had been before.

I left the dead men to the vermin and continued my journey into the dark. Tatyana's weight hardly bothered me now, and with no further sounds of pursuit or undead horrors lurking in the alcoves, I turned my attention inwards.

I tapped Tatyana on the forehead. 'Why will you not speak to me?' I asked, but no reply came.

I tried again, and a dozen more times after that, and was on the verge of venting my frustration on the next breakable thing I came across before I heard a response.

'*You.*' The voice was fainter now and her lips barely moved.

'That's a terrible answer. Why speak now, after all I have suffered? And why her?'

'*It is difficult.*'

'Difficult? Try being stabbed with enchanted spears.' There was no reply to that. There were so many questions crowding my head that choosing one to give voice to was like trying to snatch a single bee from a swarm.

'What do you want, creature?'

'*Whole.*'

'A hole?'

'*To be whole.*' These words were clearer and her lip curled into a sneer as she spoke. '*Free of you.*'

More anger billowed after these words, and I began to fear that talking to it like this was somehow making it stronger or hurting Tatyana.

'Then we have something in common,' I replied nonetheless, and saw her stiffen as the sorcerous bond between us shifted and flexed. I felt something twist in my middle, as if something was dragging itself through the coils of my guts. My mind flashed to the talons that had lain hidden within my arms for so long, and the idea of something alien swimming within me no longer felt like such a flight of fantasy. The beast's melodic voice descended into a wordless growl as it battered at the edges of my mind and whipped through my gut, but I took heart in that I had felt this all before and though it was not at all pleasant, it was not debilitating.

The beast seemed to sense it too and fell quiet soon enough, slinking back into the mental crevasse that it haunted. I pressed at the sides of my gut in its wake, unsure as to whether I wanted to be right or wrong, but all I felt were the bits that were supposed to be in there. Part of me wanted to call to it again, to try to eke answers from it rather than more questions, but caution stayed me. Its intentions seemed less than charitable and I would not provoke it while my strength was so wanting. Knowing that for all of the violence it carried, it still had a voice and a mind was a victory, whatever else happened. Mindless fury could only be fought, but a mind could be reasoned with, or such was my hope.

With my soot-smeared medallion tucked between Tatyana's limp form and the skin of my chest, I passed through the rest of the caverns without once having to gag on the reek of dark magic. I was sure the path had not been so long on the way down, but I could sense no magic befuddling my senses, only the deep, bone-eating fatigue that my impromptu meal was already struggling to keep at bay. Hunger was one thing, but the craving gnawing at my bones was the product of blood loss and too much sorcery and would not be so easily slaked. It wasn't yet bad enough to tempt me to a bite of any of the bodies that lay in the upper chambers, but I did stop to rest in the crypt itself. I didn't mean to fall asleep, only to sit down and ease some of the ache that had wormed its way into every limb, but my body took that decision away from me. I woke an unknowable time later, caught somewhere between reality and the frayed edges of the fiery dream that had woken me. My light orb had faded at some point and the darkness was absolute, and I had to take great care in kindling it once more so as not to hurt my eyes.

Tatyana was still sprawled next to me, the toll of the healing and trauma etched into the lines and dark contours of her face and I wondered if I looked as spent as she did. We needed food and rest, and the merest thought of something roasted and dripping was enough to set the drool swinging from the corner of my mouth. I moved to the doorway and listened carefully, but could neither hear any voices nor feel the tread of feet on the ground. I set my shoulder to it and forced it open as swiftly as I could, wincing at the brightness of the light that rushed in, eager to tackle the shadows.

I cautiously peered out of the crypt but the only creatures, living or otherwise, that seemed remotely interested were a pair of crows on a nearby gravestone. It was good to have the sky above me again, even if it was hidden by a solid mantle of cloud that muted the sunlight into a besmirched silver. I gathered up my unconscious charge and headed back to the necromancer's old house, the only shelter I knew of, and the ambush that awaited us there.

Chapter 37

Even though it seemed to be early in the day, the roads were largely deserted. The few people that I saw, and who saw me, stopped and stared before hurrying off. Shutters slammed as I approached, then squeaked open again after I had passed. I was perhaps two roads away from the house we had taken over when the smell of bread found my nose. Starved of anything besides the reek of spoor, mould and blood for so long, my nostrils sucked every morsel of that beguiling scent from the air and made my body follow it down several smaller paths with no little urgency until I found the source. A source whose heart was racing like a rabbit's as they fumbled with a door, the cloth-wrapped bundle clamped under their arm.

'The bread,' I said. 'I need it.' Even to my ears my voice was a growl.

The woman turned and stared at me with eyes that she somehow managed to open as wide as an owl's.

'Take it!' she shouted and threw the bundle at me before running away.

I called my thanks after her, but she vanished around the next corner before I even had a chance to pick up the bundle. I could feel the hard rounds of two fair-sized loaves in it, and it was quite a struggle not to drop Tatyana right there and then and try to fit both in my mouth. My innate discipline won, but it was a close thing. Excited beyond measure by this humble yet priceless loot, I hurried to our makeshift lair, paying little heed to my surroundings. The house seemed as empty as I remembered it, and I laid Tatyana down on the table we had eaten from.

'Are you there, beast?' I asked, nudging her in the ribs. No response came, and I had just unwrapped the first of the loaves when my newly refreshed sense of smell alerted me that there were men nearby.

I took one enormous bite from the bread before moving to find them, but only had to walk as far as the wall. They had evidently been waiting for our return and now six figures advanced upon me. I was about to spring upon the closest of them when I saw that they wore the blue sashes of the Stahrulls, rather than the red and white of the paladins. It made me hesitate, which gave the cringing messenger who waited with them enough of a chance to find his voice.

'Meneer Stratus,' he said in a voice that could have belonged to a man or woman. 'Please, stay your arms.'

'Who are you?' I said, wary that this was some sort of trap.

'Magus Fronsac sent us. I have a message for you.'

Fronsac? That was curious enough to draw some of the tension from my great muscles, and I rose from the crouch I had adopted.

'Do you have any food?'

'Food? I'm afraid not. We are from the palace garrison.'

'Can you fetch some? As much as you can carry. It's urgent.'

'Is Lady Henkman injured? We saw you carry her in.'

'Come,' I said, and headed back to the room where she still slept. 'I have healed most of her wounds but they were fairly severe. She will wake soon, and she will need food, lots of food. We both will.'

'I see,' the messenger said, staring at her unconscious form. He made to speak, but fell silent.

'I can requisition some day rations,' offered one of the soldiers. The messenger nodded and the speaker and another man sheathed their weapons and left. I silently urged them to run as I watched them leave.

'What is your message?'

'My what? Oh, yes. The message.' He swallowed and turned to face me again. 'My master says that you will know how to read it.'

'I do not read your script.'

'It's in my head. I think. I mean, that is what he told me but I don't feel any different or remember anything.'

'Are you his apprentice?' I asked. He carried no rings or amulets that I could see, nor could I sense any latent power within him.

'No, sir. I'm his cook.'

'His cook.'

'And his cousin. He said to tell you that Karl was the reason why he was sending me.'

I remembered Karl. It wasn't every day that I had a chance to wrap a wizard's apprentice up in a rug.

'I understand,' I said. 'But before I can read the message I will need to eat.'

'Of course.'

I needed no further invitation and tore into the bread with some savagery. One of the soldiers offered me a leather bottle and I took it without hesitation and poured the heavily watered wine down my throat.

'You're rather hungry,' the cook said. It was enough to make me pause and realise I was on the cusp of finishing the second loaf as well. But then there was barely a crust left so I ate that too, since such a little scrap would do nothing for Tatyana if she woke. Suitably fortified by the bread and wine, I turned my attention to the cook. My sorcery had not yet replenished itself, and, while Fronsac had earned himself a measure of respect, wizards were notoriously tricky. The last thing I wanted to do was rush into some sort of spell-trap he'd embedded in the man's head.

'What do I need to do?' the cook asked as the scent of his fear spiced the air.

'Just look into my eyes and do not panic. I will not hurt you.' Which was true in so much that he wouldn't feel it if I destroyed his brain from the inside.

He did as I bid him, and I mesmerised him easily enough. Now that he was held, I began to ease myself into his thoughts, seeking a trace of Fronsac's magic. Husbanding what was left of my sorcery slowed my progress considerably but I had no desire to go blundering about in the head of a man sent by a half-talented wizard. After some time I felt a tug of something strange in his mind and as I followed it deeper, all resistance fell away. The colours of his thoughts blurred into one, and when they stopped just as suddenly, I found myself in a chair looking at Fronsac.

'There, that should do it,' he said, setting down a bronze tablet of some sort. He stroked his beard, coughed and then spread his hands wide.

'Stratus!' he shouted, and I saw sparks flash from his rings. 'Thank you for receiving my message.' I tried to look around as he lowered his arms, but I was only a spectator in this memory and could look nowhere other than where the cook had.

'I have seen enough to know that I was right not to think you the enemy that we are being told that you are. I will be blunt, for time is against us. Novstan's army is a day's march away, two at most, and Prince Jean's ears are deaf to my counsel. There is something unnatural at work, something that thwarts my every attempt to banish it. I need your help. A sorcerer's help. Come to the palace as soon as possible. Tell Tatyana to use the north gate.' He sat back, and the memory faded away.

I willed myself from the cook's mind and left him to sag to the floor as I mulled over Fronsac's words. I wandered back into the room where Tatyana was sleeping and had just sat down when she opened her eyes and sat up with a hoarse cry. She patted her arms and looked around, breathing raggedly. I waited for her wits to return before speaking.

'I have sent for food, and I believe it has just arrived.'

'What happened?' Her voice was dry and rasping, and she touched her neck as if expecting to find a wound. 'It feels like I've been hung.'

'It will pass,' I said, although that was more of a guess than anything else. 'Wait here.'

I helped myself to one of the soldier's bottles from the next room and ignored his protests for the empty threats that they were. Tatyana drank as greedily as I had, and did not lower the bottle until it was empty. She looked across as the cook and the soldier with the food entered the room, then turned to me. I felt her heartbeat leap. Did she know them as foes?

'Why the fuck are we both naked?'

I sagged back in the chair with a sigh of relief. I needed food if I was to fight with anything resembling skill. 'Our clothes were burned, but I carried you out and we kept each other warm.'

'You kept—' She pointed a shaking finger at me but said nothing else, which was a bit confusing. She turned on the men who had brought the food, and they were quickly stripped of their cloaks and kicked from the room. She flung a cloak at me, covered herself, and then fell into a fit of coughing. Her healing wasn't reacting to it so I left her to get over it while I sorted through the food. There was some meat, but not much and not nearly as fatty as I liked it, but it would do. There was a bottle of something, but fortunately it was mead rather than strong wine as I might have struggled with the smell of it.

'How are you feeling?' I tensed, straining for any sign that the beast was still lurking within her. 'You might feel some pain from the burning, but it is not physical. I healed your burns and replaced the charred flesh, although I cannot help you with the hair.'

'Shut the Hel up,' she said in her own voice, barely pausing long enough between mouthfuls of cheese to say it.

'Do you remember anything after the Cardinal set you on fire? Not the searing, but what happened afterwards.'

'God damn it, Stratus. Shut up.'

'How about any more dreams? Have you heard any more voices?'

To her credit, I barely had time to register that she was moving before her fist landed. Unfortunately, whether ready or not, the dense bone of my face was never going to yield to those of her hands, and whatever satisfaction she took from her bizarre behaviour was quickly stifled by what had to be a painful bruising of her knuckles. She cradled her hand as she stepped away from her toppled chair, then flipped the table over, which seemed to be her favourite reaction. I stared at the spilled food, then at her, but she was already throwing her chair across the room.

'What are you doing? Is it rising? Let me speak to it.'

'Shut up, damn you!' Her face was red as she turned on me. 'This mess is all your fault!' With a wordless scream she grabbed the nearest thing and threw it at me. Fortunately it was only an apple, but it didn't seem to matter to her. She launched herself at me, thumping her uninjured fist against my chest several times. I put my arms around her to stop her from making her injuries worse and was gratified when she stopped. Rather than recoil, she pressed herself against me, her arms around my waist as if she expected to fall over.

'He burned me, Stratus.' Her voice faltered as she spoke. 'I could smell it.'

'I know.' She was shivering, and I put my arms around her.

'I saw him when he did it. That evil bastard enjoyed it. Him and that pale bastard who did . . . who . . .'

'Skibor, his name was.'

'Yes.'

'If it makes you feel any better, I stabbed him in the throat and then cut his head off with his own knife.'

Her grip tightened. 'I think I might love you.'

'That is very kind, but I don't think— '

'Shut up, Stratus.'

'You are very confusing.'

She laughed and patted my arm as she looked at the mess she had made of our food. 'That was stupid.'

'Yes.'

'Thanks.' She folded her arms. 'Now talk.'

'About what?'

'Don't play that game. Why are you so curious about what I remember and about the dreams? And why are there soldiers here?'

'It spoke to me. The demon.' I tapped my chest to help her understand.

'It spoke to you?'

'Yes. It was completely unexpected. I nearly dropped you.'

'Wait. What do I have to do with it?'

'Oh. It spoke through your mouth. The fascinating part is that it used your body to project its voice, and from the tone, it had to have altered physical aspects of your body, which means it had access to power of its own, as I certainly didn't have the reserves to do anything of the sort.' I nodded as she touched her throat. 'Yes, that's why it hurts.'

'You did what?'

From her scent and posture I knew that she was on the verge of another outburst so I quickly held my hands up. 'I did nothing. It was the beast. It somehow managed to exploit the link between us and your unconscious state.'

'That's it!' she shouted, the anger I had foreseen suddenly pouring out. 'I'm bloody sick and tired of all this. All of it, you understand? I want you and that . . . thing in your head to just leave me the Hel alone.'

'Tatyana, as I have said, I cannot reverse the bond that links us. It—'

'Will kill me. Yes, so you said. I don't care. I just got burned to death anyway.'

'You are alive.'

'And for what? So you or your "beast" can stick your magic up my arse as if I was some damned puppet every time you want to have a chat?'

'I have put nothing up your arse,' I said. 'You were willing to give your life to save mine and that is a debt that I cannot easily repay, demon or not. We are bound together, Tatyana Henkman, by both life and death.'

'Oh Hel' was all she said, adding to my confusion. She said it a few more times, each repetition quieter than the last, then threw the shutters open and stared out at the iron sky beyond.

'And the soldiers are here because they brought a message from Fronsac.'

'They did? What is it?'

I told her, and after she had made me repeat the message twice more she announced that we were to go back to the palace immediately.

315

While it was gratifying to see her being decisive, she reverted to a state of impending anger when I told her that I would not be going with her.

'He's asked for your help, and at great risk to himself. Are you going to turn your back on him?'

'Why should I not? He does not have the answers I need.'

'You need? But what about Lucien, and the city?'

'This is not my city, nor are these my people. Lucien is interesting, and I respect that you will hold true to your vow to protect him, but I must follow my own path. Go to Fronsac and tell him what we have found. It might help him, but I cannot go to him. Not yet.'

'Your supposedly great plan is suicide, and more, it's stupid.'

I felt the banked embers of my own anger flare at that. 'Stupid? Is it so foolish for me to want to know who I am? What I am? Is it stupid to want to know what this thing in my head is?' My voice was rising with my anger, but the more it rose the less I cared. 'I would rather die than live like this.' I felt the beast rising on the swell of my anger, its rage blending with mine and rejoicing in it. 'I will find Polsson, and he will tell me what I need to know, even if I have to kill every man that stands between us.'

'Even if the city falls around you?'

'Even if I have to tear it down myself.'

Chapter 38

The first of the bells began ringing shortly before sunset, but soon enough, every tower that held a bell had joined in the cacophony. I watched from the window of our lair as those few people who were on the roads hurried towards their homes as if expecting something terrible to descend upon them from the clouds. Tatyana had left some time ago with Fronsac's cook and his soldiers, and I was alone in the house as I waited for the night to take hold of the city. Before they left she had secured new clothes for me, and more food, both of which were welcome although I was more partial towards the latter.

I had spent the time trying to meditate, but the thoughts and questions crowding my mind were legion and made it unusually difficult, although I had at least managed to push them away for long enough to join with the Songlines and replenish my sorcery. The beast hadn't really subsided since my earlier outburst; I could sense its presence at the edge of my mind, like a swamp lizard watching a doe on the banks of a river. Watching and waiting for a moment of weakness.

I shook the thought from my mind. I had thrown it off before, and I would do so again. The trick it had pulled with Tatyana had been surprising, but it had also shown that it was unable to bring the strength it battered me with to bear on her. It was cunning enough to use the bond between us, but that link was never meant to carry more than occasional healing energies. What was far more worrying to me was that part of me wanted to reach out to the beast again. Now that I knew there was a mind behind it that was possessed of more than simple rage, trying not to think about it was like trying not to keep probing a broken tooth with my tongue. Did it have the answers I needed? What did it know? But was this part of me actually a part of me, or some cunning ruse on the part of the beast, left behind to weaken my resolve? Madness lurked within such thoughts and so I turned my energies to the task I had set myself.

My plan was a simple one. I would find Polsson, kill my way to him, then rip the knowledge I needed from his mind before I removed his limbs and organs. I had not lied to Tatyana when I said that I would rather die than live like I was, afraid of my own mind and unsure of anything beyond what I could see and taste. This city could burn down around me for all that I cared, and the fact I instinctively knew that it wouldn't be the first city I had seen destroyed by fire only stoked my frustration. Where were these cities that I remembered watching burn? Why had I been there, and why did I hate men so much? I was tired of not knowing anything.

Of being incomplete.

No, this night I would find my prey or die trying. And if the knowledge somehow freed the beast and killed me in turn, then at least I would die as me.

'I'm coming for you, Polsson.' I breathed the words into the wind and let it carry them away. The bells were still ringing out their ragged melody when night came. I left the house and began making my way along the streets. The clouds had been rumbling since the afternoon, and I was perhaps halfway to St Tomas when they began to empty themselves across the city, driving all but the most stalwart from the streets. I had never minded the rain, and I liked the way that it sluiced the grime and stench of so much concentrated humanity from the world around me.

As I had expected, there were more patrols and soldiers about despite the weather, and both the paladins and Jean's army were on the streets the closer I came to the city walls and St Tomas. Fortunately for me, most of them were more concerned with staying dry than what was happening above them. I could see the spire of St Tomas now, a dark shape against the last sliver of light in the west. I could hear the sonorous tolling of its great bell amid all of the others too, a deeper note that made the other bells seem somehow frivolous compared to it, so much so that I wondered whether an enchantment had been wound into it when it was first made. I clambered onto a wall, stretched myself to my full length and caught my first glimpse of the cause of all the excitement: the army of the Penullin general Novstan.

In truth I could only see a few pinpricks of firelight, but some of those distant lights belonged to his army of wizards, and there was a sense of something in the air, as if the clouds were pregnant with something more sinister than simple rainwater. I smiled at the thought of what Tatyana would say about that as I hopped off the wall and continued towards the cathedral.

I was perhaps two jumps away from the church when I saw the first rooftop guards. Unfortunately, they had seen me too, or rather heard me when I landed behind them with all the grace of a catapulted cow. I had perhaps been enjoying the moments of weightlessness as I launched myself into the air too much, as I had not paused to check the roof before I leaped. Three of the guards were already bending bows, while two others readied swords. I wasn't worried as much about these as I was the one who had run for the ladder behind them, most likely to call for help. I found my feet and charged forward, forcing the archers to loose early and spoiling their aim.

Their bows were more powerful than I had expected, and if I hadn't been so heavy the impact of the first two shafts might have knocked me off balance and off the roof. The swordsmen were running forward now, and the ladder-man had vanished. I had no time to curse before I slammed into the first swordsman, who had realised far too late that I wasn't about to stop and offer battle. My shoulder crushed his sword arm against his chest, handily driving the little bar above the sword handle between his ribs. He fell, my fists flew and two of the archers fell, their war over.

A sword flashed and hit my shoulder. I grunted at the sudden sting and chopped at the wielder's arm when he was slow to withdraw it. I felt the twin bones of his forearm snap and snatched the sword up as it fell from his suddenly limp hand. I grabbed his arm and chopped it off with his own sword, leaving him to stagger away clutching at the stump. The third archer had moved back to try another shaft, but failed to loose it before I turned and threw the sword at him. I had hoped to pin him to the wall behind him, which would have been an eloquent finish to the clash, but instead the handle hit him in the face and he fell to the ground, bawling. I left him to his misery and chased after the ladder-man.

He was about halfway down to the next landing, his arms and legs finding the narrow and flimsy rungs with a confidence that I knew I could not hope to match. Which is why I dropped the other sword down on him, and this one flew true and cracked into his skull with satisfying force, sending him tumbling to the bottom in a heap.

I breathed a sigh of relief and moved to still the archer, who was clutching his ruined face.

'No, pleash!' he squealed as I prepared to twist his head.

I paused. 'How many men are in the church?' I gave him a little shake to focus his thoughts.

'Free or four squadsh. Pleash, don't kill me.'

'What is a squad?'

'Ten, maybe twelve men.'

'How many paladins?' I gave him another shake when he started stammering, but there was an unexpectedly loud click from his neck and his legs began twitching violently. I dropped him, and went to check the swordsman with the chest wound; my luck seemed to be in because he too was still alive.

'Oh god, I'm dying,' he said, spraying blood as he spoke.

'Yes. Your lung is filling with blood. It's quite fatal. Do you know how many paladins there are in the church?' I pointed to the spire.

'I don't want to die.'

'Everybody dies. Do you know how many there are?'

'It hurts so bad,' he moaned.

I sighed. This was not helping. With a muttered curse, I called up a mote of sorcery and touched his forehead. It wasn't a healing construct, although it had a similar foundation. All it would do was scramble the sensations he was experiencing, effectively numbing his body.

His eyes widened. 'Thank you,' he wheezed.

'Yes, yes. Now, how many paladins are there?'

He opened his mouth and twitched a few times, and more blood spilled from his lips. I thought nothing much of it given his wounds, but when the tremors passed he looked up at me with eyes that were as full of blood as his mouth.

'*You fool*,' he said in a voice that was not his. Even with the wet gurgle of his filling lungs, the beast's voice was distinct. '*Your recklessness will kill us both.*'

I stared at the bleeding man like the fool he accused me of being, and was still staring when the body sagged to the ground, lifeless. I poked the body, but life had left it. I lay my hand across its face and slid my sorcery into the brain beyond, feeding it just enough energy to convince it that it wasn't dead yet. It was a temporary measure at best, as without moving blood, the amount of energy required to sustain something even as mundane as a human brain was extortionate. The base functions like movement were simple enough and required little more than a spark in the right place, but if you wanted to keep thought and memory intact it was a painstaking and meticulous undertaking. I knew because I'd had to do it to my own brain, and even then I had managed to make enough of a mess of it to paralyse myself.

I closed my eyes and let the sorcery I sent burrowing through his brain see for me. I flashed past half-glimpsed memories of a small village and a woman with straw-coloured hair and sped my energy towards his most recent memories.

A loud thump and the cracking of wood. I turn and see a man, impossibly broad across the shoulders and thick of arm, stumble into the light. My fear flashes through my body like ice. It's him! Kitan and the others are drawing their bows, and I remember my sword at the last moment. He's charging us!

The arrows fly and hit him. He staggers, but he doesn't fall! I know I'm pissing myself but I can't help it or care. I should have kept my own sword. This one feels awkward. I raise it but, oh Drogah, he's too close. He hits me, and it's a thousand times worse than when Clara's horse kicked me. I'm on my back, and it feels like there's an anvil on my chest. I can't breathe. Can't breathe. Small gasps. Oh Drogah, he's killed me.

The necromancer grabs my neck and my head, and I beg him not to kill me, even though I know I'm dying and I'll never see Clara again. He's talking, but the pain in my chest is growing. He does something then, and the pain goes, but there's something inside me now, crawling up my spine. I want to scream but I can't breathe. Clara, I love you. I should have listened to you.

Darkness swallowed his vision, but at the last moment it pulled back and I saw—

I see my eyes staring at me from the human face I created. He remembers nothing. He has made us weak and now I will never find her. We shall die an oathbreaker.

His brain died then, the memories dissolving like melting ice. I sat back and reeled the unspent energy back to me.

'So now I'm an oathbreaker too,' I said aloud, but of course no answer came from the brooding presence inside my head. 'Who is she?' I asked, shaking the corpse until the neck swung loose. I dropped it with a curse and took a deep, steadying breath. The answers were close, but I needed to remain focused.

I replayed the dead man's memory in mine, sifting past the trivia of his fleeting life to the last moments. It was a strange thing, to be looking up at myself like that. I really did look quite menacing, and I had not appreciated that the thing I could do with my eyes to see at night gave them such a red tint. I had to remember that. The moment when the beast crossed over to the body was far more interesting though; the man had been too preoccupied with self-pity to see it, but at least his brain had remembered it. It had somehow latched onto the burst of sorcery I had used to dull his pain, which was very interesting indeed. First, it meant that it knew what I was about to do, and second, it was learning from its experience of hijacking Tatyana's dreams. How long would it be until it could turn upon me in the same way?

'I wish you'd use as much cunning to help, rather than insult me,' I muttered as I made my way to the edge of the roof, squinting against the rain that was seemingly trying to erase the city.

There was one building remaining between me and the graveyard that surrounded the chapel of St Tomas on three sides, but it was further than I had so far dared to jump. Crossing the square below in secrecy was not going to be an option though. There were men scurrying back and forth, taking boxes and bundles off some wagons and putting some on others by the light of a dozen lanterns. There were too few shadows and too many eyes.

I took some time to prepare a sorcerous construct to help me with the jump. I had not attempted something like this since I had woken up, but as soon as I had begun to bind it together it began to feel familiar. I knew without having to think about it how the various elements fitted together, creating a neat web that even a base amateur would recognise as a work of no little art. Why would I be so familiar with what was, in essence, a strong gust of wind? It made me even more eager to find Polsson. It was finally ready, and after helping myself to the dead men's knives, so was I.

I walked back to the far end of the roof. I was confident I could make the distance now, but the rain had made the roof slick and a single misstep would see me hit the wall, rather than the roof. I closed my eyes, took a breath, and sprinted forward. There was no going back.

Chapter 39

I ran the full length of the roof, planted my foot on the low wall that edged it and breathed life into the wind construct as I launched myself from the building. I was still rising when a summer-warm blast of wind cupped me from below like a gigantic hand and turned the rain to a silver blur as it carried me over both the square and the building beyond. I barely had time to notice that the men on the roof weren't even looking up before I was tumbling into the forest of pale gravestones that surrounded the cathedral. The first dozen stones snapped under my weight and the speed I hit them with, sending me spinning until a particularly grand one bruised a few of my ribs as it finally brought me to a halt.

I lay there, wheezing for breath but grinning at the clouds despite the spreading ache of my latest round of injuries. I had all but flown through the air, and it had been all I could do not to shout out from the sheer joy of it. The sound of approaching men brought me back to myself and I rolled into a crouch, clenching my teeth against the pain that shot through my chest.

There were four men walking through the yard, but they were heading towards the broken gravestones with their hoods pulled up against the weather, which gave me enough time to slip away into the darker shadows that pooled along the walls of the cathedral. While they argued about what might have caused the damage, I indulged in a bit of self-healing. There was little point in having such power if my body was going to fail me when I needed it most. I wasn't so much of a fool that I expected to find Polsson without getting into a fight, possibly several, and if I was to triumph I needed a body that was in good enough condition to deal with the paladins on a physical level, letting me keep my sorcery to deal with the Cardinal's dark magics.

The first thing I had to do was find him. I didn't want to risk sinking myself into the Songlines here, for although the patterns were familiar to me now, I did not want to become distracted or lose track of time, particularly not when the area was crawling with guards. And, even if I did try, there was no guarantee that I would be able to pinpoint him. So I would need to ask someone. And with that thought in mind, I crept along the shadows and went paladin hunting.

It seemed that they had lit every lantern that could be found, and as I edged closer to the buildings attached to the far end of the cathedral it became progressively harder to find suitable shadows to hide in, but at least the profusion of light was wreaking far more havoc with their night vision than it was with mine. The contact with the Songline-saturated ground wasn't hurting either, and by the time I had reached the outermost buildings I had managed to reabsorb most of the energy I had expended on both the wind spell and the healing of my ribs.

Ahead and to the left of me were two smaller buildings, which I guessed were little houses for the priests, while on the right a neat garden gave way to a cobbled yard that led to the stables and beyond to the far grander temple buildings. The cobbled yard was a mess of activity as men came and went, some carrying things while others shouted or ran this way and that with little obvious purpose. What was of more interest to me were the paladins that stood in the centre. There were at least ten of them, all clad in their shiny armour as they clustered around another of their kind who was gesturing grandly. I waited, and my patience and cunning use of the shadows was rewarded when they split up into pairs. I ignored those that headed towards the temple buildings and stables, but was very intrigued by the two who seemed to be heading right for me.

I knew it was a ridiculous thing to do, but even so I pressed myself as flat against the wall as I could as they passed by. Neither of them so much as looked in my direction and I let them move ahead before padding after them. Once they were past the outbuildings there was a good stretch of graveyard where the only light would be from the lantern they carried. I let them reach halfway into this patch before snuffing its light out with a pinch of sorcery.

'Did you trim the wick?' asked the one closest to me, shouting to be heard over the gusting wind.

Sadly for him, the only answer he received was my fist crashing into his ear, hard enough that the result would have been the same even if he hadn't been wearing his helmet. His companion reacted with admirable alacrity, dropping the lantern and reaching for a dagger. I didn't mind him drawing a weapon, but what I did not want was him attracting attention, so I swung my leg up between his, lifting him from the ground and crushing his eggs. Men were men, even if they were paladins. He gave a croak as he curled up on himself like a spider and toppled to the ground.

I grabbed both of them and dragged them to a gap between two old crypts where there was less chance of being noticed. The one I'd hit in the ear wasn't dead, which I was pleased about as it doubled my chances of finding out what I needed to know. The first thing I did was reach out to them with my sorcery. The groaning one reacted faintly, as if touched by a waning enchantment, which was not entirely unexpected given their habit of lurking in churches and the like. His companion with the bruised skull was, however, one of Polsson's *cold* ones. I tapped his forehead, sending a jolt of energy through him that would hopefully scramble any of the worms inside it and also keep him from waking for some time. I had other questions for him.

'Where is the Cardinal?' I asked the groaner.

I could see him looking around. It was dark enough here that I would be little more than a dark shape against the painted windows of the chapel. He scuttled backwards as he looked into my red eyes, only stopping when his back hit a gravestone that time and the elements had reduced to little more than a rounded boulder. He clutched at the amulet on his chest and began muttering an incantation, although he no doubt considered it a prayer, and the cross soon began to glow. It shed little more light than a single candle, but in the dark even so mean a light would draw unwanted attention. Fortunately light spells were relatively simple things, and as so often the case with simple artefacts, it was completely vulnerable to being interfered with by someone with skills like mine. I coaxed the light to turn to heat instead, and after a few moments the paladin gave a hiss of surprise and let go of the bronze token, which was glowing as if fresh from the fires.

'If you call for help, I will ensure you never walk again.' I kept my voice low and he let out the breath he'd just drawn in a long sigh. 'Where is the Cardinal?'

'You will burn for this.'

'I certainly hope so. Where is he?'

'You will never reach him. We will cut you down, and—'

I wasn't in the mood to listen to more threats and tightened the flow of energy around his little amulet. By the time he'd finished describing how the Cardinal's special guards would cut me down, the bronze had surrendered its shape and had run between the metal rings of his tunic and began quenching itself in his chest. He almost cried out in pain but I held his mouth shut.

'If they will kill me, then you lose nothing by telling me, is it not so? Be wise and you will live to fight another day.' I drew the remaining heat from the bronze but held myself ready to heat it again if I needed to. He nodded, and I lifted my hand.

'He is in the inner sanctum, praying for the city.'

I made him describe the path to the sanctum twice, both to make sure that I understood, and that he was not lying.

'Now, tell me about this one,' I said, nudging his companion.

'What is your meaning?'

I picked my words with care. 'He is different to you.'

'He is my brother in arms. We are all one.'

'He is not favoured by the Cardinal?'

'No. Our homelands mean nothing once the oath is taken.'

'Your homelands.' I considered this. 'He is from another?'

'From Kenwin.' I gestured for him to continue as Tatyana often did to me. 'It isn't unusual for us to recruit bands of brothers from the same province. It helps create a bond between them.'

I felt a piece of the mystery unravel in my mind. 'Polsson is from Kenwin too, is he not?'

'Yes, but it matters not.'

'Oh, but it does.' I considered the man before me. 'How many among you are from Kenwin?'

'Most of the fourth cohort. Perhaps two hundred, give or take a score. But they're all here, so you can count them yourself when they cut you down.'

I sat back. Two hundred against one was not a favourable ratio, but what other option did I have? Not all of them could fight me at once, and I still had my sorcery. There was always a chance.

Perhaps I was too distracted by what he had said, or perhaps I hadn't used as much energy as I thought, but either way his companion's attack landed with complete surprise. I was lucky in that he hadn't drawn a weapon for fear of alerting me, but the gauntlets he wore made an effective mace once he'd balled his fists. The blow struck me at the back of my neck, filling my vision with a bright cascade of stars and making me bark most of the air from my lungs in surprise. I fell to the side and now he drew his dagger and fell onto me. The first thrust pierced my skin, but was deflected to scrape along a rib. He tried again, and this time I managed to grab his hand. I didn't have time for anything fancier than simply closing my hand around his, snapping his relatively delicate bones against the unyielding handle.

The other paladin had got to his feet but his legs were not yet ready to support him. I drove my foot into the side of his knee, tearing his muscles and sending him toppling back to the ground, whereupon I drove his companion's dagger through his eye, stilling his cries. The cold one with the broken hand had a similar idea about calling for help but fell to gasping instead when I grabbed him by the neck and squeezed.

'Not yet,' I said. 'You and I need to talk about wine.'

He reacted with the sudden anger that I had sensed in his kind before but, however insane he was, his body still had limits, and not having enough air to breathe rendered his renewed attempts to attack me quite laughable. I gave his throat another playful squeeze in return.

'What do the worms do?'

'You will die for this,' he wheezed in reply. 'You cannot stop what is coming.'

'What is coming?'

'The Master,' he said, and as I was watching through the red tint of my night vision, I saw his forehead bulge with veins where none had been before. I had built my own body, and I knew what I saw were not veins. 'He is bringing the goddess, and we shall stand at her side.'

A goddess?

I searched the barren hall of my memories for any trace of a goddess but found nothing.

'If he has a goddess, what does he want with me?'

'Death,' he hissed.

I had no idea if that was an answer or if he had reverted to meaningless threats. 'Answer me.'

He didn't, of course. Not then, nor in reply to any of the other questions that I put to him, and I could not say whether I finally killed him out of boredom or frustration. I tried not to feel too disappointed; at least I had a direction now, and I had managed to trim the odds a little. I stowed the bodies deep in the shadows and headed back towards the chapel.

Chapter 40

I had thought to linger unseen until the need to sleep emptied the yards of men, but the presence of the invading army seemed to have spurred them on to unnatural levels of activity. I could not fathom what they were doing for all that time. Surely there were only so many boxes and bundles you could carry from one place to another? I quelled my impatience and tried to make myself as comfortable as I could behind a sprawling green bush that smelled overwhelmingly of fox urine.

Some time later, and at about the same time that I resolved to kill them all, a new mob of guardsmen came out of the chapel, an occurrence that prompted another flurry of activity, but one that swiftly abated. The last of the interminable chain of boxes were carried into rooms, and shutters and doors were closed. In ones and twos the men drifted into the chapel and the dormitories, the doors and shutters slammed shut until all that was left was the latest group of guards. I counted two dozen, but at least there were no paladins among them.

I slipped out from behind the bush and squeezed myself into a gap left inside a nearby circle of barrels. Their leader was setting them their tasks for the night, but his directions were too confusing for me to follow, so I settled down in my new hideaway and watched and waited as they went about their tasks, silently tracking them until I was confident I knew where they all were. Getting inside the chapel was my first priority. The directions that the paladin had given me were blessedly simple after that: across the entrance hall to the furthest door on the right, then on until I reached stairs. Two flights of those, then I step out into a passage and the second door on my left opens into the sanctum and, beyond that, Polsson's lair.

Simple.

Except, of course, that it was anything but. These new guards were positioned so they could all see each other, which made the task of silencing them far too difficult. I toyed with the idea of using my sorcery to set a fire somewhere, but something in my memories warned me that men would swarm at the call of fire. The answer came in the form of a soundless blur that swept past my head to collect a plump mouse from the top of a nearby barrel. The owl vanished into the night over the heads of the wandering guards, who did not so much as remark upon it.

I couldn't fly, but my wind spells offered a fairly good facsimile of it. I looked across to the cathedral and its steeply sloped roof, measuring the distance as best I could. I had covered more distance than that in my leap into the graveyard, and even without the benefit of leaping downwards I felt confident that I could manage it. Once on the roof, I could break through it and make my way down to the sanctum easily enough. After all, the guards would not be expecting an attack from above. I waited until the two closest passed my hideaway before slipping out from the barrels and across into the shadows of the house opposite to where I'd hidden. I waited until the guards were close by before drawing a deep breath. I edged around the corner of the building until I was sure they were gone, then taking care with my footing, I aligned myself with the corner of the cathedral roof. It was quite steep, and ridged with some sort of ornamental carving, so I would need to land carefully if I wasn't to do myself an injury or bounce off.

I had perhaps ten paces clear between where I stood and a line of empty carts; the nearest guards were now up and to my right, and I kept my eyes on these as I prepared the wind construct again. I felt it snap into readiness as I fed power into it and waited. After what felt like an age, the guards finally turned away.

I launched myself forward with the great muscles of my legs, each stride stretching them to their full potential. On the sixth I leaped and released the construct. The wind drove me upwards with enough force to push my limbs out behind me like a swallow's wings. The yard rapidly fell away beneath me and for the time it took me to reach the peak of my jump, it felt like the sky belonged to me. But then the wind faded and the clouds tilted and I was falling towards the chapel which suddenly seemed ludicrously far below me.

I had fed the construct too much power.

Not only that, it had also pulled the air from all around me, tipping some of the carts over as the mass of it pushed upwards, but by then I was already over most of the chapel and falling towards the market square beyond at a terrifying speed. There was no time to replicate the wind construct except in a malformed and untidy way, but I had no choice. I threw power at it, trusting to brute force to overcome its rudimentary design. Much of it was wasted, bursting from the untidy seams of the construct in purple and green streamers as the raw energy bled into reality, but the structure held, with just enough manifesting as wind rather than sparks to ease the dangerous trajectory I was falling at. The dregs of it cushioned enough of the impact so that I could roll the rest off, but even so I shattered a good number of tiles beneath me as I skidded across the roof with little idea of which way was up. Dregs of my misdirected sorcery that had leaked from the construct burst into flame around me, blinding and confusing me even more. I bounced once, then slid across the rain-slicked roof, the cracked ends of the clay tiles scrubbing lengths of skin from me. By the time I finally slid to a halt it felt like I had rolled down a mountain made of volcanic glass. My mouth was full of blood from having bitten through my lip and my body was simultaneously numb and aching, like my feet had once felt when I had jumped over a wall and landed flat-footed. I tried to summon enough energy to heal myself but I had burned it all off in the panicked rush to arrest my fall. All that energy, wasted.

I lifted my head to try to get some perspective on where I was and felt something click painfully in my neck, the motion sending a small landslide of broken tiles sliding away to my right and over the edge that I was teetering on. My left arm was stretched out, my fingers hooked around a beam of wood exposed by a fallen tile, and I could feel the slow tearing in my shoulder and nails as they continued to hold my full weight. I braced my right hand to ease myself up, but whatever I was braced against gave way with a sharp crack, sending several more tiles into the night. I heard them shatter against something below, each as loud as a thunderclap. I eventually managed to find something more substantial to hook a toe onto and pulled myself over onto my stomach, easing the pressure on my arm.

By this time I could hear the sound of the guards below, and it was only the height of the roof that had delayed them from spotting me yet. I blinked away the last of the stars floating in my vision and looked around with a mind that was slowly starting to feel less like it had just been shot into the side of a stone building.

I was perhaps four paces from the far end of the chapel, and five from having missed it entirely and landing in the graveyard all over again. I could trace where I hit the roof by the trail of broken and missing tiles, and again some semblance of luck had been with me, stopping me from hitting the raised ridge that ran the length of the roof and breaking more than just tiles. I would need to move soon, judging from the guards' activity. I had no idea how easy it would be for them to get up here, or how long it would take, but there was no doubt that they were on their way. The trail I had left was too wide and obvious to try to cover up, so I would need to move away from it instead, which was easier said than done on such a steep and unreliable surface.

I looked up to where I had gripped the wooden beam and reached for it again. Here at least I had something to hold on to and I pulled myself up higher, my abused muscles shivering with the effort. I had meant to cross the roof and find somewhere to break through into the building on the far side, away from the area the guards would be searching, and I was within an arm's reach of the ridge that ran across the roof when the timbers beneath me gave way without so much as a warning tremble, spilling me into a musty void filled with silver cobwebs and brittle, dead pigeons.

I could hear human voices below me, and I had barely located them when a section of floor began lifting in front of me, sending a shard of yellow light to pierce the dusty gloom.

'Right, it's open,' said a voice. 'I'll go up first. You lot stand ready to follow me.'

I was behind the floor door, out of their line of sight for now, but it was a fool's hope to think that I would go unseen once they brought a lantern up. It or the hole in the roof were the only way out though. I was as trapped here as the dried husks of the pigeons that littered the floor and the spiders that watched from the rafters.

Spiders.

I had always liked them, although I would make an exception for the pale ones that lived beneath St Tomas. I knew that I had something of an affinity with them, even if I couldn't remember how or why, but I reached for that memory now, coaxing it from the murky depths of my mind with a vigour born of both anger and desperation. *Help me, damn you,* I silently raged at the beast. It seemed to work, despite the doubt that its previous refusals had left with me. I felt something bloom inside my mind for a moment, nothing more dramatic than the sense of relief when you remember a word that you had forgotten, but it was there now and it felt like it had never been gone. I looked up at the dark nests among the rafters and smiled as I felt the feathery touch of their tiny minds against mine.

I crouched down as the soldier pushed the floor open and stepped up into the space, a small lantern in one hand and a sword in the other.

'There's a hole!' he called down to his companions. He took a step forward. 'Surrender now and you will not be harmed,' he said loudly, lifting his lantern as he did so. Its light gave him a glimpse of the dozen or more dark shapes descending upon him. He shouted a curse as he swung his sword in a wild arc, cutting one of my little allies in half, but they were too many. By the time that the last of them was upon him, his sword and lantern were both on the ground and he was leaping through the door, his curses now somewhere between a shriek and a scream.

I helped myself to his sword and followed him down, albeit without the ululating scream he'd crossed the threshold with. He was stretched out on the ground, rolling to and fro as his three companions kicked out at the spiders who were sinking their fangs into any skin they came across. These three turned as I landed behind them, and the precious moments it took them to realise the import of this cost them dearly.

I chopped my borrowed sword into the closest head and threw myself at the other two, fouling their attempts to bring their weapons up. One of these rammed his forehead into my face, a cunning move that took me by surprise, and if I had been a man it might well have tipped matters in his favour.

But I wasn't.

As he reeled back from the hard bones of my skull, I ripped into the great veins on the side of his neck with my sharp demonic teeth. His companion cried out as a spray of blood from the ragged wound blinded him, and while he moved to clear his eyes I grabbed him by the throat and crushed the life from him. That left the spider-man, but freed from the crushing feet and swatting hands, the spiders had done their job admirably. He was still alive, but his heartbeat was weakening.

Thank you, little friends, I pulsed at them as I leaned against the wall and watched the handful of survivors cluster on his chest. I felt their need brush against me, and although it cost me some effort, I hoisted the man onto my shoulder and carried him up into the roof void. I closed the door and left them to their reward; it was time to seek my own.

Chapter 41

I rummaged through what the guards were carrying and silently rejoiced when I found a small leather sack of fermented apple wine and even some bread and meat, though both felt mere weeks away from becoming stone. I didn't let that stop me from eating them as quickly as I could though, softening the bites with the tart wine. I decided to risk a few precious moments to reach out for the song of St Tomas. It was dangerous, but so was blundering about in a nest of paladins with lingering injuries and no sorcery. Buoyed by the food, I managed to join with the Songlines on my third attempt and sighed in relief as I felt it begin to alleviate the vacuum within me. As soon as I dared, I drew half of the flow away and sent it into my body to boost the healing process.

My legs felt strong again when I stood up, and I was equally encouraged by the absence of men trying to kill me. I decided to let the guards' scent guide me along the passage as theirs was the only fresh scent that I could detect, and the few doors I passed were locked tightly. I slowed as I came to a junction with a larger passageway and carefully edged around the corner, frowning as I realised that there was something familiar about it. My head had stopped ringing enough for me to use my night vision again, and I welcomed the thinning of the shadows that the red tint now brought with it. The air was fresher here, and as I moved out I picked out the scents of a number of men, certainly more than two, but less than six. I could go either left or right, but both ended in another sharp corner some forty paces away. The shadows on the left were marginally thicker, so I went that way, trusting that I would hear and see any man before they did me.

I paused at the corner with as much caution as I could muster, but the hallway ahead of me was again deserted, with only a single lamp burning in a niche at the end, some fifty paces away. Four doors were set into the left, while the right was a low but unbroken wall for the full length. I wasn't particularly keen to deal with the guards, but I had expected more vigilance than this. I moved forward with care, and was perhaps halfway along its length when I heard the shrill, toneless sound of bells from somewhere below.

'Alarm!' shouted a muffled voice. 'Alarm!'

The door that I was a mere arm's-breadth from passing swung open and a naked man ran out and down the passage, almost extinguishing the lamp as he careened around the corner.

'What is going on?' came a shout a few moments later, louder than I had expected.

'Two of the brothers have been killed!' came a response.

'What? Who?'

'I don't know, but the Cardinal has ordered full quarters!'

'We only just came in!'

'That's your problem!' the voice from below shouted.

I pushed the door closed and headed down the passage after him, snuffing the lamp as I did. The passage narrowed, and the naked man was leaning over the low wall, shouting down into a partially enclosed courtyard. I felt the realisation of where I was fall into place. The room that I had been locked in when they first brought me here was on the opposite side of the void, which meant the stairs that led down to the chapel and Polsson's sanctum were not far off at all. Even as I was congratulating myself, the man turned towards me, his brow furrowing as Tatyana's often did when she was more confused than usual.

'Who are you?' he asked.

'*The Dead Wind.*' I felt my mouth move, and I heard my voice, but I didn't say it. The words spilled from my lips of their own accord.

'The what?'

'Sword. Crow. Road. Cat. Horse.' It seemed I still had full control of my mouth, and my voice was my own, so what the Hel had just happened? I felt neither the rage nor triumph from where the beast dwelt, only a sense of curiosity.

'Wait, you're *him!*' cried the naked man. He turned to the void and drew a breath to shout a warning or the like, but I slapped my hand across his face, stilling his cry, and threw him onto his back.

'What have you done to me?' I asked. The man writhed under me. 'No, not you,' I said. 'The thing inside me.'

I gritted my teeth as I felt it wake and rise, filling me with that awful sensation of something swimming up through my innards again. I sent a pulse of sorcery into the man that left him entirely stunned.

'I know you're in there,' I said to the unconscious body. 'So talk.'

He began to tremble, and soon after he opened his eyes. The whites were now as red as mine, and blood ran freely from the corner of each and his ears.

'*Fool,*' he said. '*You risk too much.*'

'The Dead Wind. What does that mean? And how did you speak it?'

'*It is part of your name, but you are too weak to know it.*'

'Who am I? Damn you, talk to me.'

I was holding the man's head, and as I spoke I saw three spots of dark blood burst across his face. I let go of him and my fingers came away bloody when I touched my nose.

'What is this?'

'*Your mind is broken,*' he said, the words bubbling through the blood that now flowed from his mouth like spilled wine. I could taste blood in my own too. '*You must let me in before it is too late for either of us.*'

I felt my sorcery rebound as the last word sighed from his lips. His body trembled more violently, then lay still in a spreading pool of its own mess and blood. I licked the blood from my lip and wiped the rest from my face.

'Wonderful,' I said to the corpse, but he had already spoken his last. 'The Dead Wind.' I said it a few times, it had a good feel to it. I didn't know *how* to say it, not so that it had the correct resonance with the Songlines, but names had a power nonetheless.

'Stratus, The Dead Wind. The Dead Wind, Stratus.' I could feel the beast's attention on me as I said it, the sense of anger and disappointment that radiated from it shot through with something else, something cooler but not yet distinct enough to name.

Another round of bell ringing and shouting rising from the courtyard below, distracting me from my musings, and I peered over the edge of the wall. Soldiers and paladins had gathered below, and a brief count told me that there were easily a score of each, and that was without counting the priests and boys that milled around the edges of the neat square the men-at-arms had made. I had to move quickly now, before they dispersed. The sound of a door opening behind me and a voice calling out, 'So what's going on?' only served to spur me on, and I was already descending the stairs when whoever had found the dead man began calling for help.

There were five layers to the building, not counting the crypts and dungeon, and I was on the fifth of these. If there was one fault I could find with the craftsmanship of the stairs, it was that they were clearly made for a time when men were emaciated midgets. I bounced and scraped against the walls as my feet slipped and missed some of the shallow steps, leaving smears of blood on the stone, and when I met the guards who were rushing up to answer the call for help, I didn't so much attack them as fall into them.

A spear cut a bloody furrow across my arm, but that was the worst of the wounds they gave me as I sent them tumbling backwards, breaking at least a few bones in the men unlucky enough to take the brunt of my fall. There were too many limbs flapping about and under my feet for me to stop them all, and by the time I had my feet firmly under me again I could hear them shouting to the massed soldiers below for help.

I cursed and, moving as quickly as I could, threw the dead and injured down the stairs, both to slow their advance and clear the landing. I stepped out into the passage beyond and hurried to the second door on my left, the paladin's directions echoing in my mind. Unlike the others, this one was of dark wood, and heavily carved with the usual plethora of skulls, runes and those oddly disturbing fat children with wings and trumpets. It certainly seemed special and, as I kicked it from its hinges, I could only hope that it did indeed lead to the sanctum I sought.

The door crashed to the ground, followed a moment later by the limp form of the priest who had been hiding behind it. I stepped over both into a modestly large room with air that was thick with years of old incense and walls that housed even more books and scrolls than I had seen in Fronsac's chambers. Another priest and another door waited on the far side of the room, and as I approached both the sharp smell of urine joined the ancient woody musk that flavoured the air.

'Good evening. Is the Cardinal in?' I asked the trembling priest. Manners cost nothing after all.

The priest lifted what I assumed to be another symbol of their god, and I caught a glimpse of gold the colour of a slumbering fire and the glint of precious stones. 'P-perish!' he shouted, shaking the symbol.

I clutched at my face as if struck, and as he lowered the symbol I snatched it from his hand in a brilliant display of speed and dexterity, leaving him staring at me with eyes that would surely have fallen out if he leaned only a little bit forward.

'This is beautiful,' I said, rubbing my thumb across the gold, and it truly was. I grabbed him by the robes and threw him to the other side of the room, where he joined his similarly insensate companion. I bounced the treasure in my hand, but before I could pocket it and kick the door in as I had intended to, I saw its gems flash with power. The priest had activated it, but I had not sensed it and had snatched it away before he could close the circle to direct its energy.

I saw the cracks spreading through it, the jagged lines dark at first but then filling with a brilliant green light, forcing them wider and wider apart until the uncontrolled surge of magic blew it apart into a thousand shards of glittering metal. They were too sharp for me to feel them cutting into me, but I felt the bone-shaking thud of the magic discharging. It was both colder than ice and hotter than lava, and even as it flayed my skin and hurled me into the wall, the shards that had embedded themselves in me were discharging their now wild magic into my flesh.

Falling to the floor, I counted myself lucky that I had landed on a cushion of books and scrolls. I clawed my way back onto my feet, my muscles shaking and jumping as the unfocused magic raced through them. I had little chance to wonder at the potency of these priests' artefacts, for even as I rose, I felt the beast rising within me with a might that I had never felt from it before. Its rage crashed through my head, all but deafening me with a roar like the world breaking, stealing the strength from my limbs and robbing my mind of its ability to control them. I felt its presence close around my mind in a tight fist, and I pushed back against it with a strength that I knew was already failing.

The beast fed on uncontrolled magic, the kind that I had just been bathed and punctured by.

It was quite an epiphany, and one that I should really have had weeks ago. There was no time for wonder or regret now as the weight of its will to dominate pressed down on me, uncaring of the blood that had begun to flow from my nose and ears, or the men who even now were coming to slay me.

Let me in, let me in, it roared in that beautiful voice, over and over again.

It needed no breath nor any other mantra, and at first its words broke against my will like the sea against a rock. But no wave was ever so aggressive or determined, and I felt the rock that was my will shift and begin to erode as the onslaught hammered it without pause.

Let me in.

I was clutching at my head in a vain and animalistic need to smother its voice, and I was still standing there like that when my armour-clad killers came for me.

Let me in.

I was only vaguely aware of them shouting, but it didn't seem important, not even when the first of them tried to press me to the ground.

Let me in.

Was I imagining it, or did it sound desperate? The grip of its rage was
fading as the energies of the shards embedded in my flesh began to
dissipate, taking much of the beast's power with them.

I spat blood from my mouth. 'I have you now,' I said to it, but it gave
no answer.

'Kneel!'

I blinked as the word was barked into my face on a breath that would
make a vulture gasp. Part of me had expected to see some terrible demon
with burning eyes and teeth of lightning, but instead there was only a
red-faced man with teeth that were further apart than the gravestones in
the yard outside.

'Kneel!' he bleated again.

I felt poorly enough after the beast's latest attack, and swallowing your
own blood is surely enough to put anyone in a fractious mood, so I
accept no blame for breaking his neck. He fell, and it was only then that
I saw the men who were standing behind him, jostling each other for
space in the chamber as they brandished their weapons at me with new
vigour and reminding me of Tatyana's warning about the twenty-one elite
paladins who guarded the Cardinal.

Let me in, the voice whispered.

Chapter 42

I took a step back, then another, and felt my back press against the door to the inner sanctum. I reached behind me and tested whether it was locked, which it was. The paladins advanced, those terrible short spears held out in front of them in a neat row, the steel gleaming and the runes upon them burning with killing potential.

I was so close, but it looked as if my story would end here, cornered in some mean and musty room. I could sense the aggression heightening in the paladins, their hearts labouring anew as they prepared to charge me down. I raised my fists and gritted my teeth as I willed the black talons to slide from my arms, and although it was faint, I was gratified by the scent of fear that drifted from the men as the gleaming lengths were revealed. They drew back, but a sharp command from one of the silver-haired ones saw them take their places again.

'Demon!' the same paladin shouted, pointing his sword at me in case any of the armoured idiots around him hadn't yet seen me. 'You have been judged by Drogah.'

In truth, I did not pay much attention to what he was saying after that. It was just another distraction, and I needed to focus if I was to have any hope of seeing the dawn.

They charged as the sky outside was lit by a flash of lightning, the strobing flash muted into a rainbow by the coloured glass in the narrow windows, painting their mindless hate into something almost beautiful for the briefest moment. Their spears were inches from my breast when I triggered the wind construct that I had hastily prepared while the silver-haired paladin had voiced his grand tirade. Their hesitation in charging me had given me enough time to bring the construct back to mind, and this time I had done it properly, maximising the effect that even a small amount of power could yield.

In the confined space of the room, the effect on their close-packed ranks was wonderful, and I shouted with glee as they were hurled into each other as the wind filled the room with a roar to wake the ancients. The patterned glass in the windows was ripped from its frame by the construct's demand for air, the sharp, brittle fragments adding to the chaos as the howling wind turned each into a flying knife. It did not last very long, but by the time I could hear the thunder outside again, the stunned and bleeding paladins were lying in an untidy heap.

I withdrew my black talons, gathered up two of their fallen spears and fell upon the dazed men, using my strength to stab the enchanted blades through two or three bodies at a time, their armour offering as much protection as their garbled prayers and entreaties for mercy did. They shuddered and screamed as I sent them to whatever afterlife they believed in, and I was glad for the open windows as their bodies emptied from a variety of holes, natural or otherwise.

My clothes were heavy with blood when I stepped back, my chest heaving as I gulped down lungfuls of the storm-fresh air until my head cleared. I rolled my shoulders and turned to the door.

It was time to end this.

I took three steps back, then threw myself at the door. My plan was simple: I would burst through low and fast, avoiding whatever trap Polsson had prepared, then throw both of my borrowed spears at him. Even if he avoided these, it would give me enough time to cross the small chamber and get my hands around his throat.

I hit the door with my full weight, and as it splintered inwards I glimpsed the flash of the hidden wards that he had set inside the doorway just as they flared to life and engulfed me in violet fire. I was not afraid of fire, but this purple blaze was not like anything I had ever felt. They hit me with a brutal force that threw me through the air even as it set to burning me with a vicious intensity, as if Polsson had somehow compressed a forest fire into each of the deceptively languid-looking flames. Even if I had not blundered into it like a fool, nothing could have prepared me for this.

I managed to roll to my knees as I tried to rip my clothes off in a blind frenzy, but it did little to stop the unearthly flames rampaging across my arms, face and legs, cracking my skin and boiling my blood into steam. It was *hungry*. I clamped my hands to my face to try to smother the flames, but I could feel them burning on, the unnatural fire alive against my skin. Every breath I took was slowly cooking my throat, and I dared not open my eyes for fear the sticky flames leaped onto them. My legs connected with something hard and heavy and I fell. I tried to crush the flames against the floor but only managed to peel back layers of burned skin against it.

I screamed while Polsson laughed.

'So you can burn. What a fine irony that I have brought you low with fire. If my master did not want you alive, I would watch it consume you.'

A kick slapped into my ribs, and as feeble as it was, the impact split my blistered skin and made me cry out loud, the ever-hungry flames scorching another layer of skin from my mouth.

'But then alive is a broad description.' Another kick, but this time I kept my teeth together and felt the flame break across them, cracking one and burning my gums away. He began to chant then, gathering his magic. Any thought I had of fighting back was eaten by the touch of the fire even before it could fully bloom inside my head. I was no stranger to pain, but this agony was an aggressive, ever-changing thing that burrowed deeper with every beat of my hearts.

Let me in.

The beast's voice rang in my mind, as clear and beautiful as it had ever been.

Let me in.

I felt no pain when it spoke, and as if hearing my silent plea, it began to repeat itself.

Let me in, let me in.

Let me in. It was a curious choice of words. To let it in, not to surrender to it nor to get out myself. It could be a command and a threat, or it could be a plea. Another kick slammed into me, and I tried to pull myself away but sagged to the floor, my muscles and will both weakened by the agony that gripped me and clouded my mind. It was getting harder to think. I needed to breathe, but didn't dare. Behind my closed eyes, the dance of shadows created by the flames bloomed into new shapes.

A mountain. A city on fire. A field of burning bones. A fortress among the clouds. A cage.

Something cold pressed into my arm, and I felt the flames and flashing images falter for a moment. I reached out, touched it. An engraved disk. The medallion, fallen from my torn clothes. It counteracted some dark magics, which meant the flames were not natural but a spell. Magic, let loose to feed on me.

Let me in, the beast crooned at me.

I felt it press against my mind, that immense rage straining forward yet unable to penetrate the walls that kept me what I was. No. Not unable; it's strength and will were far greater than mine were, than they had ever been. *Unwilling.* It was not my enemy. It was part of me, some monstrous part of me held at bay by my denial of it. But what was I? I had no name and no future. I was defeated, burning. Dying. Lost.

Let me in.

I felt my arm extending, my physical body mimicking the intention within my fracturing mind. I drew a lungful of fire and when I spoke the words, they puffed out as fire too.

'Come to me.'

Chapter 43

The pressure came first, as if my skull were shrinking, squeezing my brain until it felt as if it would ooze from my eyes and ears. There was pain, but there was always pain. Behind my closed eyes the world shattered into glittering shards, and in the sound of its breaking I heard my name, spoken as it had been when my soul was forged in the stars an age ago.

My true name.

It reached into me, deeper than any tooth or sword ever could, beyond my reforged flesh.

Stratus, the voice named me. *The Dead Wind.*

With each part of my name I saw shards fall into me, twisting and melting together and filling me with a beautiful light that flashed through me, branching like the lightning that filled the sky outside, arcing from me to the Songlines that surrounded me. I felt its deep and ancient power respond to my names, that steady harmony finding the parts of myself that I had lost, creating a discord within my being. The power flowed through me, restoring them and removing the imperfections that affected the great harmony and in so doing, mending the errors that I made in creating this body. This mind.

And the shards twisted and became something new, the terrible pressure in my head increased tenfold, and I must have screamed, but I could only hear a bestial roar that rivalled the thunder. I could feel something, an imperfection within the shards, something that was trying to find its form but that kept slipping and breaking, then coming together again. I felt myself tremble and shudder as it slowly, so very slowly, reformed, bringing together sounds that were meaningless alone to form a new harmony.

It was a word. A name. One of the missing parts of my true name.

Firesky, the voice said, and I felt my hearts stutter and then surge with new-found vigour as the Songline flashed and sent its pure energy cascading into me, its purity burning away the doubt, fear and pain that remained. It was a vortex of golden light, and I watched as a shape coalesced within it, amber amid the pale gold. I saw it and knew it for what it was as it approached me, its huge form impressing the truth that the Songlines had already whispered to me. It was the beast, but it was more. It was me, and I was it. We touched, and like the meeting of two great rivers, we swirled together and became something new and more powerful.

Stratus Firesky, the Dead Wind, a voice said, and I recognised it.

I recognised the terrible sadness and joy hidden within it as she spoke my name, an echo of the grief and madness that I had felt when she first spoke to me in Tatyana's dream.

'It's cold, Stratus, and you promised. You promised.'

I wanted to call to her, to ask her who and what she was, but before I could form the words the Songlines surged once more, swamping my mind as the power pulled me apart and remade me into a new whole. Images and sounds flashed through what passed for my consciousness in that strange reality, the part of me that had been the beast finally surrendering and providing the context for the memories that had so long puzzled me. The burning mountain I remembered was my home, our home, and the paladins that I remember surging towards me were those who had crusaded to drive us from it, every defeat we inflicted driving them to new heights of madness and ferocity.

I remembered the cage and the taunts of those who came to mock and gloat, the crackling of the cruel wards set within its bars giving them false courage. I remembered the countless years of my captivity and the cold indifference of my keepers, the descendants of Henkman himself, and my dream of ending his line for good. I laughed silently that both had now been foiled by the last of his line.

'Is he dead?'

The voice burst in on me, shocking me into a sudden awareness that my body had remained where it fell while the rift in my mind was healed. It felt cold, this flesh encasing my spirit, and as distant as it had when I had first woken in the shadow of those vultures.

'He sure looks dead,' said another voice.

'I will not take any chances again. Bind him well.' *This* voice I knew. A priest of some sort?

'Yes, Father. I have seen what he did to my brothers.'

This time, however, I did not need a Deacon to mend what was broken within me. I had made this body when my sorcery had echoed to my true name, something that the schism in my mind had distorted, severing the connection between will and flesh. I was all but whole again, and now that I understood what the problem was, I could mend it myself.

I felt myself expand as my flesh welcomed me anew, vitality flooding through every fibre and sinew. I felt the weight of my body once more, and the hardness of the floor beneath me. I opened my eyes and it took a few moments to understand what I was seeing as my mind settled. I was on my back, which gave me a view of the domed ceiling, which I had not noticed before was painted with representations of the constellations. Men stood on either side of me, one in armour with the symbol of the paladins upon his breast, the other in robes.

'Henkman?' I asked, but of course it wasn't him. He was dust, and had been for centuries.

'That ironclad whore isn't going to save you now.' The robed man looked down at me, and his scent drove the last of the fog from my mind. *Polsson. The chapel. Tatyana. The beast, the demon that was me. That is me.* My brain was suddenly alive with a thousand thoughts.

Polsson was still talking, the sound of his voice like the unwelcome chittering of an insect. 'The battle has begun, and my master shall be here soon to throw down the King's puppets. And then, my friend, then we will see how much their fine breeding and dowries mean when they come crawling to me. Begging me for my mercy.'

I reached for my sorcery and felt it respond with eagerness. My reserve of power was overflowing and begging to be released. My sorcerous abilities were inextricably linked with who I was, and with most of my true name now restored, the power I had been able to access before was a shadow of what I felt respond to me now. I reached out and snapped the chains they had bound me with. Both men leaped backwards as I stood up, the broken links clattering to the floor. I looked at Polsson and saw him for the vermin that he was.

'Kill him!' he shrieked. I stepped to the side and saw the paladin as he leaped towards me, his spear raised high, ready to strike. I used the flame from a nearby lamp as a catalyst and met his charge with a plume of fire that lifted him from his feet and sent him back the way he'd come, screaming as the fire melted flesh and armour into a single mass. I heard an echo of Tatyana's pain and terror in the sound, and felt my upper lip pull back from my teeth as the sound rekindled the rage and hatred that had sustained me for all the long centuries of my imprisonment.

'I think I have had my fill of your stench,' I said, my voice a growl.

'Burn, you abomination!' Polsson thrust his fist towards me as he ignited the power within his rings and sent a cone of the violet fire to engulf me.

'No,' I said. I drew my sorcery in, cutting through the connection to the Songlines that he drew on to let his fires burn so terribly. Artefacts were useful things, but the price of their accessibility was that their magic was both inflexible and vulnerable.

The ring had not finished discharging its spells, and Polsson had enough time to yelp before it exploded and ripped three fingers from his hand. He staggered away from me, scattering scrolls and books as he went, clutching at his hand as if surprised to discover that he too could bleed. I caught him easily enough, and before he could recover enough to try something else, I grabbed both his hands in one of mine and squeezed until I could no longer feel individual bones. His screams were nectar to me, but they brought more guards running too. More men to blindly lash out at something they did not understand. I tossed the Cardinal aside and turned to meet his remaining guardians.

The first rank died before they could aim a weapon at me, the fire that still burned in the dead paladin's fats providing the basis for a stream of yellow flame that I melded together with my wind construct, flaying them to the bone with the force and heat. The survivors quailed at the sight of their immolated companions, those at the front pushing back while those at the rear tried to go forward. I sprang upon them while the flames still burned, breaking bones with my fists and tearing out throats with my real teeth, and laughing as I did so. It left me bathed in their fluids, yet I felt content as I looked down to where the last of them lay broken at my feet.

I returned to the Cardinal and kneeled beside him. 'Everything I did here was for this moment, to know who I am.'

'You are nothing. You belong to my master,' he said, the pain of his crushed hands making his voice weak.

'Your master is but a man, and I will see him burn for what he did to me.'

'He broke you once, and he will break you again.'

'Do you really want to waste your last breaths issuing empty threats?'

Of all things, that made him laugh. 'Empty threats? He leads an army the like of which these lands has never seen. He has brought Krandin to its knees, the first to do so since the great battle kings of the Dawn Age. When it falls, this world will belong to him.'

'He'll find that hard to do when he is ash.' I leaned in close. 'And you forget who brought those great battle kings low.' My smile had little humour in it and his scent curdled at the sight of it. 'But tell me, why does he still pursue me so? Speak truthfully and I may grant you a quick death.'

'Death holds no fear for me, creature. We have conquered it.'

'It isn't death you should fear, but the manner of it.'

'It is beyond your understanding.' He spat at me. 'Blood is power.'

I snorted at that. 'Blood is nothing. Everyone has it.'

He bared his teeth at me. 'Your blood.'

'Aside from being mine, my blood is still just blood. What else?'

'You really don't know, do you?' He laughed again, and it was a sound I was quickly growing tired of hearing.

'My friend Tatyana told me a story once about a man like you that they captured at a city named Aknak.'

'That whore again.'

I grabbed his chin, pried his jaw open and ripped a few of his teeth out.

'Do not mistake my civility for either mercy or tolerance, you insect. I name her as a friend, and an insult to her is an insult to me.' I squeezed his jaw and leaned in closer. 'Insult her again and I will break you in a way that will make the dead weep.'

My nose told me that he believed me, so I released his face and sat back again. 'Like I was saying, she told me a story about a man like you, and how eager he was to explain all he knew after they applied some fire to him. And you must know how much I like fire.'

'I can't,' he said.

'Ah, but I think you can.' I conjured a ball of flame and set it to smouldering its way through his robes. It may have been because of his penchant for alchemy, but I certainly had not foreseen that his garments would burst into flame in the way that they did, and from Polsson's reaction, he hadn't expected it either. Seeing and feeling his chest aflame seemed to shatter his reserve.

'Put it out! He needs your blood but he didn't tell me why. It burns!'

'Of course it does, it's fire. I can smell your skin crisping.' It was a lie; even so close, all I could smell was the rank odour of his clothes. 'And the worms? What are they?'

'Aah! Help! They are from . . . they are the goddess. They grant power. Please!'

'Why?'

He was too busy screaming to answer, so I flipped him onto his stomach, smothering the fire, then rolled him over again, leaving a fair amount of skin on the floor. 'It isn't as much fun when you're the one on fire, is it?'

'Please, no more.'

'What power do they grant?'

'Bridge . . . They br . . .' His eyes widened a moment before his back arched with enough violence that I heard the bones crack. It lasted as long as the telling of it before he fell back, blood and liquefied brains oozing from his nose. It seemed that there were some things that the Worm Lord did not want his underlings discussing. I stared at his body in disgust, and with no little disappointment, before smashing a lantern onto it.

I rose and made my way from the sanctum as the flames danced across the surface of the oil and spread to the books and scrolls with no little greed. The storm was still raging outside, which surprised me as it felt like far more time had passed since I had entered.

I paused as I felt a sudden tug on my sorcery, or more exactly, the sensation of Tatyana's healing ability coming to life. She was hurt. My *friend*. I had not given it much thought when I spoke to the Cardinal, but our magical bond notwithstanding, it felt right, even now that I fully understood who she was. I was smiling as I smashed the rest of the window out, creating a hole big enough for me to climb out.

Stratus Firesky, friend to the scion of Henkman the Vanquisher.

That was not something I had ever thought to hear, not in all the long centuries of my life.

Chapter 44

Much of the knowledge of the Dawn Age was lost when fear and ignorance turned the kings, who we had raised so high, against our order. What price the dominion of man when the reward is a world where ignorance is celebrated? We have lost much, but we have learned much too, and I bid you to take heart for while the Destroyer remains bound, the hope for a return to an age of wisdom endures.

An Introduction to the Path of Power
by Tiberius Talgoth, Archmage

The air was cleaner than it had been since I arrived in this city, and I lingered on the edge of the window to enjoy the taste of it and the feel of the rain against my skin. I breathed deeply, letting the air expunge the stench from my nose while the rain washed the blood from me. I woke my night vision, and could not help but laugh at the memory of how it had startled me the first time I had used it in the forest.

That I had survived this long stumbling about like a clueless cub, startled by my own body, was more of a miracle than that the transmogrification of my body to this new form had worked at all. If I ever found that Deacon again, I swore to myself that I would do my utmost to spare his life, or at least end him painlessly. Without his intervention, I would have been vulture scat long ago.

I shook my head to clear it. I needed to find Tatyana before I tried to make sense of the jumble of memories that the healing of my mind had unlocked. It was not something to be resolved while squatting upon a window in a storm. I crouched, mildly amused by the sensation of knees that bent the wrong way after remembering my own legs, and launched myself into the night air. My wind construct bloomed beneath me, carrying me over the churchyard and the lines of men beyond. It was as close to flying as I had felt in an age, and had I been capable of tears I might well have shed them.

I landed in a side street with far more grace than either of my previous attempts and set to running in the direction of where I could feel Tatyana's healing calling me. Two patrols did try to stop me. I leaped over the first, leaving them shouting behind me as I sailed over a terrace of houses, and the second I blinded with a flash of light and left to wail in the dark.

I eased to a walk as the gaps between the buildings widened and the palace loomed. The gates in its outer wall were all shut and I could see guards walking the length of it. I made my way around the perimeter until I reached a place that accorded with my idea of where Fronsac's chambers were. It didn't take much beyond a purely physical effort to cross the outer wall, and I was pleased to see that it was more or less right where I had hoped to be. I crossed the small gardens and was almost at the doors before I was challenged by a guard.

'Who goes there?' he called, which was ridiculous. If he didn't already know who I was, I could say I was anybody.

'The Dead Wind,' I answered, pleased to have an opportunity to see how it felt to say it.

'The what?'

'I am here to see Magus Fronsac. It is urgent.'

'Not so fast, my black friend.' He stepped into my path and levelled his spear. 'The only place you're going is the guardhouse.'

'I said it was urgent.' I stepped forward but he thrust the spear towards me.

355

'And I said you're not—'

'Enough!' I said, closing in on him. He jabbed his spear at my chest but I grabbed the pointed bit before it could touch me and bent it back on itself with a groan of metal. He stared at me, and never one to waste an opportunity, I held his gaze and crushed his will beneath mine. It was laughably easy now.

'Take me to him, now.' I rifled through his most recent memories for anything useful but it was all human nonsense. I did, however, catch a glimpse of myself from his perspective and had him fashion me a short skirt, a kilt he called it, from his cloak and belt. Humans were bizarrely tetchy about seeing naked bodies, and I didn't want to be interrupted by them telling me the obvious time and again. I helped myself to the heavily watered wine he carried too, the tartness of it refreshing after the stars knew how many mouthfuls of blood I had suffered that night.

'He is inside,' he said, eventually coming to halt outside a remarkably unremarkable door.

I fed some power into my vision and admired the delicate and intricate web of magical wards that lay upon it. I dismissed the guard and left him to wander off, then knocked on the door. These rooms were part of the palace after all, and if the door was so heavily warded as to react to a knock, there would have been a pile of dead servants next to it.

'Who is it?'

It was tempting, but I decided to stay with the name he knew. 'Stratus.'

I was quite pleased when I saw that it was Fronsac himself that opened the door, and more so that he wasn't holding a weapon of any sort. In fact, he was almost as undressed as I was, his body marked with wards that I could sense were permanent.

'It *is* you! Come inside, quickly now.' He all but pulled me inside and I felt him reseal the wards as he shut the door.

These were his personal chambers, and they certainly felt far more like what I had expected from a wizard's rooms. At first glance, it was a jumbled mess. A wide desk stood in front of a velvet-draped window, occupying at least a third of the floor. The top of it was perhaps the only flat surface that I could see where things had been neatly stacked. Everywhere else they lay in piles and heaps, and every book had at least half a dozen feathers or scraps of paper protruding from it. One entire wall was covered in shelves that sagged like drawn bows under the weight of the baubles, bottles and jars crammed upon them. A narrow bed was wedged against the far wall and currently supported a large spar of crystal nestled in a golden cage.

Fronsac swept a stack of scrolls from a chair with stained fingers, and gestured for me to sit while he poured us each a cup of wine that was generous, even by my standards. I sniffed at it but found no trace of the worms or any sort of magic.

'I thought you were dead,' he said, lifting his glass towards me.

'I thought I was too,' I said, copying the gesture and drinking when he did. The wine was the nicest that I had yet tasted and I drained the glass, enjoying the sense of forgotten summers that it imparted.

'You're changed,' he said as he lowered his glass. 'You're stronger. I can feel the pressure of your sorcery on my skin. It's quite remarkable.'

That was impressive, but this was his inner chamber and even without exerting myself I could feel the wards layered upon the walls and floor.

'When I first came to you, I was suffering from an affliction, an old injury of sorts, one that has since been healed.'

'I am pleased for you, my friend, for we will need your strength in the coming days. I am glad you got my message.'

'Where is Tatyana Henkman?'

'Tatyana? I don't know, why?'

'I sent her to you with a message.'

'I have not seen her since that day with Jean.'

I set my cup down before I crushed it. 'She is nearby, and injured. I can sense it.'

'I swear that I have not heard anything of her. What was the message?'

357

'Do you trust me?' He didn't answer except to gesture to himself and his room, and I understood his meaning. 'Then look into my eyes and have no fear.'

He pursed his lips, and for a moment I thought he would refuse, but then he sighed and leaned forward, his blue eyes locking onto mine. I knew that he would be maintaining his wards, but they had no real effect on what I was doing since I was inviting him into my memories, rather than the other way around. I felt him as a strong and carefully contained presence, hesitant but not entirely afraid. I welcomed him and shared with him what we had seen in the tunnels beneath St Tomas, the bodies, the worm wine, all of it, right up to where I burned Polsson's body, but leaving out the touch of the Songlines and the truth of me.

That secret was mine alone for now.

When I was finished we both sat back, untangling our minds by mutual agreement. I felt unexpectedly relieved at having shared the knowledge, and waited while Fronsac drank another measure of wine straight from the bottle.

'We must warn Jean,' he said. 'Gods, what a mess.' He rose and began dressing from a pile of clothing near the door. He tossed a few pieces at me too. I found a pair of very loose-fitting trousers that must have been like wearing a ship's sail for Fronsac, along with a tunic that was only slightly snug. Both were soft and had a clean smell though, so I did not mind too much.

'That is why I sent her,' I said, dressing awkwardly. 'I will go find her. Could she be with Lucien?'

'Perhaps. Prince Lucien has taken to spending much of his time with the commanders of his new army, something I now regret encouraging him to do.' He looked at me as he lifted a heavily enchanted bracelet from an ornate box. 'Aside from the legion that Jean has passed to him, Lucien has taken command of the fourth cohort of the Order of the Sword.'

'The paladins from Kenwin.' I grimaced as the shape of Polsson's plan began to reveal itself. 'Tell me, magus, are you maintaining your wards on Lucien?'

'Of course. Him and Jean both, but my magic cannot shield them from honeyed tongues. Or forked ones, for that matter.' He tied his hair back with a strip of leather. 'But if he has drunk from the Cardinal's wine I cannot be sure how steady their foundations are, not without checking them myself.'

'I understand. I will seek him out once have found Tatyana, and I suspect the two shall not be far from each other.'

'You are changed, Stratus, and not just by having more power. I felt it when I opened the door, and now I hear it in your voice.'

'You have a good and astute mind, magus. It is one of the reasons I like you.' I smiled at the truth of it. 'The injury was to both my body and my spirit, and now that it has been healed there are other matters that we need to discuss.'

'Matters of sorcery?'

'Yes. The reason I sought out a city of man in the beginning was to speak to its wise men. Much has happened, but that goal remains.'

'A city of man.' He looked at me as if seeing me for the first time and I felt a delicate trace of magic dust my skin. 'What are you, Stratus?'

'Invigorated.' I smiled so that he would not take offence at my deft evasion. If he had asked me who I was, I might have told him then. 'We shall talk later.'

'Once we have overthrown a legion of corrupt paladins, an army of necromancers and ten thousand Penullin regulars who haven't tasted defeat in two seasons of campaigning.'

'Yes, I think that is the breadth of it. We can go for a pie.'

He laughed then, and I followed him out. 'Good luck, Stratus.'

'And to you, magus. Do not die.'

'Words to live by,' he said and strode off down the passage.

Inspired by the wards inked into Fronsac's flesh, I took some time to call my sorcery forth and prepare something similar for myself. If he survived what was coming, I wanted him to teach me about rune-craft as I had little skill in it. The wards I prepared for myself were crude copies that required a constant trickle of power from the Songlines to remain active, unlike his which could apparently remain dormant and self-contained. I felt quite good when I was finished though, the soft heat of the wards warming me like no tunic or cloak ever had, and I imagined that this was how men felt when they strapped armour to their soft little bodies.

The palace, however, remained a senseless and frustrating warren of corridors to me, and after perhaps the third time that I found myself passing along the same hallway, that frustration was turning to anger. Yet it was then that I caught a familiar scent. I slowed and took a deeper breath. **Lucien**. I followed the scent trail to another, smaller passage and saw a group of men ahead of me. There were at least a dozen of them, but I recognised Lucien from the blue on his armour. A burly paladin walked beside the prince, and when I called out it was him who turned first. He said something to Lucien before barging his way through the others and came striding up to me, the spicy scent of his aggression preceding him.

'Demon!' he shouted, slapping a hand to his sword. 'You will surrender to me, now!'

'Be silent,' I said, closing the distance between us in two swift strides, effectively trapping his sword arm against his chest armour. He tried to move back, but as he did so he met my gaze. It wasn't the first time a paladin had done so, and again I could not but wonder whether it was arrogance or ignorance that made them so careless. I wasn't one to spurn a gift though, and I quickly fed a measure of power into my gaze as he met it, trapping his mind like a bird in a net. I could feel his confusion buzzing at the edges of the unnatural aggression that dominated his mind, but paid it little heed as I sent a command for silence spearing into his head. I felt it take hold and pushed past him, leaving him to stare at my back while the confusion warred with his aggression.

'Hello Stratus,' Lucien said, a burr to his words that was not there before. 'I must admit, I did not think to see you here.'

'We need to talk.' I caught the whispers of the other men around us and added a 'Highness' to appease them. Two or more had already scuttled away down the passage and I had little doubt that they would be calling for the guards as soon as they could.

'I'm very busy. We're riding out to meet with Baron Karsten in the morning.'

'Have you seen Tatyana? Has she spoken to you?'

'Tatyana?' He rubbed his face. 'No.'

'Lucien, you must find Fronsac. Talk to him before you leave.'

'I meant to, but there's just so much to do,' he said, waving a hand at the men whispering around us, and had I not already smelled him, I would have thought he was drunk again by the way he stood and sounded. I heard the paladin curse suddenly as he shook off my command. It seemed some of his charms and blessings actually had some power. I didn't want to kill him, or more accurately, I didn't want to kill him in front of Lucien before I had a better idea if it would affect whatever it is they were doing to him.

'Lucien Stahrull, give me your word that you will speak to him.'

He stared at me as if noticing me for the first time, then nodded. 'Done.'

That was enough for me. I pushed through the onlookers as the paladin went storming up to Lucien. He would no doubt cause trouble soon enough, but I could deal with that once Tatyana was out of danger.

Once out of sight, I called up my sorcery and sent it racing through the corridors ahead of me, following the gossamer trail of the link between her and me, as I should have thought to do at the outset. After having to hoard my power like a miser for so long, it felt strange and quite exhilarating to be able to dip into it and not fear that it would soon be depleted. With my path now laid out before me in a glowing trail only I could see, I traversed the rest of the palace at a good pace.

Eventually I came to the door my sorcery was calling me to, a door that was guarded by two men dressed in the now familiar white and red of the paladins. They recognised me as I drew closer, and it came as no surprise when they lowered their spears and marched towards me. One shouted a command for me to get on my knees, but my days of kneeling to men were over.

The passage was just about wide enough for them to run at me side by side, which would have left me little room to evade them had I wanted to. They pulled their arms back for the thrust, then shouted in pain and alarm as the wooden shafts of the spears burst into flame. It was a simple enough trick, and one that I had used on archers many times over. My black talons slid out while they tried to draw their swords, but they were too close and I was too fast. I punched a talon through each of their heads and left them to kick and twitch their last.

The door was locked but not warded, so I simply kicked it open. It swung open on a single hinge before crashing to the floor. The room beyond was empty but the air was sour with the unmistakeable stench of necromancy, something that I had foolishly thought I had become inured to. I made my way across the chamber and along a passage that led to three wooden doors. The first of these was the sleeping room for the paladins in the palace, which was obvious because there were at least six of them in there, although not all were asleep. I slammed the door shut, muffling their shouts. It had a mechanical lock, and I swiftly locked it but with the added precaution of melting several of the little metal bars together. If they wanted to get out they'd need to hack through its thick timbers.

The second door led to a smaller version of a chapel that was clearly the source of the stench permeating the air. I wasted no time in throwing the wooden benches against the centrepiece and willing a fire into being among them. I didn't know where the dark magic emanated from, but I couldn't bring myself to ignore it.

I unlocked the third door and stepped inside. This final room was small and completely bare except for the woman launching herself at me from next to the door. I had time to flinch before an iron manacle bounced off the side of my head, sending a spray of stars across my vision. It would have been a tremendous and quite likely fatal blow if I had been a normal man.

'A fine greeting,' I said, dabbing at the wound as she staggered back, clutching the other end of the manacle. Her wrist was a bloodied mess from where she had forced it out of the metal cuff and I reached out with my will and accelerated the healing of her hand as I did my head, something which made her curse as fluently as ever before she finally looked up at me.

'Hello yourself,' she said, her curt tone at odds with her smile. 'You took your time.'

I looked at her, seeing her for the first time as both a friend and a Henkman, with a real understanding of what that meant. She was the last of his line, and if I was to be true to the vow I took so many years ago, I would have reached out and broken her neck where she stood. Or, if I was to keep to the letter of the vow I had made, I would have burned her over a slow fire and eaten her heart.

'What? Why are you staring me like that?'

'I remember.' Part of me wanted to laugh at the sheer absurdity of how I had come to be there, rescuing a Henkman.

'That's great. How about you remember when we're somewhere nice, rather than in a rat-infested prison cell?'

'I have already remembered. We need to talk, you and I.'

'Fine, fine. But let's talk elsewhere.' She peered out into the passage. 'What's that noise?'

'I locked some of the paladins in their sleeping room. They're probably chopping the door down.'

'It's called a dormitory. Honestly, I'm surprised you didn't kill them.'

'I wanted to find you first.' What would it feel like, to kill her? Would it be any different to the others I had slain? I had felt a sublime sense of pleasure in ending Polsson, even if it hadn't been by my hand directly, this man who had only wronged me for a matter of days, whereas Henkman's crimes went back centuries.

'Well, aren't you the sweetest demon. Come on, you big oaf.'

'I am not a demon.'

'See? I told you so. You should listen to me more often.'

I followed her past the dormitory and out into the passage where the sentries' bodies lay in a pool of cooling blood. She stopped and stripped one of them of his armour with enviable ease, all the while keeping herself away from the blood that had leaked from his riven skull.

'Damn, that feels better,' she said, pulling at various straps. 'So what's the situation? Stratus? Are you drifting off again? Did I hit you too hard? Sorry about that, by the way. The last few days have been shit.'

'No, I am not hurt. It is just strange seeing you in the garb of a paladin again.'

'Piss off,' she said, tearing the emblem and cape from the armour. 'So out with it. What's happening out there? These shits,' she paused to kick the stripped body, 'grabbed me as soon as I showed my face here. They said it was on Lucien's command.'

'I fear it might have been.'

'What?'

'I spoke with Lucien on my way to find you and it was as if he was drunk. I fear they are working to remove Fronsac's wards.'

'But he wasn't one of them?' She tapped the side of her head and I took her meaning. 'He wasn't, was he?'

'I do not think so, not while the wards are still in place.'

'I'm going to kill Polsson.'

'You are too late. Polsson is dead.'

'You killed him?'

'I set him on fire before his brain melted, then burned his corpse.'

'Well, I can't think of anyone who deserved it more. That's a story I want to hear, but we need to find Fronsac. He can—'

'Not yet.'

'What? Why the Hel not?'

'I came back to find you,' I said, watching her. 'To see how I would feel when I saw you properly.'

'What does that mean? You're going strange again.'

'As Tatyana, you have been a friend to me. But I took a vow a long time ago to erase the line of Henkman the Vanquisher.'

'What? You're not making any sense.' Her hand settled on the handle of the dead man's sword as I took a step closer.

'Little of this makes sense, but I learned a long time ago that while Fate is as cruel as it is fickle, it also has a sense of humour.'

'We're still getting nowhere on the part where this starts making any sort of sense.'

'Your kindness and courage are worth more to me than a vow made to a man who is little more than myth to you and dust to me. I spoke the words to him in anger but held true to them, until I met you. The last of his line. I suppose it is only fitting then, since I am the last of mine.'

'Who are you talking about?'

'Henkman the Vanquisher.'

'You're not making any sense, Stratus. He's been dead for close on seven hundred years.'

Had it really been so long?

'His name was Aethbert. No one seems to remember that he was Aethbert the Vanquisher before they decided Henkman was easier to remember.' She didn't return my smile. 'Your father. Did he ever talk about a circus?'

She frowned, crashing her eyebrows together in the way that she always did when she was thinking. 'Yes, I think so. It was a long time ago, in his father's father's time. He didn't talk to me about it, although I heard him speaking of it to my brother. I can't remember any of it, only that none of it made sense to me.'

'I remember the circus.' In my mind I saw the curtains pulling back from the front of my cage, and again heard the screams of the crowd outside as they looked upon me, mothers drawing their children close and men their wives. Screams of fear and hate, mingling together into an undistinguishable whole. 'Because I was there. I was the reason for it.'

'What? Stratus, what did Polsson tell you? What did he do?'

'Polsson was nothing but vermin, but he did provide the key I needed. I remember now, you see. I remember who I am and what I am, my friend. I am no demon, and I am no man.'

'Stratus, your eyes.'

I smiled, and startled as she was by the embers that had lit within my eyes, she staggered back as my real teeth filled my mouth.

'My name is Stratus Firesky, named The Dead Wind by the first men.'

'What? No. You're . . . you're insane.'

'Others named me The Destroyer and The Doom of Krandin. I burned each of your cities to the ground, and a year of celebration was announced when I fell.' My voice softened as the memories of that time crowded my mind. 'The mead flowed like a river.'

I closed my eyes and again pictured the beast as it had come to me in the Songlines' embrace, the golden light reflecting as amber from its midnight-black scales, its neck thick but graceful and its strong wings folded across its back. I looked into Tatyana's eyes, and let her see it, this most intimate secret of mine. The truth of who I was.

'Oh sweet god.' She staggered once more and fell to her knee, the sword she had half-drawn now forgotten. 'It cannot be. It was a just a legend, a story.'

'All stories begin somewhere.'

'But he killed it. You.'

'No. Your forefather failed in that and I was captured, not slain, although in the years that came to pass I often wished that he had struck true. Shrivelled and bound by the powerful enchantments of the Archmage that served him, I became the charge of your family, a glorified trophy of war to be passed from father to son.' Memories of another time rose unbidden in my mind and I swallowed the emotions they evoked with difficulty. 'I became a curiosity to be gawked at and spat upon, to be laughed at and reviled. For centuries I was displayed like something to be pitied rather than feared, my glory forgotten and my name greeted with laughter, not terror. Come and see, they would cry out while they rung their damn bells; come and see the mighty Dead Wind, last of the dragons.'

Acknowledgements

A few people have asked me how long it took to write *Infernal*, and in some ways I started writing it the first time I picked up a dice, which would make it a very long time.

The person I owe the greatest debt to is without doubt my wife Liz, for always having my corner and for bringing Stratus back to life for me in the first draft of *Banished*. He didn't survive to the final draft, but sitting there talking about him kindled the spark.

There are a lot of people who've helped shape him and the world he lives in into something real for me, but I owe the crew who fought the battle of Balfont with me the greatest debt. The magic was real, even if it was punctuated by my mother checking in to make sure we weren't being satanists or something equally embarrassing.